UP FROM ORCHARD STREET

Up from Orchard Street

Eleanor Widmer

BANTAM BOOKS

UP FROM ORCHARD STREET
A Bantam Book / August 2005

Published by
Bantam Dell
A Division of Random House, Inc.
New York, New York

Book design by Lynn Newmark

Bantam Books is a registered trademark of Random House, Inc., and the
colophon is a trademark of Random House, Inc.

Library of Congress Cataloging-in-Publication Data

Widmer, Eleanor, 1925–2004
Up from Orchard Street / Eleanor Widmer
p. cm.
ISBN 0-553-80400-6
1. Widows—Fiction. 2. Women cooks—Fiction. 3. Grandmothers—
Fiction. 4. Jewish women—Fiction. 5. Poor families—Fiction.
6. Jewish families—Fiction. 7. Cookery, Jewish—Fiction. 8. Tenement
houses—Fiction. 9. Women immigrants—Fiction. 10. Grandparent
and child—Fiction. 11. Lower East Side (New York, N.Y.)—Fiction.
I. Title.
PS3623.I35 U6 2005   2005046405
813/.6 22

Printed in the United States of America
Published simultaneously in Canada

www.bantamdell.com

10 9 8 7 6 5 4 3 2 1
BVG

To Jonah, my magical son

UP FROM ORCHARD STREET

1

Manya's Restaurant

MY FATHER NEVER felt sorry for himself because he had no memory of his father; in fact, he reveled in his semiorphaned state because it had brought him closer to his mother, Manya, and to the young girls and older women who doted on him. Born Abraham Jacob, he called himself Jack after he heard the name shouted on the streets of the Lower East Side.

He emerged a precocious, mimetic child who talked English in long paragraphs, Yiddish in short ones, taught himself to read, sing, dance and make up enchanting stories without being urged. When he was four, to keep him company Manya sent for her seven-year-old sister, Bertha, born in Odessa after teenage Manya and her groom escaped to America. Everyone assumed that Bertha was Manya's daughter. She had neither the time nor the inclination to correct them. In the crowded noisy streets of New York's Jewish ghetto, no one put too fine a point on dates of birth, names or truth telling.

Manya worked like a dervish to support the two children, starting at dawn in Greenspan's bakery, where she baked bread and scrubbed heavy pots during the day, and then racing to her night job at a gaming room on Forsyth Street, where men played dice, cards, chess and checkers and drank a burning substance concocted by the owner, aptly referred to as Tyvil, or the devil.

The sign on his window read Cold Drinks, which translated into Yiddish as *bronffin,* prepared from rubbing alcohol, whose recipe he guarded with zeal. He possessed no license to serve alcohol but the seltzer was legitimate, splashed into glasses that could have done with more zealous washing.

Manya's white hair at the age of twenty fascinated Tyvil and he hired her because she was fast on her feet and aroused desire in every man who had blood in his veins. She carried a flyswatter to keep them at bay.

Tyvil's original intention was to have Manya steal bread from Greenspan's bakery to serve with his barely fermented booze—he had often spied her coming from work with a fishnet bag filled with unsalable odds and ends of rolls, pumpernickel and rye. She refused his request and almost pushed him off the sidewalk in her indignation.

"What are you, some uptown Yankee, you won't be an American goniff?" Tyvil said, laughing.

Her blazing tongue put Tyvil in awe of her forever. "If I steal from Greenspan, then I steal from you. You want a goniff, find one, but not me."

"You're a freethinker. A woman who works Friday nights and Saturday mornings and you make a shrei about stale bread?"

"Need breaks iron," she retorted. "I have two children to feed. You want to call me a freethinker because I work when others daven, call all you want."

"You they should also call Tyvil. I'd die for that fire in bed."

Manya swatted both of his hands with her flyswatter and ran off. He pursued her. "Wait. You have the job. You'll wash glasses, serve seltzer, maybe a little something to eat . . ."

Her reputation as a cook spread without her knowledge—for the soups she brought to the bakery in a lidded tin for her midday meal, for her stews, for the scraps of dough that she turned into what the Russians called pelmeni and the Jews kreplach, dumplings stuffed with chopped meat and onions. She prepared hot borscht with beef in winter, shchi or cold borscht in summer, chicken cooked with prunes or a tsimmes with sweet potatoes, carrots and prunes.

Tyvil decided to suppress his lust and opt for Manya's cooking—he was either a bigamist with two wives, or unmarried with two mistresses. He persuaded Manya to cook one dish each night; in exchange she could keep the tips and bring her son, Jack, with her. These last two concessions sealed the arrangement. Bertha, her baby sister, did not mind sleeping with their neighbor, Mrs. Molka, until Manya returned from her night job, but Jack let out such howls of despair that she brought him to her night work.

In theory, Mrs. Molka took care of the two youngsters during the day. In fact, they drifted away from her and regardless of the weather spent whole days in the street, running between the pushcarts, gorging themselves on unwashed soft fruit that fell from the carts, or trading the ends of bread from Greenspan's for thin slices of halvah, or for ice scraped from huge blocks and doused with red sticky syrup. On hands and knees they combed the crowded streets for lost pennies, which they squandered on salted pretzels, pronounced "pletzels," or a single baked chestnut that Jack divided scrupulously.

Bertha proved to be an excellent student. Jack insisted that she drop both Russian and Yiddish and speak English only. Within six months her past fell out of her head and she became as Americanized as Jack, who had been born on Ludlow Street.

Jack told time by glancing at the sky. Once it turned bluish gray, a sign of dusk, he grabbed Bertha's hand and raced her back to Ludlow Street, up four flights of stairs to their one-room flat that faced another dingy building.

The room was dominated by one bed in which his father had died and he, Manya and Bertha now slept; a shaky wooden table and three straight-backed chairs, none matching, that came from a Hester Street pushcart. A two-burner gas ring and a tiny cold water sink completed the amenities.

The first word Bertha had taught Jack was *Siberia,* the coldest area in Russia, a punishing ground for criminals. The children screamed "Siberia!" as they entered the freezing apartment.

Then, Jack filled the dented tea kettle with water, lit the flame and placed a basin and the cheap brown bar of kosher soap on the table. With the warm water he washed his hair first, stating as always, "I can't stand schmutz in my hair," and then scrubbed the rest of his body with a rag, making certain that his skinned knees and muddy feet bore no telltale signs of the street.

Bertha's turn to wash came next. She protested that in Odessa she bathed her whole body only once during the entire winter. Shooting her a look of disdain mingled with pity, Jack retorted, "There are people right in this building who don't wash either. But we're not them. We're different."

Meekly, Bertha complied; decades later she still remembered her first American lesson in Jack's dandyism. He soaked their soiled clothes in the sink, wrung them out as best he could and hung them on the line outside the window. Sometimes the clothes from the day before had frozen solid and had to be thawed on the backs of the chairs.

Jack changed into clean unironed clothes and the hated shawl that his mother wrapped around his shoulders to protect his weak lungs. Doctors who practiced in the neighborhood prefaced every illness with the term *weak*: weak eyes, ears, throat, heart, lungs, stomach, right down to the feet.

The prospect of losing her child to the same illness that had killed her husband kept Manya in a constant state of anguish. She bundled Jack into bulky sweaters, festooned him with shawls fastened with a diaper pin, and at night covered him with the major share of the feather-filled blanket spread over the bed. Much as it embarrassed Jack to walk to Tyvil's gaming room wrapped in a shawl, the price was small compared to the joy of being there, especially on Friday nights.

On Fridays, Manya served hot cabbage borscht with chunks of beef and boiled potatoes, ladled into deep soup plates with chipped edges and a variety of pans that included frying pans.

Every table filled quickly with customers, some of them Orthodox Russians who came to drink themselves into oblivion, banged on the tables and demanded to know how Manya cooked such a mouthwatering soup from an axe.

She stood in the middle of the room and explained. "First, I take an axe and boil it in water. It doesn't have much taste, so I beg Tyvil for a little salt. He doesn't like to spend much money, so I have to get on my knees and ask him for a few wilted cabbage leaves. The meat, it's the worst kind, fatty, hard to chew, maybe it even smells bad, but I put it in the pot with the cabbage and soft tomatoes and cook it for hours and hours. And that's how I cook borscht from an axe."

The story was an ancient Russian folktale and Manya recited it in Russian, in Yiddish and in a combination of the two plus ghetto-style English. During the course of the evening she recited it at least twice and the men, already lit up on alcohol, cheered, whistled and dumped their loose change for their charming chef.

Jack scooped the pennies and occasional nickels into a miniature drawstring clothespin bag that he hid in the folds of his shawl. The secret to his mother's borscht was brown sugar, thrown in by the handful along with rock sour salt. Every Thursday night she prepared split pea soup with flanken, fighting with Tyvil because she wanted a better quality of meat.

"If you cook an axe, you get an axe," she cried in protest. "God knows where you buy this junk. A starving dog wouldn't eat it."

Even as they argued about the quality of the meat, she was chopping the cabbage for the borscht; she cooked both soups simultaneously. The split pea soup vanished within an hour; the borscht had to marinate overnight and was reheated the following evening on a low flame. Not once did Jack eat there; Manya wouldn't allow him to taste such inferior food.

Not that the soups interested him. He loved Friday nights because Joe Bloom played chess on Fridays only.

Joe, slim, wiry and not much taller than Manya, had fingertips permanently stained black from the ink he used as a typesetter for the *Jewish Forward*. He wore a blue dress shirt and his sad eyes had dark smudges beneath them. Jack wondered whether Joe rubbed his stained fingers under his eyes to create those dark circles. As soon as Manya entered, Joe would raise his hands from the chess pieces to stare at her, a bloom of red coloring the pallor of his cheeks.

One Friday night he beckoned Jack over. "Come here, I'll teach you something."

"Chess?"

"No, how to read a horse-racing form."

His chess partner left for home and Joe shut the chessboard and tumbled the pieces into a clean cigar box. Joe wouldn't use Tyvil's greasy food-stained games. He spread two newspaper clippings on the table.

"These are racing forms, one in Yiddish from the *Forward,* one in English from the *Daily News.* Take a look. First race, Jack the Giant Killer; second race Jack and the Beanstalk."

Jack peered at the words in English. "I don't see Jack written anywhere."

"So you can read?"

"Of course, whole books. These horses, you play them for their names?"

"No. I study the comment."

"The comment?"

"It's the information about the horse. How old she or he is, where he ran before, how many times he won. Also who the mother is. Horses are like people. The mother is very important."

A sigh escaped Joe's lips. He rubbed his eyes with his inky fingers. No dye came off.

"Your mother is beautiful, intelligent, and her husband, your father, he read poetry to her. She doesn't belong here. It's a rough place, with rough men. She should quit this job as soon as possible and open her own restaurant."

Jack tweaked the black curtain that shrouded the store window. On Friday nights Tyvil closed the curtain and didn't turn on the outside light, pretending the store was closed so that the Orthodox on their way to shul wouldn't hurl curses at him or spit on his doorstep for allowing gambling on the Sabbath eve.

After a long pause, Joe said, "I'm walking you home."

In fact he carried Jack to Ludlow Street with Manya at his side, and up to the top floor. Manya collected Bertha from Mrs. Molka and tucked both children into bed. A ten-watt bulb sputtered in the hallway before it went out. That instant was enough for Jack to catch the two adults kissing. Then they were enveloped in darkness.

The moment his mother curled into bed Jack poked his elbow into her ribs. "I saw him kiss you."

"So."

"And you kissed him back."

"So."

"Are you marrying him?"

She hugged her son close to her. "Do you think one kiss means marriage? In Russia and in Europe, men kiss on both cheeks instead of shaking hands. At concerts in the park, people who know each other kiss. And men and women kiss to say hello, good-bye, thank you. I kissed Joe, he waited for me to finish work, he carried you all the way home and up the stairs. Don't you think a kiss is coming to him?"

"No. You should give him a few pennies from your tips."

"A grown man, a few pennies? I can't talk more—I'm tired. I've worked all day without a stop and while it's still dark I have to creep into Greenspan's."

Too exhausted to argue, Jack resigned himself to that kiss. He felt sorry that his mother had to slip into the bakery before the sun rose. She did this to prevent the Orthodox men from taunting her, yelling "Shabbas goy" because she worked on Saturday until noon. At the bakery she opened the large oven door where dozens of pots filled with cholent simmered lazily. She shifted some of the pots around so that none were overcooked while others remained tepid.

By ten o'clock, the hungry customers had lined up outside the basement door, old cloths in their hands to prevent their fingers from burning as they transported their cholent home. Cholent was a stew known the world over by different names and in existence since antiquity. There were countless variants—it derived its flavor from beef, chicken, potatoes, beans, barley, with or without vegetables, that simmered in low heat for about twenty hours. It was the traditional Shabbas meal.

In theory, Manya admitted three people at a time to select one of the pots that she pulled from the oven on a huge plank. In fact, the aggressive ones jumped the line, pushed and shoved, and amid the shouts and curses, pot covers flew, ingredients spilled and Manya's flyswatter went into action in an attempt to maintain order.

If she was tired when she entered the bakery under a cloak of darkness, she left with no energy at all after cleaning the mess on the floor and on the basement steps. She tucked her white hair under a shawl large enough to conceal most of her face, claimed her own pot of cholent and stumbled to her building and up the four flights of stairs. There she tore off her shawl, and in the Sabbath silence went to bed.

The next day she doled out the pennies from her tips the night before to the Armenian janitor's son, Egoyan, pronounced "Eddy," and he and Jack went to the movies, mostly silent films with written dialogue. They sat through the program two or three times, after which Jack reenacted every piece of action, improvising dialogue, as he did for the rest of his life.

One Friday night, Joe Bloom, visibly excited, had no patience for either chess or horse-racing news. He helped Manya serve the men, clear the dishes, and wash and clean the disorderly kitchen, the sooner to rush her and Jack out of the gaming room. "I have a surprise for you."

"Is it a present?"

"It's the best I can give you. Tomorrow, I'll pick up Jack first, then we'll come to the bakery where I'll show you the surprise. Let Greenspan clean up the mess for once."

"If I don't clean up, he'll fire me."

"No, you'll fire him."

Joe ran off without his good-night kiss.

Too tired to speculate on her friend's behavior, Manya gathered her two charges and sank into bed with her clothes on.

True to his word, Joe called for young Jack in midmorning. The day was crisp, sunny. Bertha left with Mrs. Molka for Saturday morning services at the shul, located in the shadows of the Second Avenue El. There the men prayed in the rows of long, backless wooden benches in the front and the women huddled in the rear. Shul held no delight for Bertha. She did enjoy the other little girls, who explained "Gayn pishen" to their mothers but actually never entered the smelly, dilapidated toilet. Instead, they collected at the back, whispered and talked, showed off their Shabbas dresses, a change from their everyday outfits, and didn't return to their seats until the rebbe intoned the Sabbath blessing at noon. Bertha enjoyed the sociability; this was her one contact with girls her own age. Too busy to enroll her in school, Manya experienced no remorse, believing that her son was as good a teacher as any. In shul the little girls kept their voices low, spoke in a variety of languages, and in the absence of parental supervision experienced a chattering joy.

At the same hour, the basement of Greenspan's bakery was bedlam, the last customers calling for the bubbling pots. Greenspan, the owner, never showed his face, claiming extreme piety, while Manya dealt with the voracious crowds.

Not on this day. Once the pans rested on the tables, Joe deftly bustled Manya out of there, beaming at his own cunning.

"Where are we going? Where are you taking me?"

"Not far. A few streets. You'll see."

Holding Jack's left hand and Manya's right, Joe led them to 12 Orchard Street.

The building required finishing touches: the plasterers had yet to add the decorative cornices. But it smelled of clean wood, clean plaster and clean air. They climbed up two flights of stairs, where a bulky man with smudged glasses low on his nose announced "Weinstock-the-agent" and flung open the door of the first apartment.

They stepped into the kitchen, which faced Canal Street, and stared in wonder at a new gas range, a new wooden icebox, a half-wall of new wooden cupboards. The walls were painted white. The sun, a vast orange, hung close enough in the sky to touch. The brilliant light after the frozen north of Ludlow Street, the location on one of the best-known streets in the vicinity, the water tower in the near distance, and beyond it the grid of multiple streets, evoked from Manya two words: "Gan Edan." Garden of Eden. She believed it for the next thirty years.

Joe Bloom sat on the kitchen windowsill as mother and son inspected the front room with its coal-burning heater. One tiny bedroom faced Canal; the second bedroom looked out on Orchard Street, where no pushcarts were permitted.

"It's yours, Manya, so you can open a restaurant right here, and be your own boss and not be exploited by Greenspan and Tyvil. It's my gift to you."

"What are you saying? What are you telling me?"

Joe burst into tears, shaking uncontrollably.

"He paid the first month's rent," explained Weinstock-the-agent. "Ten dollars a month for 12 Orchard Street, for your new restaurant."

"Ten dollars a month? Every month? How will I pay it? How will I start a restaurant?"

Weinstock shrugged.

"Why is he crying?"

Regaining control, Joe Bloom replied, "I quit my job at the *Forward* yesterday. I'm moving far away."

"Where's far? The Bronx?" Weinstock demanded.

"No. Chicago."

"Chicago?" Manya leaned against the not-yet-installed double washtubs. "What's in Chicago?"

"My brother, the one who fixes watches. He's married to a lovely girl, Miriam Rosen. She has a sister, Ruchela, Rachel. I'm marrying her. Two brothers to two sisters. An apartment upstairs with the business downstairs."

He held up his dye-stained fingers. "Do you think these hands can fix watches like Spinoza?" Stumbling, eyes brimming with tears, he tackled the new steps two at a time and was gone.

"It's ba-shert," Weinstock said, nodding. "How do you say that in English?"

"Meant to be," answered precocious Jack.

The following day Manya took leave of Tyvil. Everyone said he was an evil omen. Without his talented cook business faltered. One night, the place went up in flames. Rumors circulated that Tyvil himself set the store on fire in a drunken rage. Or that one of his wives or one of his mistresses did it. Or that the Orthodox community, in a fit of religious anger, hired a *Shabbas goy,* a non-Jew, to destroy the sinful Tyvil. Poking amid the rubble, Tyvil fell and broke his leg, and then, with his wives, mistresses and his secret recipe for gut-wrenching booze, he moved away.

Simultaneously, while the gossip swirled around Manya—that she had worked for a gangster, a mobster, a thief and a bigamist—she had a visit from the Lipinskis, distant cousins from Odessa, who were childless. Husband and wife looked like brother and sister, short, dark-haired, bereaved because they were barren. They sat on two of Manya's mismatched chairs, cried into their spotless handkerchiefs, and begged to have Bertha live with them.

Gittel, the wife, gulping her sentences as she wept, offered to walk Bertha to and from school—she tactfully avoided the fact that Manya hadn't bothered to register the child as yet—to feed her the best food, to buy her seven dresses, one for each day of the week, and since Duved, the husband, sold beauty supplies wholesale, Bertha could have her hair washed and set every week in their steam-heated four-room apartment in the Bronx.

Manya listened carefully, sighed and gave her answer.

"It's not up to me, it's for Bertha to decide. This is not Russia where Jews couldn't walk the streets, learn and study with Russians, weren't Russians by law, suffered from the Cossacks. They thought each one of us was an anarchist, we didn't deserve to live. No one asked what we thought or believed. But here, a child can answer for herself. You have to ask Bertha what she wants." Manya delivered this speech in rapid-fire Yiddish, not pausing for breath.

Gittel twisted her handkerchief. "We heard you were very educated."

Disregarding the compliment, Manya addressed her young sister. "Bertha, they will love you and you wouldn't be living in the streets, sleeping with neighbors. We have this beautiful new apartment, but I'm opening a restaurant here. How I'll do it, I don't know; maybe I still have to work at the bakery. The Lipinskis, they'll give you a different life." Manya was close to tears.

Jack leaned over and whispered into Bertha's ear. He talked and talked. Bertha listened and nodded. Finally she looked up. "I'll go live in the Bronx, but only if I can come here every Friday night and stay to Sunday night."

They kept this arrangement until Bertha married. Manya made the wedding, held at 12 Orchard Street.

Manya, my grandmother, my Bubby, and her adored son, Jack, my father, left Ludlow Street and moved into the Orchard Street apartment facing Canal Street, and there she started her private restaurant, serving five-course meals from 11:00 A.M. to 3:00 P.M. It was called dinner then, the largest meal of the day. My grandmother's dinners soon became the rage with local merchants and others who frequented the Lower East Side.

Though still in short pants, Jack had the wisdom to suggest that the front room could be enlarged by tearing down the wall between it and the tiny bedroom above Canal Street. He also insisted that the front room would be better off without the coal stove and its ugly tin flue. "A coal stove," he told his mother, "is for greenhorns."

"How will we keep ourselves warm if we tear it out? The only thing left would be the kitchen range."

He bested her with one sentence: "Don't you know that coal dust gives you black lung disease?" He triumphed. Her young husband had contracted tuberculosis during the six-week journey in steerage from Odessa, Russia, to Ellis Island in New York. He died when he was twenty, leaving my six-month-old father half an orphan and my grandmother a widow. Nothing frightened Manya more than the prospect of losing her only child to a lung illness. Mother and son developed a phobia on the subject of lung problems.

My own early recollections of my father were of him shaking down the thermometer, inserting it under his tongue and then pacing on the Persian rug until certain that his temperature had registered. One degree higher than normal did not alarm them. But should it rise to a hundred, he was rushed into bed with a mustard plaster on his chest, which Bubby prepared with dry mustard and vinegar, placed in a brown paper bag, and covered with an old towel. If that failed, she sent for the barber, who arrived with a set of glass bulbs with narrow mouths that he heated with a small torch and arranged on my father's chest. The cupping brought the blood to the surface of the skin, creating circles as round and symmetrical as red checkers.

Even as a young child my father recognized his mother's anxiety about his health, and he played it like a wild card whenever he wanted something that she temporarily resisted. Getting rid of the coal stove had been a walk in the park for a player as adroit as little Jack Roth. Having the wall pulled down between two rooms required greater finesse and more ingenuity. It took him a week or more to come up with a plan.

"Weinstock-the-agent who collects the rent, he'll do it for you," Jack announced. "He likes you and your free meals. Say you'll pay for the cost, for the workers, but he can't tell the landlord, who won't like the idea. Work on Weinstock. Don't take no for an answer. He'll do it for you." Jack paused over the chicken fricassee—chicken and tiny meatballs cooked together, flavored with paprika and a dash of cinnamon, a sprinkle of sugar to cut the acidity of the tomatoes. "But he can't give you any kisses for doing you this favor."

Jack guarded his mother jealously, happy that they didn't hear again from Joe Bloom after he moved to Chicago. He hated every one of her suitors, every male visitor who dropped in for a glass of slivovitz that she prepared in a storage closet in the back of the building. Most of these men were Odessaniks, who had not known Manya in the old country but were sent to her via the constant chain of gossip within the ghetto.

What my Bubby served her customers on any given day quickly reverberated around the entire quarter. All of her purveyors—Kufflick the butter-and-egg man, Saperstein from the appetizer store, Pollack in the bakery—shared the knowledge of Manya's kitchen. Newly arrived youths still with sidelocks and scraggly beards dropped into our restaurant. She confessed that disuse had made the Russian language remote to her, and to account for the steady stream of visitors, she explained that if it weren't for them, her Russian would have long been forgotten. Yet they rarely conversed in Russian, only Yiddish. Her son regarded each man as a potential threat, including the shabbiest in their shiny jackets and worn-out cuffs, or boys hardly older than he was. Although he concocted the scheme about Weinstock, he realized there might be a calculated risk, in terms of a flirtation with his mother.

Weinstock-the-agent—few men seemed to own a first name— huffed and sweated his way up the two flights of stairs to the restaurant to collect the monthly rent and of course his free meal. He was notorious for dumping the various dishes together. Chopped liver, gefilte fish, tongue in sweet-and-sour sauce, cold salmon in hollandaise, all went right into his soup bowl.

Simultaneously he would cut up the side dishes—sweetened cucumbers in vinegar, beets decorated with slices of hard-boiled eggs, my grandmother's own cured sauerkraut—and place them in the kasha (groats) or in the mashed or roasted potatoes, along with his chicken or brisket of beef, with whatever broth was left in his soup bowl. Shrugging his thick shoulders, he would explain, "It goes in the same place, and I like the surprise of finding something new in my plate every minute."

Some of the diners refused to have their meals in the same room as Weinstock, so he found himself banished to the kitchen. Far from feeling insulted, he shivered with delight. If he ate at the kitchen table, he could grab still more food from the trays and pots that covered every surface. Eating sent his moist steel-rimmed glasses sliding to the end of his bulbous nose.

My grandmother overlooked his boorish manners not because he brought in demolition workers to remove the wall between the bedroom and living room without telling the landlord, but because she was indulgent toward all males. Even someone as crude as Weinstock elicited her compassion. "Just think of his poor wife," she said, laughing, "having to live with such a bulvan."

The enlarged room became an asset and Weinstock took the credit for the idea. At first jealously flared among the neighbors because Manya had the largest living room in the building, but they all agreed that her restaurant brought class and distinction to everyone who lived at 12 Orchard Street. Eventually the talk about the enlarged room died down.

To a significant degree Jack's vision of how life should be lived came from the movies. He attended every change of program at the neighborhood theaters and walked to Second Avenue for the latest ones. During one of those pseudo-British films in which Constance Bennett trilled her r's and said "rawther" every other minute to certify that she was a genuine Brit, she leaned against a grand piano covered with a heavily embroidered shawl with a border of luxurious fringe. Bug-eyed at the sight, Jack had to have one like it for Orchard Street. He depended on his mother to obtain the shawl.

Physically, Manya was both appealing and aristocratic in her bearing. It wasn't her copious white hair that attracted men, her flawless white skin, her billowing breasts, but the innate womanliness that emanated from her. Even when she wore her cooking clothes—a mammoth Hoover apron that she slipped on over her head and tied around a baggy dress or her cardigan sweater, a dull brown thing appropriate for shopping—she exuded a sympathetic femininity.

Manya didn't give much thought to her appearance. More often than not she washed her face and body with the brown kosher soap that contained no fat from forbidden animals, and wrapped her hair in a haphazard bun held together with several large imitation-turquoise hairpins. Her cooking shoes were splattered with chicken and goose fat, bits and oddments of duck, salmon roe, even calves' brains. Because she had been raised on the Black Sea, she loved caviar, so every now and then a glistening bead would fall upon her well-fed shoes. The smell of food on her body made her no less alluring. More than one male customer winked and said he would like to feed upon her.

When her precocious son demanded the embroidered shawl for the dining table she cried out, "Where will I get it? On a pushcart? In a store down here? Maybe we have to ride uptown. Maybe I have to put on my good shoes and a blue silk dress. You can't walk into uptown stores like a beggar."

"Someone will get it for you. But you must be charming."

"And who should I charm? Sophie Gimbel? Madame Hattie Carnegie?"

Jack began his characteristic pacing as he thought through his scheme. Abruptly he stopped and answered, "Orloff."

"Orloff, the silk man? Meshugana," his mother protested. "Everything in his store is from fire sales, water sales, damaged dye lots, with colors that no one wants and he has to sell two cents a yard above cost. From him you're expecting a shawl with fringes like in the movies?"

Jack leaned over and kissed her cheek. He loved her overwhelmingly and he often averted his glance from her lest he betray how deeply he felt. He parceled out his kisses for the same reason.

"No, Maminyu, I don't think Orloff sells a silk shawl, but he knows where to find one. I'll go with you when you ask him. I'll be waiting outside the door, or under the steps. If he gets fresh, I'll be there to protect you."

It was a well-known fact that Orloff had a crush on Manya, despite his marriage and his three children. He would have abandoned his waterlogged silks and charred remnants and rattled down the steps for one real kiss from Manya.

My grandmother tried to impose logic on her son's fantasy about the shawl. During business hours, they spread white cloths on the large mahogany table that she had bought on Clinton Street with her first earnings and on the folding tables that they put away after dinner. What need would they have in the evening for a luxury item?

Jack asserted that the shawl was necessary for their souls.

My father never explained his need for things of beauty, and although his mother realized that the shawl represented art as much as a painting, a vase or the candlesticks she had brought from Odessa, she faced the reality of her limited means. She indulged Jack in every way possible, but an item that cost three weeks of work in her kitchen— well, for once she would deny what she regarded as a temporary fancy. She had not, however, counted on the strength of his desire. Every morning when he brushed his teeth at the kitchen sink and late at night when he piled on two or three sweaters for sleeping, he asked, "Are you getting the silk shawl or not?"

Business in her restaurant came to a virtual halt on Saturday. The merchants were busy with uptown bargain seekers and stayed in their stores; they didn't take time out to eat until they closed their shops and went home. The Orthodox wouldn't handle money on Saturday and always ate with their families. Many of the neighbors criticized Manya for cooking on Saturday morning and serving an occasional customer a snack. She ignored this. She clung to her notion of acceptable behavior as she had done in the years when she worked in Greenspan's bakery on Saturdays. If men opened their stores on Saturday, why couldn't she do the same with her restaurant? Still business merely trickled in and Manya regarded Saturday as her day off.

So it came to pass that one warm Saturday morning, Manya took a thorough wash at the kitchen sink, donned the brassiere that she wore for special occasions, and pulled on her corset from the Orchard Corset Discount Center. Of her two good dresses, she selected the watery blue silk as the best for a stroll down Orchard Street. She took special care with her long white hair, braiding the strands in the front and piling them to the top of her head to form a tiara. With a tiny dusting of Coty's face powder, she sallied forth in her patent leather pumps to Orloff's House of Silks.

My father loped after her. As soon as she ascended the flight of stairs to Orloff's store he planted himself across the street, shading his eyes against the spring sun and squinting to make out the images through Orloff's windows.

At the sight of Manya—unannounced and unexpected—Orloff's bald head glistened with sweaty excitement and his beady eyes darted. "Manya, Manya, mine libbe," he cried dramatically and lunged for her lips. She sidestepped; the kiss landed on her jaw. Too polite, she did not wipe off the spot.

"Hand to God," Orloff sighed, "the Czarina was never as beautiful as you."

"Orloff, you're a married man with three children. Don't act foolish."

"For you I would be foolish, crazy, stupid, smart. What do you want?"

"I want a large silk shawl, a light color, with embroidery and fringes."

Orloff took a step backward. His pursed mouth, often smelling of garlic and chicken fat rubbed on pumpernickel bread, fell open. "Manya, you need that shawl for the opera? You're going to the opera, to the ballet?" He pronounced it "bahlee."

"No, it's not for me to wear. It's for my table, my dining room table." As if to forestall any comments about so decorative an item on Orchard Street, she added imperiously, "And I'm getting a Persian rug. You'll help me with both of them."

"And what will you give me if I help you?" He edged closer to her.

She rolled her eyes heavenward and slid out the door.

Five or six weeks later, the perfect shawl arrived from uptown. He, Orloff, had taken the subway to Fifty-seventh Street, to a shop with fancy prices, and he sold it to her at cost, hand to his heart, not a penny did he take for himself because Manya's happiness came first.

Young Jack regarded the shawl with awe. It was pale ivory silk, with cabbage roses embroidered in red, lavender and white thread. The heavy ivory fringe swept down almost to the floor. "Classy," my father said.

From a knot in her stocking Manya retrieved twenty dollars, turning chastely away so that Orloff did not catch a peek at her snowy thigh. After he consumed a meal of made-on-the-premises pickled herring, barley mushroom soup, duck with red cabbage and potato pancakes, Linzer torte and three glasses of tea with four lumps of sugar and raspberry jam on the bottom, served in a filigreed holder, Orloff pretended to give Manya a receipt. Instead he kissed her full on the lips. She shooed him out with a quick push and a slam of the door. A few months later, a rug peddler staggered in with a secondhand Persian rug, almost good as new, taken from a Turkish boat that very morning. What with the silk shawl for the table and the Persian rug, my Bubby's salon became the talk of the neighborhood.

2

Paradoxes

CUSTOM DICTATED THAT Jack have his rite of passage as a man, his bar mitzvah, when he reached the age of twelve instead of thirteen, because he had no father. Already taller than his mother and dressed in a gray suit with a white shirt and navy blue tie, he wowed the guests and the various officials at shul with his rapid-fire readings of the Hebrew text and his speech in English so elevated that he could compete with any young man a decade older.

After the services Bubby served a sit-down dinner at home for selected guests: the Lipinskis and Bertha; Weinstock and his wife, who was his former sister-in-law whom he had married when his first wife succumbed to the flu; Orloff and his wife, not as yet adapted to American ways and still wearing an outdated wig, a sparrow's nest, on her head; Greenspan from the bakery without his wife and free to grow roaringly drunk during the first hour; Saperstein, her sturgeon and caviar purveyor; and Stein the butcher, who had been the first to race to her side when her husband died. And then there was Dr. Koronovsky, fresh out of medical school and already a legend for his handling of epidemics that bore away dozens of inhabitants in a single day.

Of the many toasts in Jack's honor, the most stirring was provided by young Dr. K., who assured everyone that Jack Roth, with his gift for language, was destined to become a brilliant lawyer, possibly a judge, and undoubtedly, if Jews were permitted this privilege, a government official. After these rousing words he handed Jack a five-dollar gold piece.

Bubby shed tears of joy. Jack, slick of hair and adult in bearing, grew two inches taller from the praise. After dinner the doors of the apartment were thrown open and everyone, whether invited or not, could partake of the "sweet table": slices of cheesecake, bundt cake, strudel, rugulach, strawberry shortcake prepared with sponge cake, honey cake, macaroons, chocolate cake, Linzer torte, nut cookies, lemon cookies, sugar cookies, hamantaschen, prune Danish and cinnamon twists— mountains of everything. "Manya's affair" created buzzing gossip and conversation for years to come. What other bar mitzvah could match free food of such variety and quality?

At high school, Jack zoomed ahead, grew bored and restless with the bland subjects. Who knows whether he would have fulfilled his destiny as a lawyer if he hadn't walked over to Division Street just for laughs and been hired immediately to sell coats to women who knew little about fashion and less about speedy, eloquent speech. Within months, working only on Saturday and Sunday, Jack became known as "the man who loved to dress women."

My father was a womanizer, yet he never sustained an affair with a woman. His standard opener for flirtations consisted of, "Darling, how does it feel to be beautiful?" No hypocrisy fell from his lips. In fact, attractive women filled him with wonder and his immediate response led him to plan their improvement.

"You know," he would suggest, "green is not your best color. It does nothing for your complexion and makes your skin look sallow." *Sallow* intrigued them. Uncertain of its meaning, they submitted to the man who could express himself so grandly.

Colors were part of Jack's artistry and like a painter he expounded on them. He hated greens and browns and asserted as if set in concrete that only middle-aged women preferred purple. He dismissed white attire as "ice cream suits" but adored every shade of blue; azure suggested morning, periwinkle the afternoon and navy blue the evening.

Because many women in adjacent Little Italy rarely discarded their black mourning clothes, Jack advised black in small doses: black with a pinstripe; a black skirt topped with a white jacket à la Chanel, especially if worn with an expensive fur. "Never put a rat on your back," my father would instruct me as we rode the subway together, and he would point out every fur in the subway car. By rats he meant squirrel or muskrat, though in more confidential moments he admitted that minks and sables in their natural state resembled glossy rodents.

For my father, the worst offense was a print dress, especially fabrics that sprouted flowers. "You want flowers," he chided, "buy a hat, visit a milliner." Five minutes after he met a customer at the store where he worked, or a woman at a social gathering or in the lobby of a movie house, and he engaged her in conversation, he gently removed her lapel pin, invariably made of colored glass. He permitted my mother, Lil, to wear a long string of fake pearls that, in the current style, descended to her waist, but in general he despised costume jewelry, imitation gold bracelets that jangled, plastic buttons and flat-heeled shoes: "Like Greta Garbo out for a walk." In matters of taste, my mother conceded to my father without question.

When Jack first met Lil, he rejected her boring monochromatic attire: brown shirtwaist, long brown skirt. "The only thing to do with that outfit is burn it," he told her. We heard the story until it passed into legend of their first date, when he commanded her to lift up her skirts. They were in my grandmother's living room, the same one in which my brother, Willy, and I grew up.

"What gams," he exclaimed. "You could make it in the Follies."

My mother hung her head, overwhelmed by the grandeur of the room, the Persian rug and the embroidered silk shawl with long fringes that graced the table. She could hear Jack's mother, Manya, busy in the kitchen, an inhibiting factor.

My mother asked, "You mean that?" and dropped her skirts.

"No, I'm just an uptown guy who feeds a pretty girl a line, then forgets her." He called out, "Ma, come here."

Bubby moved to the doorway of the living room.

"What do you think?" he asked.

"Zee iz zayer yung," she said in Yiddish, to spare young Lil the embarrassment.

Throughout the many years that they lived together my grandmother defended any deficiencies in my mother with the same phrase, "She is very young."

My father wasn't asking for his mother's approval. At the age of fourteen, when he sprang up to six feet, he had started parading the young girls before his mother. She responded to them democratically: fed them, exchanged a few words of politeness, then closed her mouth as well as her eyes. Ritual taught her that the next day or the day after there would be another girl, skinny, wide-eyed, undernourished, badly dressed. Still, she paused to consider his question about Lil.

"Where shall I begin?"

"With the head."

As my grandmother later told me, she was referring to whether or not my mother could keep up with her fast-talking, quick-witted son. He, on the other hand, concentrated on the color of Lil's hair. "Blonde or red?"

"Rayt vee un Tzigeunner?"

"You're right, red is for gypsies. We'll go for natural blonde." And he marched the sixteen-year-old Lil to Pandy's beauty parlor on Clinton Street.

Did my mother protest when Jack discussed the shade of hair he desired with the beautician, Pandy? Did she ask a question, possibly offer her own suggestion? She sat there mute, gaga-eyed with instant love, mesmerized by this tall, thin young man with his gleaming black hair, his suit complete with vest, and the disarming way he appraised her.

Jack took an intense interest in every aspect of Lil's revitalized hair, holding her hand while the color dried as if she were a patient about to undergo a medical procedure that required soothing words. He told her that he, Jack Roth, had a perfect eye, the way some musicians had perfect pitch. More often than not his vocabulary confounded her, made her wonder in astonishment what he was saying. She was sixteen, and she earned her living wrapping coats and suits into tissue paper before she boxed them at a store on Division Street; she hadn't finished high school because her family of seven brothers and two sisters needed the money she earned. Yet here she sat with a City College man.

Yes, Jack had registered at college, and yes, he attended a few classes sporadically. But he was too enchanted with life, with young women, with his sporty clothes, with Broadway plays, with movies, with his desire to dress and clothe women appropriately to bother with sitting in classrooms. He read voraciously. He told Lil about deep plays that he had seen by Eugene O'Neill, or novels by Ernest Hemingway that made her blush. Later, my mother cried because God had made me take after him instead of her when it came to reading.

An autodidact, my father loved to dispute H. L. Mencken's articles out loud. He read three newspapers a day, but mostly he enjoyed the tabloids, explaining to Lil about yellow journalism. He wished he could write like Winchell or Damon Runyon, idolized Ben Hecht and Mark Hellinger.

When Lil's hair came out the exact shade he desired, Jack gazed upon her as if he had created a masterwork. In fact my mother became an ongoing creation of which he rarely tired.

A zealot about every article of her clothes, he chose her dresses and coats as well as her shoes. Though our apartment resembled a bitter hell in the winter with its windows covered with ice, he didn't allow her to sleep in flannel nightgowns. No matter if she wore a sweater over her nightie, it had to be silk or crepe, soft to the touch. "Flannel is for old ladies, older than Bubby," he declared when he lectured me on his favorite topic, "How Women Should Dress."

Once in a rash moment, he bought my mother a fur jacket made from bits and pieces of seal fur, a patchwork shortie. My mother hated it on sight, and possibly in revolt against Jack's rigid code, on arctic days she defiantly wore it to the toilet in the hall. Subsequently, she thought of a better purpose for it, namely as a partial bedspread that covered their shoulders and ears.

My father tormented himself for that mistake. How could he have made such a purchase? What was he, blind, a beggar with a box of pencils, some greenhorn off the boat conned by the bargain price? But I assumed that most people had fur bedspreads, and loved to nap under the seal pelt. My father's sense of disgrace rekindled every time he looked at it, and one day when the weather skyrocketed to unseasonably warm, he tossed the fur out the window on the Orchard Street side. Immediately, a passerby in full retreat claimed the unexpected bounty, and Jack's blunder disappeared forever.

My mother was a golden person, or at least Jack transformed her into one. Sometimes, when in a playful mood, Lil instructed my brother, Willy, and me to state our address as "Orchard Lane," bringing to mind the movie version of southern mansions surrounded by hundred-year-old leafy trees in perpetual bloom.

Not that our location really bothered Lil. Variously, she borrowed the street number of Jacob's Men's Clothing, a store on Canal Street directly under our apartment, or decided on her friend Ada's address on East Broadway, two blocks south of the *Jewish Forward* building. In bolder moments she announced that we resided in the Amalgamated buildings, an apartment complex funded by money from the garment workers' union. She had New York street smarts and could have devoured the entire city with her seductive smile and white teeth. The ethics of survival dictated how my mother acted or what she said; expedience was all.

I always cringed when sightseeing buses rumbled down Orchard Street with the bus guide shouting through a megaphone, "Here we are on Orchard Street where they sell black for blue and blue for black." Street urchins ran after the bus, the girls raising their shabby skirts to show their dirty underpants, the boys yelling, "Monkeys in the zoo, they look the same as you."

The tour buses never fazed Lil. Always fashionably dressed, she wore high-heeled shoes even when walking to the toilet in the hallway. She regarded herself as sophisticated enough to move uptown in a wink, if only she and Jack had the money. The Orchard Street apartment was Bubby's, and though Lil moved in the day she married Jack, and was to hand over her two children to be raised by Manya, she regarded the arrangement as temporary. Some act of magic would one day whisk the whole family off to West End Avenue, the middle-class Jewish mecca for which she yearned.

Every Friday, on their day off, Jack and Lil rode the subway uptown, maybe to the Palace or the Roxy, possibly to Radio City Music Hall, although the live entertainment at Radio City did not suit my father. He loved Broadway musicals with singable tunes—Ethel Merman was his favorite—and whenever possible he bought tickets to her shows. On the return trip, if a vendor was standing at the steps of the Forty-second Street subway, my father bought a song sheet printed on cheap green paper that provided the lyrics to the latest popular tunes. As soon as they danced through the door of the apartment, my mother began to sing, not stopping until she had gone through all the lyrics on the sheet.

That was the best part of Lil: singing. She sang throughout the day, accompanied by music from the radio or by songs in her head. She had neither the style nor the cadence of great women vocalists, but her voice came through without affectation and she could instinctively deliver a tune. Her greatest failure was her haphazard memory. She couldn't remember lyrics from one song to the next, and in midtune and at a loss, she didn't scat sing like Louis Armstrong; she either jumbled some nonsense syllables together or she snapped her fingers and I provided the words.

From the age of five, maybe earlier, I served as my mother's prompter. If we had guests and she took the floor to sing, I tried to remain as invisible as possible while mouthing lyrics. I memorized every song in her repertoire. Lil needed no prompting for oldies like "Margie," "You're Mean to Me," or "Melancholy Baby" and she did a fair imitation of Harry Richman singing "Putting on the Ritz." But a song like "Prisoner of Love" stumped her—she couldn't reach the line "I need no shackles to remind me" without going blank, and she botched "Button Up Your Overcoat," referring to "bootleg hootch" as "hootchey kootch." Not that anyone cared. Gifted with a cabaret vibrato that carried her along, she brought down the house with her rendition of "Are You Lonesome Tonight?"

She and my father always ended the entertainment by harmonizing the Irving Berlin standard "All Alone," although my father had to carry her through the last line, "Wondering where you are / and how you are / and if you are / all alone, too."

Once, when my father heard me singing "Button Up Your Overcoat," he stopped me in midsong. "Mother sings, you listen," he reminded me. Yet he agreed it was in my mother's best interest that I stand behind her swirly skirt and when she faltered whisper the words she needed.

My brother, Willy, and I never resented our parents' diversions and entertainments, or their fine clothes compared to our shabby ones. Glamorous as movie stars, and drawing admiring attention when they walked arm in arm through the tumultuous streets on their way to work or to the subway, they occupied their own universe. Encouraged by Bubby, who attempted to shield them from the harsher realities of the ghetto, they had the aura of visitors who sometimes invited their children to their parties.

Bubby maintained an ironclad schedule to which she was devoted. Because of chronic insomnia, she awoke at first light, turned on the gas range in the kitchen to warm the apartment, heated water in the tea kettle toward the hour when we would want to wash our hands and faces, and prepared "fendel" coffee for herself. Although her skills as a chef met no challenge, her coffee was dreadful.

We did own a percolator, which she pronounced "poker-lady," but for herself she heated water in a *fendel*—a small pan—and when it boiled she threw in a handful of ground coffee, letting the whole seethe and bubble until it yielded a noxious brown fluid. In theory, the grounds would settle at the bottom of the pan; in fact they would find their way into coffee cups. When I was still drinking from a bottle, the not-too-clean-pan in which my milk was warmed often contained coffee grounds, which I hated. Since my parents slept late, my grandmother prepared percolated coffee for them, or my father had breakfast at some diner close to Wall Street. But she herself drank fendel coffee the day long.

She ate nothing until she returned from shopping for her daily supplies. Until I started kindergarten, I accompanied her. We set out early and she carried two large black oilcloth bags, which she held in one hand, and held on to me with the other.

Her first stop was at the poultry market, where women sat plucking fowl of every kind that had been slaughtered under the supervision of a rabbi. I hated the sight of these women with their bent backs and wan faces. From the tops of their heads to their messy aprons to their shoes, they were covered with clouds of feathers from chickens, geese and ducks. Since chicken enhanced most of our soups, Bubby bought two chickens every day—one for soup, and the other for roasting or stew, and when available, goose or duck. Her notion of a three o'clock snack for me was to take a goose liver, place it on a wrinkled brown paper bag and bake it in the oven. When the liver was crisp around the edges, she peeled it from the paper and added a few grains of kosher salt. Not until many years later did I learn that goose liver meant foie gras, an emblematic delicacy for the well-to-do.

Once we finished buying the fowl, we entered the dairy store, where Bubby tasted the sour cream from a large tin milk can whose handles sported communal tasting spoons affixed to cords that had once been white but were now black. Kufflick, the dairy man, always had a cigarette between his lips and more than once as he passed the sour cream can his ashes fell in the white cream. He sported a long beard and wore a skullcap, or yarmulke, as oily as his thick black unwashed hair.

When not ladling sour cream or cutting butter from a wooden tub with a sharp-edged paddle, he spent his moments screaming at the cats that slid into his shop whenever the door opened. They lapped up droplets of sour cream that fell to the floor from the tasting spoons. Every now and then, he'd cut a thin slice of cheese from whatever round had been reduced to slivers and hand it to me. It wasn't that he liked me—he wanted to impress Manya. Then he retired to his dark room in the rear to candle the eggs, making sure that not a single egg contained a blood spot.

Since Bubby baked daily, it would have been prudent to buy a two-day supply of eggs and butter, but unthinkable for a woman European to the core. She counted on her food shopping as part of her social intercourse, to exchange news and gossip: what child had the pox, which woman had been widowed during the night, what Jewish gangster shot or arrested, what disease swept through the ghetto. On Saturdays, when she didn't shop, Bubby groaned with restlessness, bereft, as if she had misplaced an object that she couldn't find.

We could hear her sighing with relief when Sunday morning arrived and the ghetto revitalized itself, people from all over the city surging through the streets, hunting for bargains, for excitement, the endless haggling over a few cents or a few dollars. Sundays on the Lower East Side offered drama as compelling as theater. And Manya was part of it. Shopping between Orchard and Essex streets evoked a European market fair. In the bitterest weather or the most humid, she went forth with her oilcloth shopping bags. The merchants would hail her: "Manya, Manya, you should go to the Yiddish Tayater on Second Avenue, Molly Picon in *Ah Be Zum Labin*, or *Der Alta Koenik,* oh did I cry, hub ich gevanyt, such three daughters, the oldest, a tyvil, mean to her tateh."

After the dairy store we went to Saperstein's. It gave Manya extreme pleasure and me as well. Our mouths watered at the smell of the barrels of sour pickles, the sauerkraut, the red and green pickled tomatoes, at the vats of black olives. I loved the counter filled with lox, whitefish, sturgeon. Saperstein looked like a sturgeon, long, white, sharp-toothed. I marveled at the way he wielded his razor-sharp knife. Cutting a bit of translucent smoked sturgeon, you expected it to shred if you breathed on it.

Manya achieved status as his sturgeon expert. She had grown up with sturgeon, a staple along the Black Sea, and she pronounced a sample too salty, too mealy from being packed in ice, too strong in flavor, or absolutely perfect. Saperstein, a purist, inevitably felt sad that his customers did not truly appreciate his top-of-the-line products. He communed with Bubby over a slice of sturgeon or belly lox as if having a religious moment.

Even when bad weather kept customers away from our restaurant and we were low in cash, Bubby invested in a few slices of smoked sturgeon, not for her customers, but for our family. She could ignore lox, smoked whitefish, pickles or fresh herring, but she couldn't do without the weekly treat of sturgeon. To prove that he was a sporting man who approved of her taste, Saperstein created a cone from white paper and dropped in some caviar, which he kept in a tin secreted in a hole under the counter—God forbid during a robbery, the thieves would never discover his hiding place. For Manya he saved his best maslinas, black wrinkled olives almost the size of small black plums, that she prized.

Our last stop was Pollack's bakery—Greenspan had long since retired—to buy one large rye, and one pumpernickel that I carried, unwrapped. We never kept bread for the next day, giving any remnants to beggars. Staples such as sugar, flour, barley, kasha, dried beans, my mother bought at the grocery store because she didn't mind carrying those bulky items once a week.

Plodding home, exhausted but exhilarated, we finally climbed the two flights of steps to our door. Always, before she sat down, Bubby took the breads from my hands and cut the pumpernickel European-style, the bread held to her chest and the knife flashing inward instead of away from her body. Two slices of bread cut, she would root in her shopping bags, famished for some of her newly acquired purchases.

For a number of years, Negro boys, some as young as ten, entered New York via freight cars from the South. Unable to find work and starving, they went from bakery to bakery to beg for bread. If they stumbled into Pollack's bakery on Hester Street, Mrs. P. didn't spare them as much as a two-day-old kaiser roll. Instead, she directed them to Manya's Restaurant, where until she ran out of food, Bubby gave away everything that was left over from the midday dinner and the scrawny young black boys scurried down the stairs with their bits and pieces, looking like underfed birds whose skinny legs hardly seemed able to carry them.

One such youngster moved Bubby deeply. In the midst of a cold spell, with a wind that made it impossible to catch your breath in the street, he showed up in pants that were literally in shreds and with no shoes on his feet. He may have been the runt of his family's litter because though he swore he was twelve, he appeared no more than seven: short, with a washboard chest and a pinched face.

At first we thought he was mute. He seemed incapable of answering the simplest questions, such as his name or the place from which he had come. But gently coaxed by Bubby, who embraced him and whispered in his ear, he uttered his name: "Carlton." This was too difficult for her to pronounce so she renamed him Clayton, gave him some of my brother's old clothes, a jar of cabbage borscht with beef in it, and as much bread as he could carry. The next morning when she opened the door to go out to the toilet in the hall, she discovered Clayton curled up on the floor, his arms wrapped around the soup jar.

Bubby could not resist nurturing him. At first he slept under the stairs or on the hallway landing and worked for his meals. He did the afternoon dishes, scrubbed the kitchen floor, took a steel brush to the oven and burners that otherwise rarely received more than a passing nod at cleanliness. Unlike the other neighbors who kept locks on their hallway toilets, we did not because Bubby hated the idea of locks. But our customers in their haste to get away often pissed on the floor, or failed to flush the toilet with its pull chain. First thing in the morning, Clayton cleaned the toilet. Bubby bought a remnant of linoleum, which he cut and fit around the base. He found lye to bleach out the stains in the bowl and seemed to be a master of domestic knowledge. And whatever he didn't know he soon learned from Manya.

My grandmother's purveyors often cautioned her against Clayton, sure he would cut us to pieces in our sleep. To these admonitions she responded with merriment. "I lived through the czar, I lived through the Cossacks and pogroms, now I should be afraid of a little boy? Forget such foolishness!" she said, laughing.

Because of the rats that inhabited all the tenements, she worried about Clayton sleeping in the hall, so after a few weeks she walked to the Bowery and found him a room close to Chinatown that would rent to nonwhites. The exploitative rent was a dollar a week, but she admitted to me that she lied and told everyone that it cost her fifty cents. Customers would say, "Manya, that boy will take advantage. You shouldn't be so kind to him." But Clayton became a permanent fixture in our lives.

Evidence of Manya's generosity was part of ghetto lore during the weeks before the High Holy Days in early fall that marked the Jewish new year. As we grew older, the kitchen grew smaller, but every year when Rosh Hashanah came, Bubby collected or bought Mason jars that she scrubbed and stacked beneath the kitchen window, and filled with single-course meals: chicken soup with homemade noodles, carrots and chicken breasts or thighs. Three or four cauldrons simmered on the gas flames. When the contents cooled and were poured into jars, Bubby, Clayton and I set out to distribute them, together with quarter-loaves of challah.

Walking from tenement to tenement, Bubby whispered the names of the needy, those sick, without a mate or with ailing children. Clayton carried the food. I opened the apartment doors, sought the nearest clear surface and deposited the holiday meal. We left no calling cards. Almost every recipient knew the bounty came from Manya.

For days our motley little band—a white-haired woman in a brown cardigan, a small girl in an ill-fitting spotted skirt and too-small sweater, and a black boy dressed in castoffs who carried oilcloth bags full of clanking jars wrapped in newspaper—trudged from street to street. We quit only when Bubby couldn't advance another step, or Clayton had run back two or three times to replenish our stack of jars until we had given all our food away. The following morning we began again.

Bubby considered these meals sparse, and they did not compare to our own Rosh Hashanah repast: chopped liver, gefilte fish, matzo ball soup, roast chicken, brisket of beef, stuffed cabbage, sweet potato and prune tsimmis, two kinds of kugel—noodle and potato—as well as knishes and kasha varniskas. She also baked rugulach and mandel-brot.

Neither Bubby nor my parents were much for formal ritual. My parents attended Rosh Hashanah services as briefly as they could. The synagogue was poorly ventilated and men and women were separated, so Jack and Lil could not sit together in their splendid outfits. They always aroused curiosity, as if they had wandered in by mistake.

In this congregation, it was the custom for the Orthodox men to stand in place and to sway their bodies from right to left while beating on their chests with their right fists. Although the rabbi with his long beard and sidelocks led the prayers, almost everyone knew them by heart.

Then came the moment when the scrolls—the Torah—were removed from the ark. We had read that in uptown shuls built for the wealthy the Torah scrolls were lifted up for all to see, and then returned to the ark in pristine condition. Not so here. Selected elders carried them up and down every row of seats, while some congregants leaned over and kissed the sacred writing and others put their fingers to their lips and then to the Torah.

The moment after Jack touched the Torah, he pushed his way to the exit with Willy. This was the signal for the women in our family— Bubby, Lil, me—to press into the aisle to be the first females to reach the Torah, allowing us to escape quickly, too. Bubby attended services for the sake of continuity with her past, for a nod to her origins. She especially wanted to hear mention of the Book of Life, in which she hoped our names would be written for the coming year.

Yom Kippur, the Day of Atonement, ten days later was another matter. It demanded sacrifice. Bubby and Lil fasted the full twenty-four hours, not even brushing their teeth or taking water to their lips. Children were not required to fast but I did so from the age of five, finding the prospect uplifting.

At noon, just as we started to grow ravenous, our family left the shul, and rather than be tempted by food or the possibility of a nap at home, we walked across bridges during the afternoon. Our favorites were the Brooklyn Bridge and the Williamsburg, where we met thousands of other worshipers doing the same thing. The Orthodox always cast bread upon the water for the new year. Our family's version was to walk one bridge or another to cast off our transgressions. Our clothes new and stiff, our hunger palpable, we took pride in our pale faces and visibly parched lips.

Toward dusk we walked back to shul to hear the blowing of the ram's horn, the shofar, that marked the exact moment Yom Kippur services ended. Calling out "L' shana tova" and "Gut yontif," we hastened home to eat at last.

For breaking the fast we ate cold dishes. Bubby's specialty was pickled herring, which involved weeks of preparation. She personally selected the fresh herring from large barrels at Saperstein's and we carried them home wrapped in newspaper. For days the kitchen was full of fish scales, bones and discarded heads and tails.

Bubby boiled vinegar, sugar and pickling spices in an immense vat and then poured the mix into five-quart jars in which she had already placed the cleaned fish slices and countless pounds of sliced onions. We kept a daily watch on the jars as the onions softened and grew translucent and the herring lightened from gray to white. Lil was the official taster and decided whether the marinade or the herring needed more sugar or spices. Manya's pickled herring became known citywide. We could rarely fill all the orders that we received from private parties and restaurants.

We always suspected that Jack and Willy cheated during Yom Kippur, that when they ran home for a pee they gobbled a few pieces of herring, using their fingers instead of telltale forks. But Bubby invoked our silence. It was one of her "Don't tell" strictures.

Later in the evening, the table was laden with platters of food. We welcomed neighbors, a half dozen of my mother's brothers—Grandma Rae never came—friends from Division Street, Bertha and the Lipinskis, who feasted until every scrap was gone.

We opened our folding beds with relief as soon as our guests departed, climbed in, and Bubby sang into my ear, "If there is a God, he sent you to me."

The restaurant paid for the rent of our apartment and for our outrageously large gas bills. Since my father's selling job was seasonal and he rarely worked in the summer, when business was slow in the stores on Division Street, his salary went for the indulgences that he had adopted as a youth—movies, theater and clothes—often for doctors, and some for our vacations in the summer.

Bubby didn't count her labor as deserving of wages. It didn't occur to her. Accustomed to work she adored, she would have been shipwrecked without it. She didn't need praise for the sake of praise, but when a customer told her, "Manya, that's the best duck and red cabbage I ever tasted," she blushed and lowered her eyes as if the man had flirted with her. I often marveled that she could cook day after day without tiring of it. When I asked her about this, she replied, "What else would I do with myself?"

No sooner did Bertha marry well to a pocketbook manufacturer she always called by his last name than they moved to the wilds of Yonkers. She and Goodman had a house with a porch, two floors—the top reserved for bedrooms—and two indoor bathrooms. Bubby and I visited this Arcadia twice a year. Though Bertha did her best to wait on her during these visits in her Yonkers home, to entertain and pamper her, Manya could hardly wait to return to Orchard Street.

Unexpectedly, Bubby's sense of continuity, self-worth and purpose trembled when a cafeteria was installed in a vacant bank building on Canal Street; the bank had failed during the Depression. A real estate company bought the building and decided it was the perfect spot for a cafeteria.

Cafeteria! The very word caused Bubby to shudder. Still, no one in our family or in the entire neighborhood could ignore the renovations taking place kitty-corner to our apartment. Men showed up with scaffolds, drilled off the name of the bank and blasted out chunks of cement from the solid walls to replace them with clear windows.

In the beginning, Manya and her faithful customers mocked the cafeteria's prospects and laughed at the uptown boobs who invented the idea. Who would want food that sat the day long on a steam table? What did they take the merchants and businesspeople for, hicks from Hicksville, they should pay their hard-earned money for goyishe dreck?

Nevertheless, when The Grand Canal opened, we watched from our windows with alarm as hordes of people—even Jacob, who ate at our restaurant for nothing in exchange for calling us to his phone in his clothing store—shoved their way inside. Flyers had been jammed into every neighborhood mailbox, offering Grand Opening Specials and Blue Plate dinners at discount prices—thirty-nine cents for meat loaf, gravy, mashed potatoes, canned string beans.

To placate his mother, Jack scoffed, "Who would eat there three times a day? It's probably terrible stuff, worse than the Automat." My grandmother made no reply, but after ten days of diminishing lunch business, she told him, "Jack, go there and eat. And Elkaleh, too. Between your two heads I'll find out everything."

We went on a Friday afternoon for lunch. Compared to our restaurant with its wobbly folding tables, the cafeteria in the bank dazzled us—marble floors, a vast counter displaying daily specials, tables with Formica tops, dozens of spotlights in the ceiling. My father and I split an "American" sandwich, tuna on factory-sliced white bread, and American apple pie, prepared from canned apples, a cornstarch filling and a crust that my father perceived as containing lard. We could hardly hear ourselves think, let alone talk, because of the noise. Three or four busboys carted away soiled dishes and wiped off the Formica tables with white terry-cloth towels. Ice water ran from a dispenser at the end of the counter. No one drank seltzer the way they did at our restaurant, and tea meant a cup of water plus a tea bag. Tea bags! It was my first experience with one.

We raced out, crossed the street by darting between the cars and trucks, and took the steps up to our apartment two at a time. "Ma," my father called out, "the place is a mausoleum! White walls, white ceilings, white plates. I've seen people laid out on slabs in better places than The Grand Canal. And the food!" He shuddered. "The butter is so salty you can't put it to your lips, the bread is like eating cotton balls and their spring salad is cottage cheese with radish and cucumbers. A fancy name for a whole lot of nothing."

My grandmother studied me without flinching. "Und vuz zucks du? What do you have to say?"

"Everything made me sick, I have to lie down." I went into my parents' bedroom and closed my eyes. A wave of queasy anxiety swept over me. My father and I had both told the truth—the food was inedible compared to my grandmother's. On the other hand, the fancy lighting, the busboys, the ice water from a machine, even the tea bags swirled in my head. What my grandmother offered had unaccountably become dated, out of fashion, like an item of clothing relegated to the back of the closet.

Lil, without a worrisome thought to mar her seamless brow, rose to the occasion and added to the family's coffers by becoming a weekend salesgirl at Palace Fashions on Division Street. She thrived on her new status and loved walking "up the marble staircase" every week—her way of referring to the Bowery Saving Bank at which she deposited her salary.

My father proved correct about one thing—The Grand Canal did poorly at breakfast and soon decided to close after 5:00 P.M. But for the noon meal it continued to thrive, diners darting in either for a full meal or a nosh.

To nosh is to seek a treat or a snack. Consume it and it's out of your mind forever. Some men ran into The Grand Canal for commercial pastries, say, a runny éclair or so-called strawberry shortcake with tough sponge, strawberries like red pebbles and fake whipped cream. But Willy and I learned early on that a nosh meant something else to our father. For Jack it was a sexual dalliance that took no more time than it would to gulp down coffee and cake.

If his female customer was pretty and vulnerable, if she blushed when he asked her how it felt to be beautiful, if he told her she looked stunning and began to remove her junk jewelry, or remarked that the color of her new garment did not make her skin look sallow—if she seemed receptive, then he maneuvered her into the broom closet, or onto the table in the alteration room and slipped it in and out as quickly as possible. Then he ran home to report to my grandmother that he had had a nosh and like fake whipped cream, it made him "naw-shus."

It would be unfair to say that Jack was a compulsive nosher, that he noshed every week, or every month, routinely. He did not. But when the fever came upon him, whether on a snowy day in February with one lonely woman seeking to kill an hour in a store before she went home to her family, or a spring day when he felt charmed by the turn of a customer's shoulder as she shrugged into a coat, then the desire for a nosh overcame him.

Jack's easy confessions did not strike Willy or me as odd because my grandmother assured us that the incident meant nothing, like passing a little water. But my father, my brother and I were under strict rules not to hint to my mother about these noshes. "It's a don't-tell," Bubby warned us.

"Would I hurt Lil, would I hurt her smallest finger?" Jack protested as he disappeared into the dark room where we stored the beds and folding tables, took a quick wash with hot water from the tea kettle, and changed his underwear. If forced to take a lie detector test, he could pass easily over whether he had been unfaithful. "No," he'd answer with resounding conviction. "I love my wife." Which he did. And my mother, who didn't understand the word *paradox* or its implications, agreed.

3

Shanda, Shanda

IF BUBBY'S DAYS belonged to her restaurant, to the endless stream of customers, friends, neighbors, her nights belonged to me. Her past was inexplicably wed to the present and during the winter months when it grew dark early and the last visitor left our apartment, Bubby suggested that we roll our folding beds into the dining room.

A dark alcove, not wired for electricity, led off the front room. Possibly it had been intended as a bathroom, an idea that the landlord may have abandoned to save money. Instead he installed two toilets in the hall on each floor of the five-story building. The unlit alcove inside our apartment held a skinny closet with shelves for my father's laundered shirts and his vast assortment of ties. Next to them was a chest of drawers with Lil's finery: her chemises, always called shimmys, her satiny one-piece undergarments named teddies and her silk stockings. Against the darkest wall stood my brother's cot and a double folding bed for Bubby and me. The springs of our bed were soft and the mattress mushy, and a supporting iron bar under its center had lost some of its screws so that it slid from side to side capriciously. Lil, skillful with the Singer sewing machine, made a curtain from some drapery material to hide these sorry beds whose condition deteriorated with the years.

Bubby's historic feather comforter, the perrina that she had brought with her from Odessa, had a decorated cutout in its center trimmed with cotton lace. Feathers escaped nightly through this cutout. In the coldest weather we piled wool blankets and even our overcoats over it. My grandmother, strongly attached to the perrina, called it her "wedding blanket." Feeling it close to her skin brought her ever-flowing recollections of her dead husband, now gone for decades.

My fifth year had significance for me. Not only because I first began to help Lil with the words of songs, but because I tried to muddle my way through the meaning of time. My brother, Willy, always taken for younger than I, was two years older. My father had passed thirty: thirty, a vast age because I considered someone sixteen fully grown and someone ten almost out of childhood. And my grandmother related stories that happened before she gave birth to my father with the same passion, the anxiety, the rage and despair, as if the oncoming tragedy occurred on a day of the week before.

Other children of immigrant grandparents or parents may have heard tales of shtetl—village—life, marked by isolation and rigid religious ceremonies. But my grandparents came from a cosmopolitan city, a bustling trading seaport with transients from foreign lands. True, Jews in Odessa lived in a separate quarter, but many of them were freethinkers, political radicals, and among them was my grandfather, Misha.

As if it were an established folktale, Bubby told me how she met Misha as he tore through the streets of Odessa distributing anticzar pamphlets. One day, blinded by a snowstorm, he ran into Manya and knocked her to the cobblestones; his pamphlets went flying. His first thought was to retrieve the papers. With the wind at his back he jumped up and tried to catch them as they swirled like black flakes from the sky. But the unexpected contact with the young girl's body impelled him to run after her. She had already picked herself up and was plowing ahead along the storm-swept street. Misha caught up with her and asked whether he had seen her at a student meeting, or perhaps in the cellar of the clandestine printer who ran a hand-set press.

One glance at the tall young man with piercingly intelligent eyes and hair that fell in waves over his brow left Manya breathless. If she could, she would have hurled herself at him so they could tumble down again, arms and legs entwined. He must have experienced the same jolt because he seized her arm and demanded to know her name. Then he whispered lovingly, "Manya, du bist fah mir."

She was fifteen and he seventeen, a "brenfire." My grandmother never uttered *bren* alone or *fire* alone, though they both meant the same thing, a burning flame. Although the woman for whom my grandmother worked as a kitchen helper in no way boasted of royalty, my grandmother had nicknamed her "die czarina" because of her imperious manner and her arrogant condescension toward her servants. One of the first things my grandmother confided to Misha was that "ven der czarina gayt pishern, dofen mir shtanden": when the czarina goes to pee, we have to stand. Misha adored her irony. She, on the other hand, adored everything about him: his fiery looks, his ready discourse, his knowledge of the world, all of which she lapped up as she did the delicious taste of his skin. Their lovemaking verged on the miraculous.

"We both believed in frya libbe," she told me at an early age. I translated the phrase *free love* to mean that she loved him as much as possible, that is, freely. I heard the joy in my grandmother's voice as she whispered these words in the dark. Free love with Misha made her desperate years as a cook's helper in the czarina's kitchen almost bearable. As for her beloved, he was impatient, restless, always on the move. He would pace the floor holding a book in one hand while he gesticulated with his other, explaining lengthy passages of Bakunin the political theorist or the hammering words of the poet Pushkin.

During the summer, they strolled the seaport wharves, but rarely for long. Cossacks rounded up "strays" regularly, particularly Jewish students, all of whom were suspected of being bomb-throwing anarchists. Although Misha skittered around the city unafraid, he was always wary, always on the alert for possible danger.

A year after he knocked Manya down in the street they were secretly married. She continued to live with her family, and he with his. Periods of calm would invariably be followed by surprise roundups of students, who were beaten and jailed. Manya pleaded to leave for America. Misha worked at any menial job he could find to save money for their voyage— he had an uncle in New York whose address he held on to as a talisman. Yet whenever Manya brought up the subject of their migration, he would answer, "Not yet. It's not yet time." Another year went by.

Then an incident in St. Petersburg determined their fate: students rushed the czar as he rode in his carriage. The repercussions were felt from the frozen steppes to the Black Sea. Manya didn't hear from Misha for ten days, although he had no part in the attack and had not been informed in advance about the plot. It came as a relief when at last he tapped on her window in the middle of the night and whispered, "Now. It's time now."

She wrapped her feather comforter around things she regarded as her dowry: a bronze mortar and pestle and brass candlesticks with curlicued stems. She slipped into her clothes, a long shift, an ankle-length sweater, a head kerchief and an extra pair of long underwear. She neither said good-bye nor left a note for her parents. Once they discovered the vacant place left by her perrina, they would understand.

It was one in the morning, uncommonly dark, the air tinged with frost but not yet too cold. They pressed themselves against buildings as they silently made their way to the port. The sky paled as Misha motioned toward their seagoing vessel. With shaky fingers he tapped his coat pocket for their tickets.

After the hours of silence and anguish, the rattle of their footsteps on the gangplank startled them. Hastily, they scrambled below deck, where they found body crouched next to body on the cold planks. Exhausted, apprehensive, uncomfortable, they counted their every breath.

How long did they sit there? An hour? Five? Suddenly they felt the roll of the ship. The hundreds of passengers cried out in relief. Every swerve and rock of the ship meant a movement toward freedom. It was during the midst of this communal jubilation that Manya, the kitchen helper, realized that she had forgotten to pack food.

"So what did you live on?" I asked, lying close to her warm body in the folding bed we shared, as if I hadn't asked the question a dozen times before. "We lived on love," came the answer.

I neither enjoyed nor cared for the second half of my grandmother's saga, what we called "the sad part." Though Misha had contracted a mild cough during their long journey, he passed the medical tests at Ellis Island. To see whether immigrants commanded average intelligence, Ellis Island clerks handed them crude pieces of wood, a puzzle to fit into a wooden frame. Misha finished his in less than a minute and Manya followed a few minutes later.

Then, to enhance their anxiety, men and women were separated during their physical examinations. A doctor probed Manya's vagina with an iron apparatus that resembled tongs, the metal crude and un-yielding and causing intense pain. The overworked doctor poked his skinny moist finger up her vagina and the same finger examined her teeth and mouth. Then he directed her to a cage where children, young women and the elderly waited, shaking with fear.

The worst sight—and she told me this over and over—were the women with pox or coughs that yielded blood, who were told they either had to be quarantined for several months or sent home. "They screamed, they pulled their hair," she recalled, as if still seeing their misery before her eyes. "They didn't know whether they would find their husbands or parents or children again. The men too." Informed that they couldn't come into America, they cried like babies.

"I cried the whole time until I saw Misha again," Bubby admitted. " 'Animals,' the clerks called us. 'These people are animals.' "

They hadn't bathed for more than a month and cold water without soap left their hands grimy. But my grandparents were elated, expectant, eager to begin their new existence together. An indifferent clerk translated their Russian name, Rakidovski, into Roth, the formalities ended and they boarded the ferry to Battery Park.

No one waited for them, but almost every passerby on the sidewalk spoke Yiddish and directed them to the Jewish quarter. The uncle, whose name and address they clutched so proudly, could not be found.

Having exchanged their rubles for dollars, they rented a basement room on Ludlow Street. It was so dark, so dank, it reminded them of the cellar back in Odessa that housed the hand-set printing press. Their room contained a mattress, one chair and a patched-together table with a small gas cooking unit. They found a communal cold-water faucet in the outside hall near the toilet. But after the weeks of being surrounded by hundreds of others, their privacy felt like a gift. During their furtive years of lovemaking in Odessa, they had never spent a full night together.

"For two, maybe three days on Ludlow Street," my grandmother explained matter-of-factly, "we slept and made love." When they finally ventured out into the street, the daylight half blinded them. They bought black bread, one enamel cup and black tea—Russian tea, chai, that could be as dense in color as coffee.

Misha immediately found work on an ice truck, using a hammer and a pick to break off irregular chunks of ice that he wrapped in a torn burlap sack and heaved over his back. He carried the ice up and down stairs to deliver it to apartments and stores. Manya cleaned pots and scrubbed floors in a bakery located one flight down from street level. In the summer the heat left her skin dry and her hair singed. The worst day at the bakery came late on Friday afternoons, when the ghetto women arrived with their cauldrons of cholent—meat and beans, barley and potatoes submerged in water—to leave in the bakery oven to simmer overnight.

Shortly before noon on Saturday the Shabbas goy, an underpaid gentile hired to do work forbidden on the Sabbath, opened the bakery. He pulled the pots out of the oven, gave them to the waiting women, and afterward cleaned up any mess that had spilled on the floor, scraping the oven itself for food that had boiled over.

One day Manya asked the bakery owner, Greenspan, for the job. He was furious that a woman could make such a suggestion. For a woman to work in a store on Saturday was considered sacrilege. "It's a shanda," he cried. "A shame. A disgrace."

Bubby paused at this point in her narrative. "A shanda?" she asked rhetorically. "We needed the money. Misha had this terrible cough. His whole body shook from the coughing. So what was the shanda, that I should work on Saturday or that my husband should have medicine from the clinic?"

The doctor from the clinic at Gouverneur Hospital, which the ghetto inhabitants called The Hospital as if it were the only one in the city, recommended that Misha leave the ice truck job. The ice, the cold, the damp rag on his back day in and day out incited the cough.

Next he worked at a kosher butcher shop, lifting heavy carcasses and washing away the bloody water in which the meat had been ritually koshered. For families where women worked and didn't have time for koshering at home—the rabbi's stamp on the meat was considered insufficient—the meat was soaked in pans filled with water and kosher salt for at least three hours.

Carrying the heavy pans as well as the carcasses was exhausting, but Misha enjoyed the company of his boss, Stein, pronounced "Shtein." Stein encouraged Misha to read the daily papers in Yiddish and summarize the news for him. He enjoyed talking to Misha about the Russian writer Gogol, whose stories reminded him not only of Russia's lower depths but of the Lower East Side. Stein would shake his curly red hair—which had earned him the nickname "rayta hund"—red hound—and say, "Boychick, it's a shanda that someone gebilded should be working by me lifting pans with bloody water."

"Again a shanda," Bubby protested. "Always a shanda this, a shanda that. The baker Greenspan, he finally gave me that Saturday job, but I had to creep into the store in the dark so people wouldn't see me and scream 'shanda.' And Stein, Misha's boss, if he thought it a shanda that this educated boy worked for him, why didn't he try to get Misha a better job? Your grandfather and I, we didn't believe in shandas."

Finally, Misha's diagnosis came: tuberculosis. The officials with whom they dealt were either overburdened or had become hardened by so much disease and suffering that they dismissed the sick man by saying no hospital beds could be found for him. Not a single one in the city, or in that unexplored and alien region known as "Upstate" New York. One afternoon Misha hemorrhaged in front of Stein and with the greatest reluctance, Stein had to let him go. My grandmother took a second job as a prep cook in a restaurant, work she could do in her sleep and often did because she didn't give up her hours in the bakery.

Misha stayed in bed and swallowed cough syrup, nothing else. They moved to an upstairs room in the same building that had more air and filtered sunlight, then considered the absolute cures for consumption. Every spare hour Manya spent in bed with her husband. They made love feverishly. Unafraid of infection she kissed him on the mouth. She believed she could heal him with those kisses. Twice a month she went to the hospital and begged for a bed for Misha. "It's a shanda," the nurse said, "that such a handsome man, refined, should not be getting hospital care, but all I can do is move him up on the waiting list."

Yet joy smiled at them when my grandmother became pregnant. A man who could make a baby had life and strength in him. The baby! A lucky omen.

Misha sat in a chair at the window as a midwife and Manya delivered my father. The couple could not believe their good fortune and happiness. The possibility of death didn't enter their minds. Soon the hospital bed would be available; soon Misha would be cured; soon the baby would understand what a gift of God he was, a "golden mitzvah." They had an almost mythological sense of their destiny. The illness was a setback, not a tragedy. The baby brought them a new sense of innocence. And just as innocently, Misha died.

After that, my grandmother explained, she never feared death. It came, she said, as a whisper, almost silently. Death wasn't frightening. Only irreversible. Since she hadn't been raised to believe in an afterlife, she couldn't console herself with the notion that she would see Misha again. But she kept his memory alive with the tales that she spun more nights than I can remember. Often she would draw me close and confide, "Did I tell you the worst shanda of all? On the day of the funeral, some social worker came to tell me that they had a bed in the hospital. Now *there's* a shanda."

Winters tested our endurance on Orchard Street with teeth-chattering, bone-aching cold. Ice and frost covered the windows as if they had been applied with glue. The mildest rain hardened into ice; the snow that we loved to watch turned into icicles. We lined the leaky windows with old towels that grew sopping wet from droplets of ice.

Damp, frigid air seeped into every room. In the dining room the wall-paper that my parents prized buckled from the moisture.

To offset the cold, we wore layers of sweaters over our underwear. Sweaters knitted by Lil provided bulk rather than warmth. Our skin, oily and smelly, longed for a warm room and a bath. On rare occasions we bathed in a tin tub filled with water heated in one of Bubby's vast soup pots. Lil bathed at her friend Ada's, who lived on East Broadway "by the doctor," Dr. Hershel. He occupied the top floor, his office as well as his home, while Ada Levine and her family rented the apartment four steps up from the sidewalk, facing East Broadway. A visit to Ada's three-room railroad flat provided Lil with steam heat and a bathroom with a claw-foot tub adjacent to the kitchen.

Once, I accompanied my mother to Ada's for a bath, while her daughter, Shirley, and her son, Artie—the same ages as my brother, Willy, and me—played on the stoop. Ada, a short brassy blonde with brassy bleached hair, a brassy voice and a look of naked aggression, could level you to the ground with an unflinching stare. Seeing me undressed in the bathroom, she observed that my vagina resembled a "dried-out knish."

Hearing this, Bubby responded with outrage. "You, a dried-out knish? You ugly? You have more in one little finger than Ada has in her whole head. Right now you could speak with the president of the United States. If you met the president tomorrow you would know what to say to him. And Ada, that nar, all she knows is to dye her hair and to wink at men. Some married woman—she carries on like a streetwalker, a nafka." Though Ada's apartment was warm and her bathtub a treat by my standards, I restrained myself from bathing there again.

Instead, every so often on a late Friday afternoon, I went with Bubby to the public baths on Eldridge Street. The city provided the space and the boiling water for the showers. A hunched-over old crone, dripping wet from the steady stream of hot water, sat at the door and begged to cut your toenails for a few pennies. We couldn't decide whether she had been born a hunchback or whether years of sitting cross-legged at the door had caused her back to curve into a half-circle. She still wore a wig as in the old country, and a black ragged shawl over an equally black ragged dress. Moving from customer to customer, she resembled a toothless black crow. The old woman terrified me.

The water for the showers came on at intervals of three minutes and lasted for three minutes. You had to wash and rinse quickly unless you wanted to stand and wait for the next cycle to begin. Most women languished at the public baths for an hour, but my grandmother got me in and out in a hurry, lest I catch cold walking home with damp hair. She'd bundle me in a large towel, hand me a fresh *shtinik,* a white cotton slip that served instead of an undershirt, and then put on my smelly sweaters again. I soon rebelled against the public baths. "I feel shanda," I told my grandmother. I hated the cracked tile floor, the yellowing tile walls, the odd shapes and forms of strangers' bodies. During our many years together, my grandmother's policy and philosophy rested on not sabotaging my wishes. "You shouldn't feel shanda in the public baths," she soothed me. "In Russia, every Friday women run to the public baths to make themselves clean for Shabbas." "I can't stand this place!" I cried in rebellion.

"See how she opens a mouth to her bubby," a woman in the next shower complained.

My grandmother bustled me out and offered to buy me a charlotte russe displayed in a candy store window—slices of imitation sponge cake placed on a circle of cardboard and topped with fake whipped cream and a cherry.

I refused, not easily placated after what I considered a humiliating experience at the public baths. "All right," she said. "You don't want a charlotte russe, why don't you read me the signs as we walk home." Bubby knew that I enjoyed reading the letters out loud and then sounding out the names of the signs. To be sure, I had them all memorized and it wasn't much of a challenge, but afterward Bubby told everyone that even before kindergarten I could read every sign on Orchard Street. On the next to the last time that I visited the public baths, we went to a sweater store and Bubby bought me a thin maroon vest to wear next to my shtinik, and a navy blue one for my brother. "With such a nice vest," she said with a smile, "you won't feel a shanda if you have to go to the doctor and take off your middy blouse."

4

Doctor, Doctor

THE DOCTOR WAS a constant in our lives. My mother, who was diagnosed with what was euphemistically called "a weak heart," laughed and laughed when the insurance doctor told her that she couldn't obtain a life insurance policy because he detected multiple murmurs and an uneven beat. When he remarked, "You're too young to have such a weak heart," Lil thought it a big joke. "Who doesn't have a weak heart on the Lower East Side?" she asked as she skipped out of the house in her high heels, her blonde hair perfect, her dress and coat as fashionable as any woman uptown. How could she take her heart problems seriously when my father had bad lungs and walked around with a thermometer in his mouth; my brother suffered from asthma and wheezed his way through the nights; and later I contracted rheumatic fever and stayed in bed for weeks.

Nor were we the isolated few. A diphtheria or measles epidemic would spread catastrophe through the Lower East Side. When polio raged, children seemed to be carried away overnight. In fact, we were among the privileged because of our private doctor.

Dr. Koronovsky—again no first name—lived with his two sisters in a luxurious elevator apartment on Grand Street furnished with, among other possessions, a piano covered with a shawl more intricate than ours, and wall-to-wall carpeting. The doctor had his own room with a bedroom set that he had bought at Jones Furniture, which sold "the best" to uptown people; a plum-colored couch and upholstered chairs in the living room; and two radios, one in the living room and one in his private quarters. In the second bedroom his maiden sisters, Etta and Yetta, slept in twin beds—everything of the finest quality, Bubby reported. She had been in the apartment several times to cater small dinner parties.

Still, Dr. Koronovsky carried an air of sadness with him. He sported a small goatee, a vest that displayed a gold chain with his Phi Beta Kappa key as well as his gold watch, and Hickey Freeman suits in various states of disrepair. What accounted for his misery? His two sisters had made every sacrifice to send him to medical school, serving as janitors for the building in which they lived in exchange for free rent. They scrubbed the steps, pulled garbage cans to the sidewalk, mopped animal urine and feces; no job too cruel for them because their brother had to be a doctor. Their parents expected it; they had martyred themselves to send their children to America.

After Koronovsky finished his residency at Beth Israel Hospital he was offered the chance to buy into a private practice close by on West Sixteenth Street. But his sisters, tiny black-haired women with worn-out eyes and bony hands, refused to move uptown. Koronovsky, easily the best doctor on the Lower East Side, kept his office on East Broadway, charged more than anyone and did consultations uptown. To ensure his sisters' happiness he didn't marry. But he did have "a friend," a woman refined and educated whom he loved and visited once a week.

In our apartment after he diagnosed my father's bronchitis—he scoffed at the barber and his burning cups—or Lil's sore throat, Dr. Koronovsky would sit in the kitchen with Bubby to speak of his dilemma. "After what my sisters did for me, how can I bring a strange woman into the house? My wife would run my house! What would happen to my sisters?"

"Emmes," Bubby replied, "absolutely true." She paused to formulate what she said next. "But your life: you deserve a life. It's coming to you. When will you begin living, when your sisters are gone? Then it will be too late."

Dr. Koronovsky dipped rugulach into his raspberry tea served in a filigreed holder and refused to answer Bubby's question. "What about you, Manya? You didn't remarry. You had chances. Quite a few."

Bubby nodded in agreement. "More than a few, but not one meant anything to me. One man was not too smart, another couldn't hold a job, a third . . . Can you imagine . . . this man, he asked me to marry him after knowing me two weeks. He said we should take Jack, about three years old, and while he played in the park, we should sneak away and leave him there. I should forget about my one and only child, leave some stranger to find him, for that grub yung? What was he, crazy? I told him, 'Don't find your way back here, or I'll soap up the stairs and slide you down.'

"Another meshugana, almost the same story. I should bring Jack to the Hebrew Orphan Asylum and say I'm too poor to take care of him. 'Manya,' he told me, 'without your child we will always be on a honeymoon.' " Bubby leaned forward for emphasis. "Do you know what he meant by that? I should hand over the restaurant to him, he should make jokes with the customers, drink slivovitz and do nothing else. And all the time my boy, my one and only child, would be in an orphanage."

Reflection filled their temporary silence. Finally the doctor wiped his mouth and asked, "But what about Mister Elkin? A real love with no shanda."

The subject of Mister Elkin always caused my grandmother to fight back her tears. "After my husband, Mister Elkin was the only man I ever loved. The others, a hug here, a kiss there. Gornisht. With Mister Elkin, a deep love, for both of us."

"What a shanda that he deserted you." Dr. Koronovsky stroked his goatee. "A tragedy."

If Manya seemed about to cry, she didn't allow the tears to fall. She busied herself adding a few butter cookies to the doctor's plate.

"The loss of Mister Elkin, that wasn't a shanda, it wasn't a tragedy. Only sad. Very very sad. When my husband died, now that was a tragedy. He left a child without a father, me without a husband, and his own life, gone too soon. Did you know that in Odessa they called him Misha the tzadik, the wise one? Who knows what he would have become if he lived?"

Dr. Koronovsky rose from his chair. "We've had sad lives. Both of us."

"No," my grandmother protested. "It will change soon for you."

"Please, don't wish what you are thinking on my sisters."

"I'm not thinking what you are thinking. Doctor, forgive me, I don't want to feel shame for what I'm telling you, but one pubic hair is stronger than ten oxen. Just marry the woman you love and bring your wife into the same house with your sisters. You'll find a way. You'll be happy. And excuse me again if I didn't speak right."

Dr. Koronovsky blushed and added graciously, "Manya, you and I understand each other. There's no offense." He turned for the door. "See that your daughter-in-law takes the powders I left her."

The powders, crushed aspirin with possibly a dash of codeine, came in folded waxed papers and Dr. Koronovsky always carried a boxful. He distributed them for each and every ailment.

"Manya, let me know how Lil's sore throat is. If it's not better in two, three days, call me."

As it developed, Lil's sore throat wasn't the problem. She took the powders in water. She gargled with kosher salt; painted her throat with tincture of iodine, wrapped her neck in cold compresses followed by hot. The dry pain in her throat eased, but she started to throw up. Every morning. She felt sick to her stomach. Her breasts hurt.

My grandmother and mother didn't argue or fight. But when Bubby suggested, "Maybe you're pregnant?" Lil snapped at her, "What are you crazy? Do you think I'm out of my mind?"

"From your mind is not how you get pregnant."

Lil was vain about her excellent figure, the flatness of her stomach, her incredible dancer's legs. To this she added the fact that she had become a saleswoman on Division Street, in the very store in which she had packed coats into boxes. Lil had given birth to two children because it seemed the conventional, appropriate thing to do. The prospect of a third child horrified her. When she learned that she was in fact pregnant, she cried out, "How could this have happened to me? What did I do to deserve this?" as if beset by the plague.

Of course, Rocco, my father's bookie on Mott Street who considered himself the conduit through which all services flowed, crossed himself before he confided to my father. "Listen, Jack, you know I'm a good Catholic, confession every week, don't eat meat on Friday, church on Sunday, God should burn my tongue out if I don't believe that each child has a soul that will go to heaven. But you know how it is, Jack. You run across a bimbo every now and then and she's in trouble. I mean, I'm not saying who got her that way, but after all, that's life, a man loses himself for a minute and God forbid his wife or mother should find out. Anyhow, here's the story, and no disrespect to Lil, but this woman, she's clean as a whistle, immaculate and she does a perfect job in half an hour." Rocco wrote a name and address on a piece of paper. "A Mrs. O'Brady. In east New York. She wears a cross," Rocco added.

My father put a match to the paper.

Everyone admitted that the Gypsy fortune-tellers who lived right under the Williamsburg Bridge sold pills that brought on a woman's period. Buy pills from Gypsies? Jack paced the floor, chain-smoking. "Who knows what Gypsies are selling? Could be cyanide. Could be made from cat's piss, God knows what. Those pills are out of the question."

"All right," Lil sobbed, "no pills, no Irish midwife." She added wildly, "What am I supposed to do, jump off a bridge?"

As soon as the words flew out of her mouth, Lil bought a jump rope and every morning and every night she jumped rope a hundred times in the kitchen. My grandmother fanned herself with her Hoover apron. "Please," she protested, "you'll get a heart attack. You'll kill yourself with this jumping."

"I used to do double Dutch when I was a girl, up to a hundred."

"You're not a little girl now. What's worse, having a baby or having a heart attack?"

For jumping rope Lil wore an old pale nightgown that once may have been pink but now had faded into gray, the color of Lil's skin as she persisted with her rope skipping. Her blonde hair bobbed up and down as she counted with increasingly shallow breath, "Twenty, twenty-one, twenty-two, twenty-three, twenty-four." As she reached twenty-five, as if possessed by some childhood demon she called out, "Crisscross," and twirled the rope to jump inside it at one count and out at the other. We could hear her panting as she counted, "Thirty-five, thirty-six, thirty-seven . . ."

Lil went dead white. The rope slipped from her fingers as she crumpled to the floor. My grandmother ran to her side, wiping the sweat from her face, crooning softly to her, rocking her in her arms. Bubby put her ear to Lil's heart. "It goes too fast, too fast. I hear it like an ocean, rocking like the ocean on the boat from Odessa."

Her voice held a note of panic as she asked me to bring the slivovitz liqueur from its accustomed jug in the kitchen cupboard.

"A bissel," she instructed me, "a little." The whole scene frightened me. My hands shook with the responsibility of the task but I poured a few drops into a water glass. Bubby took the glass and brought it to Lil's lips. "A drop," she coaxed, "try to drink one drop." Lil didn't drink alcohol except for some Manischewitz wine at the Passover seder, and little at that. Bubby forced a few drops into her mouth, then placed the glass on the floor and sprinkled the slivovitz on Lil's lips and nose. We could see her chest heaving through the material of her nightgown but her eyes began to flutter. She sat upright in my grandmother's arms and slowly the two pulled themselves to their feet.

Lil rested in bed while Bubby hovered over her, bringing her sips of chicken broth, one or two strawberries that she had preserved during the summer served over a bite of sponge cake. "Sugar is good for you, some fruit it's very good, it will make you feel stronger."

Lil dozed fitfully, but at 7:30 she rose and took hot water from the tea kettle that seemed never to run dry. Bubby helped her sponge her entire body. When Lil dressed in a navy blue shift with an all-pleated skirt that showed off her shapely legs Bubby said, "You know, Lil, if women could do away with pregnancies by jumping rope, the Gypsies and the midwives would be out of business." Then she looked up at me and Willy and reminded us, "Don't tell!"

My father, home from work on Division Street that night said, "Lil, you look like a million bucks. Want to go out for chinks?"

My brother, Willy, and I gaped with wonder at the way my mother had transformed herself from a woman with a near heart attack to one with carmined lips and a touch of Chanel No. 5 at her ears.

But during the next several days my mother cried and cried, demanding, "What have I done to deserve such a thing?"

"What have you done? What everyone does," Bubby replied. "When I was a girl I thought frya libbe was really free. But in this life, everything costs. A kiss, a hug, it costs. A night of love, it costs the most. Look what happened to me and Mister Elkin. We would send Jack to the movies and right on the floor, on the Persian rug, we had those stolen kisses, always worried that Jack would find us.

"You know the kitchen lock, you can open it with a hairpin, so Elkin and I would be rushing and holding each other, lost in a dream. Always we thought, if only we didn't have to feel like two bandits, stealing an hour together, stealing our own kisses from each other."

Bubby kneaded yeast dough as she reminisced, running her hand over the silky dough, pulling it up high, then pounding it back into a vast lump, only to repeat the process until her hands had the feeling that the dough could soon rise. Then she placed it in a large brown ceramic crock and covered it with a towel. She had an order from an uptown customer for a braided challah and afterward, Clayton would deliver it along with a note that my mother wrote in a large childlike hand, "This bread is for Mrs. Davis at 124 West 12 Street from Manya's. The boy who carries it works for us. Oblige, Lil Roth." Clayton carried the note in case someone stopped him on the bus and accused him of stealing the bread.

On this particular day the dough for the challah served as a welcome distraction because my mother wept intermittently, refusing any consoling words. Bubby set the crock of dough on a warm part of the gas range, at its very edge.

The next moment in a last irrational act before she accepted the inevitable, my mother scrambled to the top of our small refrigerator and jumped off. She did it with such speed and such a thump that the pot of yeast dough crashed to the floor and scattered jagged pieces of crockery and lumps of dough everywhere, some landing on Lil who had fallen with her legs under her.

Tears cascaded down Bubby's face as she went to Lil. As gently as she could, Bubby tried to untangle those beautiful legs from beneath Lil's thin body, asking, "Is anything broken?" Lil shook her head. The rebellion had gone out of her, along with her drive and vitality.

Bubby ran her fingers over my mother's ankles, her calves, her thighs. "Does it hurt? Does it hurt?" Lil, eyes closed, shook her head. My grandmother lifted my mother in her arms.

At that moment Clayton opened the door. When he had bread to deliver he always came to our house early in order to fill himself with food, especially chopped liver. As soon as he saw Bubby holding my limp mother he, too, began to cry, "What happened? What happened to Miss Lillian?"

"She fell down. The pot broke, she fell over it. Please help me." Clayton carried Lil to her bed as she whimpered, "Don't drop me, please don't drop me."

The wall against which the bed stood had a huge white plaster patch, a jagged circle that covered almost the entire surface. It had been there ever since a pipe burst in the wall years before. Every year the agent, Weinstock, promised to have the wall properly mended, sealed and painted because even on the hottest summer days it felt moist to the touch. But every spring, during the season to ask for repairs, my mother refurbished the main room. After all, that was where we made our living and Weinstock's funds were limited. Some years he paid only to have the dining room baseboards and the windowsills painted. Occasionally he granted us fresh wallpaper, mottled ivory with brown strips pasted into squares to resemble paneling. Very classy for Orchard Street.

Carried in by Clayton, my mother turned to face the dirty runny patch and closed her eyes. Bubby sat on the bed and said softly, "Did I ever mention how I wanted a child with Mister Elkin?"

Lil's voice was muffled. "You wanted a baby, a real baby with Mister Elkin even though you had Jack?"

Bubby fanned herself with her apron. "Mister Elkin was the only one I wanted to marry, the only one who made me think of having a child. It happened to my own mother the same way. I left for America, she missed me. The next year she had a baby, my sister, Bertha, the one who lives in Yonkers.

"I had Bertha brought to America when she was maybe six years old. She stayed with me a few years, then she went to a cousin who couldn't have her own child. My sister, Bertha, she married right here in this apartment. I made her wedding in this house, and I bought the dress from Milgrim's," Bubby rattled on, gazing into Lil's face as she told the familiar tale. My mother gripped her hand. "Ma. I have terrible cramps. Terrible." She grimaced with pain.

"Blood, any blood?" As she asked, Bubby raised the blanket. Abruptly she left my mother, and ordered Clayton to run and fetch Dr. Koronovsky.

Everywhere on the Lower East Side, Clayton was known as "Manya's boy," as in child. When asked to bring Dr. Koronovsky, he didn't have to be told the office address on East Broadway. Bubby told him with some urgency, "If he has a patient, knock on the door. Tell him Lil is bleeding."

Bubby returned to the bedroom. My mother moaned without cease, every now and then letting out a sharp cry of pain. For once I asked Willy to turn up the music on his Zenith radio: "We're having a heat wave / A tropical heat wave." Thought it was only 3:30, the sky had darkened and the wind seeped in from every windowsill. Clayton was a fast runner, yet he couldn't make it to the doctor in less than ten or fifteen minutes. Whenever my mother screamed, I bit my lip, unable to sit still, and peered out of the begrimed windows, hoping in the gathering dusk to spot Dr. Koronovsky's dark blue Ford, familiar to everyone in the ghetto. Or I expected Clayton to burst through the door, exclaiming dramatically, "The doctor is coming."

A new song on the radio began: "These foolish things remind me of you . . ." My usual strategy when I panicked—if a rat crossed my feet on the stairs, or a drunk came out of our toilet unexpectedly with his fly open—was to run for my grandmother's lap. But she wasn't available to me now. In my imagination a full-term baby would emerge from my mother, although I had no idea how long she had been pregnant. I remembered every tale from the old country told by Mrs. Finkel, Mrs. Feldman, Mrs. Kleinfeld, about babies born with heads of chickens, babies born blind, deformed, with no arms or legs because their mothers tried to get rid of them. I was close to hysterics by the time Dr. Koronovsky called, "Manya, how's Lil?" I hadn't heard him come in.

At once the apartment filled with bustle and crackling tension both worse and better than what had preceded it. In his doctor's case, Dr. Koronovsky carried a hand brush with which he scrubbed before any examination. On this occasion he also poured antiseptic over his hands and smelled up the whole kitchen. My brother, Willy, at last detached his ear from the radio; the fumes made him sneeze. Dr. Koronovsky said, "Very clean towels, Manya."

We were the only ones in the building who used a professional laundry for our linen—tablecloths, sheets, napkins, towels. My grandmother reached for our stack of napkins on the bureau but Dr. Koronovsky shook his head. "Still wrapped in laundry paper if you have them." From the dark cavern of the storage room I brought the unopened package.

"You know that I'm going in," he said. My grandmother and the doctor exchanged a quick glance. If Bubby saw that I saw, she merely pressed her lips together and carried in a vast enamel bowl of hot water.

At the door of the bedroom, the doctor said, "Manya, stay out until I call you." Again that meaningful flicker as their eyes met. Bubby became aware that in the last hour she had failed to acknowledge my presence. "Don't cry. It will be all right. Dr. Koronovsky, he's the best. It will be finished, ended, in half an hour."

We heard a high piercing cry that stunned and rooted us in place. Not one of us—Bubby, Clayton, Willy, me—breathed during that scream. Bubby's arms trembled as she gathered me and Willy to her. "That's it. Finished."

Silence was broken by the doctor asking, "More hot water, please, and a newspaper." Bubby held on to us as Clayton brought both to the bedroom door. After another interval the doctor said, "Manya, would you come here, please." She sped inside.

When the two of them emerged a few minutes later, the doctor wiped his pink-stained hands on a fresh linen napkin and my grandmother held a tiny packet wrapped in newspaper. In his most professional manner the doctor gave instructions. "Sitz bath three or four times a day. Towels, napkins, all sanitary. Buy a very large box of Kotex. Don't use old flannel or rags. And a sanitary belt." He looked directly at me. "You'll remember these things, won't you? Sanitary belt and Kotex from the drugstore. Warm water wash several times a day. Bed rest." As if he knew or suspected that the neighbors gathered outside the kitchen door—there were no secrets in this building—he said very loudly, "Miscarriage after a few weeks. Nothing more."

His exit scattered the neighbors. Bubby reported that my mother was sleeping and warned Willy and Clayton not to go inside the bedroom until she cleaned up. Then she said to me matter-of-factly, "Elkaleh, cum mit mir."

I took her hand without question. We walked into the toilet in the hall. She said, "Don't look," but I did. A bloody mass fell from the newspaper. Did I see a form there or did I imagine it? My grandmother pulled the chain on the toilet once. A residue of pink rose to the top. She flushed again. Then she gathered my hand in hers and we walked back inside.

From under the candlestick where Bubby kept money she took a dollar and handed it to Clayton. I repeated to him what my mother needed: a big box of Kotex and a sanitary belt. Then my grandmother went into the bedroom alone, gathered the stained linens that lay on the floor and stuffed them into an old pillowcase. The pillowcase went into a crumpled paper bag and into the garbage can.

As soon as Clayton returned, Bubby gave him a handful of change and said, "You're a good boy. Tomorrow, I'll make chopped liver, fresh, just for you."

That night, my insomnia was worse than ever. My grandmother said to me in Russian, "Even the ocean is resting. Why aren't you?"

"Bubby," I answered, "is what we threw in the toilet today, was that a shanda?"

I thought she had dozed off, or possibly hadn't heard me. I didn't have the courage to ask twice.

"No," she finally replied, kissing the top of my head. "It was nothing. Just some blood. No shanda at all."

5

Shirley, Shirley and Shirley

MY MOTHER RESPONDED to her convalescence by turning it into a celebration. She languished in bed for days, accepting visitors and presents as if they were her due. Because of her good looks and slightly flirtatious air she had become a favorite with the shopkeepers and customers at our restaurant.

Pandy, her beautician, bestirred herself after hours to bleach and set Lil's hair, using basins of hot water that Bubby happily fetched from the kitchen. Mother's friend Ada brought two pairs of peach-colored step-ins with lace edges. Orloff, the silk dealer, offered a silk nightgown with a froufrou at the throat, an uptown special. "How I got it don't ask," he remarked as he planted a kiss on Manya's cheek. The neighbors chipped in and purchased a box of Loft's chocolates, parlays: cigar-shaped confections filled with walnuts and caramel and covered with milk chocolate. My father, the chocolate maven, preferred very dark Belgian chocolates, but like the rest of us, he had to make do.

Weinstock-the-agent gave the best present of all. "He took his hand away from his heart," Bubby explained. Weinstock sent the plasterers in one day to cover the massive patch on the bedroom wall. A week later the painters, pronounced "paintners" by Weinstock, showed up. My mother chose a pale yellow color that bathed the room with sunlight.

The cozy interlude pleased us. My parents slept on the floor of the dining room during the repair of their bedroom. My mother sang along with the radio, and to entertain her, my father recounted movies with heightened style. Since he was a voracious reader and had already read Theodore Dreiser's *An American Tragedy*, he combined its contents with the old movie of the same name starring Phillip Holmes and Sylvia Sidney, one of his preferred actresses because she was Jewish. When the troubled hero drowns his pregnant girlfriend, my father's version of this melodramatic tragedy had us weeping. We also adored his telling of James Cagney in *Public Enemy* and Paul Muni in *Scarface*. My father claimed these movies. They were his to embroider or elaborate on as he saw fit, telling different versions depending on his mood. He romanticized gangsterdom, as did many of his generation.

During my mother's convalescence, her friend, brassy Ada Levine, came to visit. My father disapproved of her. He recognized her as cold and stony to her core, and despised her lack of scruples at the pettiest level, observing that she would easily steal pennies from blind men who sold pencils in the street. Surprisingly, though, he defended Ada's earliest love affair at age fourteen with Ruby-the-Runner, a petty gangster of sixteen who was gunned down in the street for failing, more than once, to hand over the dimes and quarters he collected from people who bet on numbers.

After Ruby died, Ada went to work in a brassiere factory, attaching by sewing machine the elastic backing for hooks and eyes. My mother and Ada had attended the same grade school and lived next door to each other in a tenement on Rivington Street, but that could not explain my mother's fascination with her friend. Ada had no schooling, no interest in the theater the way my parents did, and the only female movie star with whom she identified was Mae West. Ada's one contribution to any party or extended conversation was her imitation of Mae West intoning, "Beulah, peel me a grape."

Ada married Irwin Levine because he rescued her from the

brassiere factory. Sappy with desire for her, Irwin worked as a shoe salesman on Delancey Street. He was good-natured, a good provider and a good dancer. Ada's one requirement as a wife concerned sex—first thing before Irwin went off to work and last thing at night. Irwin paid no attention to the fact that before she met him, Ada had lived openly with a local hood.

"Those things happen," he shrugged philosophically. "She was a kid, fourteen, so now she's a respectable married woman and lives on East Broadway and we have two children." Irwin Levine had a fleshy face and a heavy torso and sweated a lot, so he needed a freshly laundered shirt every day. Ada considered it a small demand for her respectability as a wife and mother. As for sex, no one knew whether Ada passively complied or longed for it.

Ada noisily inspected the newly painted bedroom and confided that she never ever refused her husband, even when she had her monthlies, even when she had the flu, even in the last hour of her pregnancies.

Sitting a few feet away, trying to read one of my brother Willy's books from school, I drew in my breath when I heard Ada admit in her coarse voice, "I can do it sitting down, standing up, laying down, front, back." Her raucous laughter rang with pride. "I'm a great lay," she boasted.

Perhaps she had made this claim before and it hadn't registered with my mother, whose first and only man was my father. Perhaps the recently redecorated bedroom added to sexual activity. That night when my mother thought we slept, I could hear her asking my father exactly what men considered a good lay. Weren't all woman good lays, just by being women?

I realized that my father found her naïveté endearing. He took pride in the fact that the Lower East Side, with its vulgarities in speech and aggressive behavior, had not rubbed off on her. My mother accepted the double standard without question—men had the right to sexual liberties, women did not. Lil's brothers, who visited us often, talked openly about their sexual escapades and it didn't bother her. Street language that rang with obscenities had no effect on her. Few who lived on the Lower East Side understood the meaning of repression or puritanism; the most ardent Catholic women in Little Italy accepted sex and violence as twin aspects of human existence. As a mark of her innate propriety, Lil insisted that we call her "Mother," not "Mom" or "Ma," and referred to sex as "all the good things."

"When you grow up, you'll marry a nice businessman, you'll have all the good things," she informed me. This was the extent of my sexual instruction. Between my grandmother's "frya libbe" and my mother's "all the good things," I conceived of lovemaking as a state of perpetual hugs and kisses that lasted until one tired.

I awaited my father's reply about a good lay with more than ordinary curiosity.

"It's a woman who loves it," he said slowly. "She wants it and she needs it, she admits it. She goes after sex like a man."

"That's it? That's all? I guess that makes Ada a good lay."

"Don't be ridiculous," my father shot back. "Ada lets men do it to her. That's not the same as wanting it."

"But how about Ruby-the-Runner? They did it three times a day. Maybe more. That's what she told me."

"Ada was fourteen and Ruby sixteen. At that age anyone who breathes can do it four times a day." My father laughed softly. "Here's one that you won't believe. My friend Shimon, we know each other since we were kids, I call him the other day, ask him if he'd like to come down, dope out some horses, maybe take the train to Belmont, he tells me no, he can't. I say why not and he answers, 'I always go home for lunch. I leave my dry-cleaning store and go home for lunch. Only we don't eat. The kids are in school, we do it till my thing almost falls off. I swear, Dory, my wife, can't get enough, I have to put my hand over her mouth, she screams so much my neighbors think I'm maybe killing her. That's why I married her. She's so skinny, she could do a flip in a putty blower, but in bed . . .' "

"How could we carry on like that?" my mother asked plaintively. "Your mother and the children are in the next room, and in the afternoon the customers are here."

"Lil," my father assured her, "don't you worry. You're the best. The very best." Appeased temporarily, my mother settled in quietly, though not for long.

Shortly after that conversation with my father about sex, my mother began to display a restlessness that we hadn't witnessed before. Instead of resting at home as the doctor instructed her after the miscarriage, she dressed early in the morning, slipping into her high-heeled pumps and one of her best dresses topped with a heather tweed coat whose white lynx collar could flatter any movie star. Where did she go? To S. Klein on the Square, to Russeks to inspect furs, to Gimbel's to try on hats, searching for a new identity through clothes that she didn't need and whose prices she couldn't afford.

Goodman, Aunt Bertha's husband who manufactured purses, invited her to his factory to pick out anything she wanted in the new spring line. For spring he was heavily promoting patent leather—envelope shapes a yard long, or multipocketed large purses that from a distance resembled my grandmother's oilcloth shopping bags. Goodman adored and admired my mother. Short, broad of chest, thin of leg, he was a Humpty-Dumpty of a man, generous of spirit and amazed by his good fortune, his house in Yonkers, his wife, Bertha, his two children, who thanks to his money attended private schools in Westchester. He filled an entire small carton with his samples and gave them to Lil after patting her on the behind and pinching both her cheeks. He called her *tsotskele,* little toy.

Jack vetoed most of the purse samples. The red patent leathers were too garish, the envelope shapes brought to mind a lady lawyer. He despised the fake crocodile clutches as well as the bucket-shaped "marshmallow" of fake leather. Happily, my father consented to let me keep a small patent leather purse with an imitation gold snap and a link chain handle. Lil selected an identical one in a larger size.

My mother dispensed with the rest of the purses, and donated the bucket-shaped number to her mother, my Grandma Rae, who lived on Jefferson Street with her sons.

I liked some of my mother's brothers, my young uncles who set up a roof garden at the top of their apartment house. They lived on the fifth floor and whenever we went to visit my mother rested on every second floor because of her irregular heartbeat. Grandma Rae had more children than she could handle, displayed affection for none, was a compulsive cleaner, and each and every day cooked the identical menu in a two-foot-tall cast-iron pot: meatballs and potatoes. She made me uneasy. On every visit she lifted the hem of my skirt to inspect my underclothes. They rarely met her standards, but after remarking on them or the shabby state of my middy blouse, she ignored me.

She impressed us by the cleanliness of her windows, the floor, the bedclothes. Like most apartments on the Lower East Side, even Ada's "by the doctor," you entered directly into the kitchen, and then the rooms followed each other in a row. Each was filled with beds and some straight-backed chairs. The beds in Grandma Rae's house could have passed muster in the army. Their gray wool blankets, squared at the corners and pulled tight, signaled that no one dared disturb their symmetry.

In our house, someone was always occupying my parents' double bed—my father or my mother, or I'd rush home from school, roll into the bed and begin reading. Such behavior would have been unthinkable for Grandma Rae. Though Clayton did the cleaning, the tray under our gas burners did not sparkle as hers did, and when we stored our folding beds, the sheets jammed inside every which way.

During her early married years Lil used to bring cookies and cakes from Manya's generous kitchen when she visited her mother. But Grandma Rae would respond by saying, "What is this, charity, we don't have enough to eat?" So my mother soon stopped the practice.

After three quarters of an hour at Grandma Rae's my mother would suggest that we walk along Delancey Street—she always enjoyed the weekly display of new shoes at A.S. Beck. During one of these strolls, no sooner did we stop at the window of Beck's than she sucked in her breath. In the window, leaning against a pair of high-heeled pumps, was a black envelope purse decorated with a monogram of fake gold letters. Small *a,* large capital *B,* small *s.* My mother fluffed up her lynx collar and we stepped inside to inquire about the letters on the purse.

"It's for A.S. Beck," the skinny clerk explained. "The *B* is in the middle for Beck and the *a* and *s* for first and middle name." He paused and gave my mother a grin to show a half-broken front tooth. "Here," he continued, "I'll print it for you. What's your name?"

"Lil Roth."

Carefully he printed a large *R* with a small *I* on the left. "Your middle name?" he asked. My father, born Abraham Jacob, signed his name Jack A. Roth, but my mother had no middle name. "I think it's Leah," she replied.

I pulled at her elbow and whispered. "That's your Jewish name, that's why they call you Lil. You can't call yourself Lil Leah, it's the same thing."

"Fine," replied the skinny salesman, "that's easy, *I R I*." My mother thanked him and we hurried home. "I must have a middle name," she declared. Grasping at the first one that came to her mind she asked, "How about Shirley? Lillian Shirley Roth."

I knew three Shirleys: one more hateful to me than the next. They may have been named during the Shirley Temple craze when so many of the Jewish Sarahs, Sylvias and Shoshanas became Shirley. And here was my mother, a grown woman, wanting to adopt the name for herself.

My contempt for Shirley Levine arose from her lack of brains. Like her mother, Ada, she liked to talk about dresses—when she bothered to talk at all. She would repeat endlessly, "My mother is buying me a red dress, with a petticoat to match." Neither the dress nor the petticoat materialized, a promise, typical of Ada, that she had no intention of fulfilling. For her daughter, that one sentence, "My mother is buying me a red dress, with a petticoat to match," summarized the extent of her conversation.

Yet just as I admired and feared my Grandma Rae's impeccable housekeeping, I admired and feared Shirley Levine's physical agility. She roller-skated for years, not on learners but on real skates with steel wheels, and in the coldest weather she wore socks, not stockings, a fashion my mother associated with the upper class.

The second Shirley I loathed was Shirley Mathias, who lived with her brother, Nate, and her parents above their men's hat store on Canal Street. The Mathias Hat Company had a citywide reputation and the store itself was a marvel: gleaming wooden shelves, dozens and dozens of hats stacked one on top of another: derbies, fedoras, snap-brims, hats made from real fur, beaver hats fit for a Czar, curly gray Persian lamb hats with side flaps that generals sported in movies, top hats for the opera. During the summer Mr. Mathias displayed stiff straw skimmers with tricolored hatbands, soft Panamas with perforations for air at the crown, caps for boating, caps for golf, white visors for tennis. Everything we knew about sports—and it was painfully little because on the Lower East Side handball reigned: slapping a hard ball against an equally hard wall—we learned from the Mathias Hat Company. My father, considered a paragon of sartorial splendor, always bought his fedoras—worn with the brim turned down on all sides—at Mathias.

But little Shirley Mathias possessed the tongue of a devil. Each time I walked on Canal Street she would shout, "Skinny pickle, skinny pickle," darting her head in and out of her father's store like a snake's. And as soon as I started kindergarten, she yelled, "She got left back, she got left back!" a wound not easily forgotten.

True. Thanks to the odious Ada Levine, my mother had registered me at the Hester Street P.S. 21 at the age of four. Ada always referred to me not by name but as "That one." "That one has a dried-out knish." "That one has an old lady's head." "That one can read all the signs on Orchard Street." Ada advised my mother to start me in school a half year early, to say that I was born in September, instead of January. "That one," she told my mother, "will be the smartest one in kindergarten. Get her out of the house. How long is she going to hold her Bubby's hand and go shopping? Get rid of her."

I had nothing to say in the matter. My mother brought me to register at school. She claimed she had lost my birth certificate but swore, smiling winsomely, that I had been five in September. Then, as she left me at my classroom, she repeated again, "Remember, when the teacher asks you when you were born, say September seventh." I must have appeared stricken, because she cajoled me, "You'll get all the books you want to read. Free."

On the first morning of school, no one inquired, but on the second,

Mrs. Clarke, an imperious woman with a pince-nez around her neck, asked everyone to state their name and date of birth. Automatically, I told the truth and repeated it. I was sent home immediately—the class was burgeoning with children, as many as forty-five—with a note saying that unless my mother could produce my birth certificate, I wasn't to return.

My mother screamed, "Dummy, didn't I tell you what to say? Why didn't you say what I told you? What are you, stupid?" She began to shake me. Bubby came to my rescue immediately, "What are you crazy, you have to listen to everything that Ada Levine tells you? So your child told the truth, and for this you are yelling and screaming? She's four years old, she can stay with her Bubby a little longer. She'll be a professor six months later."

"A professor?" my mother protested. "Who will marry her if she's so smart? Who, who, *who*?" And she burst into tears, crying almost as hard as when she thought she would be having another baby.

Hearing the early morning ruckus, my father left his bed and came in to settle the disturbance. "Look," he said to my mother, "does it put you ten ahead if she starts now or six months later? In a few months she'll be five, you'll bring the birth certificate, you'll behave like a lady. And you can tell your friend Ada Levine she can show her ass in Macy's window for all I care. Let her put her own daughter in school six months early." Then to soften the message, he smiled at her and said, "Come on, Lil, we'll have Danish and coffee at Ratner's, my treat."

Since there were no secrets in the Jewish ghetto, this kindergarten mishap soon reached Shirley Mathias, who rarely failed to taunt me that I had been "left back."

The third Shirley who drove me crazy was Shirley Feld, the granddaughter of Mrs. Feldman who lived in the apartment one floor above us. Mrs. Feldman, a widow three times over, admitted, "I'm burning like fire" in between mates. Her only child, Yussel, whom my father still called Yussie, had shown an affinity for fresh fruit from his earliest years. Not eating it, but lifting it from pushcarts, stands and fruit stores.

Notorious throughout the streets for his quick fingers and for the voluminous sweater under which he adroitly tucked apples, oranges, grapes, bananas, even watermelons larger than his head, Yussie made off with the fruit as the helpless vendors watched, unable to give chase because that would lay them open to ten other thieves. Yussie could drive a truck by the age of twelve, and though he was a runt, with red-rimmed eyes and a snotty nose, he was agile, fast and bursting with self-assurance. Not only did he jimmy open a parked truck, but in broad daylight he emptied out a fruit warehouse on Front Street. He couldn't work nights because he had to stay home with his mother.

Caught in the act, Yussie was convicted of two counts of robbery, the truck and the fruit, and lived "out of town" for several years. When released at sixteen, however, he confided to my father, "They beat the shit out of me," and went straight after that, as ambitious as ever, loving fruit as ever, but now conducting himself on the up and up. As an adult and married man he now lived on the Grand Concourse in the Bronx, sported a pinky ring with a large yellow diamond, wore hand-tailored expensive clothes and drove a Cadillac.

Having changed his name legally to James Feld, he opened a gourmet fruit store on Fifty-seventh Street. His gift baskets graced the best homes in the city, and were photographed in the staterooms of French liners leaving for Europe.

One Sunday every month Yussie came to see his mother in the role of the dutiful son and to expand his chest as he flashed his engraved business cards: James Feld, Fruit Fit for Royalty. Even his West Fifty-seventh Street address was catchy.

Yussie had married Martha, a girl from the Bronx, a high school graduate who had hoped to attend Hunter College before he swept her off her tiny feet. Yussie towered over her. He and his wife were perfectly matched, she docile, adoring, proud of James. But one glimpse of their daughter, Shirley, revealed that she didn't dine on her father's fancy fruit.

She wasn't pleasingly plump, just fat. Her fancy outfits couldn't disguise the short chunky legs, the round stomach, the moon face. Shirley Feld's permanent wave produced curls in the manner of Shirley Temple. The fourteen-karat gold bracelet on her wrist bit into her flesh, and the two gold rings on her left hand were buried in puffy skin.

Yussie paid the street urchins to watch his car during the hour he spent chatting with his mother on Orchard Street, yet he wouldn't part with a cent for his favorite meal, which Bubby invariably prepared for him—an entire duck with orange sauce, which he called "duck à l'orange." To display his generosity, he always brought Bubby three navel oranges for the sauce and every now and then a one-serving pocket-sized jar of commercial jelly, surely a joke. Bubby's preserves, put up in gallon jars, were famous.

But Bubby laughed rather than complain. Remembering Yussie from his early days, she didn't take his pomposity seriously.

Yussie ate Bubby's food in his mother's kitchen, but after a while the family would troop downstairs to our apartment and Shirley Feld, in a red velvet dress in winter and a red flowery one with ruffles in summer, honored us with a recitation. She took elocution lessons, a word that burned itself into my heart. Each and every time she recited the same piece. Since my parents worked on Division Street on Sundays, always a busy day, they would arrive home exhausted and the last thing they wanted was to array themselves in chairs on the Persian rug and listen to Shirley Feld. But after much stumbling and pausing, gazing down at her Mary Jane pumps, and then upward at our ceiling, Shirley managed to get through the same few lines:

> When I was a beggarly boy
> I lived in a cellar damp.
> I had not a friend nor a toy
> But I had Aladdin's lamp.

> When I could not sleep for the cold
> I had fire enough in my brain
> And builded with roofs of gold
> My beautiful castles in Spain.

My parents and my grandmother applauded dutifully. Mrs. Feldman and Yussie's wife, Martha, beamed.

But on the Sunday that Shirley Feld recited wearing a white rabbit muff on her right hand, I could bear it no longer and ran into my parents' bedroom. Shirley scarcely noticed because after the recitation she was busy polishing off an entire plate of butter cookies sprinkled with confectioners' sugar. As they got ready to leave, Yussie left his card with us for the hundredth time and Martha dramatically shook out Shirley's winter coat with its gray Persian lamb collar and cuffs.

"What a four-flusher," I heard my father say with distaste. "I wonder if he ever told his fancy wife with her fancy mink that he once stayed out of town for three years."

"Shah," my grandmother replied. "It doesn't pay to talk like that."

"But he's such a phony."

Bubby paused before replying. "Yussie has something to be phony about. He used to hitch rides on the back of trucks, the biggest goniff on the streets. So, if he wants to show off, you should laugh at him."

Then she rushed into the bedroom to find out why I was crying.

My mother hadn't noticed that I wasn't in the dining room. Standing on her high heels from ten in the morning until seven at night, Lil worked on commission only, with no base pay. On Sundays, when the store was particularly crowded, she came home with her feet aching. To her credit, it did not occur to her to envy a mink coat or a fancy car. It had to do mostly with her image. She earned her own money. For work she dressed like a movie star. In her own small world she carried more respect than Martha Feld.

Moreover, my mother was warmed by my father's love and the admiration of the men around her. When she stood up to sing at parties or social events, she felt herself bathed in a yellow light, and when the applause sounded she didn't need the Grand Concourse or a store that sold fruit baskets wrapped in yellow cellophane and red ribbons. Any day or year now we would move uptown. Lil never doubted that.

So when she kicked off her high heels on that Sunday night, I did not appear on her horizon. My grandmother came to me in the bedroom.

I was curled up in my parents' bed, wrapped in the seal fur jacket that my father would later toss out the window. "Why are you crying?" she asked me.

"Because I hate Shirley Feld." Bubby stroked my less-than-clean hair. "Why should you hate her? She doesn't have in her whole body what you have in your little finger."

"I can't stand her and her elocution. I can't stand the same poem every time."

"So you'll recite the next time. Next time you'll recite and you'll show everyone how you speak like a chuchim."

"I don't take elocution."

"Is that why you're crying? You want lessons in how to recite?"

I thought this over carefully. I didn't have to lie to Bubby because the withdrawal of love didn't exist, nor was there fear of punishment or censure. But in order to be honest with her, I had to be honest with myself. Or as close to honesty as I could achieve. It took me several minutes of having Bubby pat my hair and caress my back before I answered with difficulty. "It's the white muff. I want a white muff."

"Like a czarina in Russland, riding in a troika?"

"It's in the books with pictures, little girls in white fur hats and white muffs. They skate on ice. They dance with their muffs."

"In Russia they have dancing bears, but the bears don't have muffs."

"Bubby, don't laugh at me."

"I'm not laughing." She spoke softly. "It's like your father with the shawl for the table. It's magiicheskii," she added in Russian. "But if you want it, if you need a white fur muff, you'll have it. Uncle Goodman will be here this week. I'll tell him to find you a muff, like you want."

6

—◦◦◦—

Promises

THOUGH MY PARENTS were in the business and sold furs and cloth coats I noticed that my grandmother didn't rely on them or think of asking them for the muff. They would say, "Yes, of course," and forget. It wasn't that they were liars, but that the spoken promise meant nothing on the Lower East Side. Phrases like, "I give you my word," "my word of honor," "I promise," had no meaning. They were not brought up to understand them.

People who came to our restaurant or whom my parents met socially promised one thing or another: samples, yards of cloth, items of clothing, rides in their cars, parties. But the second they left, the commitments flew out of their heads. There was no tradition of keeping one's word. How many times had James Feld promised Bubby a basket of fruit, only to show up with three lousy oranges? Orloff had bought the embroidered shawl for the table, but he was driven by lust, by fantasies that propelled him to keep his word.

My own mother broke her promises routinely.

For some years I was enchanted by the prospect of seeing the lighted Christmas trees at Macy's. They advertised on radio that the indoor tree rose three stories tall, covered with over one thousand lightbulbs, an equal number of ornaments and three hundred pounds of tinsel. I repeated these numbers to myself and said them out loud with the radio. While my mother painted her toenails in front of the hot, open-doored gas range in the kitchen, I asked, "Mother, do you think you could take me to see the Christmas trees at Macy's?"

"Maybe," she answered, without taking her eyes from her toes. A translation of *maybe* meant *no*.

But my need to see this wonderful tree overwhelmed me. A few days later, I repeated my request adding, "Mother, if you're going shopping uptown, maybe we could run in and see the Christmas tree."

"It's all the way on Thirty-fourth Street. Too far."

A few days later, "You could try on hats at Gimbel's. Lilly Daché hats. Then across the street is Macy's."

"Gimbel's doesn't carry Lilly Daché. For that we would have to go to Saks Fifth Avenue. Too far."

"But sometime," I persisted, "just once."

"Maybe," she replied. We were back where we had started.

Possibly to placate me, she allowed me to walk with her to visit Ada, which she regarded as a treat. Ada pushed her children out of the house when she and my mother whispered together. Secrets. Whether it rained, snowed or sweltered, Shirley and Artie frequented the streets or the long hallway outside their apartment door. On this particular day neither of Ada's children was home, and Ada gave my mother a wink. As was the custom, they sat in the kitchen. Ada could brag about her dining room set but she used it for ceremonial occasions, Passover seder and the meal following the Yom Kippur fast. The table, veneered with imitation mahogany, was highly polished and decorated with two candlesticks.

You couldn't find a newspaper, a magazine, a book in Ada's apartment. I had nothing to do and she wouldn't turn on the radio for my sake—it was then believed that switching on the radio or plugging in an iron used vast kilowatts of electricity and cost a great deal of money. In our house, Bubby paid no attention to petty sums, and our radio hummed at all hours. Not at Ada's.

Lil said in a conciliatory way, "Why don't you walk down the hall and open the door to the backyard. There's a big Christmas tree there. With lights and everything."

"Really a Christmas tree?"

"I swear," said Ada. "A real Christmas tree."

Racing down the outside hall I tugged and tugged at the door that led to the yard. Something held it from opening. With all my strength I pulled until it yielded possibly an inch. I peeked through. Black coal, piled as high as my eye could see. Dull, dirty black coal.

"Mother!" I cried out, "Mother!" Then I banged on Ada's front door. My mother regarded me without guilt, shame or surprise.

"There's nothing but coal."

She paused as if she couldn't believe that I had believed her. "What would a Christmas tree be doing in a Jewish neighborhood, and in a backyard on East Broadway?" Her question, offered without malice, rendered me a fool. She felt no guilt for misleading me, because I had been silly to accept her statement.

A series of such incidents made me wary of promises, even one given by Bubby to obtain this magical muff for me.

On Saturday, when Goodman came to pick up his order of baked goods, he delivered the muff, pristine in its whiteness, with a fake turquoise bracelet attached to it and a Macy's label sewn right inside.

My mother rewarded him with a hug. Her hair had been coiffed the night before for work, and a glow radiated from her in the early morning light. "You shouldn't have," she said to Goodman seductively.

Goodman laughed. "The muff, it's not for you, Lil, it's not for the child. It's for Manya. She sent for my Bertha from Odessa, cared for her, loved her. She brought the two of us together. We had the wedding in this apartment, the chuppa, everything. We have a big house in Yonkers. We beg Manya to come for a week. We'll wait on her, take her to shows. Anything she wants. She always says no. No to staying a week, no to anything we would be glad to give her. So when she asks me for a muff for her grandchild, it's already done, it's bought, so Manya can have pleasure."

My grandmother replied, "Yes, when my Elkaleh has naches, I have naches."

Goodman always brought his own box from his factory for what he referred to as "the sweet table." That day he had left his home early because he worried about the ice that hardened on the East River highway. The temperature had fallen to twenty degrees and a fierce wind was ripping across the city. "Stay healthy," Goodman called to us and rushed to his car.

Some months before, a man who sold leather goods on Clinton Street stopped my mother and said he had a present for her. The jackets he sold, sewn from bits and pieces of leather, hung on hooks outside his door. On this day he handed my mother a pair of leather leggings.

"I don't know what they're for. It's a sample, maybe for horseback riding, maybe for a very small or skinny child. Take them. A salesman, he don't know what to do with this sample either and I saved it for you, for your girl with very skinny legs. Manya won't let me starve after she sees these leggings."

My mother tore home, elated with her treasure. The moment she saw me, she urged my legs—in dirty cotton stockings—into them. The side zippers could not unlock; the brass catches had broken off. I stood up and wiggled my bony legs inside. From the first moment it was apparent that there would be problems getting them off, but my mother was awash in ecstasy. "Horseback riding boots. Just like in the society magazines. They're warm, they're classy, they fit like a glove. Turn around. Model them for me. How do they feel?"

If the leggings cut off my circulation, if my legs felt encased in cement I would not have said a word, because those leggings thrilled Lil. From birth I disappointed her because like my father I was olive-complected and dark-haired. Often she remarked about my brother, Willy, "Can you believe it, that he has white skin that any girl would be proud of and she's dark? When they take a bath, Willy is all pink and she's all yellow."

"It's from the Odessa side, the dark skin," my father decided, ignoring his mother's milky complexion. "Maybe someone had Gypsy blood."

"How do Jews come to have Gypsy blood?" my grandmother retorted.

"Odessaniks have every kind of smarts, every kind of talent and every kind of blood," answered my father.

"And this maydel, my Elka, is like my husband, Misha, and not some Gypsy," said my grandmother, putting an end to it.

But I longed to look like my mother or at least to appear the way she wanted me to. So I wore the leggings. To school during the day, to bed at night, round the clock. On the icy morning that Goodman brought me the white imitation rabbit muff, our beds cluttered the dining room, and my leather leggings, with my dirty long stockings under them, showed beneath a ratty nightgown covered by two sweaters. The weather was miserably cold, so there was no question of giving us baths. My hair hadn't been washed for weeks, and God knows how I smelled. But the muff transformed me instantly into a girl with well-proportioned legs, recently bathed and smelling of dusting powder, and hair as golden as my mother's.

At that moment, Jacob called from the street. The windows were too frozen to open so he stumbled into our hallway and yelled upstairs, "No work today, Lil. Your store just called. Too cold. Who's going to come out on a day like this? By me the same. No business."

Suddenly maternal, my mother decided to wash my hair. This involved removing my clothes, dousing my hair with warm water from the kettle and lathering it with Lux bar soap. The whole procedure was hateful. I had to scrub ears, neck, arms and chest in the freezing apartment. Nothing was washed below the waist, because of my leggings.

I sat in front of the gas range with a blanket draped around me while my hair dried. Like my father's, it was naturally wavy. He slicked his hair with pomade, but mine fell in deep waves and my mother tried in vain to set it in bottle curls. This artificial coif neither suited me nor stayed in place. On this stormy day my mother had no patience for fiddling with my hair. She was too eager to get to Ada's and show off my new muff with its Macy's label.

My mother loved labels. If clothes were supposed to make the man, then labels made the clothes for Lil. The store in which she worked on Division Street attracted a moneyed clientele. Instead of coming to sales at Bergdorf Goodman or Henri Bendel, women patronized The

Palace with its pink spotlighted mannequins in the windows because it offered copies of high fashion at half the price.

While customers tried on the garments, the labels on their own clothing sometimes fell onto the carpet. My mother would snatch them up as if she had come upon lost treasure. To be sure, she asked her customers if they wanted the labels resewn by the on-the-premises tailor who adjusted hemlines and sleeve lengths. Usually, they didn't bother. This meant that some of the outfits that my mother bought at S. Klein's or at sales on Clinton Street had the spiffiest labels, cross-stitched by Lil herself. My mother was even more excited by the Macy's label than I by the muff.

In a magnanimous mood, she agreed to take my brother, Willy, along with me to visit her friend Ada. Willy had no desire to walk in the cold or to play with Artie Levine, a good-natured boy who looked like his father, Irwin, gorged himself on bread with chicken fat, ate potatoes at every meal, and topped everything off with one or two candy bars. He was his mother's favorite, and Ada had once pilfered an entire box of Baby Ruths from a local store to keep him in sweets.

Willy had no interest in Artie, or in any playmate for that matter. Given the choice, he would never have left our apartment at all. If my mother held the title of family singer, my brother, Willy, could win prizes as the whistler. He whistled with or without two fingers in his mouth, in perfect pitch, creating clear ringing sounds. His favorite song was "I Can Dream, Can't I?" and his rendition of it almost broke my heart. Lil, not given to praise, had to admit that he could go on the vaudeville circuit with his whistling.

Willy preferred to stay home and practice whistling, listen to the radio or print. He wasn't particularly good at school; neither his reading nor arithmetic was more than average. But he loved printing numbers and letters—he taught me how to make an eight by placing two balls one on top of another. And like the rest of us he adored movies, so if my mother had offered to "walk him" into Loew's Canal—children were not admitted without adults—he would have been happy. But a trip to Ada Levine's on a freezing day sent him into hiding, first in the dark room behind the folding beds and then behind my grandmother's skirt. To no avail.

The reason for my mother's obstinacy—she usually allowed Willy to do what he pleased because he placed no demands on her—was to show off a fake leather jacket lined with imitation sheepskin that she had bought for him from Jacob's downstairs. The black and shiny jacket weighed a ton. Possibly Artie Levine with his stocky build could have done justice to it; on Willy, it hung like a heavy wet sack, the sleeves inches below his wrists and the hem well below his knobby knees. If I was taunted with "skinny pickle," Willy was mocked as "broomstick" because of his awkward arms and legs, his concave chest and his skeletal body. Though like us all he was surrounded by mountains of food, Willy lived on clear chicken soup and Bubby's baked goods. Jacob sold Lil the jacket at cost. Usually he opted for the barter system and accepted meals from our restaurant. But business was bad that winter and paying cash from my mother's slim paycheck seemed preferable to feeding Jacob.

At last we set out for Ada's, my brother in his bulky shiny jacket and matching hat with earflaps, I in my leather leggings and last year's navy blue coat, inches too short and of no consequence compared to my new white muff. My mother, as usual, was resplendent in a mouton lamb coat, which she tried to pass off as sheared beaver.

The wind was biting and cruel. We had heard on the radio that the temperature was ten degrees, and my grandmother viewed our excursion with alarm. "Where are you going in Siberian weather?"

"A few blocks. Some fresh air. Besides, Ada has steam heat."

As usual, my brother kept his head down, barely keeping in step. I held on to my mother's arm. The three of us were out of breath within minutes, struggling against the wind and cold. We hardly saw a soul on the streets. The sky darkened and icy patches lay like traps on the sidewalk.

Nevertheless, we managed to traverse Canal Street and to cross over to East Broadway. We passed the *Jewish Forward* building. Across from the public library was the Educational Alliance, known for giving free classes in English and the arts. The "Edgies" also had offices where people could get free legal advice. The classes, as scruffy as the public schools, provided shabby textbooks, broken crayons and secondhand donations from God knows where. Once when I started to take a class in Hebrew at the Edgies my mother put a stop to it in a hurry. I would surely come home with lice, she cried, and moreover, I was already fluent in Yiddish and knew some Russian. What was I doing at the Edgies with immigrants?

That day the Edgies loomed as a welcome landmark and we might have ducked in for a moment to relieve the cold, but it was closed on Saturdays. Besides we were just two streets away from Ada's. We plowed along like runaways crossing a frozen tundra.

For once Ada's house appeared like a haven. We gasped with relief when we lumbered up the steps and were met with a rush of warm air at her door. Ada greeted us in a frayed pink chenille wrapper, her hair in tin curlers; she hadn't as yet brushed her teeth or fixed her coffee. "In this weather, you're out?" My gorgeous muff and Willy's shiny jacket escaped her notice. She yawned noisily, exhaling stale breath. My mother drew back a step. "How come you're not working?" Ada asked.

"Too cold. No customers."

"You came to take a bath?"

It was a mistake to have made the trip, though my mother pretended not to notice that Ada had stayed in bed all morning. Possibly her children were sleeping late as well. I pulled Willy to the bottom step of the stairs that led to the doctor's apartment and brushed my face against my beautiful muff for comfort. Willy's lips were blue and as cold as his nose.

"Mother, let's go home," I said. She ignored us and stepped inside Ada's apartment.

Within minutes, Shirley and Artie joined us in the hall. On this blustery cold day Shirley Levine wore socks over her brown oxfords. "Hide-and-seek!" Artie cried. Tapping my brother, Shirley yelled, "You're it!" Both Levine children dashed out the front door into the street. With reluctance we followed them outdoors. Neither was anywhere in sight. Maybe they were hidden under the steps of the stoop; maybe they were just around the corner. In fact, they had reentered the building while we were looking for them and locked the outside door from within. We tried with all our strength to open the door. We failed.

The wind stiffened. We stood on the sidewalk, Willy and I, buffeted by the wind. Our one desire was to get home and though we twisted around in the wind, we were certain we were walking in the right direction. We kept our heads down. It started to snow.

We must have walked three blocks before we realized that neither the public library building nor the Edgies was visible. We had wandered away from the direction of Orchard Street into unknown territory. Unknown and potentially dangerous. At the end of the street stood a group of teenaged boys.

"Sheeny on your own side!" one of them yelled.

"Guineas!" screamed Willy. "Guineas from Little Italy!"

It couldn't have been an Italian gang—we were miles from Mott, Mulberry, Cherry or Elizabeth streets. Reversing ourselves immediately, we pounded down the pavement as fast as we could. Did the boys in pursuit want to beat us? Did they long to steal Willy's shiny new jacket or my brand-new white muff? I was terrified for Willy. He lost his breath easily. In my mind's eye I could see those big boys knocking us down, stomping Willy to death. His gloved hand in mine, I pulled him through street after street.

We could hear the gang's footsteps behind us and we raced ahead blindly, crossing streets without watching for cars. Miraculously, no car hit us as we crossed from East Broadway to Canal. At that point we could have paused because we were back in our own neighborhood, with people who could protect us. But we thought we still heard thundering footsteps, and the cries of "Sheeny on your own side" swelled in our ears. Our tears had frozen our eyelashes; we could hardly see. We pounded on, past Loew's Canal, past Mathias Hats, Jacob's Clothing, not once glancing at The Grand Canal Cafeteria. My legs were icicles encased in frozen leggings. In yanking Willy across the streets I had fallen twice and skinned my knees and once my muff hit the slush. But all we could feel was fear—as frigid as the air and the ice on the sidewalk. Finally, our house. We rounded the corner to Orchard Street. No one followed us.

We gasped our way upstairs. Willy threw himself into my grandmother's lap. "Bubby, Bubby, the Guineas, the Guineas!" He was beside himself with terror.

Quickly, Bubby brought us to the cold water tap and ran the water over our fingers. Compared to their icy state, the cold water felt boiling hot. She removed our gloves and wordlessly wiped off our faces, our lashes still iced together, our mouths frozen.

For a woman built close to the ground Bubby was surprisingly limber. She quickly brought us her wedding feather blanket and took care of Willy first, removing his wet shoes and socks and placing her ear to his wheezing chest. "The Guineas! the Guineas!" he kept screaming. She wrapped him in the blanket, placed his feet in a basin of warm water and retrieved a bottle of ephedrine tablets for his asthma. She placed a pill between his icy lips, hugging and kissing him and repeating, "My kind, my sise kind."

Both of us kept crying. We couldn't stop. "My muff—it fell in the water," I sobbed.

"A little water is gornisht. A little water is nothing."

My coat and dress came off easily; the major problem was the leggings, covered with ice. I watched Bubby stand quietly, her hand to her head. The sharpest knife in her kitchen, a butcher's knife, could not cut through frozen leather. Then it came to her—how to get rid of those accursed leggings.

She warmed some oil in a pan and holding on to my skinny body, she poured the oil around the edge of the leggings, at least a quart, until at last I could wiggle my toes, my legs. Then she lowered my stockings and simply lifted me out of the leggings.

She worked with such unwavering concentration that she didn't utter a sound until I was free. Then a smile spread over her face. Her white hair had escaped from her haphazard bun during these exertions so she looked slightly wild but triumphant as she threw the leggings into a corner of the kitchen.

My legs were blue with cold. She rubbed their oily surface until I felt some sensation.

She acted as if no recent trauma had occurred. "Roasted chestnuts or hot sweet potatoes?" she asked as she rolled the hot potatoes over our chests as if they were poultices. Periodically Willy would cry out, "The Guineas, the Guineas," and each time Bubby would answer, "Not here. Not on Orchard Street."

Unexpectedly my mother came through the door. She seemed to take our presence for granted. "Listen," she said, "I decided to call myself Shirley for my middle name after all."

My father staggered out of the bedroom. He had been taking a nap.

"Jack, what are you doing home?" she asked.

"Sent back. Not a soul on Division Street. Now it's snowing. The radio says it's a major storm."

"Listen, Jack, tell me the truth. What do you think of Shirley for my middle name?"

My father scrounged around in an old tin box that once held Louis Sherry chocolates. He had given them to my grandmother for Mother's Day, ate almost every one of them, and since then often replenished the lavender box with the best chocolates he could afford. He had instructed me at an early age on the eating of expensive chocolates: "A Belgian chocolate is not a peanut. You don't bite into it. You let it dissolve on your palate." Now he extracted a chocolate cream—he preferred dark bitter chocolate filled with delicate cream—and let it dissolve in his mouth slowly before answering.

"Shirley is like Margie, it's like Mary. Everyone is called Shirley these days." He inspected the tin box thoughtfully. "Why don't you call yourself Sherry. You know, like Louis Sherry chocolates."

"Sherry? Is that a woman's name?"

"Of course it's a woman's name. Where do you think sherry liqueur comes from? Probably from some gorgeous woman."

"Sherry," my mother repeated. "Lil Sherry Roth." She regarded my father with awe. "Jack," she said, "sometimes I think you're a genius."

7

Misadventures

MY PARENTS STARTED taking me to the Roxy, the Palace, or to Broadway plays after Yussie Feld remarked during one of his visits that he and his wife had accompanied Shirley to a Saturday matinee on Broadway and she enjoyed it. "Oh," my mother said, "we work weekends. During the week, we treat our children all the time."

In late winter, business slowed on Division Street. On Wednesdays my parents sometimes kept me from school and we set out for a matinee. Sitting with them on the subway and then in some movie or vaudeville house uptown brought me to tears of pride.

Every act and headliner enchanted me; it was my American experience, as compared to the Second Avenue Yiddish theater with Bubby, a European event. Afterward, riding home on the subway, people noticed my father with his slick black hair, his expensive hat and a three-pointed handkerchief peeping from the breast pocket of his dark, well-tailored coat, and my mother elegant in the latest fashion. I felt awe and alienation. In my dull sailor dress and too-small overcoat, how did I relate to this sophisticated couple? I was Orchard Street; not they.

Once home, my father retold the jokes he had memorized watching the stage show. "So this man goes into a restaurant, and after he eats the owner asks him how he liked the dinner. The customer says the food satisfied him, but he needed more than two slices of bread. The next time the customer comes in the owner gives him four pieces of bread and still the man complains, 'I need more bread.' A few days later his plate holds eight pieces, eight whole pieces of bread, and the diner still shakes his head, 'More bread.' Well the restaurant owner says, 'I'll fix him' and he takes a loaf of bread as big as the table and cuts it in half and hands it to the customer. Then the owner asks, 'Well, was everything all right?' and the man answers, 'Great, great, but tell me, why did you go back to two pieces of bread?' "

Our entire family laughed. The news flew from door to door that I had been with my parents uptown to see a show, wearing my best dress. The sailor dress hung on a nail in the bedroom until the next big event.

However, no theatrical event could compare to a visit to Yonkers and a stay at the home of Aunt Bertha and Uncle Goodman. For a short period the Goodmans shared our Orchard Street Passover seder, I awkward and embarrassed at spending the evening with the teenaged Goodman children, Flo—Florence—and Henry, both of whom spoke with accents as different from ours as actors in a British movie. They used the English *a,* calling Bubby "Ahnt Manya," and my father "Cousin Jack." Every year Flo would remark, "I don't really prefer this menu."

Aunt Bertha struck me, not as my grandmother's baby sister, but as some movie star, say Kay Francis, whose high-fashion style she emulated. Ravishing furs tumbled from Aunt Bertha's coats; over her suits she draped double silver foxes, their mouths clasped together, their eyes bright brown beads. In the dead of winter she swept up our steps in a floor-length mink. She wore wide-brimmed hats, cloches, turbans of silk, hats trimmed with flowers or feathers, that she kept on her head during her visits. Her diamond rings glittered on her fingers like shiny pebbles. I was dazzled.

To obtain Bubby's agreement to visit Yonkers took weeks of urging and planning. My father opposed it on principle and Bubby did not feel comfortable having to dress up, worry about her English and forsake the routine of which she was so fond. Besides, when we stayed in Yonkers I couldn't let myself appear defective in English so I called Bubby "Grandmother." She created one excuse after another for avoiding Yonkers but finally, and mostly for my sake, she would consent to the trip.

The preparations took as much time as getting ready for a week in the country. Bubby cooked a vat of stuffed cabbage because it thrilled Goodman; a brisket for sandwiches; a challah; and every cake, cookie and strudel in her repertoire.

Goodman would pick us up on Friday night for the drive to Yonkers and my grandmother and I sat in the capacious leather-lined front seat of his black Lincoln. Once, he made a halfhearted effort to invite Willy to come along, but my brother, much too shy, cringed at the idea. Nor were my parents part of the equation. This was Manya's treat, and she couldn't conceive of leaving me behind.

Our Yonkers routine didn't vary. On Friday night we ate the food that we brought from home. But on Saturday night, Goodman, Aunt Bertha, Bubby and I went to a Hungarian restaurant noted not for its food but for its Gypsy violinist. Repeatedly, Goodman remarked, "The cooking can't compare to yours, Manya, and it's not as lively as Moskowitz and Lupovitz on Second Avenue, but we want you to have a good time."

Stuffed into her corset, her pumps and her gray-blue crepe dress, Bubby pretended that she did, but there was no pretense for me. I was transported to a world that fulfilled all my fantasies.

The Goodman house itself, its large rooms and high ceilings, impressed me. The wide outside porch with its swinging chaise, the entryway called the "foy-aye," and the living room with identical couches that faced each other reminded me of illustrations in a magazine. The grandeur of Dr. Koronovsky's Grand Street apartment, which I had once glimpsed, could not equal this setting.

I claimed the sunroom for my own. It faced the broad street sheltered by tall trees, and I luxuriated in the white rattan chaise amid plump green cushions. Best of all were the magazines: *The Saturday Evening Post, Colliers, Vanity Fair, Harper's Bazaar* and every movie magazine imaginable. Given my choice, I would have sat in the chaise or on the window seat of the sunroom and read magazines the entire length of my stay.

At home, I hated being outside, though outdoors was often less cold than our damp apartment. I rejected skipping rope, despised playing potsie, was terrified of the swings in Hester Park. My mother often threatened me with the prospect of learning how to roller-skate, a pastime that could only accentuate my awkwardness. And even if I had been able to skip rope, do double Dutch, swing up to the sky, skate down the sidewalks without fear, none of which I mastered, I would always wear the same clothes I wore to school.

At least once every visit, Goodman would ask, as if it were the Passover seder, why this night was different from all other nights. "Did I ever tell you how I happened to meet Bertha?" he said. His children listened, too polite to groan, and Goodman, beaming, went on uninterrupted.

"I was eating at Manya's, and there stood Bertha, so tall, so beautiful. I said to Manya, I said, 'Are you going to introduce me to this kretzavitz? Is she your daughter?' Manya laughed and said, 'That's my baby sister. She's an American, doesn't remember a word of Russian, speaks Yiddish like a shiksa.'" At this point Goodman paused. "Do you know what I told Bertha? I said, 'Bertha, I'm going to marry you. I'll stay here day and night until you tell me you'll marry me.' Bertha laughed, 'You'll be in the wrong place because I don't live on Orchard Street.' So I answered, 'Then I'll wait outside your door wherever you are. I'll sit on the steps and won't let you out of my sight. And I'll make you very happy.'"

Goodman glanced at Bubby. "Manya, iz dus der emmes? The truth?"

"Emmes," Manya replied.

Goodman jumped up. As Bertha toyed with the string of pearls at the neck of her blue and gray striped silk dress, he kissed her on the cheek. More than twenty years of marriage had not dimmed his ardor.

He regarded every diamond and every jewel that he bought her as a kiss from him to her; a head shorter than she, he was a roly-poly enthralled with his tall elegant princess. Aunt Bertha would cry out flirtatiously, "Goodman, you'll never change."

"And why should I change, why shouldn't I tell the woman I love that she's wonderful?" His enthusiasm, his buoyancy, his good nature carried the day. Aunt Bertha had made an excellent marriage—not one based on early passion on her part, but one that provided her with devotion and with luxury that no little girl from Odessa could have imagined.

On Saturday morning, Aunt Bertha, who did not observe our dietary laws, refrained from preparing bacon and eggs for her children. Rather, we had Saperstein's lox and sturgeon, and my Bubby's challah and coffee cake with our coffee, Bubby uneasy about not fussing in the kitchen. Then she and I went for a walk in the neighborhood, my eyes literally tearful at the sight of houses set back on wide lawns. When the plants and trees were in bloom, I would envision myself as the heroine in *The Secret Garden*.

In early evening, as soon as it grew dark, Aunt Bertha would remind me kindly, "It's time to take your shower." The words were magical. I went upstairs to the main bathroom, and with Bubby's help removed my navy blue sailor dress and enjoyed the spraying water, not ashamed as at the public baths but elated, imagining this house as the finest hotel. In Yonkers I forgot my skinny, shapeless legs and the ribs that showed through my chest. Here I poured shampoo from a bottle on my hair and afterward was bundled into an enormous bath towel.

To be sure, I wore the same underwear from the day before, but when my hair was towel-dried it fell into a natural wave, and Aunt Bertha would remark on how beautiful it was. "It's like your father's," she said. "Jack has beautiful hair, too."

Bubby washed her face before the evening's entertainment and recombed her hair. Long ago Aunt Bertha had bought her a robe called a housecoat, which remained in the guest room closet for our visits. Slipping out of the housecoat, she now pulled her dress over her head, and groaning slightly, forced her feet into her pumps. Then Uncle Goodman brought the car out of the garage and we drove off to The Gypsy Cellar.

No food at this Hungarian restaurant could reach the professionalism of my grandmother's cooking. The stuffed cabbage was watery and filled mostly with rice; Hungarian stew proved salty, as if it had been reheated. Soggy dessert crepes stuffed with apricot jam completed the meal. Bertha, the most knowledgeable diner in our group, ordered chicken paprikash, a combination of chicken, sour cream and paprika. I hardly tasted a bite of the potato pancakes and roast chicken that my grandmother and I shared, too intent on waiting for the strolling violinist.

He was dressed in a puffed-sleeved white shirt with a frill down the middle, a red cummerbund and tight black shiny pants, and he played a variety of Hungarian/Russian/Rumanian songs with lots of fancy fiddling, though most of the tunes sounded similar to my ears. The dark room, wood paneled and smoky, smelled of stale food. When the violinist came to our table, I rose, stood on the chair and without any hesitation sang, "Orchichornia." My father's instructions, "Mother sings, you listen," had no relevance at The Gypsy Cellar. Uncle Goodman hushed everyone around us so that my thin voice could be heard.

To this day I don't know whether I had the Russian quite right, but unafraid, I sang with great passion. "Orchichornia, orchiyasnia, orchikrasnia, imagushnia, suk ba yee, yavas, kok lublu yavas, orchichornia, I love you so."

Uncle Goodman led the applause. Bubby wiped tears from her eyes. Aunt Bertha said, "Manya, I see why you're so proud of her." At other tables I could hear diners ask, "How old is she? Where did she learn to sing Russian?" Needless to say, as my mother's prompter, I could sing every song in her repertoire, but at The Gypsy Cellar I feared to press my luck and simply repeated endless choruses of "Dark Eyes."

After tea and inferior pastries, we left for the Yonkers house. Uncle Goodman tipped everyone lavishly and the waiters in their Hungarian costumes, with red braid on their jackets and down the sides of their pants, complimented me, my beautiful grandmother with her white hair, and Aunt Bertha in her toque hat trimmed with feathers. All the while, little Uncle Goodman smiled, smiled, giving off enough electrical energy to light a stadium.

At daybreak, while Bertha and the Goodman children slept, we crept out and Goodman drove us back to Orchard Street. At the door, he pressed money into my grandmother's hand. She resolutely refused. He handed it to me and I accepted, another one of our rituals. Then Bubby started to bustle about the kitchen to prepare for Sunday's lunch customers and I took off my navy blue sailor dress.

On a dark February evening several months later, we set out again for Yonkers with our usual packages and pots of food but in the car I started to feel sick. Wedged between Bubby in her seal coat and Uncle Goodman, I said that I had a stomachache. Uncle Goodman assured me that I would feel better soon.

For once, the sight of the sunroom and the stacks of magazines failed to lift my spirits and I could hardly keep my head up. I lay down on the bed in the guest room upstairs. The white ceiling swam above me. I had to hold on to the side of the bed or fall off. Aunt Bertha heated my grandmother's brisket, but I couldn't make it downstairs. Bubby suggested that I sleep for a while and I did, fitfully, hearing the laughter and voices below, wishing I could be with them but unable to raise my head even when I tried. A minute or an hour later Bubby put her hand on my head and asked for a thermometer.

Years before, Dr. Koronovsky taught her to read a thermometer, and she became expert at washing it with alcohol, placing it under the tongue, then scanning the silver line of mercury. There was no thermometer in the Goodman household and the stores on Broadway, then the Yonkers main thoroughfare, closed up shop at eight o'clock. So Uncle Goodman rushed out and returned with a thermometer. I was too bleary-eyed to see Bubby's face when she scrutinized the results, but I heard her announce soberly, "One hundred and three."

Aunt Bertha, foreign to illness, offered a solution to the problem. "We'll give her an enema. We'll clean out her system. She'll be fine in the morning."

I despised enemas, considered them the worst of indignities, and in spite of my fever screamed out, "No, no enemas!" Then I sat up, repeated, "I will not have an enema," and collapsed back on my pillow.

When I said no to something, ridicule did not follow. In Yonkers, with Aunt Bertha standing in the doorway with an enema bag in her hand, Bubby gently turned her away. "I'll sleep with her a little," she explained. She snapped off the light, touched my forehead, moved my legs. Meningitis carried children off in hours. Gently, she massaged my arms and legs without attempting to remove my navy blue dress.

Abruptly, she snapped on the lamp and let out a low cry. I still couldn't see clearly, but my arms seemed pink, maybe red. She tried the thermometer again. "How much is it?" I asked, the true daughter of my father. "The same," she said doing her best to cover up her lie with excessive cheerfulness.

She sponged me with a cold cloth, looked out the window and waited for the sky to lighten. Finally she knocked on Goodman's bedroom door. He came to my side and nodded, "I'll bring the car."

My grandmother dressed quickly, and stripped the bed of the sheets and the pillowcases. Her sister, Bertha, would find the task odious. She wrapped me in the blanket and Goodman carried me down to the backseat of the Lincoln. "Manya, is it measles?" he asked. "No." Her voice broke. "She has 104 temperature."

I recall nothing of the ride home nor of the two flights of dark stairs. Bubby pushed open the door and my father, a light sleeper, heard us at once.

"What is it?" He glanced at me, cried, "Oh, my God!" and called, "Clayton, go to the doctor. Go to his house on Grand Street."

Settled in my parents' bed, I lost sense of time. Soon enough Dr. Koronovsky bent over me, and Bubby asked, "Will I need a paper on my door?"

"I have to report that she has scarlet fever, maybe something else. I'll be back in a few hours to see what develops."

"Polio?" my father asked.

"Too soon, too soon to tell. I'll be here by noon. Manya, you can't serve food today or tomorrow. It's the weekend. It won't be too bad for you. Keep her as cool as possible, and Lil and Willy stay away from her." The doctor addressed my mother, "Lil, you must be careful for the next few days. Because of your heart. These infectious diseases are hard on the heart."

Uncle Goodman, close to tears, managed to say, "Doctor, send me the bill. Don't worry about the money. Give her the best. Manya, you won't lose her. Manya, I tell you, you won't lose her."

My grandmother looked down at me, willing me to live.

Through the slits of my eyes I realized that Dr. Koronovsky was unshaven, a dark cardigan sweater covering his rumpled shirt.

"Manya," the doctor said, "I haven't been to bed yet. We have an epidemic. I lost two last night, one boy, one girl. Manya, she has 105 right now. Your apartment is less than adequate. The bedroom is freezing. She needs to be sponged every hour, kept sanitary, kept warm, kept isolated. Manya, would you consider sending her to the hospital, not the ones down here, but to Beth Israel, uptown? I could have her admitted because of my affiliation." He tried his best to persuade her.

More than thirty-five years had passed since Bubby buried her husband. Throughout those years her hatred and contempt for hospitals never waned—she could not even bring herself to visit my mother when she delivered both her babies in J. P. Morgan's Lying-In Hospital uptown. She didn't hesitate now. "No," she cried, louder than I had the night before when I refused to submit to an enema. "No, I will do whatever you tell me, but no hospital."

It seemed odd to me that Goodman pushed forward into my parents' bedroom and asked, as he inspected the overhead light, "Are there any other electrical outlets?"

We had one electrical outlet in the dining room that had been installed at my grandmother's expense. There Clayton would set up the ironing board and the electric iron to do my mother's personal clothing.

Instead of answering Goodman's question, Bubby wiped her flushed face on her apron. "Tell us what to do."

"A sponge bath every hour, medium warm water with alcohol. The alcohol stings, but it will also dry up the rash and keep it from getting infected. Fresh nightshirt after every bath—old soft shirts. If you have a way of heating this room, place her in that tin tub—but the room is too cold now. She's also dehydrated, needs lots of liquids. Get some paper straws, and make her sip water every half hour. Buy some Jell-O, any flavor, and dissolve it in water. Don't refrigerate it; use it as a drink, to get some sugar into her. And keep that head and hair clean. Sanitation is very important, because I don't know what else, what other disease is in her body."

My grandmother nodded to everything, and my father, whose memory always startled the family—he remembered the words to hundreds of songs, could summarize the plots of every book he read, absorbed the racing form at a glance—repeated, "Sanitation, sponge baths, Jell-O in water, head and hair clean. Doctor, what about meningitis, what about polio?"

"No signs, yet. Any stiffness in neck, shoulders, arms, legs, call me at once. And remember, Willy and Lil can't enter the bedroom." Koronovsky paused. "Manya, no meals to anyone but the immediate family. Jack, put up a handwritten sign." Willy provided one of his school tests and my father wrote on the clean side, Closed for Vacation. He pried a rusty thumbtack from the kitchen cupboard to fix the notice to the front door.

No one would accuse us of lying. The neighbors knew Bubby, my parents, my brother, me. They accepted the excuse of a vacation as they accepted any strategy that helped them to live. Dozens of witnesses had watched me carried up the stairs; countless others could testify to Dr. Koronovsky's car, to Uncle Goodman's car. Before Clayton left to buy Jell-O and straws, everyone had heard of my illness, knew my exact temperature, knew about the children less fortunate than I who had died in the night.

Sipping water from a straw caused intense pain; my throat seemed composed of shards of glass. Bubby promised, "I'll make you the telle fun himmel, the plate from heaven," and I smiled and slept for many hours after that. I didn't open my eyes until Goodman was standing at my bed, holding up a large box. "I bought you a present," he said, bubbling with enthusiasm. "I bought you an electric heater."

"Also," he added, "from my factory, I got the electrician. On a Saturday." He was elated.

My father had many talents. He was a natural writer, could compose words to popular songs that sounded as if they had been done by a published songwriter. But he literally could not change a lightbulb nor wanted to, either because he wouldn't soil his hands or because he regarded himself as above such mundane tasks.

When Goodman trooped in with the electric heater the neighbors buzzed with news. Who had heard of such an object on Orchard Street? The electrician, a man in a railroad cap and a mackinaw, came prepared with yards of extension cord, which he attached to our one outlet in the dining room and carefully tacked along the baseboards leading into my parents' room. The plug fit neatly into the electric heater.

I was too weak to applaud but everyone else did, as if he had turned on the switch to the stage at Radio City Music Hall for the holiday extravaganza. Moreover, the electrician also brought with him an entire roll of felt, and holding a dozen nails in his mouth, he discarded the sopping wet towel on the bedroom windowsill and installed felt along the entire window frame. "Airtight" was the single word he said.

Dr. Koronovsky was appropriately impressed when he returned to a warm room with an electric heater and a window sealed from drafts.

Short little kind Goodman rocked on his skinny legs and asked Bubby, "Goot gedavend? Did I pray good?"

"Very good," Manya answered, as if she had been praying in shul and her prayers were answered.

Everyone remarked on the swift skills of the electrician. His job completed, my grandmother asked him if he would like a bite to eat. He mentioned a ham sandwich. Without a moment's hesitation, she cut some brisket of beef very thin, added lots of kosher salt, lathered it with mustard and served it on rye bread with a kosher pickle. The handyman declared it the best ham sandwich he had ever tasted. She gave him another to take home.

In spite of the sign on the door all the neighbors, even the Polish woman on the fifth floor, Mrs. Rosinski, gathered to appraise the electric heater, the beautiful wiring and the felt along the windowsill. Bone-tired from the hectic, worrying day, Jack, Lil and Willy "made night" early, sleeping in the folding beds in the dining room. Everyone except Bubby. For the second night in a row, she kept vigil over me, sponging me, forcing me to swallow a few spoonfuls of liquid every few hours, but mostly moving my arms and legs and examining me for stiffness in my neck. "You'll be better," she assured me. "Besser, mine kind."

Unexpectedly, Dr. Koronovsky burst into the apartment before sunrise to speak to my father. "Jack, there's a new drug on the market called sulfanilamide. We don't have it down here, but one of my associates at Beth Israel can get me some. Your daughter's heartbeat is accelerated, either from scarlet fever or maybe it's the onset of a touch of rheumatic fever. I want your permission to try the drug. It may not help her, but I assure you there aren't side effects. A written consent is necessary. The signature must be yours."

My father paced up and down, smoking one cigarette after another. Nurtured by cups heated by a barber, homemade mustard plasters, and those powders of aspirin and codeine that Dr. Koronovsky dispensed by the boxful, he had a problem with this strange new drug, not even available on the market. Confronted with a decision, he hesitated. "Does it help polio?"

"No, as far as I know, it doesn't touch polio."

"Then what is it good for?"

"Infection. It wards off further infection. It prevents the outbreak of more bacteria. It allows the body to heal. Whether it will cure this one I don't know. But there's nothing to lose."

For once, my mother who regarded all such decisions as the province of men, spoke up, "I think we should try it. You should sign the paper. If it can't hurt her, what's to lose?" My mother hesitated. "Does it cost a lot? The medicine? Is it expensive?"

"Don't give it a thought," Dr. Koronovsky replied, stroking his goatee. "It will be taken care of without costing you a cent." My parents readily accepted this half-truth, not pursuing the question of whether Goodman or Koronovsky paid for the sulfa drug. My father gave permission, signing "Jack A. Roth" in his elegant cursive handwriting. Obviously relieved, Dr. Koronovsky announced that he would return at noon with science's latest miracle.

Bubby sponged me, took my temperature, fed me water, and at

6:00 A.M. donned her brown cardigan sweater and crept out of the house. She walked slowly to Little Italy and paused at the first open butcher shop, disregarding the pigs' heads in the window, pigs' feet on display at the counter and the salamis and sausage links that hung from the ceiling.

On the Lower East Side, everyone was a polyglot. Italians knew the Yiddish words *goniff, schmuck, putz, shiksa* and *momser*. Jews knew the words *puta, bambino, madre*. When my grandmother entered the butcher shop, she said, "Mia bambina e malo." She pointed to her face, neck and hands. "Fetz," she added. The butcher, eyes half-lidded and not quite awake, called, "Nonna!" and the Italian equivalent of my grandmother came out of the back room. The eyes of the two women locked in understanding.

The Italian grandmother showed my grandmother two types of pork fat, one a cube and the other, a loose gray mass, straight from the pig's stomach. She suggested a little of each. My grandmother nodded, said, "Thank you" in English, paid for the package and walked from Cherry Street to Orchard Street without a backward glance. She experienced not a moment's fear. White-haired women in baggy cardigans had no cause for anxiety on these streets. She stopped off to buy an Italian olive and sucked the pit all the way to our door.

My parents hadn't even stirred by the time my grandmother entered my bedroom and said, "The Polish lady, Mrs. Rosinski, from upstairs, she told me yesterday that fetz fun a choser is sayer goot."

"Bubby," I cried out in protest, "where did you get pig fat?"

"Cherry Street," she said and began rubbing me first with the stuff pressed into a square, then with the loose fat from the pig's belly. The loose fat smelled awful, a greasy mess on my hot skin. So my grandmother abandoned it and stayed with the square, rubbing it over my legs, my vagina, my stomach, chest, neck and face. Then she covered me up to my chin with a blanket and raced into the kitchen to prepare coffee for my parents and to get Willy off to school.

A few hours after my pig-fat massage, Dr. Koronovsky arrived with the new miracle drug. As soon as he walked into the bedroom, he sniffed the air. "What's that terrible odor?" He pulled back the blanket. "Ah," he said wearily, "that old idea about pig fat curing rashes.

Manya, I don't want to embarrass you, but that's a superstition, and you are the least superstitious woman on the Lower East Side."

My grandmother blushed. "I was worried. I wanted to do something, try anything."

"Try these." He shook the box with the sulfa pills. "Two at once, and one every four hours after that." The doctor sighed deeply. "Manya, bring in the tub and bathe her. Be sure to disconnect the electric heater while she's bathing. Wash her very carefully because the fat may contain bacteria." He glanced up at Bubby. "No damage done. We'll get her through this."

I survived the scarlet fever, but as a result I developed rheumatic fever, or as the doctor put it, "a touch of rheumatic fever." The phrase "a touch of" softened the blow for parents. My heart had a murmur, and there was minimal swelling in my joints. "Bed rest," Dr. Koronovsky replied. "She can't go to school for a month or six weeks."

"Does she have a heart like Lil?" my father asked, worried.

"She'll outgrow it. Lots of children do. When she returns to school, in bed immediately after. No lifting, no straining."

The advice to rest, rest and more rest defined my childhood, or more accurately, brought me to a new level of mental activity. Uncle Goodman bounded into our house one day, huffing and puffing, under his arm a carton of books that his children had outgrown: *The Bobbsey Twins, Nancy Drew, The Hardy Boys*. After I finished reading my second Bobbsey Twins book, I told Bubby, "I can do that." I was seven and about to start my first novel. But in order to begin I needed paper and pencil.

Bubby immediately ironed out the wrinkles from some old paper bags, cut off the tops and folded the bags to resemble little creased booklets. She sharpened the stump of a pencil with her kitchen knife.

The most curious thing about the Bobbsey Twins' Thanksgiving holiday was the strange food. What were mince and pumpkin pie? I asked my mother. Lil pursed her mouth and answered, "I don't know, ask Daddy." My father replied, "Some goyisha dreck. Once I took one bite of pumpkin pie, in some diner near Wall Street. Feh! Orange glue with no taste."

"And mincemeat?" I asked. "And giblet gravy?" I pronounced the *g* as in "give."

"Why are you breaking your head over these things?" he asked, which meant he didn't know the answers. "Just write what Bubby cooks in her kitchen. How could you go wrong with a Thanksgiving dinner like that?"

I covered five or six of my little booklets writing about the best Thanksgiving in the world with Bubby's specialties. Unlike the Bobbsey Twins, we had no car, but I could describe the Goodman house and our visit to The Gypsy Cellar.

Dr. Koronovsky dropped in daily. After my rash subsided, I went back to sleeping at night in the folding bed rolled into the living room, but during the day I stayed in my parents' bed, on which lay an inordinate output of stories on folded, brown paper bags. One day, viewing my bed as he listened to my heart with the stethoscope in his ears, Dr. Koronovsky inquired, "What are these brown papers? Why is the bed covered with them?"

"They're my stories," I answered.

He picked up one of my booklets at random and read my cramped writing, with as many words as possible covering the wrinkled brown paper. "Very nice," he said, smiling. An hour later he returned with a gift for me—a fat notebook from Harber's and a pencil box, complete with four number-two pencils, a gum rubber eraser and a pencil sharpener. On the front page of the notebook, he wrote in his scrawl, "To a good writer from her admirer, Mordecai Koronovsky." I was stunned by this gift from our idol, our doctor.

My mother had a child's reverence for presents and the pencil box overwhelmed her. Then I saw a frown cloud her pretty face and she tossed her blonde hair nervously.

"Doctor, I'd like to ask you something." She formulated her words slowly. "What do you think about her reading so much? Do you think it's bad for her?"

"Do you mean that she may need glasses because of the poor light?"

Lil fidgeted. Her green eyes were darkened by the gravity of her question. "I mean, what man will want to marry a girl who reads too much?" She hurried the words, stricken by her deep-seated perplexity.

In all the years that he had taken care of Jack's weak chest and Lil's weak heart before Willy and I had been born, Dr. Koronovsky confided his personal woes only to Manya. So it came as a surprise to us that on this expansive day of gift giving, he answered, "My fiancée is the medical librarian at New York University. She reads all the time. She's charming."

Characteristically, my mother blurted out, "But will you marry her?"

Quickly my grandmother led the doctor into the kitchen, exclaiming loudly as they went, "I baked two apple coffee cakes. One is for you and your sisters." Once he was safely away from Lil, she asked softly, "Is it time for a mazeltov?"

"Soon, Manya," the doctor answered. "I think soon."

We talked about this subject for days. Was Dr. Koronovsky finally getting married, and how would his sisters adjust to his wife?

My father, who loved all women in the abstract, immediately wrote off the potential bride. "Did you ever see a classy librarian? They have no style, wear flat-heeled shoes, no makeup, and glasses."

"What are you talking about? Those librarians from years ago? Then isn't now," Bubby protested.

"Then and now is the same," Jack retorted. "Have you met a librarian with an M.R.S. in front of her name?" He glanced at my mother, sipping tea at the dining room table with her legs crossed, her high-heeled shoes enhancing her ankles. "A stunner like Lil he's not getting."

The conversation was cut short by that rarity, a delivery boy with a box from Macy's. A card signed "From Flo and Henry" in Aunt Bertha's handwriting lay atop the play clothes for me in the box. There was a light blue coverall appliquéd with white sheep in pink bow ties and a two-piece shorts-and-blouse set, white blouse and red shorts. My father, mother, Bubby and, finally, Willy fingered these unusual clothes. I weighed less than fifty pounds, and I had a leak in my heart, a skin slowly clearing of red spots and unabashed tears in my eyes.

In addition to the box of clothes there was another wrapped parcel containing a battery-operated game intended for Willy, called "Geography." On one side were iron studs and questions beneath them. You pressed an electrical wire to the prongs on the other side to find the answer. Easy questions such as "How many states are there in the union?" required no battery-driven wires for answers. The dopey questions amused us the most: "How do you find the Rocky Mountains?" Answer: "Over small rocks that grew taller." "What is the capital of California?" All of us cried out, "Hollywood." Wrong answer: "Sacramento." Sacramento? Where was that? My father replied with New York arrogance, "On some ranch somewhere in California."

We loved the Geography game and played it by the hour—in fact, Willy and I were closer than we had ever been. He whistled for me every day, not just "Bye Bye Blackbird" or "Kiss Me Tonight in Dreamland," but a tune that my mother sang faultlessly, "I'm forever blowing bubbles, pretty bubbles in the air." It was a benign and wonderful period for everyone in the family, except that our restaurant business was experiencing a steady decline.

The Grand Canal Cafeteria could not be blamed, just our location. Increasingly busy shoppers from uptown wouldn't enter our hallway. If they asked for the bathroom, they would be too horrified to use it, no matter how spotless. Customers had to wash their hands at the kitchen sink and hot water came from the kettle on the stove. No one faulted the cooking or the service, but to an uptown clientele the private restaurant in a tenement proved neither appealing nor, to many who were directed to us, acceptable.

One Sunday, we had exactly two women customers for lunch. Both were slumming for downtown bargains; both adored the food and recoiled at the surroundings. Bubby sighed more than usual that day and, for once restless, Willy donned his slick long jacket and went across the street to stand in front of the Mathias Hat Shop, one of his most beloved stores. He liked to peer into the window, staring at the hats. I was sitting in the living room window, watching him, when I saw Shirley Mathias, the owner's daughter, come out from the skinny space between the stores. She carried a board from one of the hat crates and without any warning, she whacked Willy over the head. He fell to the ground, howling. Red blood gushed from his ear.

Crowded Canal Street heard Willy's cry of pain. Every merchant on the street rushed out, and each one yelled, "Manya! Manya!" Bubby was headed for the street in an instant and she ran to Willy's side faster than I thought possible. But Mathias, the store owner, ran even faster, putting his fingers between his teeth to whistle as he ran toward the El in search of a taxi. Before I could think about joining them, my bloodied brother and Bubby were hustled into a taxi.

I assumed they were on their way to Dr. Koronovsky, but Mathias yelled up to me standing at the window, "Koronovsky is uptown. They went to the hospital for stitches." He darted back into his store. First I cried, then I waited. After an hour I drew a sweater over the frail nightgown I wore, one of my mother's, cut off at the bottom and not hemmed.

It had been more than a month since Goodman carried me into the house, more than a month since I had been outdoors. My legs were weak, and my head swam from the effort of descending two flights of stairs. Slowly I made my way into the street. Had a tour bus observed me, would the driver announce that I was the Little Match Girl or an abandoned child wandering in rags? Jacob, in the clothing store below, was waiting on a customer when he spied me. "Darling, the telephone is in the back. Just pick up the receiver and ask for the number." I did exactly that, calling my father at Farber's Ladies Coat and Suits. He answered on the fifth ring.

"There's been an accident," I shouted, unaccustomed to a phone. "Willy and Bubby are at the hospital. Willy needs stitches on his ear. Shirley Mathias hit him with a board."

"As soon as possible, I'll be home. We have lots of customers," he said urgently. He hung up.

Finished with the phone, I returned slowly to the apartment. No one offered to help me. It was Sunday, a big day for business on the Lower East Side.

I had to lie down from the exertion. My legs shook. Never had I been in the apartment by myself. No neighbor came to inquire about me.

I must have fallen asleep because it was dark when the silence of our apartment compelled me to leave the bed. Turning on the lights in every room, I could feel my heart pounding through my nightgown. Jittery, nervous, I listened for every sound. At last, the slam of a car door, a taxi. I stood on the landing yelling, "Bubby? Bubby?"

She carried in Willy, his head completely bandaged, his left ear thick with tape. He had been given something for pain and slept, claiming the place of honor in my parents' bed.

Like crows, the neighbor women gathered when they heard Bubby arrive. "Twenty-three stitches," she told them. "He could have lost his ear."

"So why does he go there? Why does he stand by Mathias? Why does he go by someone who don't want him?" Mrs. Feldman asked.

"Libbe," Bubby answered.

"Libbe?"

"Er hut lieb Shirley Mathias."

A bomb exploded in my head and heart. The instant the neighbors left I cried out, "How can Willy love that terrible girl who told everyone I had been left back when I wasn't? Who hit him with a board that had nails in it?"

"If we knew the answer to why we love someone," Bubby said, "we wouldn't need a philosophe."

We couldn't continue our conversation because two of my mother's brothers, who had heard about Willy when they were playing handball in Hester Park, came to give advice. George, at seventeen, was in training for the prize money in a Golden Glove competition, and danced around the bedroom, jabbing with his fists as if he were in the ring. He told the bandaged Willy, "I'll buy you some boxing gloves. I'll teach you to box. Like Georges Carpentier." He pronounced the name "Georg-es Carpenteer."

Abe, two years older, had wiser counsel. "We thought we would take up a collection at the social clubs where Lil used to sing, so we could give you the money for a telephone. You need a phone. To call doctors, to call Jack and Lil at work."

My grandmother cringed at the word *collection*. Arriving exhausted after Division Street closed down, my parents heard every detail about the assault, the long wait in the emergency room, the twenty-three stitches, Abe's offer of a collection for a telephone. The next day my father called the telephone company and requested Orchard 4-2333. He asked for and received the number in honor of the number of Willy's stitches. For him, it was a lucky omen. He bet 233 in combination. It won ten dollars.

8

The Wedding

IN THE ENTRYWAY to 12 Orchard Street were our rusty mailboxes, some without lids, none with a name. We had had our name written in my father's elegant scroll and pasted on the first box, but the rain, the snow, the winds and the heat curled the paper and inevitably it fell to the floor. After a while, the mailman stuffed the gas and light bills for everyone's apartment into our box, along with an occasional letter from the old country—we ourselves received mail from Odessa relatives every nine months. My job was to bring up the mail and deliver the bills or letters to each tenant in the building.

I loved the top floor, the fifth, because the skylight let in beams of light, murky or sunny as the case might be. The first time the Polish woman on the top floor, Mrs. Rosinski, invited me into her apartment I was filled with wonder and fear. As soon as I stepped into the kitchen I beheld pictures tacked to every inch of clear space: of the Virgin Mary, of Jesus on the cross, Jesus with a halo of gold, Jesus weeping, Jesus in rags and sandals, holding a staff, Jesus extending an upturned hand,

Jesus in the clouds. Cut from magazines, faded, the edges of the paper ragged, they covered the walls and cupboard doors.

To show me how much she appreciated my mail delivery—a letter from Poland—Mrs. Rosinski took my hand in hers and drew me into her tiny front room, with a sewing machine where she stitched men's work trousers paid for by the piece. The most festive item of furniture was a small table on which she kept a crèche, a ceramic nativity scene, the year-round. A candle in a battered tin cup burned in front of it. Two or three rosaries hung from a nail hammered into the wall. I could have cried at her poverty. A stack of men's trousers lay on a neatly cut slab of cardboard. In front of the altar I recognized a piece of carpet that had once been in my parents' bedroom; Bubby had given it to her.

She said one of the few words she knew in English, "Nice?"

"Very nice. Beautiful."

I longed to escape, to be downstairs, surrounded by food and people and our Persian rug and the embroidered shawl, and away from the eyes of Jesus whom we had been taught to fear. Simultaneously, I wanted to fill her empty counters with the riches from our kitchen.

She must have sensed my thoughts because she smiled at me tenderly, "Manya nice, you nice." She bent to hug me.

Bubby smelled of food; my mother of Coty's powder and Chanel No. 5. Mrs. Rosinski smelled of poverty, a slightly sour breath, the perspiration under her tired arms, the iron odor of the men's work trousers.

"I hope your letter is nice," I said. Like many who spoke English poorly, her understanding exceeded her ability to express herself. She walked me to the door and waited until I descended the steps. "I'm okay," I called up to her. After that experience, every week I made sure that Mrs. Rosinski was fed.

One afternoon Mrs. Feldman leaned against the kitchen wall as I ladled some bean, barley and flanken soup into a jar. "To that Polish woman you're giving soup? They kill Jews."

"In every country someone kills Jews," I retorted, "but Mrs. Rosinski is not one of them."

"Don't begin with her," said Bubby, laughing. "Don't begin with my grandchild. She's a brenfire."

The telephone in our dining room had the status of a rare art object but its glory faded in the glamour of what I discovered in our dilapidated mailbox: a large square envelope, its flap edged in gold, addressed to "Manya Roth and Granddaughter." I took the steps two at a time and yelled, "Bubby, it's a special letter for both of us."

We opened it carefully, making sure that the gold trim did not tear. The invitation read:

MR. AND MRS. WALTER HESS
REQUEST THE PLEASURE OF YOUR COMPANY
AT THE WEDDING OF THEIR DAUGHTER
PHYLLIS ANNE
TO MORDECAI ABRAHAM KORONOVSKY, M.D.
CEREMONY EXACTLY 2 P.M., MAY 3, AT 682 GRAND STREET
INTIMATES ONLY
THE COUPLE WILL LEAVE IMMEDIATELY
FOR PARIS, FRANCE, ON THE ILE DE FRANCE

On the bottom Dr. Koronovsky had scrawled, "Manya, you will be our honored guest. Thank you for encouraging me to do this. Please bring my favorite patient, your granddaughter."

I began to screech, "Bubby, can we go, can we go, can we go?"

"Ich ken dus nischt glaben," she replied.

"Why can't you believe it?"

"Because of his sisters, because his bride is an uptown girl, because he's having the wedding in his house, because, because . . . *alles,* everything!"

"What about Mother and Daddy, what about Willy?"

"They aren't invited. It's for family and a few friends."

"Aren't Mother and Daddy friends?"

"Yes, but in a different way. I knew Koronovsky when he studied to be a doctor, when he would laugh at me for using bonkas, those red-hot cups on your father's chest for his weak lungs. Who taught me to be a good nurse if not Koronovsky? Who kept my secret about me and Mister Elkin?"

Bubby sighed, "I'm happy for him. It's coming to him, this happiness." She fanned her face with her apron. "The world doesn't stand still. It goes too fast."

"What do you mean, Bubby?"

"Mathias the hat man is moving to Battery Park, Koronovsky is getting married, Goodman is making wallets. Then there's my restaurant . . ." Her eyes met mine. "Do they think I don't understand? Everything has to end. I want a few more years. Just a few. I'm not giving up yet. It's too soon."

"We'll have business. We will. And Bubby, can we go to the wedding? Can we go?"

We heard the sound of shortness of breath from climbing the stairs that characterized my mother's entrance. "Whose wedding?" she asked.

"Dr. Koronovsky to Phyllis Anne Hess. Here's the invitation. It's for Bubby and me. Just the two of us."

Bubby waited while my mother scrutinized the invitation. "What does this mean, 'intimates only'?"

"That means family and a few friends," I offered. "They're going to Paris for their honeymoon."

My grandmother may have been on the verge of relating the news with more diplomacy when my mother lashed out, "That's enough from you, blackness."

Blackness! Did the word come from the expression "Ah schwarz yur"? From the color of my hair? From the fact that I had pneumonia almost at birth and was expected to sink into black oblivion? Involuntarily I shuddered. Bubby signaled me to remain silent.

But Lil was no longer concentrating on me. She called Ada Levine, who had a telephone installed a few weeks after ours. Especially when agitated, Lil tended to shout on the phone. "Dr. Koronovsky is getting married! And listen to this. Jack and I were not invited. Only Manya and her granddaughter."

Dr. Koronovsky's wedding became the talk of the entire Jewish ghetto and of Little Italy as well—more than once he had stitched up the wounds of Italian teenagers slashed on the streets. Remarks of wonder at the doctor's sudden acceptance of matrimony were tinged with envy directed at me. No one questioned my grandmother's right to attend, but why I should be singled out remained a mystery.

I stayed out of Lil's way, since the discussion centered on Bubby's outfit for the wedding. In bed at night I spoke to her in whispers, not once daring to ask what I would wear. At every store that sold food to Bubby and with customers at our restaurant, the same question was asked, "Nu Manya, you bought already a goldenah dress? You know how to dress swell?"

"Ah zayvah gut in Odess, like God in Odessa."

Lil spoke to Aunt Bertha about Lane Bryant's for Manya's dress.

"Lane Bryant?" Aunt Bertha cried with distaste. "That's for old women. Manya has to look like a fashion plate."

Uncle Goodman suggested that they try the fancy department store that he called Bergdorf *and* Goodman. Like so many whose names were similar to those in high places, Uncle Goodman convinced himself that he was related to the department store owners, though he hadn't troubled to find out.

Lil and Aunt Bertha began on Thirty-fourth Street, and made their way to Fifth Avenue, searching for the dress for Bubby—nothing on Clinton, Delancey or Fourteenth Street would do for this event. They ventured into Bergdorf Goodman without success. Day after day my mother returned, exhausted but enthralled, to describe dresses of satin, taffeta, lamé, organdy. Bubby cooked and baked, not once venturing uptown. She listened to my mother, nodded, assured her that she believed they would find the perfect dress, and kept herself apart, uninvolved. The search went on for one week, then two. Lil forgot her hurt at not attending the wedding and was consumed with a desire to show

Dr. Koronovsky how "stunning"—my mother's favorite word for clothing—Manya from Orchard Street could appear.

One day she and Aunt Bertha glided through our front door as if waltzing on air. The large box had the name of a specialty shop on Fifty-ninth Street stamped on it.

Aunt Bertha handled the problem of trying on the dress. "Manya dear, I'm sorry you don't have a shower, but a little spritz with warm water would be nice. In case the dress doesn't fit, you know what I mean. And also, your good corset, your fancy bra."

While Lil took Bubby into the bedroom with hot water, soap, undergarments and towels, Aunt Bertha called Jack at Farber's.

"I think this is it. Can you get away from the store for ten minutes?" Known as "a Jewish ten minutes," this could extend for an hour and still be designated as ten minutes. Jack had the final say about the wedding dress, not as the nominal head of the family but as an artist.

My mother and grandmother seemed to be taking forever to come out of the bedroom. I wanted Bubby to resemble Cinderella—a touch of a magic wand and she would emerge transformed, a princess.

Aunt Bertha called out, "Jack is here," and my mother answered, "We're ready."

Out stepped Bubby. The dress fell from the shoulders to her ankles. The underslip of pale blue taffeta and the dress itself, gray lace, had hemlines of scalloped edges. The blue of the slip enlivened the gray lace while the long sleeves had the same scallops as the hem. Bubby's hair was done up in a braided tiara. She wore the gifts from Mister Elkin: seed pearls and tiny diamond earrings.

Aunt Bertha burst into applause, but my father fought back his tears. "May Robson has nothing on you. You'll be more beautiful than the bride." He ran to kiss her on the cheek and then on the lips.

"Isn't it stunning?" my mother asked.

"Stunning. Bertha, Lil, I couldn't have done better myself. That dress is pure class."

No one asked about the cost. Uncle Goodman's treat.

One detail bothered my father—his mother's black pumps. "Black pumps are good for the theater, for a visit to Yonkers," he declared with frustration. "This is an evening dress and it needs an evening shoe. Gray satin, or light blue satin. Maybe with a small buckle."

Lil thought the task of the new shoes would fall to her but Jack announced, "I'll take care of the shoes." He intended to consult Rocco.

Rocco owned Little Italy. His business included a shoeshine stand with three chairs, enclosed on two sides and covered with an awning; a spaghetti and meatball café presided over by his mother, whose features were identical to Rocco's: straight nose, black hair low on the forehead and sprinkles of tiny moles on the chin. Rocco often insisted that I have a free shine, but the iron molds for the feet were wide apart, which meant holding down my skirt so the shoeshine man couldn't stare at my underwear. Though I declined Rocco's shoeshine, I did accept his mother's meatballs, placed over spaghetti thick with chunky tomato sauce. Rocco called me "the kid," and he would always urge me to accept a shine, or meatballs, or lemon Italian ices prepared by his uncle Nico across the street.

Since I had been raised in the restaurant business and recognized that chefs lived on compliments, I praised Mrs. Rocco's meatballs lavishly, though the heavily garlicked tomato sauce with its unfamiliar spices was hard to swallow. I declined the butter but delighted in the dense ciabatta country bread served with my meatballs. And from that day to this I never tasted better Italian lemon ices, creamy and cool, the perfect antidote to the spaghetti sauce.

The neighbors on Orchard Street marveled that I took a chance on Italian food. The Orthodox condemned me—surely pork must have been hidden in those meatballs. But compared to the soggy tuna fish sandwiches on doughy white bread served at The Grand Canal, Mrs. Rocco's home cooking had genuine appeal.

My father brooded about his mother's lack of appropriate shoes for the wedding until Friday, when he took me with him to Rocco's. Almost the entire block of Elizabeth Street consisted of bridal stores, all of them equipped with sewing machines to produce wedding gowns and dresses for bridesmaids, for flower girls, for confirmations. In Rocco's shoe shop, a gnarled Uncle Salvatore, who spoke no English and whose fingers were rainbow-hued from dyes, devoted himself to coloring shoes.

Holding Bubby's pumps in his hands—she had broad, short feet—Rocco showed them to Uncle Sal, who after much searching and grumbling, came up with a pair of evening shoes in my grandmother's size. They were white satin with curved heels, flat at the bottom, bulging in the center, tapered at the top—European. Then Uncle Sal painted various shades of blue and gray dye on a sheet of white paper until Jack decided on the color combination he desired: a watery blue pastel. He sighed with relief. So great was his need for perfection that he would have remained in the shoe store until midnight if necessary to get the right shade, and here in less than an hour he had both the right size and the color.

"You want a buckle?"

Jack hesitated. He disliked fake jewelry and the prospect of a shoe buckle studded with gaudy glass caused him to scrunch up his face. But Rocco, like a man long accustomed to panning gold, swept away most of the pompous junk. Digging deep into a carton, he brought out an oval sterling silver buckle, small, unobtrusive, fit for Marie Antoinette in the movies. Jack smiled with delight.

"How about the kid?"

"What about the kid?"

"She got a dress for the wedding or not?"

Jack lit a cigarette and drew on it rapidly, too fast-witted to admit that he hadn't given it a thought. "You have something in mind?"

We walked two blocks, my father tugging at the sleeve of my sweater to pull me along. A sign on the window read Girls' Party Dresses Girls'. Jack hesitated. Through the window he could study yards of eye-blinding purple, cerise, lemon, green.

"It has to be conservative."

"What does it cost to look?"

Frilly party dresses lay on sewing machines, on the floor and in racks that lined two walls. Jack dismissed them with a glance. At the back of the room, where the colors dimmed and the flounces diminished, one dress caught his eye: fine white organdy with tiny red polka dots, a Peter Pan collar banded with the merest hint of red satin, a wide red satin sash, and a stiff, layered red petticoat.

I had to bite my lip to keep from crying. It was my dream dress. It wasn't even suggested that I try it on. My father held it up to my throat. "That's the one," he announced crisply. I didn't dare tell him how much I loved, adored and worshipped this dress. Jack scrutinized the hems and said disapprovingly, "Machine-stitched. They have to be hemmed by hand. One of the girls near Farber's does beautiful hem stitching."

"Hey, Jack," Rocco berated him, "you take me for a cheap chiseler? We got hem stitchers right here. It figures that Mister Jack would want hand stitching for his kid for a wedding. We go for coffee, it's all done."

The prospect of leaving the dress behind sent me into a panic. On the pretext of watching the young stitcher—twelve years old, a little gnome with bad teeth and skin that rarely saw daylight—I stayed behind. The petticoat seemed to be a circle within a circle, but the girl worked miracles, content to hunch over other people's party clothes, and finished before the two men returned.

"Hey, where's the step-ins?" The reason Rocco ruled the streets was that, like my father, he kept the inventory of every store in his head. As soon as he located the polka-dotted underpants, we left, Jack carrying the dress wrapped in tissue paper over his arm. No money passed between Rocco and my father. Rocco might treat to a few meatballs or a lemon ice—just common courtesy—but my grandmother's shoes and my dress were paid for either in hard cash or with an LY—last year's styles from Farber's store, which went to Rocco's wife or a lady friend. Rocco didn't mix Jack's betting with any other transaction.

Nor did Jack bargain or haggle over price. Rocco named the sum, Jack nodded. Both had come up from the streets, where it was unmanly—not to mention life-threatening—to screw around for pennies or go back on your handshake, your marker.

Proudly, I crossed over the Bowery without holding on to my father. He kept a cigarette in one hand and my outfit in the other. Motes of dust fell from the cracks of the rails of the Third Avenue El overheard. My father, who prided himself on reading women from ages six to seventy-six, realized that I was dizzy with happiness. As we walked home together he said nothing to intrude upon it.

❧

Bubby had Lil call Dr. Koronovsky to ask how many guests were expected for the wedding. She intended not only to bake the wedding challah—sweet and with golden raisins, consumed by the guests as soon as the mazeltov resounded to signify the legality of man and wife—but the "sweet table"—the desserts following the food. Lil expected to speak to one of the sisters, Etta or Yetta—their names, like their appearance, were almost identical—but Dr. Koronovsky answered. Somewhat thrown by speaking to him in person, she discovered that the entire wedding party would consist of no more than thirty.

"Manya needs to know because she's baking the wedding challah. Is that all right?"

"I wouldn't have it any other way."

"And the sweet table."

"Please tell Manya not to bother with sweets. We have to rush off to make the boat. Friends from the wedding party are coming to see us off, so there won't be time for eating."

Lil relayed the message to my grandmother word for word, but she pretended not to hear. "Wine they'll have to drink, so they could have a piece of strudel, or a nut cookie, or a tiny rugulach, I'll make them very small. Maybe fifty each, no one should be like my customer who was having ten women for coffee and ordered ten rugulach. When I asked her what she would do if someone wanted an extra one, she laughed and said, 'She can't ask for what's not here.' "

Jack tried to intercede. "Ma, at such a rushed wedding, no one will eat three of everything plus the challah. If you baked fifty pieces of strudel and thirty cookies it would be more than enough."

"Ich ken im nisht fah shaymen. I can't shame them."

No one could argue with her about the baking, which started on Wednesday so as to be ready for delivery on Saturday night. Clayton cracked open ten pounds of walnuts and pulverized them in the mortar and pestle brought from Odessa. A gallon of Manya's own apricot preserves and another of raspberry were opened. Clayton carried home several dozen eggs and then returned to the store for fifteen pounds of flour. Lil, the expert in tissue-thin strudel dough, worked her skillful fingers for two batches. For once she did not wear high heels while pulling the dough across the entire length of the dining room table. We rushed our lunch customers, but they didn't complain. A news item about what Manya planned to bake for Dr. Koronovsky's wedding appeared in the *Jewish Forward*. The announcement of his forthcoming marriage was printed in the *New York Times*.

Even with two helpers, Bubby stood on her feet for hours, her cooking oxfords stained with flour, jam and egg yolks. The miniature rugulach proved more arduous than she had anticipated: cutting tiny triangles of rolled-out yeast dough required patience and care. Willy, Clayton and I lived on "the cripples," the rugulach or cookies slightly twisted or not perfect in shape, and the strips of strudel that had been kept in the oven too long. The odor of baking swept over Canal and Orchard Street like a heady balm. From hour to hour for those three days neighbors popped in, hoping for a handout. For once Bubby was too busy to respond.

The wedding challah came last, baked Saturday morning. The tray took up the entire oven and Bubby worried over it, careful to check inside the oven every half hour. At the exact moment that the bread turned golden, neither too pale nor too dark, she took one side of the pan and Lil the other, both holding their breath during the bread's short journey from oven to kitchen table. Uncle Goodman brought us several fresh cartons lined with tissue paper for the sweets, and an especially large one for the challah.

Everyone in the building came to view the results of these labors: a mountain of strudel, a white lake of confectionery sugar for the crescent-shaped nut cookies, a hillock of rugulach with glistening apricot jam peeping through the centers. Distributing the last-minute cripples, Mrs. Feldman in a moment of rare generosity declared that Manya's baking was not only the best in the city, but "über der ganzer veld."

We waited until 1:30 before my grandmother and I set out for the public baths. Although I hated the experience, few women showed up on holy Saturday—the big rush came on Friday, before the Sabbath. If some of the sidewalk mavens mocked us as goyim as we trudged toward Eldridge Street, our towels in a big Macy's bag, we paid no attention.

Happily, the old crone who cut toenails wasn't there. We chose an isolated corner where my grandmother washed her long hair, which was dusted with flour and other residues of her baking marathon. Lil had brought home shampoo from Pandy's, which we carried in a jar. The green stuff felt wonderful, slippery and clean, not just in our hair but on our bodies.

In the steamy public room we sat on a waterlogged cracked bench and hand-dried our hair before walking home slowly. In a rare instance of resting, Bubby napped in my parents' bed in the late afternoon. I sat in the living room mesmerized by our dresses, the gray lace and the red polka dot, their hangers hooked on nails pounded into the bedroom door.

Before dark, I walked with Clayton to Grand Street where we hailed a cab—no one would stop for him alone. Abe Abramovitz with his twice-broken nose and greasy cap was our preferred driver. One of Bubby's many schnorrers, Abe gladly helped Clayton load his car with its delicate cargo. On his return, Clayton held up a nickel, what the Koronovsky sisters tipped him for bringing in a half dozen boxes.

We started dressing at eleven the next morning, Lil attending to Bubby's brassiere and corset, silk stockings and those incredible satin shoes. Pandy came over to do her hair, to back-comb the top and push it forward against her cheeks before arranging the long heavy braid with hairpins, so that it stood up like a crown. A small boy knocked on the door and handed over a white box with a single orchid, a present from Rocco.

After Bubby slipped the taffeta undergarment and then the lace dress over her head, Lil pinned on the flower with shaky fingers. "Ma, I've never seen you more beautiful. Definitely, you'll be more beautiful than the bride. Turn around just once . . ."

I was accustomed to thinking of my mother as our movie star. But on this day with her diamond earrings, her pearls, the ravishing dress, the festive shoes, the orchid, the Chanel No. 5 behind her ears and on her wrists, I couldn't imagine any grandmother more dazzling than mine, not in the movie magazines, not in the movies.

Soon I slipped into my polka-dotted underpants, my red slip and my polka-dotted dress with its wide satin bow. For the occasion I wore white socks with lacy cuffs and black patent leather shoes. My mother put a tiny dab of rouge on my cheeks. "Perfect," she said. "Who has better taste than Daddy? From hundreds of dresses he picked the perfect one for you."

Exactly at one-thirty my father left Farber's and drew up with Abe Abramovitz and his rattling taxi. We walked carefully downstairs, my grandmother holding her right hand in mine, clutching her evening purse from Mister Elkin's theater nights in the other. We were followed by a retinue of neighbors in the building, all of them, including Mrs. Rosinski, the Polish lady, and everyone applauded as we entered the car.

Jack handed Abe a dollar tip for the short drive to Grand Street. "Take care of my two girls." His voice broke with pride.

Once in Dr. Koronovsky's apartment we realized that we were the only ones from the neighborhood. The chuppa had been set up against one wall of the living room. A heavyset middle-aged woman in a flowered print dress rushed up and asked Bubby, "Are you the mother of the bride?" Bubby shook her head. The bride was nowhere in evidence, but Bubby could have won a prize as the most beautiful woman in the room. All of the men were of medium height, inclined to be paunchy, and wore blue suits and white shirts. White yarmulkes were affixed to their heads. A short white-haired man and the rabbi, from an uptown shul, covered their shoulders with silken tallisim.

Dr. Koronovsky could have pierced the gray sky with his smile. I knew the word *ecstatic* from books, but I never knew what it meant until we came face to face. "Manya, Manya, how splendid you are. And Elkaleh—what a beautiful dress. Both of you, utterly beautiful." The small, slender man with white hair proved to be the bride's father. "This is Walter Hess, my father-in-law," Dr. Koronovsky said with pride. "And this is the famous Manya."

Mr. Hess extended his pale white hand. "Manya, I have a confession. I couldn't wait and already ate a piece of strudel. The best I ever tasted. Do you give out your special recipe?"

Bubby blushed. I realized it wasn't only Orloff whom she excited, but a courtly gentleman like Mr. Hess. "Thank you," she said modestly. "Ah shayna dank."

"I love people who speak true Yiddish, deep Yiddish." Bubby's hand relaxed in mine.

A man with a huge stomach bounded up and declared, "Bernie Frankel. I understand you're a master chef. Eating is my hobby. Any executive chef is a friend of mine. Manya, if you give me your address I'll be in your restaurant next week."

How could my grandmother reply, "12 Orchard Street?" She smiled instead. "Any time," she said carefully.

Bubby had been right. The guests were either doctors or those who worked with the librarian bride, everyone happy but subdued, no one laughing loudly, all of them smiling but not joking, and I the sole child there. Dr. Koronovsky's sisters hovered in the background, wiping tears from their eyes with crisp white handkerchiefs that contrasted with their long, shapeless, tan dresses. The moment we came near them they burst into fresh tears.

"You heard? He took a practice uptown, but two days a week he'll see patients down here. If you get sick Muntik un Dunerstik, you have your old doctor. Otherwise it's a bus to West Eighteenth Street, God knows where. This apartment, it's now just for us. He pays double rent. For us, for them, by Fifth Avenue. On the two nights when he has patients, he sleeps by us. Ah klug tsu dem ganza veld."

We couldn't reply. Mr. Hess, followed by an equally small Mrs. Hess, walked into the bedroom to fetch the bride. Waiters in short white jackets, bow ties and black pants unfolded chairs. The rabbi from uptown said in a British accent, "Would you kindly take your seats. As you know, the bride and groom leave for the pier in an hour."

Bubby and I sat in the second row, on the aisle. Dr. Koronovsky stood under the chuppa, his bar mitzvah tallis over his shoulders. There was no music. We craned our heads to see the bride as she walked in with her father. Slim and brown-haired, she wore a pink suit with pink satin buttons, appropriate for the wedding and for her honeymoon trip to Paris on the *Ile de France*. Her pink satin shoes matched her pink cloche, which had a veil that covered her brow but not her eyes. Later, when my parents asked, I told them that the new Mrs. Koronovsky looked intelligent.

"How can a woman look intelligent?" my mother wanted to know.

"Her face wasn't pretty, only lively. Her eyes were intelligent."

The service, repeated twice, once in Hebrew and again in English, was our first wedding in which several non-Jews were among the guests. As soon as the rabbi announced, "You are now man and wife," Dr. Koronovsky stomped on the glass under his foot and some of us called out, "Mazeltov." The non-Jews applauded.

Immediately the chairs were whisked away and we gathered in the dining room. On the highly polished table were two crystal candlesticks and Bubby's wedding challah between them. At the right, piled high on china platters, were the dessert pastries. To the left, a waiter presided over a turkey. Before attending to the bird, he swiftly cut wafer-thin slices of the challah, then cut these in thirds. In my own lifetime of watching my grandmother wield a French knife, I had never beheld such swiftness and dexterity. The minuscule bites of challah were passed to everyone, together with flutes of champagne. I was given ginger ale in a champagne glass.

Bernie Frankel of the big tummy offered a toast, "To Mordy and Phyllis. As the Duke of Windsor said when he gave up his throne for the woman he loved, 'At long last.' Many years of joy to them and a huge mazeltov. But I have equal luck because after all of these years I finally persuaded Mordy to come into practice with me. So let's toast to a wedding and a new prosperous career."

Guests nibbled at the challah and sipped lots of champagne. The waiter sliced the turkey—I heard one of the sisters remark, "God knows if it's kosher"—and everyone lined up for slices of turkey to place on their challah. The champagne flowed freely and I took a sip from Bubby's glass.

Another toast was proposed by the woman in the print dress who had mistaken Bubby for the mother of the bride. "It's an honor to be here among this company," she said in a quavering voice. "Phyllis is the head of our medical library in the nominal sense and in the spiritual sense. So I am happy to tell you that she will be returning to work right after her honeymoon and we hope for many years to come." Her colleagues called out, "Hear, hear."

Dr. Frankel, happily tipsy, kissed every woman on the lips and that included me. He said Bubby was a ravishing creature and he kissed not only her mouth but her hands. "That's some challah, that's some nut cookie."

Then the wedding cake was brought out, covered with hardened white icing. The bride and groom stood beside it, Phyllis holding the knife, and a flashbulb went off once, twice, six times. The same waiter, who could have cut strips from tissue paper, he was so deft, cut the wedding cake. It set my teeth on edge with its sweetness but it had no flavor, not even as much as a slice of Drake's cake. But no one had time to finish the tasteless wedding cake before Bernie Frankel, the sergeant-at-arms, called out, "The cars are downstairs. They're waiting."

"Tell them we need ten minutes."

Dr. Koronovsky came from behind the table to introduce his bride: "This is Manya and her granddaughter." Phyllis smiled at me. Her pointed face and large intelligent eyes were luminous. "I have heard so much about both of you," she said. She took both of Bubby's hands into hers. "We hope you and your family will come to visit us in our new apartment." The photographer snapped a picture of Bubby and me with Phyllis.

The speedy waiter whom I nicknamed Kid Lightning brought Phyllis a package wrapped in several layers of pink tissue paper and tied with pink, white and yellow ribbons. "It's your strudel, Manya," she said to us. "We're taking some of it to the *Ile de France*. We'll eat it on the way to Paris."

Her father, who stood behind her, held up a small white box tied with white cord. "Manya, I couldn't resist the strudel. There's a whole carton in the kitchen. I hope you don't mind. We helped ourselves."

Guests started to rush out of the front door to find seats in the cars and taxis that would take them to the pier. Half of the challah and most of the cookies and rugulach remained untouched. Dr. Koronovsky stepped back inside. "Manya, thank you for what you did for my wedding, and so much more," he said, giving her one last hug, and faded from view.

Instantly his sisters let out piercing wails. They stood at the kitchen door, crying and keening. Bubby went to comfort them. My heart fluttered at the sight of the untouched rugulach with their glistening apricot eyes, the cookies, the half-moons of white, brighter than the bride's suit. "I'm going to the bathroom," I called out.

Ordinarily, I would have washed my hands with Dr. Koronovsky's fancy soap, wiped them on his embroidered towels and remarked to myself on the depth and splendor of his bathtub. Except that now I headed straight for the bedroom. Luck was on my side. There was an empty shoe box on the bed, along with wads of tissue paper and ribbons of every color. I tiptoed into the dining room and filled the entire box with rugulach. They couldn't all fit into the box but there were enough to appear that Bubby's heroic efforts were not in vain. I wrapped the box in tissue paper and tied it with ribbons.

The cookies were trickier; they crumbled. Leaning over the table so that the white superfine sugar wouldn't get on my polka-dot dress, I gobbled up as many nut cookies as I could. It hardly made a dent in the platter. No doubt a paper bag could be found in the kitchen, but I couldn't risk having Bubby see me. I returned to the bedroom, put several layers of tissue paper together and filled them with cookies. A decorative, shiny, elongated bag abandoned on the bedroom floor rescued me. Miraculously it had a handle of twisted cord. I slipped the box of rugulach and the cookies inside and covered the opening with ribbons. My heart—the one with the leak after rheumatic fever—might have sprouted another leak because I moved so quickly, fearful of being caught, but in minutes the danger passed.

I entered the living room with racing pulse. The two sisters and my grandmother, deep in conversation, didn't notice the bag hanging from my wrist. Etta said to Bubby, "You want your schwartze to have that wedding cake? He should come and take it. To me it was poison."

"It's Sunday, he went somewhere. He'll come tomorrow, first thing."

"Then we're throwing it out. And the turkey. A goyishe turkey in a Jewish home."

Bubby paused, formulating her words, "Der leben gayt nisht glach."

Life doesn't go in a straight line. The thought sent the sister into fresh paroxysms of tears. As we walked out, Bubby glanced briefly into the dining room.

We left the building and emerged on Grand Street. Passersby yelled, "You went to the wedding? A good wedding?" Or, "Manya, you're a regular swell. So how come you're walking, not by a taxi?"

My grandmother remained self-absorbed. We walked hand in hand, not talking. Her beautiful satin shoes were not intended for the long walk home, but it's doubtful that she minded the discomfort. At the corner of Grand and Orchard, Abe Abramovitz spied us in his taxi. "Hey, ladies, hop in. I'll take you right to your door."

"It's only a few more blocks," Bubby started to protest. I pulled her inside the cab.

"So how was it? Fancy by the kikes?"

"Everyone said Bubby was the most beautiful woman there and also the bride took the strudel with her on the boat, to Paris. Wrapped in pink paper for the ship. Bubby's strudel."

In front of our building, my grandmother reached into her purse but Abe stopped her. "Hey, mark this one on ice." As he came around to help Bubby out of the cab I dashed upstairs and hid the bag in my mother's closet. The neighbors came pouring in. "Nu, nu, how was the affair?"

"They took Bubby's strudel with them on their honeymoon, all the way to Paris."

That story made the rounds, not merely that day but for years to come.

9

The Young Doctor

AT NINE O'CLOCK on a Saturday morning two weeks after Dr. Koronovsky's wedding, while he was still on his honeymoon in Paris, our phone rang. Jack had begun to wash his hair over the kitchen sink. Bubby poured warm water from a tea kettle over his hair while he lathered it quickly with Palmolive soap and rinsed it equally fast. Then she wrapped a clean towel over his head.

I loved my father's hair, its natural wave, its black color tinged with dark auburn. In the manner of the day, he parted it on the left side, wet his fingertips with water and dipped them for an instant into a Vaseline jar. When he slicked back his hair the watery Vaseline kept it in place. His hair was sleek, always with a perfect trim, cut slightly long in the back to avoid the appearance of a fresh haircut. During our bitter winters, Bubby contrived a tent from an old sheet to guard her son carefully as he washed his hair. Heaven forbid, there should be a breeze that could bring on a cold that would threaten his lungs.

My mother answered the phone. She had became more articulate since she started to sell coats at Palace Fashions, and she expressed herself with greater ease. But she still grew flustered if a question posed to her was out of her realm. After listening intently, she furrowed her brow and replied, "You'll have to speak to my husband."

With the towel over his head, Jack came to Lil's rescue. "Listen, whatever your racket is, we're not interested," he said.

We thought my father would hang up, but the speaker at the other end of the line managed to catch him off guard.

"You want us to have free examinations and Dr. Koronovsky gave you our number?" I could see he was listening impatiently, drying his hair with his free hand. "We're all fine, never better." He knocked wood on the telephone table. "No, we're not available right now. My wife and I are getting ready for work. Sunday? Listen, sonny, what did you say your name was? Scott Wolfson? Listen, Wolfson, whoever you are, you haven't been on the Lower East Side or you would know that the most business we do with the uptown trade is on Sunday. My day off is Friday. Sure, sure, we'll wait for you. But what is this Columbia Pres? Oh, Columbia University Hospital? I have a cousin who goes to Columbia, but I don't have time to talk."

My mother had no curiosity about the conversation, but Bubby did.

"What did he want? He's a friend of Koronovsky? Did you ask if he's already a doctor? Maybe Koronovsky wants him to take his place down here?"

"How could a man named Scott make it as a doctor with Jews? Scott. It's a last name, like Randolph Scott the cowboy actor."

My father flew to the door, dapper in a gray double-breasted suit, white shirt, blue tie with small gray squares. "Ma, spit on my two dollars for good luck."

Then it was Lil's turn to wash up and dress. Willy hid in the bedroom to avoid the perfume of Coty's powder and Chanel No. 5, which started him wheezing. We said in unison as she left, "Knock 'em dead."

Although my mother had set up two card tables with white cloths before she left for work, I hoped the lunch business would be slow, and I settled myself at the kitchen table with my notebook and pencil. I had gone through two or three notebooks since Dr. Koronovsky gave me my first one. They sold two kinds at Harber's—one with very rough paper whose sheets contained wood pulp, the other with a mottled black cover and smooth sheets. When I bought the cheap one out of guilt, Bubby insisted that I return it. "What's cheap always costs more in the end," she advised me. "For an extra few pennies you can write on good paper."

My contentment that day derived from a brand-new notebook and the smell of Bubby's brisket of beef; it remained our best seller. By then I had learned how Bubby prepared every one of her dishes, but unlike my mother, we were not required to set a table or clear dishes. Willy was exempt because of his awkwardness and I because Bubby wanted to indulge me.

Willy camped out in the bedroom playing Geography and I was writing rapidly when Mrs. Feldman barged in. The neighbors didn't knock. I glanced up briefly and sensed her anger.

Mrs. Feldman identified herself as Orthodox and thus unable to violate the prohibition against using the phone on Saturday. She treated me and Willy as if we were Shabbas goyim, able to carry out her demands while she kept her piety intact. But today, instead of saying what she really came for, she lashed out at me in a harsh voice. "Do you know why you got sick with scarlet fever, why now you have a bad heart? God is punishing you for writing on a Saturday. It's a sin. God may strike you dead."

Bubby dropped her cooking fork. "What are you saying to my grandchild? Your son keeps his fancy fruit store open on Saturday. Your Shirley takes lessons on Saturday."

"But writing is different. It's in the Torah—you can't write on Shabbas."

My grandmother opened the door and literally pushed Mrs. Feldman out.

Crying, I ran to Bubby. My pencil and notebook cascaded to the floor.

Bubby said soothingly, "You know Mrs. Feldman. She's a fahbissener. She's mad at Yussie, he hasn't been here for over a month, she screams at you. How many times has she seen you writing on Saturday? Now all of a sudden she's telling you these crazy things."

"But Bubby, she said it was a terrible sin."

Bubby carried me to the kitchen chair and held me in her lap. "Listen to me. God has plenty of things to do. He has business all over the world. Do you think it bothers him that a little girl holds a pencil on Saturday? If you were Catholic, living in Little Italy, a few blocks away, you could write from morning until night, it wouldn't be a sin."

"But we're not Catholic. We're Jewish. And a sin is a sin."

Just as Bubby didn't believe in shandas, I don't think she believed in sins. She and my mother always kissed the stale bread before throwing it out, an ancient ritual in which bread was considered holy. A woman who calls her son's occasional infidelity "a nosh" is hardly likely to insist that writing on Saturday is a sin.

Yet I could not be consoled. I knew about atonement from Yom Kippur and having my name inscribed in the Book of Life. Did writing stories on Saturday mean that my name would be withheld from the Book of Life, that some disaster would befall me?

Bubby rocked and kissed me, sang hoarsely about the golden calf that brought presents to children. Still I kept weeping, insisting that I would not hold a pencil in my hand on Saturday again. Finally Bubby suggested, "If you want to tell yourself it's a sin, I can't stop you. But I have very broad shoulders and I will take the sin on myself. You go into the bedroom and write, this Saturday, next Saturday, all the Saturdays of your life. It won't insult God."

The twists and turns in logic, especially that Bubby would accept a punishment in which she had little faith, eventually calmed me down, though my pencil remained untouched. Bubby went back to her brisket. I fell asleep in my parents' bed.

The phone rang. I leaped up to answer. It was my mother, who shrieked, "You'll never guess what happened! A customer of mine gave me two tickets for *Du Barry Was a Lady,* a musical with Ethel Merman, Daddy's favorite. Two orchestra tickets, my customer can't use them, she has to leave for a Philadelphia wedding. And guess what else? Mr. L. has his wife's short mink in the store, to put it in storage for the summer but he's letting me wear it tonight. I said to him, I said, 'Who wears a mink in May?' He answers, 'Women who own minks wear them over their dresses in July. A mink goes anywhere anytime.' It's a mink with a shawl collar. Just stunning. Tell Bubby we're going straight from work to the theater. Wait up for us."

My mother's happiness made me forget Mrs. Feldman, made the three of us as excited as if we expected to see the musical ourselves.

As soon as the sky darkened, we played cards, casino, at the kitchen table. I hated it when I drew an ace for fear that I would lose it when I built a five and an ace for a six of hearts that I held in my hand. Also I cheated, because Bubby couldn't see too well and couldn't tell the difference between a jack and a king. She'd ask me, "Is this an old one or a young one?" If I needed the king for myself I would say, "That's a young one."

Whether my brother perceived that I lied about the jack and the king, I didn't ask. He lapsed into himself, distracted in midgame, losing focus. Bubby threw her cards to enable him to win, if not the game, at least some points. Soon enough, he wandered off by himself into the living room to play the radio that he loved and to practice whistling the latest tunes. He fell asleep by pulling two chairs together and resting on them in the dining room.

Bubby busied herself by baking a yeast coffee cake while waiting for my parents to return from the musical. As a hardened insomniac I had no problem staying up until midnight. By 11:15 we started listening intently, in case the show had let out early. Maybe they made the subway train immediately or walked from Canal Street station in a hurry. A few minutes later we heard a car door slam, heard my mother singing, and as if by magic she turned on every light on every floor of the building.

She swept into the kitchen twirling in the short blonde mink coat, her blonde hair flying, a golden top, spinning around and around until she was out of breath. Then she and my father said in unison, "What a show, what costumes, what music!" My mother looked ten years younger than when she left that morning, perhaps as young as when she first came into Bubby's living room at age sixteen. We warmed ourselves in her glow.

Once she caught her breath, the two of them sang in harmony, "It's friendship, friendship, such a perfect blendship." When my mother hesitated at what came next, my father carried her along: "When other friendships have been forgot, ours will still be hot." They burst out laughing, then sank onto the kitchen chairs.

"How did you get home so fast?"

"Abe Abramovitz. He drove us right from Division Street to the theater."

"And he was waiting for us when we got out, right there in front, and the other taxis and swell cars behind him. Ma, what a thrill to have a taxi waiting."

The fact that Abe's cab was full of dents, its front end straightened out by a crowbar, meant nothing to Lil. The Cole Porter songs rang in her head and she announced with confidence that she had memorized most of the dance steps. During her nonstop account of the dazzling outfits in the audience, she didn't remove her fur coat. It transformed her into a shimmering presence until she suddenly slipped it on Bubby's shoulders. "Oh, Ma, with your white hair it's so becoming!"

Bubby removed it and wrapped me in it. "All the girls in the family need mink, even Elka," she said. We laughed and laughed at the sight of skinny me trailing golden mink on the linoleum kitchen floor.

Finally, we rolled out the beds and Bubby lifted Willy onto his narrow cot. He had slept through the festivities.

The following morning my mother remained asleep, but the three hardened insomniacs—Bubby, my father and I—remembered the workaday world. On Sunday, Bubby cooked blintzes and stuffed crepes, relying on the brisket of the day before if anyone asked for meat. No one did. The blintzes invariably sold out.

Happily Clayton showed up early on Sunday. He folded the bedclothes, rolled the beds into the alcove, sprinkled the rug with kosher salt and blew up dust with the frenzy of his sweeping. Willy retreated to the bedroom to avoid an asthma attack. Clayton wiped the dining room table with oil and set up the card tables while my mother dressed. After we sang out, "Knock 'em dead," my mother went off to work until dark, and my father returned the mink when Palace Fashions opened.

Clayton had started to smoke, and puffing on a Camel, he whispered to us that he had had sex all night, twice with women, once with a man. A man? Yes, a man. Willy and I were too shocked to speak and wondered how we would ask Bubby about it. "Don't get me wrong," Clayton explained. "I love titties and long legs, but a dick between my legs ain't bad at all." He began scrubbing the kitchen, neither explaining nor apologizing for his absence the day before. "Bubby," he cried, "blintzes! Will you save one for me?" "For you I made three extra." She studied him closely. "Too much schtupping and not enough eating."

"There's no such thing as too much schtupping," he answered and took the scrub brush and bucket to the toilet in the hall.

There wasn't a minute to ask Bubby about Clayton's daring revelation about sex with a man. Business was unusually brisk: we sold all the blintzes, the gefilte fish from Friday, the brisket from the day before. Lots of dollar bills lay under the Odessa candlestick—Bubby didn't have a moment to place the money in a knot in her stocking.

On this golden Sunday when there wasn't enough room under the candlestick for all the dollar bills, Bubby remained in an extravagant mood. She prepared fresh blintzes for my parents when they came home from work and what she called "a false beet borscht," without meat, just grated beets, sour salt, sugar, a beaten egg and at the last minute sour cream. For dessert, she bought fresh strawberries. She had just started on the dough for sponge cake to serve with the berries when we heard Yussie Feld.

For once he had come without his wife and daughter. "We're having a few friends over, maybe a little rummy, maybe dessert," he announced.

"Yussie, why didn't you phone? We sold out today. Not enough to feed a mouse. You can see I'm making a dairy borscht for Jack and Lil."

Yussie's eyes swept the kitchen table. "Not even one rugulach?"

"Yussie, for you I always have something even if I have to bake late. But not today. We were up half the night. Lil and Jack, they went to see Ethel Merman."

Bubby was not speaking to Mrs. Feldman because of the incident about my writing on Saturday but the news about the play and the mink coat had swept through every apartment. No doubt Yussie would hear about it again from his mother. His regret at not reaping his usual harvest of baked goods showed on his pinched face. His thin lips resembled his mother's and his eyes were cold marbles.

To overcome his disappointment, Yussie withdrew a printed sheet from his wallet. "Miss Sussman, Shirley's elocution teacher, she's putting on a performance. It's a talent contest. We're sure that Shirley will be in it. Come if you can." Bubby read the flyer carefully and repeated, "Yussie, next time you have guests, call me and Willy will write it in the order book." She folded the leaflet into small squares before slipping it into her apron pocket. Then Yussie visited briefly with his mother and drove away. My parents barely did justice to their evening meal and went to bed exhausted from the day's labor and the lack of sleep the night before. It had been quite a weekend.

At seven the next morning, there was a loud knock at the door. It was too early for beggars, for peddlers, for a building inspector who showed up intermittently with an official note from the fire department. What we needed was a rat inspector, but if such a person existed, he would have recommended sliding the entire neighborhood into the East River even as the rats attempted to swim ashore.

Bubby, already dressed and heating water for our quick morning wash before school, asked with a tremor in her voice, "Who is it?" She held her hand to her heart, fearing a cablegram from Odessa with bad news. In bounded a young man in his midtwenties, dressed entirely in white—white buck shoes, pants and a doctor's jacket. His eyes were bluer than May skies, his hair light brown and curly. The sight of him invoked all the things about summer that I had read about: the sun, summer breezes, lazy golden hours, sunflowers taller than sheaves of corn, buttery vanilla ice cream, everything creamy and smooth.

"I'm Scott Wolfson," he said, his smile showing faultless white teeth. He pointed to a badge with a picture of himself with his name under it, followed by the letters *M.D.,* pinned to his white jacket. He extended his right hand. In his left he carried a doctor's bag and a clipboard with a half dozen sheets of paper neatly typed.

"You must be the chef," he said to Bubby. "I spoke to your son the other morning, on Saturday, I told him about my project. Dr. Koronovsky supplied me with the names of everyone in the family and your medical histories. I couldn't wait to start. It's tremendously exciting for me. I came early to see the children before they left for school."

Something about Dr. Scott Wolfson's easy manner won over my grandmother. "Come in, come in," she said though he had already clasped her hand. "Yes, the children are up, but maybe you could tell me a little more, why Dr. Koronovsky spoke about us."

"It's a study about one particular family and the serious illnesses they cope with."

"Serious? Other families have worse."

"Yes, certainly. But four out of five of you are American-born, all are literate, can read and write, and all have some form of accomplishment."

I hadn't really bathed since Dr. Koronovsky's wedding, or washed my hair, or changed my flannel nightgown. To most in the neighborhood that would have been considered clean enough. But something about this white-clad doctor with the golden voice and open face urged me to at least brush my teeth. I wondered whether the laundry would be delivered before I left for school. I longed for a clean if unironed middy blouse.

The young doctor found my page in his clipboard. "Ah, the reader, the articulate one. How's the rheumatic fever? Any swelling in the joints lately?"

I shook my head.

"Good, good. But what do you do for it, for the condition?"

"After school I stay in bed and read. Sometimes I walk to the library first or go to the movies, and then I get into bed." I edged toward the kitchen, anxious to brush my teeth, run a comb through my hair.

"Just rest? Any regime of exercise? Do you walk a great deal, bicycle, swim, play tennis?"

The last question was incredible. The only thing we knew about tennis was what we saw in the movies. Real tennis was uptown. Anyone could have told that to Dr. Wolfson.

I shook my head again and asked, "May I brush my teeth?"

"May I? I'm very impressed."

"That one speaks some English," Lil offered. "It's from constant reading. She can read from morning to night. She keeps this up, she'll need glasses soon."

My mother had slipped on her fancy nightie, the present from Orloff with the ruffle in the front. Her purse with a comb must have been in the bedroom because her hair was neatly combed.

"You must be the singer. The one with the heart condition."

"My weak heart? It's nothing. Only when I walk up a few flights of steps or carry something heavy."

The young doctor asked, "Who's first, the reader or the singer?" Quickly I brushed my teeth and washed my hands and face, aware of my nightgown's sour smell. "May I change my clothes?" A semiclean *shtinik* hung from a nail on the bedroom door. For once my mother divined my embarrassment. "I'll be first," she said to Dr. Wolfson, and she handed me the slip.

The doctor placed his stethoscope into his ears and listened to my mother's heart, his face grave. "How long have you had this condition?"

"Since I was a child, after diphtheria. I was very sick. My mother had eight children. She brought me to the clinic. They told her I should eat an egg once a week. But I ate the soft-boiled egg on the fire escape and it fell out of my hands. So that was that until I married and came to this house. My mother-in-law, she takes the best care of me. Also Dr. Koronovsky. If my throat is sore he tells me it's bad for my heart. I'm his favorite patient," she added, blushing girlishly. The young doctor timed my mother's pulse. She enjoyed that, glad she had put Chanel No. 5 on her wrists on Saturday.

She did what she could to reassure him. "Doctor, don't be nervous. I was turned down for an insurance policy years ago. But I'll live out a full life. The insurance doctor said that, said he was sorry he had to say no to my application, but I could still live out a full life."

"Do you take any medication, see a cardiologist? A heart specialist?"

"Isn't that what you're here for?" Lil gazed steadily into his blue eyes.

"You're very beautiful," he said.

"And my heart?"

"It's . . . it's very brave. You have a brave heart." His hand trembled as he wrote on Lil's sheet of paper.

My mother pushed me forward. Scott Wolfson listened to my heart. "Not too bad, not too bad. Small murmur, but with the right care you'll outgrow it."

"The whistler," he said. "I must see the whistler next." Fully dressed, Willy hung his head as he usually did in front of strangers. The doctor extended his hand to Willy, who after a second's hesitation extended his.

"What's your name?"

"Willy," came the whisper.

Dr. Wolfson squatted on his knees to reach Willy at eye level. "Listen, son," he said, "everyone is shy with strangers. It's okay. Now I'd like to hear your full name."

"William Michael," his voice still softer than usual.

"He's named for his grandfather," my mother sang out.

The young doctor raised his hand. He still squatted, staying as close to Willy as possible. "Willy, I hear you're a great whistler, can whistle any song. I bet if I took you to a concert you could whistle classical music."

With his chin still scraping his chest, Willy said, "I can whistle Caruso. From an old record." The doctor stood up. "Great, fantastic. A handsome family and everyone with talent."

The laundry man opened the door and threw in two bundles wrapped in brown paper. One of linens: towels, sheets, tablecloths, napkins, the other our personal clothes. With experienced rapid movements, Bubby extracted a clean middy blouse. She smoothed it out with her hands. The hem of my skirt had unraveled. Pleated from men's coat material, it resembled a crippled umbrella. The doctor asked, "May I walk these children to school?"

He glanced up at Bubby. "I'd like to take your blood pressure before I leave." He placed five fingers across the left side of her neck, then quickly retrieved his blood pressure cuff from the black bag. He smiled into Bubby's eyes as he pumped the blood pressure bulb hard. "Say, chef," he laughed, "how many glasses of water do you drink a day?"

"Water? I hate water."

"And salt. How much salt in your diet?"

"Like everybody else."

He ran his hand over her beautiful soft cheek. "Eight in the morning and already a bloom in your cheeks. Any lower back pains?"

"From standing on my feet all day, from carrying food, of course."

He said casually, as if we had been acquainted our entire lives. "You're everything Dr. Koronovsky promised and more. So, tell me something, were those cats running from the building?"

"Doctor, you live in New York, you don't know what a rat looks like?"

On the short walk to school, he spoke mostly to Willy, asking him casually, "About your asthma, does it start when you inhale something that irritates you? I mean when you smell certain things does it start up?"

Willy didn't answer. The doctor bent down close to Willy's face. "What brings on asthma?" I started to speak but the doctor said reassuringly, "Willy can answer." At last: "Powder, perfume, dust."

"Very good. Excellent. Anything else? I mean when you're frightened." Willy hung his head, casting his glance at me.

"A gang chased us," I answered.

"We thought it was the Guineas," Willy whispered.

We had reached the corner. "Don't you have a safety guard at this street to keep the trucks away?"

Even Willy smiled at that. "I'll see you soon," Dr. Wolfson called out. "In a few days, we'll talk again."

At school, because of Dr. Wolfson I misspelled the word *receive*, though I had memorized the rule: "I before E except after C or when sounded like A as in neighbor or weigh." My teacher, Mrs. Nash, didn't let us cross out the words if we caught our mistakes. I wrote it carefully along the side of the misspelling, but she gave me a ninety-nine instead of one hundred.

I bemoaned my ninety-nine in spelling, my knowledge of Clayton's sex with a man, mostly my meeting Dr. Wolfson. That day, when I came home from school at three o'clock, I didn't find Bubby alone. A yeshiva boy came to be fed, a Yiddish writer waited to read his poetry, and Clayton showed up for a delivery that wasn't quite ready. Not until we were in bed with the lights out did I unload my grief.

"Bubby, when I grow up, do you think I could marry someone like Dr. Wolfson?"

"Of course. You and a doctor would be perfect."

"No, that's not it. I don't need a doctor. Just someone like Scott." I couldn't believe I called him by his first name. Bubby realized what this intimacy meant. She pulled me closer to her warm body. "So tell me slowly, not like a fire engine running through the streets, what do you like about him? The most important."

"He's very clean."

"That's his best? He's clean?"

"Everything about him is clean. Not his clothes, his hands, but inside. He doesn't know a rat from a cat. He talked to me about tennis. He laughs a lot. He wouldn't dare sell blue for black or black for blue." I paused, searching for the right words. "He's not like Daddy, not like Rocco. He's really worried about Willy. He wants to help him."

"Didn't Dr. Koronovsky want to help the whole family, the whole neighborhood?"

"Yes, but Dr. Koronovsky is from here; Dr. Wolfson is from someplace else, not our world. He trusts everyone."

"How did you see this in a few minutes? How did you fall in love so quickly?"

My heart flip-flopped. She knew. I didn't have to tell her.

She sat up on the lumpy mattress. "To love, it makes you years younger, makes you feel you can jump to the sky, play music on any instrument, lift up cars, trucks without feeling it. I haven't forgotten one thing about falling in love. But there's a sad part."

"You mean if he dies or runs away like Mister Elkin?"

"No, it's what you said before. Different worlds. For a little while Dr. Wolfson takes an interest in us. Then his clean heart takes him away to a clean place."

I sat up. "Bubby, I was very embarrassed today when I saw this clean man. So I want you to help me be clean. In the summer, for our vacation, Mother buys me fresh underwear so Aunt Bea or Uncle Geoff won't laugh at us. But I want you to buy me new underwear tomorrow and a new nightgown. I'll wash my things every night. I won't wear a nightgown for two weeks anymore. And I'll iron my own middies, not like Clayton on the ironing board, but the way I see them doing it at the Chinese laundry when I walk with Daddy to Pell Street. They iron on a big table. I watched them and I can do it. And you'll help me wash my hair. And those terrible skirts from that terrible material, you have to tell Mother I need a real skirt, for real money. You'll buy me those things, won't you? Bubby, I need them."

She didn't hesitate. "You'll have everything. Tomorrow. After school, we'll buy what you want. Lil and Jack, maybe they know more about clothes, but we'll look carefully. People from everywhere come to shop here, we'll shop, too.

"Thank you, Bubby."

"For me, it's not coming a thanks. My head was tsumished. We should have done this long ago."

"And one more thing, Bubby. Clayton said he slept with a man. Is that true? Could such a thing happen?"

"It happens. In the old country, in villages, men got lonely, they made love with sheep, with horses, with God knows what. Of course it is forbidden to Jews and also I came from a big city." She searched for the correct phrases. "In Odessa we heard of everything. And for the ninety-nine in spelling, it only shows what happens when you fall in love. You'll get a hundred hundreds. And tomorrow you'll start to be clean. You'll shine like a new one."

Bubby kept her word and I kept mine. I rinsed out my underpants in warm water every night. I ironed my own middies on the kitchen table, flat out, as in a Chinese laundry. We bought a plain but nice blue skirt and two blouses. My mother complained mildly about the expense, but she knew better than to cross Bubby once she made up her mind.

10

The Return of Mister Elkin

THE YOUNG CLEAN doctor wanted each of us examined by a specialist: sending my mother and me to a cardiologist; Willy to an allergist; my father to a chest doctor and Bubby—well maybe to a urologist. He promised the best care available in the city—all free, because he had what he called "a grant" that paid for the tests. In his new red Chevy he would drive us to the various doctors if we agreed.

Lil, who loved the idea of driving with the young doctor, asked, "How could it hurt? Free is free. We have nothing to lose." My father remained suspicious.

His work year would soon end. Division Street went dead from mid-June until Labor Day. Though he knew it was not the same as charity, my father hated standing in line to apply for unemployment insurance with what he referred to as "the dregs of society." He ridiculed the small amount of the checks—pocket change he called it. Mostly he despised the grilling they gave him each week about where he had searched for work, what stores he had tried for employment. Patiently he would explain that summer was the slow season, that he had a job waiting for him when the new season started in September.

Each week a new girl at the unemployment agency on Church Street read him the rules. He would grit his teeth not to tell her to take the unemployment insurance and shove it up her ass sideways. Lil didn't qualify because her weekend job didn't bring in enough money, and during these summer doldrums, my father worked at Farber's on weekends on commission, without a salary.

For him, Dr. Wolfson's offer of spending hours in doctors' offices held no appeal. "Tell Wolfson we'll decide when Koronovsky comes back from his honeymoon," he shot out angrily. Bubby agreed.

My mother begged to be allowed to relate this decision to Dr. Scott Wolfson the next time he came to Orchard Street. For the occasion, she went to Klein's and bought a blue summer dress with white polka dots, a V-neck and a circular skirt. Since my father believed that only hicks wore white shoes, she selected a tan T-strap sandal and swung her lovely legs over the seat of the chair as she talked to Scott Wolfson.

"If it was up to me I would see a heart doctor, of course, why not. What's to lose, an hour of my time and with such lovely company? But if Manya and Jack say wait for Dr. Koronovsky, that's it. Those two are Tammany Hall, you can't fight them."

The young doctor may have anticipated this response because he didn't argue. He replied, "Willy should see an allergist now. He's the one I selected until Dr. Koronovsky returns from Europe."

"It won't hurt," Willy stated. "Dr. Wolfson said it won't."

My mother regarded her son as if they had been introduced recently, as if he were a stranger to whom she had to be polite. "You want to go?"

"Yes. I'm not scared."

In this initial act of assertion, no one dared to deny Willy. Dr. Wolfson drove him to an allergist on lower Fifth Avenue and kept notes in his book about Willy.

After each visit, he bought Willy a Dixie cup or a Fudgsicle or a Mello-roll. He told Willy he could eat the amount he wanted. "Foods are like flowers," Scott Wolfson said. "Good to look at, to smell, but when the flowers are wilted, you throw them out."

Food as flowers! My mother decided to adapt that phrase as her own. Waiting on a customer whom she had to convince to buy a new coat or suit, she reported, "Your old garment is like a flower, when it's wilted you have to throw it away."

Still, Bubby could scarcely wait to speak to Dr. Koronovsky. By that time he had returned home from Paris, as his sisters weepingly lamented at the kosher butcher shop. Yet he didn't come to Grand Street or to his office on East Broadway. We heard he was busy with his new practice.

In fact, he had brought in a substitute, a roly-poly Dr. Solomon who appeared at his office, smiled a lot, and waited patiently for patients who didn't show up. For several weeks, whether ill, in danger of dying or morbidly paralyzed, they anticipated the return of their healer, Dr. Koronovsky. One Tuesday, at last, his familiar blue car drove up on East Broadway. A line formed outside his office within minutes.

Bubby didn't dare call him during his first day, but at about six in the evening, when the June sun cast an amber light on our streets, he phoned and said, "Manya, I'm taking an hour off. Are you busy?" Bubby removed her Hoover apron, washed and slipped into a clean cotton house dress, loose, with buttons down the front.

On the last day of school I had discarded my middies. My periwinkle blue skirt was in perfect condition—I hung it up on a hanger each night. Bubby had bought me two blouses, one white, the other pale pink. This evening I chose the pink. Two days ago, when Dr. Wolfson brought Willy home from his treatment, I had worn this outfit and the young doctor grinned broadly: "Don't you look spiffy." I blushed to the edges of my teeth.

As soon as Dr. Koronovsky bounded up the stairs he cried, "Don't you look spiffy," then rushed to hug Bubby. For reasons I couldn't fathom, they both wept. Not huge sobs, not waterfall tears, but unable to speak from emotion, choked up, eyes brimming.

Dr. Koronovsky sat close to Bubby on a kitchen chair, his face suntanned. He had shaved off his goatee.

"What have you done to yourself? You're ten years younger."

"I owe that to you, Manya. For years you told me, get married, your sisters will live, they'll manage, and I was afraid. But now it's come true. Every day with Phyllis is a blessing. I see her in the kitchen or in the living room reading and I can't believe in her sweetness, her softness, her gentle ways. And our love life is the same. In bed, sleeping, making love, it's a dream. Why did I wait so long? Why did I deny myself happiness? Only you, Manya, told me the truth, told me to have courage.

"Also my practice. Here I treated children from the minute they were born, often until they died. And young adults, middle-aged, old, every kind of disease. You remember Bernie Frankel from the wedding? He's a cardiologist. If their hearts are too fast or irregular I have a machine right in my office and in ten, twelve minutes I read the printout and send them to Dr. Frankel. For severe stomach problems they call on a gastroenterologist, that's a stomach man, or a urologist—" He broke off.

"Manya, Scott Wolfson is concerned about you and I feel very guilty. All those years I concentrated on Jack, Lil, the children, and I didn't take your blood pressure, never did a urine analysis, because I saw only your inner strength."

"You're listening to that pisher, he doesn't have a practice yet."

"Take my word for it, Manya, he's brilliant. Young and brilliant. He knows more than I do."

"So now the eggs are teaching the chickens?"

"I have practical knowledge, practical experience. He has theories, ideas. I started going to seminars. Every night I study like a schoolboy. Down here, you try to hide the truth. Uptown they expect to be educated. You explain to patients everything about their conditions."

I could see the pulse in Bubby's neck begin to pound. "Then you should tell me the truth about Willy. Why does Wolfson take such an interest in him? From everyone in the family, he picks Willy. The boy, maybe he's a little quiet, maybe he's not brilliant like his sister, but what does he think, I mean the young doctor?"

"Dr. Wolfson, he's in a new field, not only a child's specialist, a pediatrician, but a pediatric psychiatrist. It means how the mind can change what happens in the body."

"Vus zuch du? Willy is meshugah?"

"Dr. Wolfson thinks that Willy's allergies, his asthma, are related to . . . Well, let's put it this way. Willy is allergic to the Lower East Side, to the harshness, to what's expected of young boys down here. I remember your Jack when I was a medical student. Confident, flirting with girls, not afraid of anything. Too bad Jack didn't finish college, go to law school. He decided on the easy way out . . . Still, because of his close relationship to you he thought he could conquer the world."

Dr. Koronovsky sat quietly but inner turmoil deepened the creases on his face. "You give Willy all the love in the world. But he is aware that you're not his mother."

"He thinks I wouldn't put my arm in the fire for him?"

"You would, but it's different. You love him, you protect him. But he's not first with anyone."

"First, second. What is this, one of Jack's horse races?"

Dr. Koronovsky laughed to ease the tension. "Dr. Wolfson will tell you more. It's his specialty. Also he's a blessing to the whole family. If I had one gift to give you, it was Dr. Wolfson. Trust him." He coughed to hide his embarrassment and reached into his jacket pocket.

"Speaking of presents, Phyllis and I bought you a present. From Paris. Phyllis picked it out. We appreciated how hard you worked for the wedding. And also for our years together, for our long conversations. Anyway, here it is."

The gift lay in a maroon velvet box, stamped Cartier, Paris, France. Bubby opened the box. A flush appeared on her cheeks.

"It's a tortoiseshell comb for your hair, when you wear your braid on top. And, Manya, that's a real diamond in the middle of it."

Speechless, her hand shook as she placed the comb at the top of her white hair. "It's perfect for you," he said. "Manya, from my mouth into God's ears. May you have the love you deserve."

Everyone who inspected the comb with its quarter-carat diamond regarded it as a lucky omen: my parents, customers, the bosses, the neighbors.

So when I searched the mailbox and brought out a typed postcard signed "Mr. Elkin," the news was instantly telegraphed across the ghetto and received not as a thunderbolt, but a sign of what had been predicted by the fancy comb from Paris: a lucky omen.

The typed postcard read: "Dear Manya: After so many years, it's time for us to meet again. Unless you write me otherwise, I will be at your house at twelve o'clock for lunch, June 20. Sincerely, Mr. Elkin."

I read it to myself once and out loud to Bubby twice. She sat in the kitchen chair immobilized. As in the game "Simon Says" where if you forget to ask "May I" you have to hold the position you're in until your turn comes around again, she put both of her hands to her heart and sat utterly still.

"Bubby, Mister Elkin is coming to see you. Are you glad, Bubby, are you glad?"

It was Friday. My parents had slept late and then taken the subway to the Roxy. Willy was off with Dr. Wolfson having his allergies tested. Clayton was delivering the week's bakery orders. I shook her shoulder. "Bubby, are you all right? Why don't you say something? Do you want to see Mister Elkin?"

She didn't answer. Maybe she was waiting for her heart to slow down. Finally she said, "Ich vayst nisht."

"You don't know if you want to see him or not?"

"I don't know."

"But Bubby, you always talk about Mister Elkin . . ."

She let out a long sigh. "Talking is one thing, seeing is another."

I jiggled from foot to foot. "Don't you love him anymore?"

I was accustomed to yes or no answers. When my mother uttered "maybe," "perhaps," "I'm not sure," "I'll think about it," it translated into "no." My daily existence was organized by simple guidelines. For Bubby to tell me that she didn't know how she felt about Mister Elkin threw me into profound confusion. I desperately longed for her assertiveness. "Do you want me to call anyone? Shall I call Uncle Goodman?"

"What can he do for me, but sure, why not? Call him at the factory."

After the phone rang three times, I hung up, not wanting to waste a call if someone else should answer. Then I dialed zero for the operator and asked for the Yonkers number. Flo, Aunt Bertha's daughter, picked up on the first ring. "Is Aunt Bertha there? Tell her we had a postcard from Mister Elkin. It's important." Flo yelled, "Mother it's important, a call from Ahnt Manya."

I handed the phone to Bubby. "Mister Elkin cumt nexten Shabbas."

Aunt Bertha's cry of disbelief almost cracked the phone. "Goodman and I will be down in the morning, maybe ten o'clock. We'll talk about everything. Manya, how are you taking this?"

"I don't know."

My grandmother may have been uncertain, but my father's response left no room for doubt. "That lousy two-timing con man, that chiseler, that snake, that goniff, rats in sewers, a whole wall of roaches, bedbugs big as red grapes are better than that vermin, Mister Elkin. He took every cent of your savings, every penny of yours to go to South America to make a fortune, so he could marry you. Then he disappeared. It was a miracle that he didn't come back in the middle of the night and take back those pearls and earrings he gave you.

"Don't you remember how we tried to find out if he sailed for South America? How could you be so naive, so gullible, so foolish to not even ask him *where* in South America? Brazil? Argentina? Were you fainting with such love that you handed over your money to that swindler, that Ponzi, that schemer? For those kisses, you paid plenty. Every cent you had, not to mention that you actually wanted to marry him. A man with no character, no sense of right from wrong. Let him hang himself in front of Macy's window." My father took a dollar bill from under the candlestick, and put a match to it. "May he burn in hell like this dollar. He'll never step foot in this house. Not if I have anything to say about it."

Except that Jack had no control over this event and he knew it. All of us knew it. He could pace the floor, he could chain-smoke, rave and rant, refuse to eat, exhaust us with his rage, but he didn't have an ace to play.

My mother, whose reading limited itself to movie magazines and the entertainment section of the paper, fell back upon the movies. Fred Astaire dancing with Ginger Rogers, Ruby Keeler dancing off with Dick Powell, or those heroines who sacrificed themselves for love: Irene Dunne living in Back Street because her loved one couldn't get a divorce; Margaret Sullavan coughing out her lungs from tuberculosis.

But what movie had a story like this one, where the man disappears for fifteen years and suddenly returns? Lil believed in clichés: love conquers all; love is sweeping the country. As much as my mother was capable of loving, she loved Bubby and wanted the best for her. But my father guided her perceptions. Was Mister Elkin what Bubby needed? Lil had no answer.

Aunt Bertha showed up in the morning with Uncle Goodman at her side. She removed a small notebook from her purse and read from her list. "Of course you have to see Mister Elkin. For your own satisfaction. Either start again or put an end to it."

At these words, my father, dressing in the bedroom, slammed out of the apartment without acknowledging the Goodmans, and since he was unemployed, went to kill some hours at Rocco's, where he bet the last of his cash to ease his anguish over his mother.

"First," Aunt Bertha continued addressing Manya, "the restaurant will be closed that day. Goodman and I will see that the apartment is in the best shape possible. You'll wear the dress you bought for Dr. Koronovsky's wedding. It's a little dressy for the afternoon, but he said he would see you for lunch. Maybe he wants to take you somewhere, maybe the Lafayette, some nice French restaurant. If you cook, prepare one course, poached salmon with pureed split peas on the side. No appetizers, no soup, nothing fussy. A man doesn't like to make love on a full stomach. No neighbors here, especially not Ada Levine. In the kitchen, only Lil. She'll serve lunch. The children should be out of sight. If I'm right about Jack, he'll stay in the bedroom and not come out for a hello.

"Goodman will be here tomorrow with John, the handyman from our factory. John will measure the kitchen and Lil and Goodman will pick out a nice piece of linoleum on Clinton Street. The kitchen is a disgrace, but it's very small and can be fixed up in a hurry. We'll buy curtains for the dining room windows." Her lip curled at the sight of the short skinny curtains that hung like limp rags at either side of the two windows.

"And we need something for the table," Aunt Bertha continued. "Look at that shawl. You gave it to clean for Passover and it came back in shreds. I can't buy a new one. It's out of style, like flapper dresses from the twenties."

Then her tone softened. "Manya dear, don't worry. We have a week. It's enough. And also, Manya, only you should decide about Mister Elkin. Jack shouldn't influence you. When you see Mister Elkin, you'll know."

She smiled at my mother. "Lil, Goodman will drive us to Macy's for the curtains, and you can hem them. We'll buy long ones, almost down to the floor, to cover the walls. And we'll find something for the table. You can take the subway home when we're through shopping, and to-morrow Goodman will come with John and bring the packages."

Jack decided to give Farber a day of work without a commission, and early Sunday morning he left the house before Goodman showed up in his car, followed by John the handyman in his truck. Goodman told John, "You shouldn't move the refrigerator—God knows what will creep out from under it—and measure around the stove; you'll get a hernia if you try to push it."

He did instruct John to take out the kitchen table, and the two chairs and throw them on his truck. The table had three legs, each propped up to level it with bits of old soggy cardboard or the dented boxes that had held the matches for the stove. Even with our beloved table gone—at which we had played cards, listened to poems in Yiddish, served Bubby's many charity cases, the kitchen was pitifully small. Uncle Goodman had brought a stack of soft old pajamas and clean rags. "That's for Clayton for later," he said.

I sat beside John in his truck as my mother and Uncle Goodman led the way to the linoleum store on Clinton Street. We had never made purchases without my father. My mother bit her lip, agitated about choosing the linoleum. Uncle Goodman ruled out a white pattern be-cause it would show the dirt, green because my father considered the color a jinx, red and gray because it was similar to the current dreary floor covering. He chose a modern pattern, dark yellow boxes, like tiles, each with a corner of navy blue. "Very classy," Goodman said. He added to the store owner, "I don't have time to bargain. Give me a fair price and no hondling. But you have to cut it for me right now, and a small piece or two for the toilet and for extras." My mother trembled with uncertainty. "Do you think Daddy will like it?" she asked me. "Is it too much of a vanilla ice cream color?" I agreed with Uncle Goodman: "Classy."

While the linoleum was being cut we went across the street to a small furniture store. Lil protested that we could do better at the Allen Street secondhand shop where she had bought the telephone table, but Uncle Goodman discarded her entreaties. "We're doing this once, we're doing this right. No secondhand." The problem was to find a table small enough to fit into the space that had once held two wash-tubs. Uncle Goodman settled on the first one that would not crowd the kitchen, imitation pine with a high sheen. "It's junk," he said, shrugging, "but it's clean. Clean is a must."

Lil suggested we could ask Weinstock-the-agent for the kitchen paint. Again, Goodman pinched her cheek and laughed. "I have this one day to give you. Next year I won't remember what I spent. A few dollars more, a few less, the mind forgets, the eye remembers." Lil borrowed that sentence about the eye as a selling point, to use along with "food is like a wilted flower."

Clayton staggered in as John was carrying the linoleum up the stairs. His hair was filled with feathers, and he smelled terrible, outdoing even the smells of the toilet and hallways.

Of the events that made up this busy day, none seemed as crazy as what happened next. Goodman went into the dark room where we stored our beds, withdrew the tin bathtub, set it in the hallway outside our door, filled the tub with hot water and told Clayton, "Get into this hot water and scrub yourself all over. Then put on these pajamas."

Without a murmur of protest, Clayton stripped off his clothes. We took note of his dark uncircumcised penis, his flat behind with black hairs crawling from beneath the crack. He scrubbed himself with the brown bar soap bought for the floor, followed by Palmolive for his hair. Then he eased himself out of the dirty water, wiped himself with one of the soft rags and stood naked in front of me and Willy without the slightest urge for modesty. His penis seemed large enough to touch his knees, or so we imagined.

Uncle Goodman was short and fat, Clayton tall and skinny. He donned Uncle Goodman's pajamas and with his shins bare, lifted the tin bathtub and sloshed the dirty water down the stairs. Then he began to paint the kitchen wall where the old table had stood. It was rank with dirt, caked with food that had to be shaved off the wall with John's hand drill before they could start painting. John did the cabinets; Clayton the hard parts, up and down rhythmically: the wall, the filthy surface above the sink, under the sink, the wall again. Uncle Goodman cried, "It needs two coats, maybe three, but it's better than before, cleaner. And we don't have time."

"Tomorrow," Bubby offered, "Clayton can paint the kitchen again."

Goodman shook his head. "Tomorrow he has to paint the toilet, maybe twice. John goes home as soon as he puts down the linoleum in the kitchen. You know that movie with Charlie Chaplin, *Modern Times*? That's what we're doing here. Shnell, shnell, gefinished."

The patterned linoleum with its small and large squares and touches of blue at the edges was beautiful. It transformed the entire kitchen, the shining yellow reflecting light, reflecting newness. Hundreds of roaches had emerged in a flurry when the old linoleum was ripped off; they ate green killing powder for breakfast. But the paste applied to hold down the new linoleum killed each and every roach. "So why didn't we do this before?" Uncle Goodman demanded. "Did we have to wait for Mister Elkin to come back before we could make these improvements?"

Compared to the kitchen, with its fresh paint, linoleum and new table, the dining room appeared doubly shabby. Clayton slept on the kitchen floor the entire week, ready to help Lil install the new peach curtains, diaphanous and summery, that hid the glare from the outside but could not disguise the stained dining room seats, the balding carpet, the buckling wallpaper.

In the twitch of an eyelash, it was already Friday night. For reasons that I couldn't fathom, I decided to clean Bubby's cooking shoes. I needed a knife to scrape off the dirt from the soles and two or three coats of Shinola paste followed by liquid shine before the leather was clean. I held them up for Bubby's admiration and said, "Bubby, you'll need clean shoes when you go with Mister Elkin."

My father, who had spent the week killing time, suddenly raised his voice to me.

"Listen," he told me. "Why are you so excited about Mister Elkin? You're supposed to take after me, to be the smart one, but you're the dummy, a moron, an ignoramus. Don't you realize that if Bubby decides to marry Mister Elkin that she's finished with you? What do you think, that she'll take you along on her honeymoon? That you'll live with her on Riverside Drive while the rest of us stay here on Orchard Street?

"Mister Elkin doesn't know you and doesn't care about you. He wants Bubby, alone to himself. Why do you think I've been upset? If you're smart, why couldn't you figure this out? If Bubby gets married, it's not like when you go with her to Yonkers. It's the four of us, stuck in this dump. No restaurant, no bakery orders, no nothing. But especially no Bubby. Put that in your pipe and smoke it."

His words had the effect of an intense physical blow. My hair stood on end. My throat constricted. My heart burned with anguish and fear. "Do you think she will take you on her honeymoon?" rattled in my head until I felt dizzy, blinded by the knowledge that everything I had relied on since I was born would terminate. I dropped the shoes I had been cleaning, ran into the hallway toilet, sat on the new toilet seat and shed enough tears to fill a bathtub if we'd had one.

For days we had been playing a game called, "What does Mister Elkin look like?" Was he fatherly like Lewis Stone? Suave like Warren Williams? Intelligent like Lionel Barrymore? Sitting in the clean toilet smelling of the two coats of fresh paint and the new linoleum, I understood my father at last. Why had we bothered sprucing up the house if it meant losing the person who gave it meaning? Lying next to Bubby in bed at last, I was deadly silent. So was she. Neither of us did much sleeping that night.

Because of the general tension that pervaded our home—my father's hostility, my mother's conflicting attitudes that changed from hour to hour and my sudden secret sorrow—I hadn't paid attention to what I would wear when Mister Elkin came calling. I settled for my periwinkle blue skirt and pink blouse.

My mother dressed Bubby in her gray-blue lace, with the tiny diamond earrings and the seed pearl necklace that Mister Elkin had given her. She did not show off Dr. Koronovsky's comb in her hair. She smelled wonderfully of Chanel No. 5 and a dusting of Coty's powder. At the last minute Uncle Goodman drove up with two dining room chairs, on loan from his house in Yonkers. The seats were covered in black and gray brocade material and they had carved wooden armrests. Seated in the handsome chair, Manya appeared composed and regal.

As Aunt Bertha predicted, Jack sequestered himself in the bedroom, chain-smoking. More accurately, every few minutes he stepped out on the fire escape where he could see the length of Orchard Street to Allen Street, the better to spot the arrival of a car. My father was the only one who could recognize Mister Elkin. To the rest of us he was an imagined figure.

At last, we heard the words, "He's here." My mother put her hand to her heart. So did Bubby. I almost cried from nervousness. Each of us listened for his footsteps. A quick knock at the door. My mother opened it and in a falsetto voice asked, "Mister Elkin? I'm Manya's daughter-in-law."

"How do you do?" he said in perfect English. We had been instructed not to peek but both my brother and I did. We saw a man in a well-cut double-breasted banker's gray suit, a matching vest, a white shirt and a conservative blue tie. He was gray haired, big chested and even featured, and his eyes blazed with a cold steady light, slightly demonic. I could have founded a religion on the basis of Bubby's eyes, but not on Mister Elkin's. Some thought, some image behind Elkin's eyes flickered mysteriously. It had captivated Bubby once; maybe it would again. Compared to Bubby, he conveyed a high degree of Americanism.

As if he had left her side only a short while ago, he entered the dining room and cried out, "Manya, Manya. More beautiful than ever."

Bubby arose from her chair and immediately Mister Elkin kissed her lips, her eyes, her throat. "Manya, my love." Within seconds his eager hands dug into her dress and extracted the mountainous white breasts. My mother leaned against me for support. Were they going to fall to the floor for frya libbe?

Bubby pulled herself together and chastely covered her breasts with her hands. "Elkin, all these years, where have you been?" Caught up by his passion, he blurted out the truth. "Right here in New York. I have a business. I manufacture industrial belts for big machines."

He was on his knees, petting her, kissing her hands, then burying his head in her breasts.

"You never went to South America?"

"I thought about it and changed my mind."

"And you never came to see me, never wrote me?"

"I couldn't. Whenever I thought of it, I was ashamed, afraid."

"You afraid." She paused. "Did you ever marry?"

His eyes, those deep unreadable eyes, shifted from her face. "Manya, I couldn't stop thinking of you. How many nights I didn't sleep wanting you. And you, Manya, what did you do when I disappeared?"

"I waited, I suffered. I waited some more."

"Oh, Manya, Manya, after all these years, you can still break my heart."

"Mine broke long ago. I tried to find you. Everywhere we looked. We put a letter in 'Der Bintel Brief' in the *Forward*. We hired a detective."

Mister Elkin rose to his feet, pulled the other fancy chair close to her and sat down. "Manya, you hired a detective? You hired a detective like I was some common thief?"

"I was only trying to find you. I thought maybe you died in South America, maybe you got sick on the ship and died."

"A real detective?"

"What then, a false one? Of course a real detective. For real money, for a real two years."

Mister Elkin smiled. I could see a tremor shooting through his right hand and to cover it he straightened his tie and patted his carefully barbered hair.

"Manya, I bought a present for you. In my excitement I left it in the car. I'll get it for you. Less than five minutes."

Mister Elkin didn't look to the right or to the left, didn't say goodbye. On the fire escape, my father watched him walk briskly to his

Oldsmobile, get in and drive away. None of us stirred. We waited ten minutes, fifteen. My father emerged from the bedroom. "He's gone. He won't be coming back."

"His soul is like a raisin," Bubby finally said. "Sweet on the outside, nothing inside." She kicked off her blue satin shoes and called to me, "Elkaleh, bring me my clean cooking shoes." Not once did she return to the subject of Mister Elkin, another case of "up gevishen der lippen und shah"—wiping your lips and remaining silent. Whatever she thought or felt she kept to herself.

11

Prelude to Connecticut

MOST SUNDAYS MY father sought out my Uncle Jack. Of my mother's seven brothers, only Uncle Abe had kept his original name. At an early age, all the rest adopted names they preferred. My Uncle Jack took my father's name when Jack Roth was courting Lil. No one could remember Uncle Geoff's original name. In Yiddish it was Yuffie, but when Gene Tunney dominated the pugilistic scene, he decided that Gene sounded more manly. Though he liked Jeffrey he didn't want his name confused with the cartoon "Mutt and Jeff." After much tinkering he came up with Geoffrey as suitably distinguished.

The brothers were divided between the light ones, meaning fair of hair and complexion, and the dark ones. My mother, originally one of the dark ones, credited my father with transforming her. The brothers were also divided between the smart and average, and Uncle Geoff and Uncle Jack towered over the rest. My father influenced their reading and dressing habits, their interest in movies and theater. Everyone agreed that not one of the Simon brothers could compare in wit, repartee or writing to my father. But Uncle Geoff forced himself to become cultivated and Uncle Jack had natural artistic abilities and loved classical music.

Uncle Geoff was the first one in the family to buy a small house. It was in the Midwood section of Brooklyn and when my mother took us there, she invariably remarked, "Children, today is a day in the country." To her, Brooklyn was as much the country as Yonkers was to me.

Uncle Geoff had no artistic talents though he forced himself to learn the violin, which he tortured rather than played. But he did enjoy reading and he had a special bookcase in his house for what he called "erotica." The bookcase, kept under lock and key, contained such treasures as *Fanny Hill,* Joyce's *Ulysses,* D. H. Lawrence's *Lady Chatterley's Lover* and Gertrude Stein's *Autobiography of Alice B. Toklas.*

My father tolerated Uncle Geoff in small doses, and found his conversation sometimes stimulating, but he didn't like him. Too cold, too self-serving, arrogant, Geoff lacked heart. Besides, he kept a steady mistress in an apartment, a new one every year. In spite of my father's freethinking, he couldn't conceive of ongoing infidelity, or of a woman to whom he paid money. My mother pretended not to know of her brother's arrangement because she and Aunt Bea had been friends as neighborhood children. Bubby advised me not to reveal Uncle Geoff's separate life. "Up gevishen der lippen und shah," she told me. I considered Bubby's confidence in me as sacred and kept up the charade.

A fanatic about proper word usage, Uncle Geoff went berserk if someone called the sidewalk "the floor" instead of "the ground." He agonized over his children's names. His firstborn, a son, was tentatively called Robert because Geoff believed that the short version, Bob, sounded blond American. But his younger brother, Reuben, quickly appropriated Robert for himself and then another brother, Isaac, decided that he, too, needed the name Robert. Thus there were two Simon brothers, one Bob, one Rob, both officially Robert Simon. To avoid confusion, Isaac took his former first name as his middle initial, and became Robert I. Simon, occasionally called Robby. Reuben assimilated to Bob but not Bobby.

Having the name Robert debased by two of his brothers meant that Geoff had to begin over again for his son, and after much pondering he decided on Leonard, for Leonardo da Vinci, without any diminutive—Geoff addressed his child as Leonard. Aunt Bea, his mother, wanted to use Leon, but my father always called his nephew Lenny, and so did we.

At the birth of his daughter, Geoff hastily selected Elsie. Within twenty-four hours he realized he had blundered, switched to Elsa—too European—then to Elissa, as in Elissa Landis, the movie star. So he retreated to Alicia, and in a rare moment of common sense settled on Alice. Aunt Bea had nothing to say about this matter.

Cousin Alice was older than I, but just as people assumed that Willy was my younger brother, everyone took it for granted that Alice had been born after me. Uncle Geoff with his steely gray-green eyes and bullying manner terrified Alice and she could scarcely say her name or answer the simplest questions. Her father repeated, not once but a hundred times, that Alice had inherited the dumb side of his family, and he pinned his hopes on Leonard, who had to bear the burden of his father's ambitions. Ironically, Lil would have been satisfied with a daughter like Alice because of her conventional prettiness, light hair and fair skin, and pudgy but well-turned legs. Alice sat quietly and did as she was told, and though her eyes stared vacantly except when tears welled in them, my mother considered her a perfect candidate for marriage.

I had no complaints about Alice except that she was an aching bore. Every summer, our family and the Simons went away together. During the two or three weeks that we spent together, Alice didn't open a book, squirmed when we watched a movie and couldn't master the simplest card game. But she excelled in dancing, and could execute the steps to the latest dance craze as readily as my mother.

My father and Uncle Geoff always decided where and when we would travel without consulting Lil or Aunt Bea. He accepted his family's need for a vacation, not only because the city sweltered in July and August but because family pride and status would suffer if it had been otherwise.

This pride was bought at great sacrifice: with a loan from the Morris Plan, a banking firm that lent to the poor at exorbitant rates; and going to the hock shop to leave my mother's Singer sewing machine and Bubby's fur coat, earrings and pearls for several months.

Uncle Geoff, the ultimate snob, did high-quality printing, some of it for small book companies, so he considered himself part of the artistic world. For a man who owned a two-story home, had well-behaved, well-dressed children, his boyhood sweetheart as a wife, and a mistress whom he could turn over like a found penny, vacation spots had to elevate his status.

One year we traveled to Long Branch, New Jersey, another year to a small hotel in Atlantic City. My mother sang, "By the sea, by the sea, by the beautiful sea," but the ocean or any body of water terrified her and thus Willy and I expressed terror as well. Cousins Alice and Leonard splashed at the water's edge, but as soon as Lil felt the cold Atlantic lapping at her ankles she cried out, "My heart! my heart!" and convinced us that swimming or dunking brought on heart attacks.

Still, if Lil failed at the water's edge, she triumphed as a non-bathing beauty, eliciting praise for her "stunning" figure in the bathing suit that she chose with such care. Each summer she affected a large straw hat and sat on her beach towel in various studied poses. She was the envy of most of the women and the object of lustful stares from men. After dinner at our hotel when we strolled along the boardwalk, my mother's flirty swirly skirts, windblown blonde hair and pride in her appearance created a stir.

By comparison, Aunt Bea was plain, her hair thin, her nose broad; while she had good legs, she did not project energy or sexiness. Uncle Geoff's philosophy, "There's no such thing as love; there's only sex," led us to assume that Aunt Bea made him happy in that area. During each summer's vacation, either on Sunday night or early Monday morning when the men returned to New York City, Geoff would race to his mistress, Jack to his mother.

One day in late June, the Simons showed up at Orchard Street. Uncle Geoff was carrying a book entitled *The Inns of Connecticut.* "Our next vacation spot," he announced, "a farm that takes guests." My father wavered and my mother looked alarmed. "Connecticut?" she asked. "Where is that, upstate New York?"

Uncle Geoff explained, "We could go native there," and winked at my father. But Jack was not won over readily, so to persuade him,

Uncle Geoff suggested we take the ferry to Staten Island and talk it over. Connecticut had fired Geoff's imagination. Any outing made my heart beat faster. Since I was in my clean phase, with underpants washed every night and a fresh blouse ironed by me, I no longer had to be ashamed of appearing like an Orchard Street urchin. For once my Aunt Bea, almost as uncharitable with compliments as Ada Levine but not as harsh or vulgar, complimented me on my shiny hair.

We crammed into Uncle Geoff's Packard. I sat on my mother's lap, Alice on Aunt Bea's, Leonard up front with the men and Willy in the back with the girls and our mothers. The children were not allowed to speak or utter a sound when we were with Uncle Geoff.

Once on the ferry, we left the car to stretch our legs and inhale the "sea" air. The two fathers leaned against the railing and immediately turned to the subject of Connecticut and the farm. "It's far away enough and close enough," Geoff argued. "And it's very inexpensive. You can stay for a month for what it would cost us in Atlantic City for a week. The kids don't need fancy clothes, just some overalls and shirts. There's not been a case of polio reported there."

Polio was a nightmare terror in those years, and the very word struck fear in Jack's heart. He carried his thermometer in his vest pocket in case he or anyone in our family felt the slightest chill. An inexpensive vacation with open spaces, one that required no fancy clothes, did not appeal to him as much as the absence of polio. "But I hate the sticks," he protested. "What do they do in the evening? They don't even have sidewalks to pull in after dark."

"There's a big hotel down the road and Pankin's Farm has a piano. You and Lil can sing your hearts out."

"Who will we entertain, the chickens?"

"No, their guests come from New Haven and New London. Eugene O'Neill loved New London."

"Puts me ten ahead."

"You can educate them. Give them some of your razzmatazz. Besides, it's a different experience. Unique."

The word *unique* caused Jack to capitulate. As he leaned against the railing of the ferry, I could see him dreaming up skits and songs. Grudgingly, he agreed. "It's on your head if we hate Connecticut."

In a moment my spirits, ten feet off the ground, crashed into bruising reality. A white-uniformed man on the ferry sold ice cream sandwiches, kept frozen in the square white container slung over his shoulder by a thick strap. Uncle Geoff treated Aunt Bea, Leonard and Alice to ice cream. Jack, absorbed in the book about inns of Connecticut, paid no attention. My mother pulled me roughly by the arm and hissed into my ear, "Don't ask for ice cream. If Uncle Geoff treats on the way over, Daddy will have to treat on the way back."

Standing on the ferry, I swore to myself that I would not ever emulate my mother. She was beautiful. Yes. She could melt your heart with her singing. Yes. I could not equal her ease with men. But I didn't want to grow up and be like her.

We waited on the ferry until it reversed direction for the return trip. I kept silent as we drove to Orchard Street. My mother was content; my father hadn't had to treat for anything and Bubby would soon supply everyone with hot food. In any case, we would be going to Connecticut, to Pankin's Farm, and staying at least two weeks, possibly three. I folded up my rage against my mother into a tiny packet, no larger than a dime, and stored it away in some remote corner of my brain.

Before we left for the country two major events took place that changed my mother. The restaurant business, still slower than usual, persuaded Bubby to fill her days by buying fresh fruit—cherries, blueberries, strawberries, mulberries—and preparing jam. The house smelled sweet and her gallon jars—scrubbed, boiled and filled, then sealed with paraffin—provided jam for the coming year.

For a week or two Clayton and Bubby were out on Hester Street as soon as the fruit pushcarts came into sight. He carried home the black oilcloth bag stuffed with fresh fruit in one hand and a ten-pound sack of sugar in the other. For her summer customers, Bubby cooked a lot of dairy: schav, called sorrel soup by Americans; cold borscht; blintzes; salads without dressing. Every fruit—bananas, strawberries, blueberries—was served to our diners with mountainous quantities of sour cream. Any money that came into the restaurant was plowed back into fruit or saved for the rent.

For weeks Bubby had saved the sheet of paper Yussie Feld had given her, the one with the name of Shirley Feldman's drama teacher, the one planning a recital for her students. Bubby spoke to my mother softly and persuasively about calling the teacher for me. Did I deserve less than any of the three Shirleys, one now living by Battery Park, the other for the whole summer in the mountains, the third skating up and down the streets straight to the East River?

"But Ma," my mother protested, "we don't have the money. We have to save every penny for the vacation."

"These lessons, they don't start until September. By then we'll all be working."

"And if not?"

"If, if. If I had a man's you-know-what I'd be the children's grandfather. I can't live on *if*. We'll have the money. Gut vil zine unser tateh."

My grandmother rarely invoked the help of God; my mother realized she was serious. Still, she did not give up easily. "What does Elka need it for? She speaks fine. We don't have to show her off the way Yussie Feldman shows off Shirley, Miss No-Talent."

"That's right; Shirley Feld has no talent. But your daughter has. Speaking, it's not. It's acting. Boris Tomashevsky, Jacob Adler, Muni Wiesenfeld, now they call him Paul Muni, you think they didn't take lessons?"

Bubby waited a moment. Then, without the slightest hint of threat, she went on, "You won't have to call the teacher, my sister Bertha will call her. Bertha and I will take care of it."

My mother promptly reached for the phone and called Miss Claire Sussman. The result was not what either my grandmother or mother anticipated.

"I'm sorry," the drama teacher replied, "I'm not taking any new pupils. I hold auditions the first week after Labor Day. I can't make any guarantees. Besides, what's the rush? She can audition with everyone else in September."

"All of us work," Lil replied. "We have to settle this now. We can't bring her for auditions in September, the beginning of our season. We want you to see her this week, before we leave for Connecticut." Miss Sussman hesitated. Lil pressed her advantage with a Division Street tactic. "You'll regret it for the rest of your life if you don't come to see her this week."

"When do you want to bring her to my studio?"

"I can't. I'm at business all week. But you can come to see us."

"And where do you live?"

"Canal Street."

"Canal Street downtown?"

"Miss Sussman, James Feld, his mother lives in our building and he recommended you. If you teach someone like Shirley Feld who recites the same poem month after month, year after year, you can't say no to my daughter because of our address."

"You've worn me down. Friday afternoon, 3 P.M. What's the address?"

"The entrance is on Orchard Street. Twelve Orchard Street, but the apartment faces Canal."

Too exhausted to protest, Miss Sussman capitulated.

The house was a mess. In spite of the new paint and linoleum in the kitchen, in spite of the linen runner on the table instead of the old shawl, the house hadn't been cleaned since the day that Mister Elkin drove away in his fancy car. One morning Clayton hauled fruit and sugar for Bubby as usual, and the next day he didn't turn up. Nor a week later. In the old days it was easy to search for him, because Bubby paid his rent. Now he stayed with friends, lived in Harlem, God knows where. We didn't lack for Negroes to clean the apartment—they showed up daily asking for food. But Clayton was part of our history. Bubby needed him, she loved him. She asked every Negro man who came to our door, "You know Clayton? He's tall, he's skinny, one of his eyes is a little funny?" No one replied.

"Maybe he's out of town," Jack suggested.

"Maybe he went to California. He always talked about Hollywood," I offered.

"Without a good-bye? Without telling us? Never." But time passed and he didn't call or write.

My designated meeting with Miss Sussman immediately flew from my mother's head. She had had little interest in my drama lessons to begin with and an unexpected phone call from her boss, Mr. L. from Palace Fashions, threw her into a tizzy. While buying coats on Seventh Avenue for the fall, he had met a buyer from Saks Fifth Avenue and she asked if he could recommend a saleswoman as an "extra" for their store.

"No offense," the buyer added, "but we don't want anyone who lives down where your store is."

"I have just the girl for you." Mr. L. laughed. "She works for me, yes, but she lives in Yonkers, has two children, and her husband is the manager of a retail store. She's beautiful, well-spoken and would be a credit to Saks Fifth."

Palace Fashions was known citywide, as was Mr. L. When my mother walked into his store he chucked her under the chin and laughed, "Are you interested, Lil?"

In fact, the thought terrified her. "Me, working at Saks Fifth Avenue?"

"You can do it, Lil. Definitely you can. Jack will help you, he'll walk you through the interview. The first thing is to not look too flashy and the second is to call yourself Miss Lillian, not Lil. Give your aunt's address in Yonkers, and on your application write that you finished high school. Don't worry, they won't check.

"You'll need another reference about your work. Just tell them Missy Modes on Broadway. I'll call my friend Phil Glasser and he'll vouch for you. Also about your hair. Tone it down a few shades, not so blonde. Pale, not red lipstick and don't forget white gloves." He paused. "I forgot to mention a very small hat, straw, businesslike. And keep your hands in your lap when you're talking."

Lil was a wreck when she got home, her head spinning from all the instructions. Later, Jack called Mr. L. for the details. The only thing Lil had remembered was to tone down her hair.

Jack did not care for this turn of events. He preferred his mother in the house and felt a similar anxiety for his wife. Having her on Fifth Avenue once or twice a month upset the routine that was so necessary for him. He listed all the negatives, not with the venom that he reserved for Mister Elkin, but with reasoning that my mother could not refute.

First negative, the early morning rush hour subway ride to Forty-second Street and the local to Forty-ninth, an hour each way. Admittedly, the store hours, nine to six, improved on the late Division Street nights. But who would she talk to, kibbitz with? Whenever my mother had a free minute she dashed outside to wave to Jack or speak to him at Farber's, across the street from Palace Fashions.

True, Sophie Gimbel owned Saks but they rarely hired Jewish sales help—ask anyone, they would tell you. And what about the no-pressure selling, standing around, saying as little as possible to the customer? Why the hell did she need a job carrying suits and coats into the dressing room, not to mention recoloring her hair, dressing like a librarian and talking like one? Jack had no difficulty falsifying Lil's school record, but hadn't Mr. L. warned her to say that a garment was lovely instead of stunning? Why bother? "What's in it for you?" he demanded.

Jack's arguments increased my mother's hysteria. It had taken her years to learn how to sell on Division Street, let alone at Saks where she was too terrified to buy a lipstick. Yet, she couldn't rid herself of one thought that she expressed without fear. "If I put in one day there I can always say I worked for Saks Fifth Avenue. From Division Street to Saks Fifth. That's really something."

"And don't customers who shop at Saks come to Palace Fashions? It's no big deal."

My grandmother, who remained silent throughout this discussion, said quietly, "Trying is not the same as getting. If she wants to try, let her."

"Ninety/ten she won't be hired."

"So what's the tsimmis? A ride uptown in a nice dress isn't hard. You'll go with her. And all those questions she has to answer, you'll write them out for her on a piece of paper, she'll copy them. Then the two of you can walk down Fifth that afternoon, maybe meet Aunt Bertha for lunch. Whatever you want. It's an honor Mr. L. thought of Lil."

Temporarily placated, my father pondered for a minute. "The navy blue dress you bought last year for Atlantic City with the kick pleats. No jewelry on the dress, only your small gold earrings. Tell Pandy to part your hair in the middle and comb it into a French roll or a small bun. Something classy."

That afternoon Lil was about to leave for Pandy's to have her hair darkened when Miss Sussman knocked timidly at the door. We barely heard her. She stepped inside. "I'm Claire Sussman." Short, dark of hair and face, neither striking nor attractive, she stood with an erect posture and pronounced each word as if giving a speech lesson. My mother made short shrift of her plain summer suit but admired her hat, white straw that covered only the front of her head and dipped down over her right ear.

"Your hat is stunning," my mother said and corrected herself. "I mean it's lovely."

A few customers had eaten their meals, but Lil, too distracted by her hair appointment and her Monday interview, hadn't bothered to clear the tables, and Jack, who ordinarily accompanied her to the beauty salon, had left for his odious appointment at the unemployment office. I was keenly aware of the dishes with half-eaten food on the table, the crumbs on the unswept carpet, Bubby with flour on her cheeks, and my mother in an old summer dress that she wore only to Pandy's.

"Perhaps I have the wrong place?" Miss Sussman was what my father labeled a City College type. She reined in her aggressiveness by hard-won good manners. It turned out that she had been too short to appear in major Broadway productions, so she had opened her own successful studio for children.

"No, you're in the right place, and here's the elocution girl. Only, I have to run to the beauty parlor."

"Mother!"

Miss Sussman widened her dark round eyes. I could tell she was impressed that I had addressed Lil as Mother. Bubby signaled my mother by raising her voice unnaturally: "Pandy isn't running away." Lil stepped back inside, tolerating the next few minutes with awkward impatience.

Miss Sussman claimed the one clean chair in the dining room. "Have you prepared anything for me?" she asked. "Is there a poem you can recite?" The word *poem* came in two syllables, *po-em,* not *pome,* the way we pronounced it.

" 'The Children's Hour.' May I begin now?" The "may I" was also a big hit.

It's doubtful that Lil heard a single word I spoke. Bubby removed her apron and looked in my direction, providing so much assurance that I began without hesitation.

> *Between the dark and the daylight*
> *When the night is beginning to lower*
> *Comes a pause in the day's occupation*
> *That is known as the children's hour.*

Mrs. Thomas, my teacher at P.S. 12, had drilled us to pronounce *lower* to rhyme with hour. Miss Sussman nodded.

> *I hear in the chamber above me*
> *The patter of little feet*
> *The sound of a door that is opened*
> *And voices soft and sweet.*

Miss Sussman held up her hand. "That's enough. I'm impressed. The trip down here was dreadful. This tenement is dreadful. But your daughter is talented."

She handed me a typed sheet of paper: "Sweet are the uses of adversity / which like the toad / ugly and venomous / wears yet a jeweled crown on its head." I stumbled on *venomous* but sailed through *jewel-ed.*

"Very impressive," said Miss Sussman.

Lil softened. "Look, Miss Sussman, I have an interview at Saks Fifth Avenue on Monday. Could you give me five minutes' help? How should I sit? What should I do with my hands?"

A smile spread over Miss Sussman's alert, homely face. She stood up, then carefully lowered herself into the chair, her back straight, her head leaning forward slightly. She crossed her feet at the ankles rather than at the knees as my mother did. Her hands rested demurely in her lap.

"There's nothing to it. Just remember what I showed you."

My mother was a quick study, and went through Miss Sussman's motions, but out of habit she placed one knee over the other.

"You have beautiful legs but for an interview you must be modest about them," Miss Sussman instructed her. "If you forget, keep both feet on the floor and your knees together. About your speech, don't worry about your pronunciation. Be natural, be yourself, speak in a soft voice. Smile slightly to prove that you're pleased to be there, and keep your eyes on the person who is interviewing you. It doesn't make a good impression if you're shifty-eyed or glance elsewhere."

My mother asked me, "Did you get all of that? What she said?"

I nodded.

"How did you raise a daughter in this environment?"

"Don't ask me, ask her grandmother, she brought her up. This is Manya, the famous chef. You must of heard of her."

Miss Sussman said, "Must *have,* must *have* heard of her."

"I love your hat," Lil continued without noticing the correction. "Where did you buy it? It's what I need for the interview."

Miss Sussman removed the hat pins from her hat, and smiling, handed the wisp of woven straw to my mother. "You may borrow it. Here's my card with the address of my studio. Return it to my studio after the interview. And good luck with it. About your daughter . . ."

My mother carefully placed the hat on the bureau. "Speak to Manya. My hairdresser will kill me, I'm late already, she has to do a new style for me." She left, not bothering to thank Miss Sussman for coming, for the lesson in interview etiquette or for the use of the hat. And she got away with it. Her surface rudeness did not hide either her fragility or her vulnerability.

"I'll expect to see your granddaughter in September. I can do a lot for her."

Manya nodded. "Thank you," she said.

There was no talk about money or the cost of the lessons. Miss Sussman studied me for a moment. "That typed page I gave you. Did you know it was Shakespeare?"

My reply was one of the few things I had learned from my mother. "I thought it might be."

Miss Sussman sighed with delight. So did Bubby.

Jack accompanied Lil to Saks Fifth Avenue on Monday. Her honey-blonde hair, parted in the middle, was pushed forward in a wave at both cheeks and caught in an easy bun at the neck. The white straw hat rested lightly on her hair. Jack had been absolutely right about the navy blue dress. She carried a small navy blue purse, courtesy of Uncle Goodman's factory, and white gloves. The heels of her pumps were possibly too high but not outrageously so. "You look stunning," Jack said.

"Lovely," Lil replied.

Jack put her through her paces on two questions only. "Why do you want this job?" Answer, "I've always admired Saks and it would be a privilege for me to work here." The word *privilege* came with difficulty, so Jack changed it to *honor*. "It would be an honor for me to work here." To help her, he added, "Just think of a judge. You address him as 'your honor.' So you say, 'It would be an honor for me to work here.' If she asks you where you buy your clothes, say 'On sale at Palace Fashions and at specialty shops like Missy Modes.' "

Jack walked Lil to the door of the employment office on the second floor of Saks. He had prepared a fact sheet with my mother's name, including her maiden name, her date of birth, her address and phone number in Yonkers, the year she graduated from Seward Park High School and the years she worked at Palace Fashions and Missy Modes.

He didn't prompt her very much—it would serve to confuse her. Besides, he believed in the proverb "The face sells the merchandise." And she had the face in spades.

Still, he could sense that her confidence was faltering as he left her. Retracing his steps, he assured her again, "I'll be outside on the Fifth Avenue sidewalk, waiting. Your appointment is with Miss Sullivan. You'll do great. Very uptown." Uptown was the code word for "not too Jewish."

Jack longed for coffee but he would not leave his post. He stood there and chain-smoked the entire hour.

Lil emerged radiant. "My handwriting was very neat, and, Jack, you know the questions you asked me, why I wanted the job and where I buy my clothes? My answers were perfect. She asked what days I would be available, so I said whenever they needed me, even Sunday. That was my only mistake. Miss Sullivan, this cold fish, she answers, 'We're not open on Sunday.' Of course I was thinking of Division Street. And another thing, I crossed my legs at the knees but she didn't mind. She asked me if I could learn the stock fast and I said yes, she asked if I kept up with the latest fashions and I said yes. What did she take me for, the wife of a plumber?"

"Did she say if she hired you?"

"Oh, no! She said I would hear from them. Not when, not how, just I would hear from her and thank you for coming. I said 'Thank you' and that was that." She pressed my father's hand. "I didn't do too bad. What do you think?"

"I think we should have coffee. There's a Schrafft's a few blocks from here."

"Jack, we shouldn't spend the money. We need it for Connecticut."

"The extra few cents won't make or break us and why should we eat at a diner today?" His interpretation of the interview was that she would not hear from Saks again. Her interpretation was that she had the job.

"Listen," Jack reminded her, "after the coffee we'll have a nice long walk to Miss Sussman's studio. We'll return the hat and I want to look the place over."

My mother asked plaintively, "Do I really have to return it? Miss Sussman gave it to me."

"Lil, don't be foolish. She told you to return it after the interview and you will."

"But why? I love this hat. She probably has a dozen more. And since when did you become Honest Abe?"

"Since I want to look her and the studio over. Besides, you won't wear the hat again. You're going with the cows and chickens for the summer. The teacher came all the way to our house and didn't ask for money, not even for her subway fare. Lil, you have to learn to be classy. You want to work at Saks, act like it."

Much as she wanted to keep the hat, much as she believed her desire justified it, she didn't argue with Jack on matters of class. He was the mentor, she the student. They walked over to Seventh Avenue and slowly down Broadway. Tears came to her eyes at the prospect of renouncing the hat that she cherished for the moment. Aunt Bertha, who wore hats daily, would provide Lil with any hat in her closet, but Lil wanted this one because she associated it with the interview at Saks.

They found Miss Sussman's studio in a building with a sign that read Art Studios. Inside the small hallway with hexagonal tiles in the floor, a notice board listed Sussman Drama Studio as 1A, easily reached by a slow-moving elevator. Neither of them had thought to call in advance. Jack rang and when silence followed, Lil's spirits lifted. Maybe she could keep the hat after all. Then Miss Sussman opened the door.

In my father's assessment, she was a *meiskite,* a homely one, too small, too dark, too lacking in sex appeal for him to contemplate how he could improve her appearance. The studio, with a window on noisy Broadway, contained a piano, a small stage and several cheap folding chairs. Posters from Broadway plays—he recognized Gertrude Lawrence in Noël Coward's *Private Lives*—decorated the walls.

My mother handed over the hat with what graciousness she could muster. "Thank you for lending it to me. And this is my husband, Jack Roth. He's the manager of a ladies' retail store."

My father nodded at the poster. "I saw that play."

Miss Sussman smiled broadly. She had been tidying the studio. Her forehead glistened with sweat. My father rarely lost an opportunity to impress women, even one as unimpressive as Miss Sussman. "The theater and concerts, they keep me busy when the family is away," he offered. "This summer they'll be in Connecticut." The concerts referred to the ones he attended at Lewisohn Stadium with Uncle Jack Simon. They would kill a Sunday night sitting on the cold steps of the stadium, seeking young attractive women with whom they could kibbitz and possibly score.

"Do you like classical music?" she inquired.

"I'm bored to death with Chy-kow-sky's 'Refrain from Spitting.' "

The smile left Miss Sussman's face.

"I beg your pardon."

My father hated the implied rebuff from this oily-skinned drama teacher whom he doubted ever had a good lay in her life.

"Nothing, a street joke, not worth repeating." It irritated Jack that he had been caught in a smart-aleck crack that didn't go over uptown. Miss Sussman shifted gears.

"I'll be in touch with you in September."

"If the class is on Saturday," Jack pointed out, "we'll send my daughter with our cab driver. I don't let her ride in the subway alone and my wife and I are at business."

"I look forward to working with her."

"The pleasure is mutual." Jack prided himself on the way he closed a sale. He took equal pride in closing the conversation with Miss Sussman.

Still, this did not keep him from feeling out of sorts. There were only a few coins jingling in his handsome summer suit, and he had put a great deal of effort into the morning of my mother's interview; with little to show for it. Once home, he searched the mailbox for his unemployment insurance check. Not there. At loose ends, he called Uncle Jack at his office on Maiden Lane where he did hand engraving for wedding invitations. "Tell me," my father asked, "what's wrong with saying 'I'm bored to death with Chy-kow-sky's "Refrain from Spitting" '?"

"In the first place, it's Chy-kov-sky pronounced with a *v,* not a *w.* In the second, it's a mark of ignorance to make a bad joke about a famous work. It's uncouth."

"Uncouth? What did you do, swallow a dictionary?"

"Jack, you're having a bad day."

He was. He consoled himself with the idea that Lil was rid of Saks Fifth Avenue forever, though he confided to Rocco that she would be a steady extra for the fall season. The word spread across the Italian and Jewish quarters within hours. My mother accepted congratulations with due modesty, because why would Jack say such a thing if it wasn't going to happen? Dr. Scott Wolfson complimented her, too, saying the job would make her summer in Connecticut. It did.

The week before we left for Connecticut, Aunt Bea traveled to Orchard Street to buy overalls and short-sleeved shirts for Lenny and cotton jumpers or pinafores for Alice. Aunt Bea pointed out to my mother that each child needed two pairs of overalls, one that could be washed while the other was in use. My mother widened her eyes at such extravagance. "One overall is plenty," she remarked.

Nor would she budge when it came to buying me some pinafores for the evening. She had her own ideas. I tried on my dresses from the summers before that she hoped to restore for another season. She attached a yard of lace to the short hems. I was wearing one of them when Ada Levine came to pick up Lil to go shoe-shopping. She regarded me in this apparition of a dress and said, "That one looks like a lampshade." Bubby flushed and the vein in her neck beat visibly.

"Lil," Bubby said, "for once Ada is right. How could you send your child for dinner at a hotel in that narad?"

"On Alice it would look lovely," replied Lil.

The physical characteristics of her children remained a source of continuing grief to my mother. She of the ravishing legs had children with knobby knees, no curve to their calves and thighs as puny as lead pipes. Willy, under the encouragement of Dr. Wolfson, declared that he wouldn't wear shorts. I caught the pain in my mother's eyes when I wore them. Standing in the dress with the wobbly lace hem, I didn't bother to glance down—I could visualize my shapeless legs.

"All right," my mother sighed, "take it off." She opened a box of odds and ends of material saved for such purposes—too small in size to make anything for herself, large enough for one or two jumpers.

It should be said on my mother's behalf that she could cut freehand, with no pattern, any outfit she had in mind. She found scraps of cotton material, took her shears and cut out two shifts, basted one quickly, and had me try it on. Then Ada interrupted her by asking, "Are you going for shoes or not?" My mother wanted a low-heeled summer sandal for walking on unpaved country roads. She said, "We'll finish this later," and left me standing in this tentlike garment as she and Ada dashed out.

Except when we went to bed, our kitchen door stood open all day during summer—not for air but for easy access to the street and for sociability. We were the first to view who came and went, whether it was the matchmaker for Mrs. Feldman or the Polish Mrs. Rosinski with her bundle of men's pants. Summers were Mrs. Rosinski's high season, and every morning she walked to the factory in Chinatown and returned with dozens of unfinished men's trousers.

I was standing in our kitchen in the unfinished tent dress when Mrs. Rosinski came up the stairs, huffing and lugging her two sets of trousers. She left one package at our threshold, and climbed on up, resting at each floor, until she reached her tiny immaculate apartment. When she came back down to collect the package, she and Bubby chatted in several languages, mixing them up like a heady exotic stew. The "two Mrs. R.s," as I called them, spoke a bit of Russian, Polish, Yiddish, English, and understood each other perfectly. A glance at me in the basted sleeveless dress made her beckon me to come with her. "I gefinish," she said to Bubby, and holding the second unfinished pinafore in her hand, Mrs. R. and I plodded up to the fifth floor.

At the side of her sewing machine she had contrived a makeshift series of shelves. From the top shelf she took a Louis Sherry tin that Bubby had given her, which had her needles and pins arranged on a blue velvet lining, possibly a gift from Orloff. Speaking to me in multilingual phrases, she quickly pinned the sides of the pinafore and the hem of the skirt. Her skin was ashen, and the dried sweat under her armpits gave off a scent like the bottom of Bubby's mead barrel, but saw her narrow face radiated happiness as she pinned the dress.

In her bedroom—empty but for an iron bed and an overhead light — she located a towel, gray and threadbare, and covered my shoulders after she removed the dress. I watched her sew, marveling at her stitches, each tiny and exactly the same size as she pulled the thread through, her hands fluttering over the material like birds. She sewed the sides of the dress by machine. The top straps and the hem were hand-stitched so fine that a single stitch would have been the envy of any expert.

Then she retrieved a set of tiny wooden hoops from another box, and clamped them close to the neckline. From threads of every color, she chose red, deftly sewed the outline of a strawberry, and filled it with a hooked stitch that raised the height of the embroidery. She moved the hoops from place to place until the entire bodice of the dress was covered with red strawberries, one smaller than the next. "Like?" she asked.

To prevent myself from crying, I gave her kisses identical to the ones for Bubby, ten on each cheek and then one on her parched mouth. She hugged me with delight. "Go you," she replied, and I skipped down the flights of stairs to show my embroidered jumper to Bubby. "Isn't it beautiful? I mean the strawberries, and you can't imagine how fast she does it. I gave her a thousand kisses, that was all I had."

The following morning she brought down the shift I had left with her and a new dress with puffed sleeves. Where or how she came by the material—whether she had it in a drawer in her house or she bought it for me—we never inquired. But there it was, small red and white checks with a stitch called faggoting across the chest, large perfectly spaced stitches, each one following the other like birds resting on high wires. The collar and the trim at the edge of the puffed sleeves were white and the hem had perfect cross-stitches. Mrs. R. stood there watching me, her face as golden as the summer light on one of her religious pictures. Without shame I took off my nightgown and slipped the dress over my head, afraid to move lest I spoil this perfect moment. Bubby applauded.

Finally, it was the night before we were to leave on vacation. Lying in bed with Bubby, my belongings all packed, I couldn't close my eyes.

"Vus tract du?"

By then, everything had jumbled together in my mind: the vacation, the separation from Bubby, the prospect of not seeing Dr. Wolfson for three weeks, Clayton's disappearance, my always-present fears for Bubby's health. What I blurted out came without bidding: "Bubby, are you sorry about Mister Elkin?"

"How sorry?"

"That he left in such a hurry? Did you want to go away with him?"

"Ich vayst nisht."

"Whenever I ask you about him you say, 'I don't know.' Why do you say that?"

"Because I don't know."

"How could you not know?"

"I loved him long ago. Later you can't remember if it was a dream, a fantasia, a story you made up in your head."

"But when you saw him again, what did you think?"

"Right away, it started with kissing. Who could think? I can't answer. It went too fast. My lips were wet with his kisses when he rushed to leave me because I said 'detective.' He didn't like that. Maybe I thought of him as a swindler, a common thief, a man with secrets, maybe with two families, not one. It happens, in this life it happens."

Neither of us spoke. Her words weren't complicated, only hard.

"Do you still love him?"

"No. When the dream goes, when the fantasia goes, it's gornisht."

"But when you talk about Misha, I hear love in your voice."

"Elkaleh, Misha was a brenfire. From the minute I met him, fifteen years old, there was a fire between us. When I leaned on his shoulder, already the heat could melt Odessa snow."

I thought this revelation would keep me awake. Instead, I burrowed myself deep into my Bubby's warm body and dropped off into dreamless sleep.

12

Summer in Connecticut

COLCHESTER, CONNECTICUT, WAS 120 miles from midtown Manhattan. The food my grandmother prepared for the trip—sandwiches, hard-boiled eggs, cold chicken, slices of cake, cookies, cherries, strawberries, peaches, plums—could feed us for days. Lil, a great fruit lover, often ate the summer's harvest with bread. The fruit and bread were stored in a large basket, a gift from Yussie Feld delivered empty. "Heaven forbid," Jack had said ironically, "he should fill it with fruit from his shop." We lacked for nothing except cold drinks, which increased our anticipation when we stopped for them en route.

Surely Dr. Wolfson would have suppressed a laugh, as I did, when Uncle Geoff walked in at nine in the morning sporting a navy blue French beret on his thinning blond hair. He handed my father an identical beret. Instead of mocking the notion of wearing a beret to the country, Jack clapped it on his head, though he had decided on casual dress for the occasion: no tie, turned-up shirt cuffs and gray gabardine trousers that had seen better days. Thus attired, he lifted one of our two suitcases; Uncle Geoff carried the other. Willy insisted on lugging the basket of fruit, while Bubby, accustomed to heavy loads, brought down our lunch in a corrugated box.

Cousin Lenny ensconced himself in the front seat of the Packard between the two men, while Aunt Bea, with Alice in her lap, sat in their customary places in the back. Allegedly, the car once belonged to a bootlegger. How else account for the secret storage compartment under the seats? Our suitcases went in there. I gave Bubby, usually the recipient of my unlimited kisses, the barest peck on the cheek, lest I cling to her and start crying at the prospect of leaving her behind. Jack, on the other hand, peppered his mother's face with kisses until she drew away, dabbed her eyes with her apron and urged me in a quavering voice, "Zulst mir schrieben." We waved at her until she diminished in view on the sidewalk. Willy and I, on our knees in the backseat, continued to blow kisses to her from the rear window as the car moved beyond Canal Street.

Directions for our journey were accompanied by a crackle of the road map Uncle Geoff had marked in red ink. He and my father discussed the roads by number: 64, 22, 37. Once out of the city, my elation swelled like a giant balloon that could have floated to the sky. Cousin Alice, who rarely spoke out loud, cupped her chubby hand over Aunt Bea's ear and whispered that she had to do number one. Aunt Bea dutifully relayed the message to Uncle Geoff who roared, "No number one or number two until we finish twenty miles."

"But Geoff," Aunt Bea protested.

"No ifs, ands or buts." He flashed his cold green eyes to the backseat. "We're making five stops. I worked it out with precision. If she really has to go, I'll pull over to the side of the road. But she can eat anytime."

Aunt Bea had instructed her daughter as a baby, "Chew and swallow." But repetition has nothing to do with learning, and Alice took large bites of whatever she ate, pushed them to the back of her mouth and swallowed. Within a few minutes, she could polish off a meat sandwich that Willy and I shared for two meals. Slipping off Aunt Bea's lap, she rooted around in the corrugated box for a sandwich with enough beef brisket for two of our restaurant's entrees. She made short work of it, folding the waxed paper neatly when done. The fruit basket had been placed on the shelf behind the backseat and Alice finished off every single peach. Later, when we stopped and Uncle Geoff asked for a peach, Aunt Bea covered her daughter's gluttony by explaining, "All of us ate them." Not easily fooled, he raised his hand, reached back with a glancing blow to Alice's head and commanded, "Don't do that again, dummy, moron." She had learned not to eat in front of him, so became a secret eater, gorging herself as soon as her father turned away.

Despite his best intentions, Uncle Geoff made several wrong turns and we had to retrace our path, so it was late afternoon when we reached a fork in the road and saw a sign that read Colchester. Coming upon the village, all of us, except for the sleeping Alice, were deeply moved. From one end to another lay a swath of green, perfectly mowed. There was a church with a white steeple, and a squat white stucco building flying the American flag that signified it was the school. The drugstore and the public library nestled side by side, like cutouts in a book. People walked along the narrow paths, straight-backed and spare. They looked like characters in a silent film. I worried that our New York cadences would shock the locals. Even arrogant Uncle Geoff spoke softly when he stopped to ask a passerby, "Which way to Pankin's Farm?"

"Straight to the end of the village, first dirt road to the right."

Aunt Bea straightened Alice up, combed her hair and wiped off the thumb she had been sucking throughout her long sleep. We bumped onto the first dirt road, wobbling a bit over harrows and potholes. "If this isn't the sticks, what is?" Jack commented. We drove slowly for one mile, then two. A vast gray barn rose like a prehistoric creature on a small hill, the words *Books B-o-o-k-s* painted on every side. Small farms came into sight, the cottages surrounded by livestock: cows and chickens. We said in unison, "Cows," as if we had made a discovery known to our eyes only. Then came a burst of voices and the sounds of bustling: Pankin's Farm at last.

The photograph in *The Inns of Connecticut* did not do justice to the main house. Painted white, five broad steps led to a veranda that encircled the entire house. The roof, far from being flat, was pointed like a steeple, and beneath it I saw the round dormer window of a small room that I wanted to claim as my own for reading. As it turned out, a young couple had taken possession of it for three weeks while they were studying for the Connecticut bar examination. I knew more Russian and Yiddish than I did words like *bar examination,* and the fact that the young woman occupant studied every day until four o'clock gave me pause. Then we discovered that all the waiters were second-year med students at Harvard. Hal Pankin, the oldest son, who greeted us, leaped down the front steps in two casual jumps, hardly the hick my father anticipated.

He was thin, wiry, muscular, with thick black hair worn naturally, not slicked back. His deep-set eyes assessed us at a glance. If our New York speech startled him, he did not reveal it, but we had to accustom ourselves to the way he spoke: ahnt, cahnt, yahd, cah. There were no r's in his sentences.

"The Roths and the Simons," my father announced. "Jack and Lil, Geoff and Bea." We children remained nameless.

"I'm Hal Pankin, Hank Pankin's son," he replied with an infectious grin. "Your waiter and valet is Gabe Solomon. Gabe plans to be a surgeon so watch out when he cuts your fish or meat." Gabe, red-haired, his pale skin dotted with freckles, arrived as Hal said this. "I'll take up your bags and then I'll pahk the cah," he said.

Lil ascended the porch steps with no effort, but when we entered the tiny lobby we confronted a flight of stairs that went straight up, almost to the attic. "You're in the original house," Hal explained. The steps, very old and very steep, required more than usual effort, and after a half dozen, Lil had to pause and catch her breath. Hal, who had run up, saw her gasping and raced back down.

"Mrs. Roth, I'm so sorry. If we had been told, we would have put you in one of the new cottages." Carefully, gingerly his fingers tapped her pulse. I half expected him to pull out his stethoscope but he only asked, "Atrial fibrillation? Tachycardia?" Lil smiled at him seductively. The terms meant nothing to her, though Dr. Wolfson may have explained them. "Lil. Please call me Lil. And it's nothing. A weak heart from childhood."

Hal placed his arm under her elbow. "We'll do this slowly. Lead with your right foot and bring up your left. Take each step with your right. Pause. Right. That will be less strain for you. The first cottage that comes available is yours."

But we never moved to one of the newer buildings. Not that summer nor the summer thereafter, especially when Lil learned that our bedroom formerly belonged to Maurey, the youngest son. The Simons were given Hal's old room.

I loved our room at sight. From the side window we could view the barn and the small back window framed cornfields and beyond them tall stands of gnarled fruit trees, more summer fruit than on all the downtown pushcarts combined.

There was a double bed for our parents and twin beds at right angles for me and Willy, as well as a sink. The toilet was outside our door.

"What's the sink for?" asked Willy.

"To take a pee," my father answered. "In the middle of the night you don't want to step outside, you pee in the sink."

"Jack," my mother protested, "the sink is to wash your hands and face. We'll get a milk bottle for peeing."

Uncle Geoff and Aunt Bea had better accommodations, and paid more for them. One of their closets had been converted into a bathroom with a tiny toilet and a shower.

"Dinner is at six to six-thirty, New England meal," said Hal, who had returned to inform us. "The salmon came in fresh from New London this morning."

"Do you think they make gefilte fish from salmon?" Lil asked.

My father fell on the double bed with relief. Maybe we would have taken a nap after our long journey, but Aunt Bea came in without knocking. "Geoff made a schedule for showering. The women and girls first, in and out in a hurry, so we can dress for the dining room. Then Lenny and Willy and last the men."

"We don't need a shower," my mother lied smoothly. "All of us bathed yesterday."

Uncle Geoff overheard my mother from across the hall.

"Please don't show your origins," he snapped. "We're covered with dust and sweat. All of us will shower every night before the evening meal. We don't pay for the hot water or walk to the public baths. Come on Lil, there's soap and shower caps on the bureau."

We hesitated to reach for the hotel soap and shower caps. We wanted to squirrel them away and take them home to show them off during the coming year. But Uncle Geoff planted his short legs firmly at our door, hands on hips, eyes green like my mother's but harder than aggies. In my mind I always thought of him as The Ice Man, cold and needing a pick to touch his heart.

Aunt Bea asked Lil, "Where are your children's robes?"

"They'll run across the hall in their underwear," Lil answered.

"Be sure that the underwear is fresh," Geoff barked, and returned to his own suite.

"I can't wait until he leaves," said my mother under her breath.

My father leaned over and tried to tussle her onto the bed. "I'll be gone, too, and what will you do without your hot papa?"

"Jack, the children," my mother protested, suddenly full of propriety.

"What, they don't know their origin?"

We hastened into the Simons' quarters to shower. The Camay soap, tiny hard squares, didn't lather.

Fortunately for me, my mother paid no attention to my choice of dress, the one embroidered by Mrs. Rosinski with the red strawberries across the chest. I was not beautiful, not cuddly like Alice with her blonde, Louise Brooks short bob whose front ends curved upward naturally. No dress could disguise my bony legs, my too-wide mouth, my dusky skin. Still, I had my father's lustrous hair and my brown eyes were flecked with orange. In my new dress I felt important, even without Bubby to praise me.

My mother and I did not resemble each other in any feature. She was easily the prettiest woman in the dining room, with her golden hair, her shapely figure and silk dress. If I had been introduced as my mother's niece, no one would have given it a second thought, or Willy as her nephew. Still, we looked as well as we could; my mother had no need to be ashamed of us.

The dining room, to the left of the stairway, occupied an entire side of the house. An upright piano stood against one wall, which had French doors that led to the veranda. Tables covered with white cloths lined both sides of the room and extended to the far end of the building. Since we had eight in our party we didn't have to share a table.

As we were to learn, this area had once consisted of a formal parlor, a dining room and two bedrooms. When his wife died, Mr. Pankin retired from his construction company in New Haven and moved here, to the country, with his teenage sons, Hal and Maurey. Within months he started to renovate, tearing down walls, adding bathrooms, and finally building new cottages with modern conveniences.

As we entered the dining hall, Hal played some chords on the piano and introduced us, the Roths and the Simons, each by name. Some guests nodded to us, others said, "Good evening."

The young couple studying for the bar exam came in last. They had a table to themselves in front of the French doors. Her brown hair was long and frizzy and she wore a sack dress such as Bubby donned for cooking; I could tell she wasn't wearing a bra. Her not-quite-clean feet were shod in backless clogs, as if she meant to cast them off in a hurry. Her husband or boyfriend—we never discovered which—had sopping-wet hair. We discovered that he customarily jiggled the rusty handle of the outdoor pump, doused his head, and then stepped through the French doors to their table. The fact that water was running down his neck and shirt seemed not to concern them. They held hands across the table, ate in great haste and bolted out as soon as they finished. We could hear their laughter as they hit the dirt road for their nightly walk.

Gabriel Solomon, our sandy-lashed, red-haired, soon-to-be-surgeon waiter, recited the night's menu: salad, broiled salmon, boiled red potatoes, sliced tomatoes and corn on the cob, all served family style. A vast slab of butter lay on a white plate next to baskets of bread—white Wonder bread and buttermilk biscuits, neither of which had ever touched our lips. There was a bottle of Hershey's chocolate syrup in the center of the table, a novelty for Jews who didn't mix dairy foods with meat. "The milk is from the farm's cows," Gabe explained. "It's pasteurized but it doesn't taste like city milk. If you'd like city milk, it will be delivered to you. But try the farm milk. Some guests love it. The children seem to enjoy it with syrup." Gabe paused. "I forgot to ask you, do you want your salad dressed or undressed?" Jack immediately replied, "Undressed of course," and winked.

My mother worried about having fish with rolls and butter. "Fish is dairy," my father pronounced, immediately an expert on Jewish dietary laws. "With meat it's no butter and no milk for the children."

Lil kept fidgeting in her straight-backed chair. "What kind of food is this?" she asked softly. "What do they call it?"

"American," the two men said in unison.

Within minutes Gabe brought us a bowl filled with iceberg lettuce, butter lettuce, red oak lettuce. "These are grown right here, in our own garden. We pick the greens daily. I brought you some oil and vinegar on the side, and a gravy boat of sour cream for the tomatoes. Take a look at these tomatoes." Each one was the size of a small melon, blood red, virtually seedless. Our would-be surgeon sliced them, one-two-three. We had not encountered such tomatoes before. "Beauties, aren't they?" asked Gabe.

Jack held to certain eccentricities in his summer food. Without fail he sprinkled sugar over tomatoes, sugared his melons no matter how ripe and spread his corn with mustard—mustard! A cup filled with lump sugar sat next to the chocolate syrup. He asked for sugar he could pour on his tomatoes. Gabe Solomon replied, "Coming up, sir," and sped into the kitchen. Lil poked into the lettuce bowl. "What is this with red on the ends?"

"Some kind of American lettuce," replied Geoff, as if explaining an anthropological excavation. "I think I'll try my salad with the dressing," he announced. His decision obligated his entire family to do the same; he allowed his wife and children no individual choice. Our parents permitted Willy and me the same freedom we enjoyed in our restaurant.

Willy and I were accustomed to wasting our food. At home, I often added four teaspoons of raspberry jam and four lumps of sugar to my tea and then did not drink it; or asked for chicken and beef and sampled only a bit of each. Since we rarely ate with our parents or dined with them in restaurants, we had no one to define what was appropriate behavior at the table. At our first dinner in Connecticut, Willy poured a great deal of syrup into his milk, stirred it with his spoon, took one sip and pushed the milk aside. I buttered a roll, found it too dry and discarded it. Neither the tomatoes nor the salad interested us.

A small salmon followed the salad. At other tables people oohed and aahed, but we didn't because there was no yellow sauce, no thick smooth Hollandaise, to accompany the fish. The lemon wedges, which everyone else seemed to enjoy squeezing over their salmon, would have been sport for Willy and me but we were afraid of antagonizing Uncle Geoff. Boiled red potatoes hadn't the slightest appeal, but like everyone else, we applauded when the platters of corn appeared—each ear almost a foot long, golden and steamy.

It was impossible for me to finish an entire ear, but I did try and its natural sweetness lingers in memory as one of the best treats I ever had.

The adults at our table ate two each, my father's lathered with mustard. Not knowing whether or not to be embarrassed, I raised my eyes to Lil. She was still struggling over the issue of butter, but finally she capitulated, making swooning noises as she ate her buttered corn. But the real one to watch was Cousin Alice.

Holding an ear of corn firmly between both hands, she ran her teeth along the entire length and swallowed. For once, absorbed in his own gratification, Uncle Geoff did not admonish her, and to her credit, Aunt Bea leaned over and wiped Alice's mouth with a paper napkin after she finished gobbling each row.

Our family found paper napkins unacceptable. In our restaurant, we carelessly threw cloth napkins into the laundry bag after a perfunctory wipe. As his mustardy paper napkins piled up on his plate, Jack laughed. "Roughing it in Colchester," he said.

Ours was the only table with leftover salad, salmon, potatoes. Hal Pankin, who spun as quickly as a top from table to table, landed at ours and asked if we had enjoyed the food.

"Very much," my father answered, "but we're a little tired from the trip. By the way, the corn was sensational."

"And you ate it with mustard?"

"An old European custom."

"My younger brother Maurey is in Europe now. Maybe he came across mustard with corn in France."

"Could be." My father was being charming, his eyes alight with mischief. "By the way, do you have cloth napkins?"

"Always on weekends. But there was a mix-up at the laundry. It sometimes happens."

Terrified, I prayed that my father would not forget himself, wise-off and say, "If it doesn't happen on Orchard Street, why should it happen here?" In full control, he agreed with Hal: "It certainly does."

Hal called out with enthusiasm, "Fresh peach ice cream, made right here from our own peaches and cream." The announcement brought on applause. Hal studied Willy for an instant. His head was scraping his chest. He had been sitting too long, with closed eyes. A kindly woman with red hair left her table and came over to ours, saving us from further scrutiny.

"I'm Estelle Solomon," she said, introducing herself, "Gabe's mother." She laughed courteously. "Actually, I'm Estelle Solomon-Sullivan. My late husband, Ed Solomon, was in law practice with Phil Sullivan and after Ed died of heart disease . . . Anyway, I'm Estelle, and I'm fascinated by the stitchery in this dress."

My mother smiled her appreciation.

"She is your . . ."

"Daughter. She's my daughter."

"I do stitchery as a hobby, and I wondered whether the embroidery is the French loop."

French knots in hair, French labels in coats and dresses, French movie stars Lil comprehended. Not embroidery. She reached for a word that came often from my father's lips, "Possibly."

"I would love to know who embroidered that dress. The stitch is unique."

"It's my grandmother's friend," I offered. "She sews for a living. Not my grandmother, she's a famous chef, but her friend. She has every colored thread, and she sews so quickly, you can hardly watch her fingers. She's from Poland, and she keeps letters from Poland in her embroidery box."

Estelle patted me on the head, "If you find out the name of the stitch will you let me know?" She paused. "I hope your service didn't disappoint you. Gabe and Hal are very distracted tonight. They're expecting their girlfriends."

"Oh?"

"Gabe's girl is prelaw, but Hal's is premed. I'm not sure it's best when both do the same work. I helped in my husband's office two days a week. Now that I'm Mrs. Sullivan, I'm banned from the office."

Since Jack and Lil thrived on sharing talk about fashion, my mother opened her mouth and then closed it. At the piano Hal began to play "The Sweetheart of Sigma Chi," one of my mother's specialties, and almost in a trance she walked to the piano. She began to sing with such purity that everyone stopped to listen.

> *The girl of my dreams / Is the sweetest girl*
> *Of all the girls I know / Each fond caress . . .*

She hummed when she didn't know the next phrase, "fades in the afterglow."

> *And the gold of her hair / And the blue of her eyes . . .*
> *Are ala la la la lah*

Jack saved her. He stood up and in perfect harmony sang:

> *And the moonlight beams / On the girl of my dreams*
> *She's the sweetheart of Sigma Chi.*

The guests clapped. More than for the New England dinner, more than for the corn or the peach ice cream. Then both did an encore, Jack allowing my mother to sing most of the song and humming in the background. Lil was transformed when she sang. She held her hand to her heart as if fearing that it would stop suddenly if she didn't. Her toned-down hair color enhanced her appearance, as did the blue polka-dotted dress that she had bought to flirt with Dr. Scott Wolfson. There were calls for still more singing, but she returned to the table—and from that moment on, my mother owned Pankin's Farm.

After dinner, Aunt Bea and Lil sat on the lawn in rattan chairs and chatted with Estelle Solomon-Sullivan. The young law students returned from their walk and leaped up the stairs to their dormer room in the attic. Bits of grass and hay clung to the girl's legs, arms and hair and the young man's hair was disheveled, the fly of his pants squished over to one side. Jack took one look and asked, "What did they do, boff in the road?"

"Yes," Hal replied matter-of-factly. "After a long day of studying, they eat, take a walk and make love."

"Why not in bed? Why on the hard ground, with God knows what? They must smell like a stable."

"Non disputandem est. Who can argue with taste?"

The sight of the two young lovers had a strange effect on Uncle Geoff; nothing would do but a guided tour of the barn and the surrounding land. But each time a car drove by, Hal would stop and run his hand through his copious hair. In the last rays of the sun I could see his fingers trembling. Even as he talked he seemed to be listening for the car that would bring his beloved.

"When we first moved here," he began, "the place was rustic, circa 1910. My father, Hank, in deep mourning for my mother, couldn't operate the farm. After a while he pulled himself together. There was actually an outhouse here, the first thing to go. Then came central plumbing and heating.

"The land here is very rocky, hard to cultivate. We brought in tons and tons of topsoil and planted corn, which Maurey and I sold in the village to tourists on a day's outing. Every now and again people would drive up and ask if we knew of a room to rent for a night. That's all my father needed to hear. He called his old buddies, builders and contractors, and began remodeling. He loved the idea of summer guests, because during the winter it's pretty quiet, not much to do."

We had a glimpse of the barn. "This is my father's most recent project. He added a whole dormitory upstairs, facing the road." Two tall skinny ladders were propped up against the east wall. "My friends and I like this arrangement because none of the guests or their kids climb up. We study every day from two to four, quiz each other on anatomy or diseases. And we take in some underprivileged children, four at a time from Front Street—you know, it's a bad slum."

Jack nodded. He of the beautiful songbird wife, whose address was theoretically in Yonkers, could nod sagaciously about Front Street as if it didn't exist in the market area close to Fulton Street in downtown Manhattan.

"The Front Street kids have separate quarters below us," Hal continued, "but not this weekend. We tucked them in next to the kitchen because our girls are coming, Gabe's and mine for sure and maybe Ronny's. They're driving from Cambridge."

My father and my uncle exchanged glances.

"I'd like to take a nap in the hayloft sometimes," said Geoff.

Hal raced out because he heard a car, but the vehicle drove on without stopping.

It had grown dark. We were exhausted from the long day. Having dined on a slice of tomato and peach ice cream, I dreamed of my grandmother's Friday night kitchen with its chicken soup, roast chicken with roasted potatoes, the summer fragrance of fresh fruit simmering in cauldrons. I loved this farm: the barn, our sleeping room. But I feared the things I could not mention, our real address, our true lives in New York. The tissue of half-truths or outright lies encircled me. Like a claustrophobic, I had to be on guard every minute. None of these things bothered my parents. They could spin any sort of fiction as easily as breathing.

We went upstairs early, my mother taking each step slowly. Willy fell asleep immediately, as did my mother. I was counting on my insomniac father to stay awake and possibly whisper to me, but he, too, was sleeping soundly. I stared out the window at the yellow light that illuminated the barn. The hotel grew silent. Doors didn't open or close, bathrooms didn't flush. I wondered if this would be one of those nights when I couldn't close my eyes until dawn.

Then a crunch on gravel, and the slamming of a car door. I saw Hal race across the lawn. Two young women literally spilled out of the car. They stumbled to the grass, righted themselves. Gabe and his friend vanished from view, but I could see Hal with his arms around his girl. He lifted her skirt; her underpants were white and clingy. He placed his hand on her behind in a gesture as natural as the ardent kisses they exchanged. Obviously he couldn't wait to get her up the crazy ladder that led to his dorm. He carried her to the barn, leaned her against a wall. She lifted her legs and clasped them around his waist. Like a puppet on a string her head lolled back and forth, forth and back, and Hal, his shorts around his ankles, raised on his toes and lowered as if they were dancing.

I had not seen anyone make love before, let alone in dim light, in the open air, against a barn wall. I could scarcely breathe for the sight of it, the naturalness of it. They seemed to continue forever until her head flopped over Hal's shoulder, and slowly her leg dangled to the ground. Hal lifted her and carried her away.

I fell back on my pillow. How could I write all of this to Bubby? Our home address presented problems for me: 12 Orchard Street. Everyone at the hotel could read it. What if they did?

Experiencing a moment of complete rebellion, in my fantasy I went from table to table in the dining room and declared, "We're from 12 Orchard Street. We have rats in our building and millions of roaches, icicles in the winter and the toilet is in the hall and we bathe in a tin bathtub, and every one of us has an illness, and my Bubby's business is falling apart, and my mother hasn't worked a single day at Saks Fifth even though she wants to, and Mister Elkin left my grandmother, and we had to hock everything we owned in order to come here and we're as poor as the children you take in for charity on Front Street. Only different. Because my mother sings, my father wears hand-tailored jackets, my grandmother's cooking is better than anything here, we flushed the pregnancy down the toilet, and Clayton hasn't come back."

Then the solution to the mail blinded me: I'd walk to the post office every morning. The sentence for the first card flew into my head. "In Connecticut, all the good things are everywhere." Bubby would understand. Having decided what to write and how to mail it, I fell asleep.

13

All the Good Things

THE RATTLING OF our doorknob and the presence of Aunt Bea awakened us. "Breakfast is from 7:30 to 9:30. We're starving."

Jack turned over in bed and murmured, "What the hell is this, getting up with the chickens?"

Both Cousin Alice and Cousin Lenny appeared on the threshold perfectly attired in pressed overalls and white short-sleeved shirts. "I'll take the children down if you want to sleep late," said Bea, then added to Willy and me, "Put on your overalls and don't forget to brush your teeth."

Aunt Bea's bossiness drove me crazy. If Uncle Geoff reminded me of the Ice Man, she was the Ice Pick that chipped away at us. In that sense they were perfectly mated: they thought they knew better than anyone how to behave and what was appropriate for what event. Though it hadn't been that long since Uncle Geoff had left Jefferson Street, a few blocks away from Orchard, he treated us as if we were savages. I had no memory of Uncle Goodman ever being anything but kind and understanding about how we lived and why, but the Simons attacked our social limitations without cease.

From our suitcase I withdrew my overalls and handed Willy's to him. The material was stiff, unyielding, rough. Willy attempted to thrust in one leg and withdrew it immediately. "It scratches. It feels terrible. I can't wear them."

Not fully awake, Lil had one arm over her eyes. "Willy, you'll get used to them. Put them on."

An opportunity like this sent Aunt Bea, who was waiting in the doorway, into the stratosphere. "Lil, didn't you wash the overalls before you packed them? First of all, they have dirt on them from the store and second, the label says, 'Wash at least twice before wearing.'"

Lil rolled over in bed. Jack reached for a cigarette and lit it.

"Who reads labels?" Lil asked and added quickly. "I thought Manya would take care of it."

Jack glowered at Bea. "Why are you making such a tsimmis over a pair of lousy overalls? If I had my way, I'd put a match to them this minute."

Willy began to cry. "I can't wear them."

"Then wear your regular pants. Where is it written that because we're in Connecticut boys have to dress like hicks?"

To avert a further scene, I slipped into mine. The stiff material itched and scratched. I could hardly take a step without being aware of it. I patted the right-hand pocket with confidence. Yes, my dollar was hidden there. Bubby had given it to me before we left. One dollar for me and another for Willy. It was a don't-tell. If our mother suspected we had the money we wouldn't see it again. A dollar each was a lot of money for us. I would wear these overalls from hell if only to protect my fortune.

Willy donned his pants from the night before and we left for breakfast with Aunt Bea. Midway down the stairs I remembered the postcard I meant to write to Bubby, and ran back. Behind the closed door I heard my mother laugh, "Jack, my heart!"

"When I get to your heart I'll stop."

Quickly I turned away.

Neither Hal Pankin nor Gabe Solomon appeared in the dining room. Instead, Margie, the day girl from the next farm, carried in the heavy trays from the kitchen.

Margie could have been fifteen or thirty. She had a broad face and a broad body, stocky, without a defined waist, and the straps of her bra dangled from the armholes of her cotton dress down her muscular arms. "Juice, cereal hot or cold," she recited. "Farina or Rice Krispies or cornflakes. Any style eggs. Soft-boiled is the best, fresh from the farm." She breathed heavily. "Potatoes, too. Best is country fried."

Willy and I rarely ate breakfast, but we especially hated soft-boiled eggs, which my father called "snotty eggs." On Sundays when Bubby cooked dairy, she would sometimes have a request for scrambled eggs. She beat them with her indispensable broken fork until bubbles formed on top, then added a dash of sweet cream and several chunks of cream cheese. She cooked the eggs over a low flame, stirring constantly. The result was a mountain of fluff, creamy, smooth and delectable enough to tempt us. Glancing at Margie's tray, I could bet the scrambled eggs had been mixed in the pan, with the whites separated from the yolks. Cold cereal seemed our best bet.

One minute my parents lounged in bed, the next they were sitting at our table, my mother wearing striped wide-leg pants called daytime pajamas and a matching top. In their haste to join us my father had not slicked back his hair and it fell in its natural wave.

"Daddy, I love your hair."

"For breakfast I decided to go native. Do they have any Danish?"

He repeated this to Margie who stared at him blankly. "Danish pastries," my father said, "with coffee." "Toast is all," she finally replied. "All right," Jack said with authority, "two eggs sunny side up, once over lightly. Country fries."

We didn't drink juice. Why I can't tell you. Maybe because our apartment was too cold; maybe because my father hated pits and Bubby strained the squeezed orange pulp haphazardly. My mother ate sliced oranges midday, often with bread. For breakfast she drank coffee with something sweet from Bubby's oven, or a slice of challah.

Captivated by the individual boxes of cereal that Margie brought to us, we couldn't eat our cornflakes once we poured milk over them. "The milk smells," I said. My father confirmed that milk straight from the cow had a funny taste and smell. The Simon children didn't dare mention country milk, but Uncle Geoff told Margie in his usual stern manner, "City milk for our table from now on."

The preparation of his eggs displeased Jack, but he loved the country fries. As soon as my mother reached for one, he lost his temper. He hated to have anyone eat from his plate. "Don't do that again, Lil," he commanded, but to soften his reproach he quickly ordered fries for the table. Since we had eaten little for dinner and rejected the cold cereal because of the milk, we gobbled up the round, thin, crisp potatoes, eating with our hands, ignoring our uncle's stare of disapproval.

"Do you fry these in butter?" Lil asked Margie.

I could die of embarrassment from Lil's questions.

"Erl," Margie replied. "You can't get 'em crisp from butter." Beads of sweat dotted her upper lip. As she moved her arms the odor of cow's milk emanated from her. Uncle Geoff's nostrils twitched. "Do you help with personal laundry here?" he asked.

"Yes sir, but not on weekends."

"Take care of some overalls when you have time." He slipped a silver coin into her hand.

"Are the chicken and meat kosher?" Lil continued.

"We got a rabbi in Colchester. Everyone comes to him for the kosher stuff," Margie answered.

As soon as I could, I fled. "I have to write to Bubby," I explained, and ran up to our room, pulled out a postcard and scrawled, "I love Conn. The food is not too good. You see all the good things everywhere. Lovelovelove E."

Slipping the card in my overall pocket, I went down the stairs, turned to the rear of the house and slipped out the back door. The trouser legs rubbed against my skin like sandpaper. I walked on the diagonal away from the hotel, climbing down a slight embankment until my Keds hit the dirt road. I craned my neck as I walked, searching for the barn that advertised books without finding it.

I felt lighthearted. It was a relief to be free of my parents and the Simon family, to be away from everyone, even Hal, whom I liked the best. I wondered what it would be like to live here the year-round. I devoured the sky, the greenery, the quiet, and when I walked for over half an hour and came to the village, tears filled my eyes. I couldn't believe the green green lawns, the white storybook buildings. I found the post office and slipped my card into the red-and-blue mailbox.

Relieved, and mildly proud of having put my plan into action, I started back quickly. My unwashed trousers were killing me and I toyed with the idea of taking them off and walking in my underwear.

A car honked. I jumped to one side. The horn sounded again. Hal Pankin leaned out the window of his beat-up dusty truck. "Hey, what are you doing here all by yourself?"

Having seen his bare behind through the yellow light of the barn the night before made me feel close to him. I decided to be as honest as possible.

"I went to mail a postcard."

"I saw you. Hop in."

Easier said than done. A klutz like me couldn't scramble up that high step to the seat beside him. Hal leaped out and lifted me up. "Hey, those overalls are stiff as cardboard."

"They're terrible."

"We'll be home in five minutes. Have Margie rinse them out for you."

"She said she's too busy weekends."

"Yes, we have guests every Saturday, day people who drive up for our Saturday night dinners: fried chicken with honey, and fresh pies. I just ordered two dozen blueberry from Mrs. Eldridge."

I almost said, "That's the name of the street near where we live," but didn't.

"Did you know that we have a country mailbox right outside the hotel?"

"I wanted a walk, and I was looking for the barn that sold books."

"Have you seen our library in the game room? It's not great, but I think we have some Nancy Drews, some Bobbsey Twins."

I didn't mean to laugh out loud but I did.

"Don't you like those books?"

"Aunt Bertha gave us a whole box when I had rheumatic fever. I read all of them three or four times. I read the Hardy Boys out loud to Willy."

He slowed down and put his hand on my bony knee. "You had rheumatic fever? How did you get it?"

"After scarlet fever. Two doctors take care of me, Dr. Koronovsky and Dr. Scott Wolfson." I always said "Scott Wolfson" as if it were one word.

The noisy truck shook on the bumpy dirt road. The stick shift wobbled.

"Have you read *The Secret Garden, Little Lord Fauntleroy*?"

"Yes."

"Do you like *Treasure Island*?"

"No." But Hal wasn't really listening, thinking of something else, concentrating on the old rusty truck.

He yawned. "Your mother sings beautifully. And she's very beautiful. Has she ever been on the stage?"

"I think she sang with the bouncing ball in movies. You know, at the singalongs. She stood near the piano and sang. My father sings, too."

"So you're a musical family?"

"I'm not musical, but Willy is a great whistler. He can whistle anything, even Caruso."

He patted my head. "You're a funny duck," he said.

I waited before asking, "What's your girlfriend's name?"

"Sybil."

"I haven't heard that name before."

"Her mother read it somewhere. Gabe's girl is Susan, Susan Bergen."

Because he was sleepy, he didn't pay attention to the large hole in the road. The truck bumped abruptly and tilted to one side.

He came wide awake, thrusting his arm to keep me from flying out of my seat. "Are you okay? Have you been hurt? Is your heart skipping a beat?"

"I'm fine. Just tired. I didn't sleep much last night. Insomnia."

"Insomnia?"

"You know, hard to fall asleep."

"How come?"

I shrugged. "My grandmother, my father and I, we have trouble falling asleep. But I nap every afternoon."

"You're something else." He ran his index finger over my thin cheeks. "Shall I take your pulse?"

"Because of this little bump? You can if you want to. Dr. Scott Wolfson, he does it all the time."

"Is he a child specialist?"

"I think so. He wants to be a child psychiatrist." I had a trick for remembering that word but Hal didn't ask me about it. Instead, he started up the truck again. "Would you like to be a doctor when you grow up?"

"Never. Too sad. Lots of children die when there's measles or scarlet fever. Now there's polio."

The silence between us grew uncomfortable. Then he asked, "Who takes care of you?" Since I had already mentioned my doctors, I assumed he meant the person in my family.

"My grandmother, she's a chef. When I come home from school, I rest in bed and she brings me all of these wonderful things to eat. Baked goose livers, chestnuts, her own jam on warm kaiser rolls."

"That sounds very cozy, very loving. I'm glad we made it home without having to push this heap of junk. Be sure to take off those hot overalls. Your legs need air. And get some rest before dancing. Dancing is in the dining room, a little exercise before lunch."

I shook my head. "My mother loves to dance. She can dance with Cousin Alice. I think I'll read upstairs."

Instead of searching for a book in the library, I tore upstairs and pulled off the hateful overalls. My legs were covered with a rash. The room was quiet, clean and tidy. A miracle. My main concern was to hide my dollar bill. If I put it in my notebook it might fall out. I pushed the folded bill into one of my socks and fell on my parents' bed. Then nothing.

I don't know how long I had slept when a faint knock on the door brought me awake. Through the slits of my eyes I could see Hal and Gabe. Hal whispered, "She's asleep. Look at the rash on her legs. I don't think we should wake her for lunch."

"Shall I tell her mother?"

"No, I will. Her mother presents heart disease and the girl rheumatic fever. I feel terrible that I stuck them up here."

"Except for the steps it wasn't a mistake. It's quiet, isolated. No one will bother her if she takes a nap every day. I'll bring her some lunch."

"I'll pick out a book for her. She laughed in my face when I suggested the Bobbsey Twins."

"And what did she recommend, *The Collected Papers of Sigmund Freud*?"

"Don't underestimate her. But the family doesn't like our food. The grandmother is a professional chef, European. I guess they like European cooking. The mother, Lil, is the singer. Talented but not maternal."

"And the father?"

"Quick-witted. But the uncle is a pompous ass."

They closed the door. At the moment I didn't know who I loved more, Dr. Scott Wolfson or Hal Pankin. I didn't bother about his girlfriend, Sybil; it no longer mattered what I watched last night, it had nothing to do with me. I fell asleep again.

Possibly an hour later, Margie touched my shoulder. Her face was flushed from galloping up the stairs. Her cotton dress clung to her, and there were small islands of sweat under her armpits and across her bosom. "Dr. Hal says for you to try to eat."

The tray held half of a tuna sandwich and a carton of milk with a straw. Just like the dreck at The Grand Canal Cafeteria.

I didn't venture downstairs for the rest of the afternoon, but my parents and Willy came up at about four o'clock. This turned into my favorite time, all of us together in the big bed, my parents gossiping, relating what each had said and done with the other guests.

Lil had enjoyed talking to Estelle Solomon-Sullivan. Her husband, the hotshot lawyer, didn't come up on weekends—too crowded, too unrestful. "And do you know what, Jack," Lil explained, "on Sunday, he takes the train to New York and he goes to see a matinee, a play, like you. He prefers Sunday afternoon in New York in the summer. Mr. Sullivan, Philip, he loves the air-conditioned theaters or he sees the latest movie. And I said, 'That's what my husband does when he doesn't come up for a visit.' And Estelle said, 'I'm glad we have so much in common.'

"I said, 'My husband loves Talullah Bankhead,' and she answered, 'So does mine, he thinks she is fabulous. He loves her voice. But it's hard to catch her in the summer. She's usually on vacation herself.' And one more thing. Estelle's thinking of going back to teaching. She did that a long time ago. With a grown son who's going to be a doctor she wants to do something with herself." Lil took a deep breath, "Estelle said, 'meaningful.' She wants to do something meaningful. You would think that with a rich husband and a son who's away studying, she would take it easy, but no, she needs meaningful."

"I wonder why she didn't have more children."

"They tried. They couldn't."

As always, my father boasted, "I could make ten children in my sleep."

We laughed. My father's old jokes, his old quips found a welcome audience with us.

I waited a moment before asking, "Did you meet Hal's girlfriend?"

"Shiksa type," my mother said dismissively. That meant no makeup and hair that wasn't waved at the beauty parlor.

Below us we could hear the scraping of furniture on the wooden floors. Jack frowned. "What's the racket?"

"It's for the day people," I explained. "That's what Hal calls them. They drive up for the fried chicken on Saturday night. Then they take a walk or sit around and drive home. Hal told me."

"I hope they don't serve butter with the chicken."

"Mother! At breakfast you asked Margie if the chickens were kosher. Last night you worried about butter and fish."

"The girl is right," said my father. "What are you, some kind of mockie? You're American-born, seen the best plays in New York, interviewed at Saks Fifth. One day in Connecticut, and you're acting like a rabbi's wife."

My mother bit her lip, fussed with her hair. "I don't know. Everything is different here."

"How different?"

"The women. One goes to law school, one wants to do something meaningful."

"If you mean they're not like your dumb bimbo friend Ada, you've got that right."

"Jack, just because of what Ada did when she was fourteen, living with a boy from the streets, doesn't make her a bimbo."

"You shouldn't be mingling with such a low element. The women here, they're like the women you wait on at Palace Fashions. How about Aunt Bertha with her Lilly Daché hats? You fit right in with her."

"Aunt Bertha knows about us. We don't have to put on an act."

"You worry about an act? First off, you're a businesswoman. Second, you could be on Broadway right now if you wanted to."

"In the afternoon they read books, they talk about books." Worry glazed my mother's green eyes. "Connecticut, it's not like Atlantic City."

"Atlantic City is full of New Yorkers, that's why you liked it. But if you're not happy, we'll pack up and go home."

Terrified that we would leave, I cried out, "Everyone loves you. Hal told me you were very talented and asked if you sang on the stage."

"He said that? He meant that?"

My father delivered the punch line. "Lil, you're a knockout. Just remember what your favorite, Mayor Jimmy Walker said, 'No woman was ever seduced by a book.' Forget about those books. Just be yourself."

That night I learned that the acceptance or rejection of food has nothing to do with the meal itself but with the memories that surround it. Never having been anywhere near fried chicken, we heard little else during the day except that a Negro woman from the South who lived in Colchester started to prepare it right after lunch. For the dinner, which attracted dozens of visitors, the med students spruced up with white shirts and black pants. They carried out steaming platters of plump golden chicken with a crunchy skin we could sink our teeth into, along with two sugar holders filled with golden honey to be poured over the chicken. A golden dinner: chicken, honey, corn, cornbread.

My mother behaved herself, didn't ask what the chicken had been fried in, ignored the butter, was silenced by the wonder of the meal, the best we had since our arrival. Like everyone else, we tucked our napkins under our chins. People made humming sounds as they ate, not concealing their appetites. For us, each dish was new, remarkable, impossible to forget.

When we thought we could eat no more, Hal and Gabe rolled in the dessert carts, dozens of blueberry pies with lattice crusts over freshly picked berries, our initial taste of true American pie with an American crust. For years afterward my grandmother tried to duplicate these pies, and didn't succeed. She could perform wonders with yeast, but American flaky crust, not the commercial junk at The Grand Canal, eluded her. Two pies for our table, ice cream optional. Not to be singled out as lacking in American savvy, my mother did not refuse the vanilla ice cream. From that moment on the triumph over ancient dietary laws stayed with her. It would become part of our family's legend, my mother eating blueberry pie with ice cream after chicken.

Dinner over, the road outside the hotel was thronged with guests strolling back and forth, walking off their dinner. The grounds were filled with day people. Those too full to walk fell into the lawn chairs.

Standing on the porch watching the Saturday night spectacle, I felt a tap on my shoulder and a young woman said, "I'm Sybil. Let's talk." She led me to the back of the house, though she had no intention of sitting on the veranda. Instead she lifted two rocking chairs to the ground, to a shaded spot, hidden by a tree. Sybil was slim and muscular and she wore what my father called an ice cream suit, a long white skirt and a short-sleeved white jacket. Her hair, and best feature, was a tangled mass of chestnut brown, and she had lively, inquisitive eyes that darted everywhere, not missing a detail.

"So," she began, "how do you like it here?"

"I love it. I wish I could live in Colchester the whole year."

"But aren't you from New York? Don't you miss it?"

"I hate New York. My parents and grandmother love it. My mother and father, they love the plays, the movies, the musicals. New Yorkers born and bred. That's what my father says."

"Do they ever take you with them to plays?"

"Of course. On Wednesday or Friday, their days off, sometimes they take me with them. And my grandmother and I go to the Yiddish Theater on Second Avenue."

"That's very cosmopolitan, seeing plays in two languages. What do you like the best, comedies or dramas?"

"There's one play in Yiddish about this king with three daughters and he loses his kingdom and two girls are very mean to him, but the third one, well he loves her best, but she dies and then he dies of a broken heart."

"*King Lear*. You see *King Lear* in Yiddish?"

Sybil's arms, slim and suntanned against her white cropped jacket, marked her as "uptown." Her body and face were tense. She went on: "Then why don't you like New York? I would love to live there instead of Cambridge."

"Because it's cold, and I hate the streets in the winter and I can't stand the subway and the crowds."

"Don't you think it would be cold if you lived in Colchester in the winter?"

"Yes, there would be snow, but no slush, no icicles on the windows." I stopped myself. I talked too much.

"You're a funny duck."

"That's what Hal says."

"He told me to speak to you. Said you were nine going on nineteen or maybe ninety."

She began to rock her chair. Her slim fingers clutched the clawlike ends of the chair arms.

"What's your favorite thing to do?" she asked.

"Read."

"Don't you like to swim or play tennis or ride a bike or skate?"

Sybil came from Dr. Scott Wolfson's world with her tennis and swimming.

"Not much," I said neutrally.

"What does your mother think about your reading?"

"She's not too happy about it." For once my fear of betraying my mother evaporated. "When I stayed home because of rheumatic fever, she went to the library for me and picked the same book I just returned."

"Why does it bother her?"

I waited to answer. "Did you meet my cousin Alice? She likes girls like that. My cousin Alice, she's a very good dancer. And Shirley Levine, she wears socks no matter how cold it is in the winter and she's a great skater."

Sybil started to laugh, slowly, then harder. She rocked her chair faster.

"I hate Saturdays at the farm." I heard bitterness in her voice. "Hal won't be done for hours. And we have so little time together."

"It will be quiet when the day visitors leave. My father and uncle drive home tomorrow."

She stopped rocking. "I won't be here tomorrow. I'm leaving at midnight to meet my parents. I promised I'd drive with them to the Cape. You'd like the Vineyard. Everyone reads and swims and there are lots of girls like you, all in shorts, riding bicycles.

"Of course I promised my parents, but if Hal agreed to travel with me to Europe these next two weeks of vacation, my parents would understand. I begged him last night, I begged him. This may be our last chance because of the political situation in Europe. I wanted to see Venice or Florence, just for a short while, and on the boat we could have a honeymoon, but no, he's tied to this farm, to this awful place. Sometimes I think that when he finishes med school he'll come back and practice here."

The encroaching dark provided a cover for my recent fantasy. "Are you going to marry Hal?"

She gained joy from her mockery. "Aren't you the bourgeois?" she said.

My father said that word often, but with a different pronunciation and a different meaning: dumb or stupid or silly. "That's a lot of bush-wah," he'd say.

Sybil's tone cut hard, implying uptown against downtown, my origins.

Perhaps she realized my confusion because she added, "Hal has to finish med school, his internship, his residency, more work for his specialty or research. These types of men are familiar to me. My father is one of them. An oceanographer. He'd stay in Woods Hole forever if my mother didn't complain. But I'm the restless type. I'd like to quit school and travel to Europe before it explodes. Or sail to Alaska or Easter Island. I love Hal but his idea of our future is too confining. My family and I went to Europe every other year in the summer. My father gave lectures there. We loved Austria. But now my father is afraid because of the Nazis. Hal isn't afraid. He just loves the farm too much. But wait until you meet Maurey. You'll fall in love with him. Everyone does."

I sat without moving. Sybil had forgotten me, rocking, rocking. Finally, as the darkness increased, she said, "Good-bye," and disappeared. I never saw her again. Neither did Hal after that night.

We didn't bother with breakfast the following morning. My parents enjoyed sleeping late at home and early rising on their vacation made no sense. Besides, we had consumed twice what we normally ate the night before and food didn't tempt us. While my parents slept Willy and I played Casino and then twenty-one.

For once Aunt Bea didn't come knocking at our door to boss us around. With our parents asleep in the big bed we felt a sense of intimate security. When we tired of playing cards Willy whistled softly, "I Can't Give You Anything But Love," followed by "Tea for Two." I wrote about yesterday's events in my notebook.

It wasn't until noon that we sauntered downstairs and bumped into Hal. If an emotional scene had passed between him and Sybil, he showed no sign of it. "I've been looking for you," he said, laughing. "The Simons left for the lake, but Ron can run you down there if you're interested."

Because of my parents' aversion to water, especially my mother's fear that she would have a heart attack if she moved past the shoreline, we avoided bodies of water from the Atlantic to swimming holes. Uncle Geoff, an accomplished swimmer, liked nothing more than to show off his skills, which he learned in front of open fire hydrants and later in public pools where he could take out his aggressions by whacking other boys on their heads to ensure space for himself. I think we were happy to be rid of the Simons for a few hours. Lil, adorned in shorts and a halter-top created by sewing together two red bandannas, devoted herself to her tan, lying on a chaise. Jack kibitzed with one of the men about the 1929 stock market crash.

During one of his more adventurous periods some years before, my father had bought Philip Morris stock, mostly because of the ads where the uniformed bellhop cried "Call for Philip Morris," rather than for any practical information. His investment may have been three hundred dollars, possibly less, with the rest on margin. But to hear him tell the story he had been wiped out of a "small fortune." On the day of the stock market crash he came home and reported to Bubby, "The Jews took a beating today." Bubby answered, "Never mind the Jews, how did you do, my son?" Jack shook his head. "It was a pogrom. For me, too."

We could repeat every line of that saga but Jack enjoyed retelling it, embellishing the facts and giving the impression that he had lost massive amounts on U.S. Steel, the Lackawanna Railroad, Texaco Oil.

Eager to see that his guests were occupied, Hal suggested to me, "Maybe you'd like to take a walk in the orchard." Willy and I exchanged guilty glances and I flushed. During the period when my mother instructed us to give our address as Orchard Lane, it conjured up visions of the movies we watched of the Deep South. Now I caught my breath. "I'd love to read in the orchard," I said and quickly headed for the library converted from a sun porch.

It had been haphazardly cleaned after the night before, and books lay scattered in disarray. Estelle Solomon was examining a bookshelf as I came in. She wore a yellow-orange sundress that complemented her hair. "I see that some of the guests made off with the more recent books. These are from the year of the flood." She pointed to Charles Dickens's *David Copperfield;* the name and date on the flyleaf read "Elizabeth Morrow, 1910." As soon as Estelle opened the book, yellowing pages fell from the binding. Both of us sneezed.

"Maybe tomorrow I can try the public library. I saw one in the village."

"Tomorrow we'll drive you to the Book Barn. My treat." She regarded me thoughtfully, but didn't call me a "funny duck."

"You're not swimming with your cousins. Where are you off to?"

"A walk in the orchard." I could say the word without hesitation or stammering.

By then Willy had met up with Pudge, a coarse overweight boy from Front Street. They were sitting cross-legged tossing cards on the lawn. I walked slowly past the vegetable garden, the cornfield, the wild field of hay that fed the cows, and finally came to the fruit orchard: trees with tiny green pears, pink, red and yellow apples, rosy peaches. I caught my breath and sat under a pear tree, marveling at its perfect dark green leaves stirring faintly in the breeze.

The sky was luminous. Happiness rose up in me for my great luck in being alone on this day, in this place. It wiped out Orchard Street as if it never existed. I nearly forgot my grandmother. A leaf drifted lazily to my feet. I curled up and without intending to, fell asleep.

When I awoke, I thought of writing a story called "The Tree That Made You Forget," but I didn't have my notebook with me. Overwhelmed with sudden anxiety—suppose my parents worried about my disappearance—I started running away from the trees, through the hay, past the vegetable garden. The farm seemed asleep, becalmed in the summer heat. A glance at the porch revealed my father playing knock rummy with the man from the stock market. My mother was dozing in the shade, like a child, with her thumb touching her lips. Many of the guests had retreated to their rooms to nap.

Pudge, the charity boy, appeared out of nowhere, seized my arm between his fat fingers and dragged me to the ladders against the east wall of the barn. "Up there," he said, "it's a free show."

He hauled me up from one rung to the next as the ladder shook violently. When I looked down I panicked. "Bubby!" I cried out. "Bubby, save me!" It wasn't Bubby who came to rescue me, but a young man: Gabe Solomon.

"Hold on, hold on," he called. Then his arms encircled my skinny body. I cried into his chest as he carefully carried me down. "Don't cry, you're fine, a little afraid of heights." His tenderness, his loving concern, caused me to cry harder.

Gabe called up to Pudge, "What the hell is the big idea?"

"I wanted her to see you fucking. That's what you were doing up there. I was giving her a free show. Fucking, fucking, fucking," Pudge cried out, his moon face delighted by his prank, his fat body like an inflated balloon veering back and forth on the ladder.

The profanity reverberated across the afternoon stillness. Though on firm ground now, I could still feel the shaky ladder beneath me and continued weeping. Gabe carried me to a cool patch behind the barn. "Don't cry, sweetie," he said. No one had called me sweetie before. Even Hal couldn't do better than "funny duck."

Then Gabe jogged back to the ladder and yelled up at Pudge, "Get down here at once. If you don't, I'll come up and drag you down."

"I dare you, I double dare you, you Jewish faggot."

The other med students, who may have been studying or resting in their loft dormitory, swarmed out of their quarters, plucked Pudge from the top of the ladder and began to heave him, heavy as he was, into the air holding tightly to one arm and one leg. "Apologize!" they cried in unison. "Drop dead, you fairies," he answered. They allowed him to catch hold of the ladder and scamper down.

"Pack your stuff," Gabe shouted at him. "Hal will be back from the lake and he'll call your social worker."

I sat behind the barn in the shade where Gabe placed me, and when my heart returned to its normal beat and my head cleared, I realized that I was also in love with Gabe. I loved Dr. Scott Wolfson because he wandered into our lives from another world; I loved Hal because of his energetic concern about me; I loved Gabe because he was gentle and tender. Wouldn't it be wonderful, I thought, to be with a man who called me sweetie, brought me water, bathed my face, and didn't care that back home the phrase "skinny pickle" taunted me.

So I wasn't paying attention to anyone but myself when out of the back door of the barn came Uncle Geoff, standing in the brilliant sunlight buttoning the fly of his pants. He didn't see me, he couldn't see me in the shadows of the tall grass. Margie followed close behind him, scattering hay from her skirt. Her half-opened blouse revealed flesh as soft as goose down and wisps of hay floated from her bosom into the air like feathers. Uncle Geoff strode directly to the main house. Silently, Margie slid into the fields.

When I was sure they had both gone, I ran to find my mother. Neither Willy nor my father were in sight, but I found Lil dozing on the chaise. I cupped my hand over her ear and whispered. "Mother, Mother, Uncle Geoff came out of the barn with Margie. With Margie, Mother, and he was closing his pants."

Lil bestirred herself. The buttons of the thin chaise pad had pressed their shape into her cheek. She didn't bother to sit up. She kept her eyes shut as she said, "Don't be silly. You imagined it."

I recognized the impossibility of her accepting the truth. She always managed by molding reality to her own needs, to the dictates of the moment. She set her face away from me. I shrugged and walked up the porch steps, feeling faint. Too much had happened in a single afternoon and I hadn't had a bite to eat all day. In the kitchen, Belinda, the Negro woman who prepared the fried chicken, was moving about slowly, pitting cherries, soft peaches, soft plums—throwing them in a pot of boiling water. "Hey, girly girl," she said cheerfully, "you want a snack-sickle? You starving?" I nodded.

"How about a juicy plum?" Belinda asked. "Juicy plums goes good this time of day." The plum juice squirted down my chin. She came from behind the table and wiped my chin with a soft rag. "Girly girl, how come you don't have fat on those bones? You come in here any time, I'll fatten you up."

During the short period that I rested in the kitchen, my mother managed to navigate the steps up to our room. When I opened the door, I found her sitting on the bed with my father. "Guilty as sin," he pronounced, "I tell you, he's guilty as sin."

On his bed Willy was studying the pictures in an old *National Geographic*. His eyes didn't meet mine. He must have watched what Pudge did to me in the barn, but he needn't have worried. I wouldn't tell my mother that Willy was too in awe of Pudge himself, too anxious to please his first real friend, to come to my defense. I couldn't betray Willy in his first act of betrayal toward me.

A sharp rap on the door was followed by the appearance of Uncle Geoff. "Jack, can you be ready to leave in half an hour, forty minutes? I thought we'd get an early start."

"Didn't you want to wait until the Sunday traffic calmed down? Don't you want to have a bite to eat?"

For once Geoff studied his shoes instead of issuing orders. "We don't need their dinner and if we're stuck in traffic, at least we'll be in our own beds tonight." He pulled his winning card from his sleeve. "Manya will be glad to see you. You can be home with your mother by midnight."

Jack jumped up and started to throw his shirts into his fake leather suitcase. My uncle said, "As soon as I shower, we'll take off."

Jack didn't bother to shower. He said philosophically, "Guilt is stronger than love." In less than an hour both fathers were gone.

14

The Arrival of Maurey

INVARIABLY LIL SHED a few tears whenever Jack left her; this parting was no different than the others. Like the Gershwin song that began, "I could cry salty tears," she shed a few outside the farm when she acknowledged that Jack would not be returning in the evening.

I was less than three years old when I sat on the dining room table while Bubby fed me chicken soup with noodles, as two ambulance men carried Lil to the hospital because of double pneumonia. The windows were caked with ice; the walls dripped with water; the kitchen oven could not create enough warmth to seep into the bedroom. Dr. Koronovsky had no alternative than to suggest a warm hospital. Jack cried, my mother cried, and Bubby, whose fear and hatred of hospitals had been imprinted on the entire family, busied herself with me rather than walk alongside the ambulance gurney.

But she cried, too, cried until her tears fell into my soup and I asked, "Bubby, is this tear soup?" She stopped feeding me, drew me to her copious breasts and assured me, "It's from cutting onions." Bubby talked about "tear soup" for years, and whenever a financial or health crisis befell us she announced with the little cheer she could muster, "Today we'll have tear soup."

As we entered the dining room in Colchester after my father left, Lil sighed, "I guess we'll have tear soup for dinner." Tear soup would have been an improvement on the Sunday evening dinner: tomato slices and watery cottage cheese, which Margie referred to as spring salad, and bowls of blueberries for dessert. Willy and I ate our berries with sour cream in time-honored Russian fashion, but Aunt Bea regarded sour cream as lower class and poured sweet cream over the berries for Leonard and Alice. Since their father was not present, they let out a howl of protest that the cream smelled funny, followed by a sirenlike sound from Cousin Alice: "I'm hungry, I want a sammich." Her sentiment was repeated throughout the dining room. Gabe had left to return Pudge to Hartford; Hal was cloistered with his father discussing the wisdom of following Sybil to Cape Cod.

Ronny and Sam, two med students who served a different corner of the room than ours, did their best to quell the rebellion, which was made more difficult because several women who had been bidding farewell to their husbands now came late to their tables. Ronny Silver, a nice young man studying internal medicine, called out, "Tuna sandwiches coming up." He and Sam Green ran back into the kitchen, presumably to open cans of tuna.

With reluctance my mother made herself a tomato sandwich on "goyisha" Wonder bread and called it a night. "Good thing Daddy isn't here," she said. "He wouldn't open his mouth for such food."

It took forever for the tuna sandwiches to be brought out, lathered with Hellmann's mayonnaise. Cousin Alice wolfed down her first and grabbed a second. Lil nodded at me. "Want to take a walk? Willy, how about it?"

He had found a cardboard puzzle in the library, a map of the United States, and since it was similar in shape to our game Geography, he said he would rather stay upstairs to work on it. But not before he shot me a pleading glance, afraid that I'd inform my mother about his role as a conspirator with Pudge. "It's a don't-tell," I whispered. His skinny face melted with relief.

My mother, who was wearing her striped pajama outfit, walked briskly with me down the road. Instead of wandering in the direction of the village, we decided on the first left, a deserted patch of road where we wouldn't be bothered by cars leaving for their city homes on Sunday night. My mother hooked her arm in mine and leaned against me.

In New York, when we walked to Ada's on blustery days, my mother "crossed me over," that is, she held my hand as we crossed the busy intersection. On occasion, I walked beside her when we went window-shopping, but she didn't loop her arm with mine or allow me to lean close to her body.

"Did you ever eat such dreck in your life?" she exclaimed. "We haven't had soup once. The fried chicken I could go for right now."

"Maybe they think it's a health farm where people try to lose weight."

"Where do you read such things?"

I didn't answer because just then we spied a dilapidated farm, the slats of the gate broken, the grass wheat-colored and uncut. A swarm of children was running about, six or seven of them, their mouths purple either from berries or grape jam, their blond hair filthy, their undershirts torn and too short to cover their belly buttons. As we watched, two little boys peed against a tree, then one squatted to do number two. A boy no older than three, with long whitish hair, danced on the edge of the tumbledown porch, pulling on his penis. Simultaneously, he jutted his pelvis forward and screamed "ahhh." The older girls yelled, "Ma, he's doing it again! He's doing it again!" No adult voice responded.

"Maybe the mother is Mary the Sugar Bum, drunk—the charity case Estelle told me about," my mother said. "Her husband's a fisherman. He comes once a year, gets her pregnant and then leaves. The county supports her. Mr. Pankin gives her leftover food. But the children, what a shanda! That little boy, playing with his birdie in public. Let him go in the bushes and play with his birdie all day long, who would care? But no, the mother doesn't teach him that much."

When we rounded a turn in the road, we glimpsed a half-destroyed hammock, its seat a mass of loose strings, the ropes attached to the trees frayed and in danger of throwing the occupant to the ground. We caught a side view of the mother, swinging slowly back and forth.

"What is she dreaming of?" my mother asked.

"Maybe her husband."

"That's it! She's dreaming of her husband's brand." Lil resorted to this phrase often. "She likes his brand," she'd remark, as if sex were a product like Palmolive or Lux, something you could buy from a shelf. "She likes his brand, so she lets him make her pregnant and she doesn't care what the children do."

We walked on leisurely, the sun at our backs. My mother's arm in mine was golden, relaxed. I marveled at her gleaming hair that hung down to her shoulders, the face without makeup, those incredible green eyes. I didn't envy her good looks as much as admire them. I knew Lil wasn't motherly; I accepted that she had little understanding of her children, but she emanated a light, like a full moon that draws the tide, like a remote but heart-stopping falling star. She cleared her throat. "What I wanted to speak about is . . . what you saw with Uncle Geoff, that's a don't-tell."

"Who would I tell? Cousin Alice? She's a moe-ron." I pronounced it the same way my uncle did.

"Don't be silly, a moron has spit coming from his mouth. Alice has a good appetite. She's a terrific dancer. She doesn't say much, it doesn't make her a moron. Anyway, don't tell Aunt Bea. Don't tell anyone."

"Daddy will tell Bubby."

"Bubby knows and hears everything. She won't tell. Besides, that's how men are. What does Daddy call it?"

"The double standard."

"That's right. One rule for men, the other for women."

"Yes, but the men are doing it with women."

My mother stopped. "That's what Estelle Solomon said. She doesn't believe in the double standard because the men are having affairs with women. So both are cheating."

At the last fork in the road we reversed our steps.

"I don't believe in the double standard either," I said.

My mother's mouth fell open. "What are you talking about? No matter what Uncle Geoff does, he provides a wonderful life for Bea and the children. They have a car, a beautiful home with upstairs and downstairs, nice clothes, vacations. Aunt Bea graduated high school as a bookkeeper, but she didn't have to work, not once from the age of seventeen, the day she married."

My silence confounded my mother. We walked three or four minutes without exchanging a word.

"So how come you're not saying anything?"

"I would hate Aunt Bea's life. You live on Orchard Street but you have a better life."

"How can you say that? I would love Aunt Bea's life."

"You wouldn't. You'd be crying all the time, because everyone is afraid of Uncle Geoff, and you're not afraid of Daddy. Daddy doesn't give you a house and a car, but he's proud of you. He loves the way you sing, the way you look. He told Rocco a hundred times about your interview at Saks. Uncle Geoff treats Aunt Bea worse than a pushcart peddler."

My mother dropped my arm. "How can you say such things? How can you think such things?"

I studied those innocent green eyes. Lil had acquired some street smarts. She could charm men. Yet, standing under the summer sky, in a golden universe, my mother appeared childlike.

"Do you know what Sybil told me, Hal's girlfriend?" I replied. "That she wants to live in Italy, see the world before there's a war, that she hates Colchester and Hal loves this farm too much."

"What has that to do with Aunt Bea and Uncle Geoff?"

"Uncle Geoff won't let Aunt Bea think for herself or say such things."

The farm loomed ahead of us. Unexpectedly Lil announced, "Estelle says you're unusual. Is that good or bad?"

"Does she mean unusual like smart or unusual like looney tunes?"

"Not looney tunes."

We laughed together. When we got back we found many of the guests in the dining room area listening to the Sunday night radio shows—reruns of Eddie Cantor at the moment. My mother joined them. I went upstairs immediately, homesick for Bubby yet torn with longing to live here forever.

I loved the farm on Monday, not merely our first one there, but every Monday that followed. A quiet descended, a calm that I couldn't experience anywhere else, not even in Yonkers.

Some of the guests left with their husbands. Some women busied themselves with hand laundry and took turns at the iron in the laundry room next to the kitchen. Standing midlawn, I listened to the swaying of the leaves, the quiet hum of the bees, and shared the sense of laziness that descended on the farmhouse.

My notoriously thrifty mother washed and rinsed our overalls in the laundry room, scrubbing them on an old-fashioned washboard with a corrugated metal surface. Uncle Geoff had tipped Margie in more ways than one, and she attended to the Simons' clothes in an old washing machine cranked by hand. My mother enjoyed hanging our clothes, a lot easier here than when she was a little girl balancing herself on the roof to help her mother with wet sheets and bushels of diapers.

We found Estelle Solomon on the shaded porch in her sundress, leaning forward, listening intently for the car that would bring her husband, Philip Sullivan, and her son, Gabe, back to her. Having deposited Pudge in Hartford, Gabe had driven on to New Haven and stayed at the apartment of his mother and stepfather. Estelle wasn't a beauty—you wouldn't notice her in a crowd except for her red hair—but her expectancy made her appear girlish. When the Buick with her husband and son chugged over the potholes she ran down the steps of the porch rippling with laughter.

Phil Sullivan reminded me of Orloff: short, thick-chested, bald. He carried a briefcase and wore a seersucker suit, a white starched shirt, no tie. His navy blue tennis shoes were his only concession to country living.

Estelle kissed him gently on the mouth and asked, "You didn't bring your work, did you?"

He winked affectionately. "Just the Sunday *Times* and a few back issues of the *Wall Street Journal*."

Gabe unfurled himself from the wheel of the car. "Breakfast on your terrace or in your room?"

"Terrace," Estelle answered and she and her husband walked arm and arm to the new cottages. Gabe parked the car, but before racing toward the kitchen, he called, "Hey, sweetie pie, did you miss me?"

I nodded my head but he disappeared quickly, to return in a few minutes with a tray laden with a pot of coffee, scrambled eggs, toast and a fresh jar of orange marmalade Phil had brought with him. The last glimpse I had of the Solomon-Sullivan couple was at the table on their terrace. After breakfast, they went inside their room and weren't seen again until he left before dark that night.

As if reading my thoughts, Hal appeared and explained, "They read the whole Sunday *Times* down to the crossword puzzle, then take long naps."

I hadn't caught a glimpse of him since noon yesterday. Obviously he had decided not to follow Sybil to Cape Cod. I had been afraid to ask. "I spoke to your mother," he smiled, "and she's fine about our going to the Book Barn. I'll bring the truck around."

"I hate that truck," I said.

"Good for you. It's one of the things Hank and I discussed last night. We're ordering a new one today. We thought we'd wait until Maurey came back because here it's one-man-one-vote on everything dealing with the farm. But it would be a nice surprise if we picked Maurey up in a new truck, with all the extras."

"May I run upstairs for a minute?"

"Don't run, walk."

But run I did. For my dollar hidden in my sock. Hal lifted me into the front seat.

"You'll love this barn. Wait until you see it. People come from every part of the country to browse there. It has thousands and thousands of books. Jenkins the younger spends his time at book auctions; Jenkins the elder minds the store. The place is old and musty. Anyone can take junk from the stall marked 'free books.' When Jenkins the elder buys an estate, he gets junk with the good stuff."

The vast Book Barn smelled of ancient pages and bindings, the floorboards creaked. Neither Jenkins was in sight, but young men with uncut hair and bare feet sat around in chairs, some reading, some taking notes, glancing up every now and again. Signs, freshly painted, or dim, read Best Sellers, Children's, Junior Adult, Foreign Language, followed by specific subjects, Africa to Sanskrit. Books ranged from First Editions to Out of Print. At the head of the stairs, an arrow on the wall led to "Rare Books: ask for key." The peaked roof was at least four stories high, and the aisles of books covered a space several times as large as the public library on East Broadway. Hal brought me up to one of the young men who sat reading. "We'd like to start an account for this young lady with a deposit of five dollars."

"I have a dollar. My grandmother gave it to me for spending money."

"Put your money away." Hal's hair fell over his eyes and he tossed it back. "This is from me and Gabe and Estelle. We want you to have an account here."

"But five dollars . . ." I didn't finish my sentence. My parents gave five dollars for a bar mitzvah or an anniversary present. It bought more than two tickets for a Broadway show. My mother sweated over an old washboard in order to save a quarter by washing our clothes herself, and Hal proposed a five-dollar gift at a bookstore. I would have been content to read the free books or to buy some at a dime each. What were they thinking?

"We want to do this for our one and only child reader. If you don't spend it during the next few weeks, you can buy some books and have them sent home or keep the money in your account for next year."

I hesitated, red-faced, remembering a writer from the *Forward* who remarked to Bubby, "Manya, you're a great giver. You give away everything. But you have to learn to accept presents graciously." He had bought a carving knife with a fake ivory handle as a gift. Thinking of his words I said, "I accept, but only for half the money."

"Done," Hal laughed. "Two-fifty it is, you funny duck." He guided me away from the free books and within a few minutes he selected Charles Dickens's *Great Expectations* and Charlotte Brontë's *Jane Eyre*.

"These are for tenth graders," Hal said, "but the reading isn't hard and they will keep you busy for days."

I could see myself rereading them on cold winter afternoons in my parents' bed with Bubby hovering over me, bringing in warm kaiser rolls filled with her strawberry jam.

Back in the truck hugging my two books in my lap, I asked shyly, "Why did you pick these two books?"

"I love those crazy English names. Like Pip and Miss Havisham in *Great Expectations*. And the women are named for the months of the year, March, April, May and August. Or Fiona. I love that name. Have you ever met a Fiona?"

"I met a Sybil." My face reddened.

"Don't worry about mentioning her name. I struggled for hours last night, trying to decide whether to follow her, race off to Europe, live a more unstructured life. But it's not me. It's not what I want. Sybil deserves her adventures. I'm not the type. She's right when she says I'd like to practice medicine here. Why not? Hank would love it."

And so would I. To change the subject I asked, "What's your father's real name?"

"You mean his original name? Herbert. He hated it. Hated Herb and Herbie. He thought Hank sounded more manly."

The truck shook, trembled, stuttered over the slightest bump in the road. We headed for the village. "What's your father's original name?" he asked.

"Abraham."

"Abraham Jacob? Is that where the Jack comes from?"

"No, he heard it in the street when he was a little boy. He's been Jack ever since."

"And your Uncle Geoff?"

"I don't know. All my mother's brothers have different names. My Uncle Jack liked my father's name so he took it for himself. Cousin Alice, she has two Uncle Jacks, my father, Jack Roth, and Jack Simon. There's also two Roberts. Only my Uncle Abe, he never changed his name."

"And your mother, Lil, is she really Lillian?"

"Oh, no! Something horrible like Gussie or Tessie, something she hated. At the store where she works they call her 'Miss Lilyan,' with a *y* in it."

We approached the main street when the postmaster, with a watermelon stomach and a thatch of white hair, waved an envelope and cried out, "It's a Western Union, from Maurey. He'll be here Wednesday."

The truck stopped on a dime. Hal leaped out and tore open the telegram. "Arriving Wednesday. Can't wait. Love Maurey."

Hal seemed to forget our reason for being in the village. He reversed the truck and gunned the engine. "This truck is held together with spit. What a relief to buy a new one tomorrow." We zoomed back to the farm, the books bouncing in my lap, Hal bouncing up against the small head space.

"Has Willy ever shown dislike for you?" he asked.

"Willy?" The question startled me. "Why should he?"

"Because you are everything he's not. I used to feel that way about Maurey," Hal replied. "My mother's favorite, good to look at, a born charmer. He rarely studied and got A's. Everyone adored him, he didn't have to work at it. He's a natural. Do you know what that means?"

The truck stopped dead, as if it was incapable of moving another foot. Hal jumped out and pulled me with him, racing up the steps of the porch. "Dad," he called. "Dad, a telegram from Maurey. He'll be home tomorrow." Father and son escaped into the kitchen.

My one desire was to start reading one of my books in the fruit orchard, but my mother stopped me. "Daddy will be calling soon. He and Bubby want to speak to you." This reminded me that I hadn't written to Dr. Wolfson. I galloped up the steps quickly and pulled a postcard from my notebook.

Dear Dr. Scott Wolfson
There's a big barn that sells books, I got C.
Dickens and C. Brontë. Both of their names
start with C. See? Love it here and you too. E.

I wished my handwriting was tiny and neat. Postcards were too small for me. I had forgotten to tell him how healthy I felt. I wrote his name and address at the hospital neatly and was debating writing him a second card when the door burst open. Hal lifted me under one arm and carried me down the stairs.

"It's your dad. Lil is speaking to him on the phone in the library, but you can talk to him on the extension in the kitchen." Extension. A foreign word to me. Hal lifted me onto a stool and handed me the receiver attached to the kitchen wall. Everyone in my family except Jack screamed when we spoke into the phone, but especially for long distance, I heard my mother, a few rooms away positively shouting. "So where is Farber going, where, where?"

"To the Catskills for the weekend. Mister Big Shot, he's taking his wife for three days and I have to open and close Saturday and Sunday. God knows if a single customer will walk in, it's hot enough to fry an egg on the sidewalk. I have to do it and besides on Friday Dr. Wolfson is taking Manya to a kidney specialist."

Dread flooded me. Bubby was a *shtarka* from Odessa. How was she capable of having a serious illness?

"Maybe it's nothing. Maybe she needs less salt in her diet," Jack tried to convince himself and Lil. "So I won't be coming this weekend. Geoff is driving up. The following week I'm bringing Manya with me. Geoff said it would be fine."

"Where's Bubby?" I shouted.

"Mine shayna kind," she crooned, and I tried not to cry but I did. "Vayn nisht. I'm coming soon. You'll tell me everything." I heard her smack her lips to send me a kiss.

"We miss and love you!" I yelled. Jack hung up.

My mother put my hand to her heart when we met in the lobby. It raced like a horse at Belmont Park. "Let's go upstairs and rest." Willy had not spoken into the phone, nor did he expect to. He enjoyed staying in the room during the afternoon.

We were resting there when Hal knocked and poked his head in. "I forgot to mention that Monday is movie night. Want to go?"

"Of course," Lil trilled.

"Dinner is a half hour earlier because I'm treating everyone to a soda before the movie. And you," he laughed pointing to me, "get to ride in the rumble seat. Have you finished reading a hundred pages by now?"

We could hear his laughter as he bounced downstairs.

In my notebook I started a list of new words I learned since coming to Connecticut. Some I spelled perfectly, others I wrote as they sounded: med school, bah eggzam, eggstenshun phone, Ford rummel seat, black and white: chocolate soda with vanella ice cream.

The last two I added when we returned from the movies. Lil loved Kay Francis, her hair parted in the middle, her height, her glamorous clothes. But she hated the end of the picture. Instead of choosing her stage producer who lived in a penthouse and wanted to take her around the world, Kay Francis renounced her career as an actress and returned to her secret husband, in jail for holding up a store when they were poor.

Still absorbed in the movie, Lil was startled when Aunt Bea turned on her once we entered our rooms.

She stood in our doorway, legs wide apart, and glowered at us. "The end of the movie was true to life," she announced in her no-nonsense manner. "A woman is married, she stays married. That's the way it should be."

Lil shrugged her shoulders. "I would pick the producer. He had everything. Money, a British accent, beautiful clothes. He would give her anything she wanted."

"Do you mean that you would leave Jack for a man like the producer in the movie?"

Lil replied, "My Jack *is* the producer."

The answer infuriated Aunt Bea. I saw her face swell with rage.

"What are you talking about? Jack plays the horses. He spends his money on good times. You'll stay on Orchard Street forever."

"What are you talking about? Always the same thing, Orchard Street, Orchard Street. Jack has the best taste. He's six feet tall, taller than any of my brothers. And he's so smart. Tell me one person you know that's smarter." There was a brief pause when Lil ran out of words. "And anyway, why are you so excited about a silly movie?"

"Because I don't want my Alice to be treated like an orphan."

"What? What are you talking about?"

"Why didn't Hal buy Alice a book today?"

"Buy Alice a book?" Lil choked on her laughter. "I know Alice since she was born and not once did I see her with a book. Besides, you would have to be crazy to want a daughter who reads and maybe needs glasses, and doesn't go in the street because she is reading."

"Alice likes to look at the pictures. And that's not the point, it's the principle of the thing." Bea stormed into her room, shooting arrows at us with her eyes.

It didn't help matters the next morning when Estelle Solomon-Sullivan came over and sat with us at breakfast. "I feel so blue since Phil left yesterday," she confided. "I really wanted to pack up and go home with him, but it's not much longer to Labor Day and I should stay with my son. Once school starts Gabe is either in classes or at the hospital and when he comes home he sleeps and sleeps. So I decided to be here with him." She attempted a smile. "He's off with Hal to New London to pick up the new truck and tomorrow everything will be crazy getting the farm ready for Maurey."

She placed her hand on Lil's arm. "Lil, I hope we see each other in New York. I take the train there two or three times a year. Wouldn't it be lovely to have lunch together?"

It was more than Aunt Bea could endure. Like a frog, her face puffed up to the point of bursting. My mother and I exchanged uneasy grimaces. Suppose Aunt Bea blurted out, "Be sure to call them on Orchard Street and not in Yonkers."

Orchard Street! Why had it become such a problem? In Atlantic City or Long Branch when other vacationers asked where we lived, we answered, "New York City," or Jack diverted them with an anecdote. No one cared that much about us to ask detailed questions. Here in Connecticut, though, we established immediate friendships. Hal had only to sweep his hair from his eyes and call me "funny duck" for my heart to quicken. Gabe asked, "How's my sweetie?" and I blushed. As for Estelle, I could tell her my deepest secrets and not be afraid. Yet I couldn't confess to her that we came from Orchard Street. The entire family, with our uncle reminding us not to show our origins, had created a Yonkers identity for us. We had no power to destroy it and I was on edge lest Aunt Bea in a fit of rage reveal our secret.

But her anger soon evaporated. The mail arrived early and a letter from her husband pleased her. She called, "Lil, can I see you for a minute?" Lil went to her on the porch. I followed.

"Geoff is coming for the weekend and he'd like Lenny and Alice to sleep in your room Friday and Saturday. He wants us to have privacy. You won't mind, will you?"

"Of course not, it's no trouble. The girls and I will sleep in the big bed and the boys on the cots."

Because of Aunt Bea's abrupt change in mood, I couldn't withhold the words that flew out of my mouth. "Did he have a fight with his steady girlfriend?" I asked Lil. "Is that why he wants his children in our room?"

My mother's outburst was swift and went for my jugular. "What are you, an old lady, maybe fifty years old? What did I do to deserve this?"

I backed off, shivered slightly, then left on a run, carrying my notebook and *Jane Eyre,* sprinting past the vegetable garden and cornfields to the fruit trees. Once I started to read I forgot everything except the story—the orphaned child, the mean auntie, the dreadful boarding school. Nor was I aware of hunger, thirst, or of the time of day. The grass rustled; I didn't lift my head.

"Hey, you funny duck. I thought I'd find you here. You skipped lunch. We called and called. You didn't hear us."

It took me a minute to shift from Jane Eyre's sad, bitter, lonely existence to the beauty of Hal's suntanned face, to his muscular legs in his shorts, to the floppy hair that I ached to touch. Emerging from the book was like coming out of an intense, complicated dream into daylight.

"Come see the new truck," he said. "It's like a piece of sculpture, a Ford and a beauty. Shiny black. You'll love it."

We came from a family that had little connection to cars. Uncle Geoff owned one and of course so did Uncle Goodman, and John, the handyman for Uncle Goodman, drove a truck, but I couldn't tell its name or year. When my father remarked on the subway or in the street that "it's a Ford," he meant that a woman wore a coat or dress that had been copied from an original and reproduced so often that you saw the same style on dozens of women. To me a Ford meant a garment, not a car.

By now, everyone at the hotel had gathered to survey the new truck, parked in front of the barn. Estelle climbed up, put the key into the ignition and maneuvered the wheel. "It handles beautifully. Better than my own Buick."

Estelle was the first woman we knew who drove a car. Aunt Bertha hadn't bothered to learn.

With his father in the passenger seat, Hal maneuvered the new truck into the garage. We watched as Hank leaned over, hugged his son and kissed him on the lips before tousling his hair. I had to turn aside. That gesture of love came from my fantasy.

On Tuesday after dinner, guests played bingo. Children were allowed to play but I sat next to Lil and helped her. She had forgotten her outburst at me—one of the best characteristics of our family was not to stay mad for more than the batting of an eye. Lil wanted desperately to win—not a good card player, she found bingo to be her style. But in the first round Aunt Bea won.

Her prize consisted of five picture postcards with Colchester in script printed across four of the views: the village square, the lake at sunset, cornfields under a blazing sun and the fruit trees. Aunt Bea, ecstatic with her prize, didn't offer us a single card. No doubt the postcards made up for the imagined slight to Alice at the Book Barn.

During the games and in honor of Maurey's arrival the med students soaked the front lawn with hoses, washed the chairs and hosed the entire veranda. Margie began her sweaty task of oiling the floor of the lobby, the banisters and the steep steps.

None of us could sleep late the next morning. Several youths with rusty lawn mowers shaved the grass, up one lane, down the next. Two women from the village scoured the kitchen while the med students Bon Amied the French doors and windows in a spirit of high fun and low humor. The laundry room was off-limits—Mr. Pankin didn't want drying laundry fluttering like flags when Maurey walked by.

Cousin Alice waved one of the postcards her mother had won at bingo the night before, fluttering it like a fan. Much as I wanted one of those cards to send to Bubby, I suggested, "Why don't you write that card to your father?" She stared at me blankly. "With words on it," I explained. "Like 'Dear Dad, How are you?'" Alice communicated with her mother by cupping her hand to Aunt Bea's ear and whispering. Aunt Bea rummaged through her purse for a discarded envelope. "Practice on this first," she instructed.

Watching Alice write was like seeing some aged horse pulling a wagon too heavy for its creaky bones: you expected it to drop to the sidewalk foaming at the mouth. She covered most of the writing space on the card with the salutation and half of the first line. The pencil fell from her sweaty fingers, and the exertion reddened her face and throat.

Alice burst into tears. "There's no room," she cried.

She ran to her mother, sobbing, just as a yellow taxi drew up to the hotel. Its occupant leaped out. "I'm home!" he called. "It's Maurey!"

Hal and his father burst onto the porch. Maurey embraced both men for an instant before kissing his father on the lips, on both cheeks, on the lips again. Then he reached for his brother and did the same, lips, both cheeks, close body hugs. "It's so great to be back, to be home!"

Maurey, very tall, very slim, wore his streaked blond hair long, curling at his shoulders. When the *New York Daily Mirror* ran the novel *Ivanhoe,* by Sir Walter Scott, as a comic strip, Willy cut it out every day and pasted it in one of his ledgers until he had the complete story. That's what came to my mind at first sight of the youngest Pankin, with his pageboy hair and strong, suntanned arms.

Jack kissed Manya daily, sometimes on the cheek, often on the mouth, particularly when he needed a lucky omen as he left to bet a horse at Rocco's. The kisses Maurey bestowed on his father and brother were different, grown-up, stemming from joy at his homecoming. Neither Lil nor I had ever witnessed an outpouring of affection mingled with happiness like this. "Sunny, darling Sunny," Hank

Pankin murmured. Later he explained, "The name is not S-O-N-N-Y but Sunny, for the sun he brings to us."

At that moment, Estelle came out of the cottage and she and Maurey locked eyes. He did not dash down the steps—he placed one hand on the railing of the porch, vaulted clear of the house and ran to Estelle.

He was wearing tan pants and a blue button-down shirt, with a striped tie in red, gray and blue stripes. He didn't run, he flew, and he picked up Estelle in the yellow-orange sundress and whirled her around, crying, "My dearest heart, my darling love." He spun her at a dizzying rate, doing some crazy step, covering the lawn with his feverish antics. Their clothes melted together like multicolored Popsicles, with blue yellow orange red swirling together.

"Maurey," Estelle cried out, "I'm going to faint." His long blond hair fanned out. "Great it was this dawn to be alive," he shouted, "but to faint with Maurey is heaven." He fell to the ground, Estelle with him. Breathless.

Estelle rested; Maurey jumped up. "I have a present from Paris, from Chanel, just for you." Dr. Koronovsky's comb to Bubby came from Cartier's. To us Chanel created suits and perfume. We were now to learn differently.

Leaping to his suitcase, Maurey tumbled his clothes until he found a flat box wrapped in white, silky paper bordered in black. It had a red double intertwined *C* in the middle, for Coco Chanel. "Wait until you see what I have for you," he cried as he ripped the paper from the box. He tossed the box aside, and held aloft a long scarf in a dark brown and dark orange abstract design banded by gold thread. In the center was the double *C* in glittering satin.

Maurey placed the scarf over Estelle's red hair, then around her slim shoulders. "How do you like it, dearest dearest heart?"

"Maurey," she replied, "you're incorrigible."

The scarf didn't ignite desire in me; the wrapping paper did. I needed that paper more than any gift from Paris, more than the maroon box with Bubby's comb from Cartier's. It was a strange obsession, this need for paper to write on other than wrinkled paper bags, my desire for notebooks without bits of wood pulp to mar the smoothness of the writing. I longed for picture postcards, sheets of Uncle Goodman's company stationery, the clear side of engraved invitations from weddings.

Pretending to tidy the lawn, I crept along the grass and began to harvest the wrapping paper. Maurey smiled at me. His eyes were azure blue—I recognized the color because Jack had taught me the names of every shade of blue. Since I was my parents' daughter I tried to think of a movie star whom he resembled, but he was an original. "You're a dear girl," he called out to me—not a funny duck, not a sweetie pie, but a dear girl—as I smoothed the wrapping paper with my hands and with shaky legs walked to the porch.

I didn't want to appear obvious, to rush up the stairs with my treasure. Before I could sidle up to my room, Maurey finished his shower in Estelle's cottage and emerged with a towel wound around his waist, his long wet hair dripping in rivulets across his suntanned back. From the instant Maurey appeared, Lil's eyes followed him. Without the slightest bit of self-consciousness, he crossed to the barn and started to climb the ladder to the med students' dorm. "Dad," he called out, "any chance for Belinda to cook some fried chicken for tonight? And I'll nap in the loft instead of the cottage."

"Of course, Sunny, of course. I'll pick her up in the truck."

Maurey stepped through the door of the loft. "Where's Gabe?" he called, sticking out his wet blond head. "I forgot to kiss him."

As Estelle crossed the lawn, she waved to Lil and said, "Maurey, he's the freest person in the world."

Slowly I ascended the steps, heaved a sigh at being safe in our room and turned the white jagged pieces of Chanel paper over and over as if they could radiate sparks like diamonds. Then, carefully, I put them in my suitcase. I kept those scraps for many years, until they began to disintegrate.

15

A Fearful Week

FROM MY UPSTAIRS window at the farm, I watched the grass and leaves, the bushes and the top of the barn blacken under the beating rain. A streak of lightning scratched the sky; the thunder shook the house and subsided. Lil was writing to Ada in her large, childlike handwriting. Willy had dozed off and my mother whispered, as she handed me the note, "This is what I have so far."

"Dear Ada, this is not such a hick place. The waiters are young doctors. The food is terrible accept for sat. nite. Not much to do. Having a good rest."

"What else?" she asked me. "Anything else? Shall I tell her Bubby and Jack are coming next week?"

"No, suppose she wants to come along?"

"To a farm?"

"For the young doctors."

Lil studied her nails. Anxious to give herself a manicure, she had heeded Dr. Scott Wolfson's warning that nail polish remover could start an asthma attack in Willy and had colored her nails outside, on the porch. "Should I cross out the sentence about the doctors?" she asked.

"You have to recopy the letter. Ada will figure out that the crossed-out sentence was important. Just end it with 'See you soon.' "

Lil wrinkled her brow. "If she reads about the doctors, she'll be jealous. Men are the only thing she cares about."

This did not come as news to me. When Jack and Lil quarreled over some nonsense, he always called Ada a "who-a."

My mother busied herself copying the letter, to which she received no reply.

Fried chicken, prepared at Maurey's request, was our pleasure in the evening, but none of the waiters appeared. Mr. Pankin and Margie waited on tables. The rain stopped. My mother urged me to walk with her. The roads were soft rather than muddy. She linked her arm in mine.

"Let's play 'Favorites,' " she said.

We sauntered past the dilapidated house with its neglected blond children and realized the grounds were deserted. The front door banged open and shut in the evening breeze. The fence more gap-toothed than ever and the tall dry wheat-colored stalks had taken some battering in the recent storm. Not a child was in sight.

"Maybe for once they went on a pitnic," Lil said. She used the New York pronunciation that put a *t* instead of a *c* in the middle.

"Maybe their father is visiting and the whole family is in Middletown."

"Maybe they moved. Got tired of this dump and moved." Lil stepped carefully over a soft, waterlogged rut in the road. "So are we playing 'Favorites' or not?"

"Favorites" was a simple child's game where you had to name your favorite color, first name or movie star. One player was the caller, who yelled out one two three four five six seven; you had only seven seconds to answer or else you were "out." No color or name could be repeated, and when it came to rivers or states or names of presidents we usually collapsed. But we were quick to respond to movie stars, popular songs or movies.

Lil did not have our ordinary categories in mind. "Favorite person," she suggested. "Who's Bubby's favorite?"

"Daddy," I answered cautiously. "Jack, her son, is Bubby's favorite."

"Photo finish," Lil replied gaily. "Who else is her favorite?"

"Me and Willy."

"No, just you. Daddy and you."

She bubbled with excitement. I could see the pulse in her wrist beat against her thin skin.

"Aunt Bea."

Without hesitation, "Cousin Alice."

"More than Geoffy? You should have seen them when they were going steady. Bea lost ten pounds just from hugging and kissing. She couldn't rest. She couldn't eat. I say it's Geoffy."

"Does that mean I'm out?"

"A few more, a few more." She wore last year's blue sailor pants and a blue-and-white knitted top, and could have passed for my older sister. "Mr. Pankin's favorite?"

"Hal."

"Not even a photo finish with Maurey?"

"Maurey and Hal."

My mother blushed. I thought she would progress to Estelle Solomon, or on more familiar ground, Aunt Bertha or one of her older brothers. But the game was over when she asked, "Who's your favorite, Hal or Maurey?"

"I don't know about Maurey. He just came here this afternoon."

"Don't be such an old lady. Pick one."

"Hal. He brought me two books, he found me when I was reading and missed lunch . . ."

"But he calls you 'funny duck' and Maurey calls you 'dear girl.' 'Dear girl' is much nicer than 'funny duck.' "

"You're right," I said. I kept my eyes straight ahead. As we approached the main house we heard laughter and shouting from the dorm over the barn.

"I wonder why they laugh so much?"

"Maybe Maurey is telling stories about France."

"Maybe he's telling about the girls he had there."

The sky changed and a light mist enveloped us. On the porch the two overweight women friends were playing mahjong. I went upstairs and Lil followed, taking one step at a time. Aunt Bea's door was open. Willy and Lenny were shuffling cards while Aunt Bea filled a sheet of paper with tasks to be done before her husband paid his visit on Friday.

"I found out that there's a good beauty parlor in the village," she said to Lil without preliminaries. "I'm having my hair done Friday morning, shampoo and set. Want an appointment?"

"I'll wait until next week when Jack and Manya are here."

"You went for a walk?"

"You know that family with those children running around? No one was there. Not a soul."

"Didn't you hear? She's in the hospital to have another baby and the social service from Middletown came and took all the children away."

"To a home, to an orphanage?" Lil expressed the New Yorker's fear of social workers, of charitable agencies, of meddling do-gooders.

"You'll have to ask Mr. Pankin. He's on the board of some charity organization. The children ran around like wild Indians. They want the mother to get fixed so she can't have more and to put the new baby up for adoption."

"That's terrible," Lil protested. "Look how many in my family, no one took the children away. We were poor but honest."

"Those were different times, and besides, Rae was very strict and you cleaned and scrubbed and hung clothes on the roof. Not for Jack and Manya, you'd still be there, slaving away."

Lil grew pensive. "I think I'm one of the luckiest women in the world. I love Manya with my deepest heart. And of course Jack."

Nevertheless, Lil hastened to my bed, kneeled on it and stared out of the misted window at the dorm that housed the young men. "Do you think we'll see any of the waiters tonight?"

I didn't answer, and I didn't want to think about what my mother meant when she asked the last question.

Maurey showed up late for breakfast, wearing shorts with deep pockets front and back held down with large silver snaps. He introduced himself to everyone, bending down to kiss a hand here and a cheek there. The male guests found him as captivating as the women, asking him about France, inviting him for cards, treating him with easy camaraderie.

We noticed his long, straight, well-developed legs with their fuzz of golden hair. "We have a date," he told Lil. "Ten o'clock sharp. I have to hear the golden voice that everyone is talking about. I'll sing with you, we'll do duets."

"I only do that with my husband," she replied without irony.

"Then you'll sing by yourself. You name it, I'll play it."

Promptly at ten, Maurey came looking for her. She had gone upstairs to shower and dab her precious Chanel No. 5 on her wrists. "Stay with me," she whispered when she came down. With the most natural movement, Maurey led her to the piano. "What shall it be?"

" 'Margie,' " she replied without hesitation. She closed her eyes and belted it out, clear, fast, without artifice. "Margie, I'm always thinking of you, Margie . . . I have bought a home and ring and everything for Margie . . ."

He joined in, "After all is said and done, Margie you're the only one. Oh Margie, Margie, it's you."

He had a young boyish voice, nothing special, but his piano playing was. His long fingers barely touched the keys. Unlike Hal, who tended to bang on the keyboard, Maurey called his playing "The Rubenstein touch." He played some chords and crossed his hands to conclude.

"Does your voice come from your throat or your diaphragm?" he asked.

Lil blinked. The last word was unfamiliar. He placed his long elegant hand directly beneath her throat. I saw her jump, steady herself. "Does your voice come from here?"

"Oh, I couldn't hold my breath for that long."

He slid his three middle fingers to her chest. "From here?"

"I guess."

"Lil, I'm going to make a torch singer out of you, better than Libby Holman, better than the other Lilian Roth. Do you know the song 'I Still Get a Thrill Thinking of You'?" She shot me a hurried pleading glance. "Not every word," I answered for her.

"Dear girl," he asked, "are you the prompter?"

I nodded.

"Fine, then prompt away." He faced Lil. "The key to being a torch singer is to sing slowly with a lot of vibrato, you know: sort of a gargle, in the lowest register. Like this." He did a poor imitation of a cabaret singer, "I still get a thrill thinking of you." He instructed, "Go very slowly, one word, one sound at a time, don't rush. Sing, 'I still get a thrill,' then pause, rest, nod at the audience, then continue with, 'thinking of you.' The phrase 'thinking of you' has to mean something. You want everyone to believe that you're thinking of *him*. The words to hit are 'thrill' with a gargle and 'thinking of you' as slow as you can."

"Are you a music teacher?"

He pouted his lips before replying. "No, but in France, I had contact with lots of vocalists and I went with them to their lessons." His blue eyes never left hers. He tossed his long blond mane. "Have you ever had voice lessons?"

She shook her head. "I used to sing with the bouncing ball in the movies. You know, during intermission, they would have sing-alongs and I would start the singing."

"That's fine, I was curious." He laughed into her eyes. "Do you know what George Gershwin said to Ethel Merman? 'Never take lessons, it will ruin your singing.' "

"Ethel Merman is Jack's favorite."

"But you're a Libby Holman type." He placed his hand over hers. "Courage," he said in French. Lil understood what he meant. "Now let's see if you can nail this song."

Lil's hand trembled, but she prepared to sing her heart out. As slowly as she could, and with her voice in the lowest register, she began, "I still," pause, "get a thrill," pause, "thinking of you."

"That's it, that's it. Once more."

She growled deeper, her voice trembled more than her hand.

"You know I still," pause, "get a thrill," pause, "thinking of you."

He thanked her with a grandiose hug. She nearly toppled from the piano bench. "You're going to be wonderful, wonderful," he said and kissed her on both cheeks.

After the music lesson, Maurey sauntered outside where his father was waiting for him in the shiny truck. They drove off toward the lake. I stood on the porch, confused, gripped by a sudden unshakable anxiety. I grabbed *Jane Eyre* and headed for the fruit trees. Lunch held no allure. No matter how meaty and sweet the tomatoes, how fresh the vegetables from the garden, I had tired of them.

An hour might have passed, possibly two. I could hear the voices of Mr. Pankin and Maurey in the fields, and the wind carrying Maurey's exclamations of "great" and "amazing." He said the word *amazing* like two words, aye-mazing. His father's reply faded along with his receding footsteps. Had Maurey gone with him? I listened intently, and could detect soft thuds spaced between the silences, like pears falling from the tree under which I sat.

I couldn't stay there forever. My legs had grown stiff. Trying to be inconspicuous, I scurried with my head down, only to discover Maurey standing amid the corn, devouring one after the other, discarding the cobs by tossing them over his shoulder. He cast a shadow against the afternoon light. His blond hair lay against his bare shoulders, his shirt was jammed into his shorts. His blue eyes settled on me and he called out, "I was hoping it was you, dear girl. Come here, I'll pick one for you that's young and sweet."

Nothing in my background prepared me for standing in a field eating uncooked corn from the husk. Maurey placed my book into his waistband, selected a small ear of corn for me, pulled away the silk and peeled it as if it were a banana. Then he handed me my prize.

"Sweet as sugar candy," he cried. "Every day I spent in France, I dreamed of this cornfield, of standing here eating. Go ahead," he winked, pleased at sharing this secret with me, "make a fool of yourself."

I dug my teeth into the raw kernels. They were, in fact, better than candy. He watched me closely. "What did I tell you? Ecstasy. Right? I've had five or six of them. Allez!" he commanded.

It seemed impossible to deny him. We chomped in unison, he making humming sounds. He signaled to me that he was sated by pulling my book from his waistband. He entwined his fingers over mine and led me into the clearing. "I have a date with one of our guests, Si Ratoff. He thinks because I'm starting law school at Yale that I can help him with his legal problems. He's a sweet old man."

Then he switched gears. "Your mother must be very proud that you're such a good reader."

"Yes," I lied.

"She must be giving a lot of thought to your education."

"Yes," I lied.

"I'm sure your parents want you to attend the best university possible."

"Yes," I lied.

"You know," he explained, "that's how we happened to settle in Colchester. When my mother was alive, my dad tried to please her in every way. Trips to Europe. Trips across the country. One year we went to California. Days and days on the train but Los Angeles was aye-mazing, open, free. You could eat pancakes for dinner, wear shorts at night, never have to worry about being polite or saying what was expected of you. It was like a frontier city except glamorous. We were crazy about the place.

"After my mother died, my father became distraught. I mean off his rocker. He wanted to leave anything that reminded him of her and for one wild week he kept insisting that we pack up and move to California.

"Do you know who stopped him? Estelle Solomon—my mother's best friend. She said, 'Where will the boys go to school? What kind of education will they have out west?' Dad knew she was right. Hal and I studied at Choate. We came home for the funeral, but we didn't finish the term there. We couldn't bear to leave Dad and he couldn't bear to let us. So we searched for a retreat and bought this place. We actually went to Colchester High. At Choate I was reading De Toqueville in French as fast as I read the comic strips, and here they didn't have a science course, just some world history books from before the Johnstown flood. It didn't matter. Hal decided on med school because of Mother's cancer. He wanted to make a difference in medicine. We built up the farm and then went to the best universities anyway. Choate helped."

Maurey held my hand in his, swinging it as we walked. He spoke as quickly as a New Yorker, yet I had to strain to remember his words. He had gone to a school named Choke, and read some writer like the comic strips. In New York we called them "the jokes." Willy and I loved "Terry and the Pirates," but we *hated* the Dragon Lady. I started to say this to Maurey and held back. With Hal I had no trouble speaking the truth and half-truths. Maurey closed down something inside me. His beauty, his naturalness made me ill at ease. But I wasn't surprised when he said, "Your mother is very talented and very beautiful."

"Yes," I replied without lying.

Si Ratoff waved to Maurey. "See you later, dear girl," Maurey said and trotted off to meet him.

In the evening Maurey suggested a hayride.

"Hayride?" Estelle clapped her hands. "Don't we need a wagon pulled by a horse?"

"We've tons of hay to fill up the bed of the truck and we can pile in a dozen people." With Maurey the deed was done the moment the idea struck him. He backed the truck into the barn; the med students filled it with hay.

Estelle and Aunt Bea and the two women playing mahjong bestirred themselves for once and agreed to come with us. They had stout legs, overhanging stomachs and wide behinds. They drove from rural Massachusetts to vacation in rural Connecticut. Smoothing their beltless sack dresses, they hopped into the rear end of the truck with surprising agility. A few of the guests' children came, too. We sank into the hay, chattering with excitement.

"Once around the lake and then the village for ice cream cones. My treat," Maurey announced.

The sole person to hold back was Lil. "I don't think so, I have to do my nails, write postcards." Subdued, she kept stepping backward as though to turn around and run. The forlorn expression on her face must have caught Maurey's attention. His golden head popped through the truck window. "We're not having a hayride without you." Gabe jumped out of the front seat and wordlessly lifted my mother up. The broad-assed mahjong women wriggled to make room and Estelle hugged Lil in elation.

"What shall we sing?" Hal asked and started the first round of a song: "The clarinet, the clarinet goes do a do, goes do a det . . ."

We drove around the small muddy lake, then past Grey's Hotel, imitating drums and violins, until we were hoarse.

At the village drugstore, we tumbled out, disheveled but radiant, covered with hay.

"Show of hands. How many for chocolate, how many for vanilla?" Hal did not pronounce the flavor *ella* the way we did in New York. "Any for coffee ice cream?"

Willy and I had drunk coffee from earliest childhood, so Willy selected coffee, I chocolate. Maurey handed Lil a sugar cone filled with strawberry ice cream. "Can I have a lick?" he asked and before she could answer, he dug his white teeth into the top of her cone and darted away.

We finished our treats before we started back. Some of us were thirsty, some sticky, all tired. Lil was among the first off the truck, disappearing into our room with haste. "Did you like it? Did you like the hayride?" Willy asked her, his enthusiasm a rarity.

"Yes," she answered, "only I wish Daddy and Bubby would come here tomorrow instead of next week."

Despite the hectic air that pervaded the hotel over the weekend, Maurey remained an island of calm. The one concession he made to the bustle around him was to insist that Lil take her music lesson immediately after breakfast. He led her to the piano bench, with me standing to her right. To warm up his slender fingers, he played and sang softly, "But How About Me?" "And one day, a baby will climb upon your knee and put his arms around you, but how about me?"

There was rarely a moment when he wasn't smiling, showing off his white teeth, chatting with men and women, on top of the world. I wondered if he ever confronted a sad day, despaired, cried, felt less lionhearted and more heartbroken, whether he was capable of coping with the stress that accompanied our family hour to hour and day to day: bad health, poverty. True, his mother had died, but Maurey had been blessed with some kind of magic.

"All right, Lil. Lots of vibrato, sing slowly. Let's start where we left off yesterday."

More nervous today than the day before, she edged away from Maurey on the piano seat and wiped her sweaty palms on her bare thighs. But she was a trouper, a natural performer, and when she wobbled on the opening notes, she took a breath and started again: "I still," pause, "get a thrill," pause, "thinking of you, and I still," pause, "feel your lips," pause, "kissing me too."

"First rate. I'm impressed. Very impressive." He picked up her left hand and covered it with kisses. "Want to sing more?"

She didn't know the words.

Maurey understood this, and repeated offhandedly, "Although our love affair wasn't to be." He didn't have to instruct Lil when to pause: she blushed violently on the words, "our love affair wasn't to be."

"Wonderful, perfect. Now from the top, all three lines."

She repeated them twice. He praised lavishly, told her she was wonderful, that she would knock everyone out of their socks, that if he wasn't entering law school, he would be her manager and make her a star. Abruptly, he asked, "Want to see the cows?"

Lil and I asked simultaneously, "What cows?"

"The cows that give us milk, cream and butter. The ones who eat the hay in the barn."

I had covered every inch of the property without meeting a cow. Why hadn't I noticed that?

"They're at the next farm. Gladkowski's farm. He keeps them for us, puts them out to pasture, milks them, has the milk pasteurized. But this is our last year. Too many requests for city bottled milk. It's no longer cost-efficient for us. That's what Dad and Hal and I talked about. Projects for next year. Eliminating the cows, giving them to Gladkowski and remodeling that part of the barn for guest rooms. Anyway, off we go."

He walked between us, taking my mother's hand and mine. Anyone seeing us would believe we had traversed this road for years. A taxi whizzed by with Aunt Bea, Alice, Lenny and Willy on their way to the beauty parlor.

Gladkowski's farm was overgrown with trees, bushes and vines that made it impossible to glimpse from the road. Maurey led the way as if hacking through a jungle. "Watch out for the chocolate patties," he warned.

We crouched beneath the drooping limbs of lopsided trees and the stench of cow flop twitched our nostrils. Through the open door of a small cottage we could see a rustic kitchen. Sparks and the sound of crackling wood came from the blackened kitchen stove.

A bulky woman lifted one of the heavy iron covers to feed more kindling into the oven, her hair pulled back with a rubber band and her cheeks the color of flame. She wore a man's denim shirt whose sleeves had been cut off at the shoulder.

"Hi, Olga," Maurey called out.

The woman's face grew redder than the flames.

"Maurey. Margie said you was home. I been baking bread for you."

"You shouldn't in this heat."

She wiped her hands on a soot-covered apron. "I should. For my favorite fella."

"Olga, all that flirting will get you in trouble someday." They laughed to acknowledge their familiar banter.

"This is young Margie's mother and these are guests from our hotel," he said. The woman barely nodded; she couldn't take her eyes from Maurey.

"Where's Gladdy?"

"Maybe in the barn, maybe in the pasture. I baked six loaves. You want to carry them back with you?"

"Just what we can eat. Hal will pick up the rest later."

The entire place—the farmhouse with its slanted roof, the barn that leaned to one side, the crooked rusty fence—gave the impression of sinking inch by inch into the ground. Yet the field trembled with wild-flowers: white Queen Anne's lace, yellow buttercups, random sprouts of red that appeared to have sprung up by accident. In the midst of this luxurious wildflower carpet the cows chewed and shat simultaneously. One cow, black and white, looked like a cutout in a cardboard puzzle; another was rusty brown, sleek-shiny like a horse; the bull was menacing, ugly, square-faced, with vacant eyes and a body as gray as the rocks beyond. In the distance two more cows sauntered lazily.

We shuddered when the bull lowered its head and approached the fence. To steady us, Maurey circled his arms around our waists. More, he cupped his chin over Lil's right shoulder. She put her hand up in an attempt to remove his face from hers. He responded by placing his hand over her hand, locking her body close to his as he leaned against her. She pretended nothing had happened, a casual meaningless gesture.

The embrace lasted only moments. Like a spell in a fairy tale we stood rooted to the spot, incapable of moving.

Farmer Gladkowski broke the tension and Maurey's grip on my mother. "Maurey, you no-good bum, whatcha doing in my pasture? France is not good for you no more?"

Maurey spun around. He hugged his tall, skinny, wrinkle-faced neighbor. "Gladdy, I missed you."

The farmer smelled of unwashed overalls, cow shit, warm sour milk, salty sweat, greasy hair. "We got your card, but couldn't read it. Olga and Margie, they cried over it."

The two men abandoned us, walking from the pasture to the house. As we rounded a corner, Olga pressed a freshly baked white bread into the crook of Maurey's suntanned arm. Her hands were swollen paws, burned in many places from handling the black iron lids of the wood-burning stove, scarred from knife cuts, from thrashing through overgrown brush, from carrying old milk buckets to the ancient pasteurizer.

"The cows are in great shape, and we're giving them to you," Maurey explained. "Buying store milk next year."

"You go to France, you come home crazy." Mr. Gladkowski wiped his face with a shredded bandanna.

As we departed, Maurey broke off chunks of bread and handed them to us. Lil hadn't uttered a single word during our visit to Gladkowski's farm.

A steady stream of cars was heading to Pankin's hotel. Car doors slammed; families greeted each other noisily.

"The Gladkowskis, they saved me and Hal when we first moved here," Maurey explained as he hurried us along. "I would wake up screaming for my mother and then Hal would start crying, too. Sometimes in the middle of the night we'd run to the Gladkowskis' house. Olga cooked us breakfast at three in the morning. We got used to her bad smell and the stink of the outhouse. That was the first thing Dad did for them. He installed a bathroom in the house with a toilet and shower. How did they live without an inside toilet or shower? How could anyone?"

My mother and I remained silent.

As we neared the main house Maurey broke into a trot, his blond hair flying. "I'm here, I'm back," he called and lost himself handling luggage and directing newcomers to their rooms. Lil breathed hard. She considered herself a woman with New York street smarts, a flirt for the purpose of bargaining, getting something for nothing. But she had never been with any man except Jack. She was adrift, rudderless, confined to a silence she couldn't break. Instead of climbing up to our room, she dropped into a wicker chair at the side of the house. Whatever her thoughts she didn't share them with anyone.

16

Staying Until Labor Day

ON FRIDAY, WE expected Bubby, Jack and Uncle Geoff. Jack had called Mr. Pankin to say that his mother was bringing dinner for everyone in the hotel. Like the wildflowers in the field that submitted to every stray breeze, word spread from guest to guest that a famous chef from New York was preparing a special Friday night dinner.

Willy marked off each hour with a Waterman's pen he had found in the grass, which he shared with Lil. Our ethic did not necessitate returning anything we found or inquiring about who lost it. "Finders keepers" was the rule instilled in us from birth.

On Thursday, the day before we expected Bubby, I sat under my favorite pear tree and finished *Jane Eyre*. I was sad, and ready to let the tears fall when Hal came in search of me.

"Hey, you funny duck." He hadn't had his hair cut in weeks. It flopped over his forehead and ears; it curled down his neck. He sat beside me.

"Estelle tells me you're on a retreat, reading, reading, reading. Finished *Jane Eyre*?"

I nodded.

"Like the happy ending?"

I meant to say, "Not really happy." I nodded again.

"Then why are you sad?"

One or two tears wet my cheeks, which I hoped he didn't notice. "It's not the book. I just . . . I just don't want to go back to New York."

"Like it here, do you?"

"Not like. Love."

"What do you love best?"

"Our room, the trees, the people."

"You care for Estelle, don't you? And me and Gabe and Maurey?" He didn't wait for a reply. "We like you, too. Estelle said that knowing you was the best thing that happened to her in years."

"You mean my family, my mother?"

"We think Lil is great. Beautiful and talented, a charmer. But no, you funny duck, we mean *you*. Of the many guests, you're the most interesting."

How to accept this compliment, from a man, particularly from Hal? Dr. Scott Wolfson, whom I had loved first, hadn't said he found me interesting.

"Estelle and I wondered if you'd like to go to the Book Barn today. A farewell gift, something to read when you're home."

"I still have *Great Expectations*."

"We thought a few more Dickens."

"What about Charlotte Brontë?"

"You've read the best. The others aren't so fascinating. Her sister Emily wrote a good one. *Wuthering Heights*. It's harder to understand, at the beginning."

I preferred Hal to the others because he didn't speak down to me. He treated me as if I were an adult, accepting my silence or my sadness. Finally, "Well, how about the Book Barn?"

"I'd rather wait for my Bubby. I want her to see it."

"Does she read a lot?"

"Her friends do, and her husband, my grandfather, he read to her every day. Pushkin. Do you know that Russian writer?"

"No, but I always wanted to have a dog with a Russian name. Don't you think a dog called Pushkin would be great?" We both laughed.

He nudged me with his elbow. "Hey, cheer up. We're open for Thanksgiving you know." Hal waited. "I suppose your grandmother's restaurant is reserved for Thanksgiving, Christmas and New Year's Eve, too."

"Yes," I lied.

"How about making a date right after New Year's? I'll take you to the Radio City Music Hall and then we'll have dinner."

My secret about living on Orchard Street caused me despair. I loved and trusted Hal, but a description of our dwelling was out of the question.

"Sometimes we get sick in the winter," I said.

"Everyone gets sick in the winter. Besides, you have a young energetic doctor. You told me so yourself." He helped me to my feet and carried my book. "If you won't drive to the Book Barn, come see the room we fixed up for you and your grandmother."

It was a small single room and bath, the smallest of the cottages. Everything was white: the walls, the double bed, the coverlet, the dresser, the night stand. Color came from a large vase of flowers—not flowers from the fields but from a shop—and the shining glory was a basket wrapped in yellow cellophane filled with fresh fruit and tied with yellow ribbon.

"Where did these come from?"

"Secret. We have our ways."

"I wish I could stay here forever," I said, or thought I said. Maybe I told it to myself and didn't utter a word.

One thing was certain: I didn't sleep much the night before my father and Bubby drove up. I washed and dried my hair in the morning, combed it a dozen times and selected my dress with the embroidered strawberries. Lil didn't bother me about breakfast. I stood on the porch, watching the unpaved road. Guests must have said "good morning" or "hello" but the sound didn't reach me. I didn't hear the delivery trucks, the slamming of the front door, the guests talking or laughing. I waited with patience for the black Packard to come into view. At last it did, drawing to a stop exactly at the porch steps.

Jack, seated in the back, jumped out first and led Bubby out of the front passenger seat. The instant I spied her, I didn't run down the steps of the porch, I jumped. I flung myself off the porch and into Bubby's arms. Her beauty took my breath away. Aunt Bertha's black-and-white-striped dress had been cut short. Bubby wore it loose without a belt. Broad shoulder straps crisscrossed in the back, and the square neckline revealed her flawless white skin.

Pandy had done Bubby's hair with her braid as a crown. Her feet were shod in white flat-heeled shoes with black patent leather heels and tips. Since her diamond earrings and pearls had been hocked for the summer, a simple gold chain—Aunt Bertha's—adorned her neck. I buried my face in hers with my legs wrapped around her waist.

It had not been my intention to cry. But once I felt Bubby close to me, warm, sweet-smelling, erect and elegant, I couldn't stop my tears.

Every sound on the farm came to a halt. Every activity ceased, as guests watched me and Bubby. Finally a voice said, "Look at that child with her grandmother," and another, "She's beautiful, like a movie star, what's her name, May Robson?" "No, more aristocratic." The last comment was Estelle's.

I lifted my head. Lil didn't crowd us; she waited her turn, smiling. Someone asked her, "Is that your mother?" Lil replied, "Yes, that's my mother."

She skipped down the steps. "Ma, you look beautiful." Noisy kisses followed. Lil's relief at viewing shiny-haired Jack obliterated my fears.

"The food!" Geoff cried in his most commanding voice. Hal and Gabe appeared and from the trunk hauled two-foot-high stainless-steel cauldrons packed in "magic ice" by Moe of The Grand Canal Cafeteria. Three vast platters held cold salmon surrounded by Bubby's signature marinated beets. One heavy cauldron was filled with stuffed cabbage; another with beef brisket. Challahs large enough for many guests sat on cartons filled with gallons of fresh fruit compote, strudel and rugulach. Hal and Gabe groaned under their loads as they staggered to the kitchen, and Mr. Pankin rushed out to greet Bubby personally.

"Mrs. Roth, it's an honor." I held my breath as Bubby answered without a trace of Yiddishisms, "It's my pleasure. Please, call me Manya."

As soon as we could we walked across the lawn into Bubby's room, our family crowding inside to comment on the fruit basket, the fresh flowers, the white coverlet. Jack removed his mother's shoes. My mother lifted her dress over her head to keep her hair in place. Swiftly and expertly, Jack opened her suitcase and hung up her skirt and blouse for tonight and her outfit for Saturday night, packed professionally as only Jack could—he prided himself on his ability to fold women's clothes so they emerged without a wrinkle. Her sundries went into the bathroom and the medicine bottle with white pills rested on the white night stand. The summer robe with sprigs of flowers that she kept in Yonkers had been laundered professionally.

"Ma, don't forget to drink a lot of water. Two glasses would be good." Jack kissed her on the cheek and left the room with Willy. Lil helped Bubby remove her fancy rose-colored corset and a new satiny bra. "Ma, you look like a bride," Lil said, laughing, "only thank God you're not." It had not occurred to me before that Bubby bought these undergarments for Mister Elkin's arrival—that these were part of her trousseau.

"Would you like me to bring you a bottle of soda?"

"Things I loved, maslinas, lox, sturgeon, caviar, soda, they're bad for the kidneys. No more lifting, no more carrying heavy bags with chickens and geese."

"What do they expect you to do? Retire? They must be crazy."

"Not retire, only to take it slower. Pavolinka."

Bubby let out a sigh as she slipped into her robe. "It's wonderful to see you. This summer, it was hard without you."

The sight of Bubby brought Lil to a familiar plateau in the universe. The confusion that had rested on her brow for days vanished with this simple speech.

"You bought so much food. Clayton came back to help you?"

"For three days we worked. It kept us busy. We couldn't put you to shame."

"You, shame us? You look like ten movie stars." Lil didn't ask who had paid for the food. Surely it didn't come from Jack's unemployment check. "Try to take a nap. You don't have to dress until five."

Bubby regarded Lil closely. "You're happy here?"

"I won't be the same again." Without waiting for a reply she tip-toed out.

At last we were without the others. It was Bubby's turn to study me. I tumbled off the bed to hide my confusion.

"So who do you love that you're falling from the bed?"

I settled on the pillow beside her. "Hal is my first favorite. Not because he buys me books but because he wants to practice medicine here in Colchester. I would like that."

Of the many extraordinary aspects of my ties to Bubby, the most unusual was that our intimacy never unraveled. It stayed intact whether we were apart for a few hours or a few weeks. We picked up exactly where we had left off without a heartbeat of awkwardness or hesitation.

"You want to be with a man like him or you want to live in Colchester?"

In my daydreams about Bubby's visit, I intended to have this conversation about Colchester the second day. I imagined we would drive to the Book Barn, and walk around the village square, and while we rested on a shaded bench I would suggest, plead, beg her to consider moving with me and Willy to Colchester. The moment came a day too soon but I couldn't squander it.

"Bubby, listen. Do you think you could possibly move here with me and Willy? There's a school in the village and when it snowed we could walk in clean snow like you did in Odessa. Bubby, there's a tearoom next to the post office. It's open only in the summer. You could rent it and serve dinners there weekends. People would drive from all over Connecticut to have dinners at Manya's. We would live in a house near the village and Mr. Pankin would drive us. He's very lonely in the winter when his sons are in school. It would be peaceful and quiet. Wouldn't that be a lovely life? Wouldn't it? Wouldn't it?"

Bubby sat up. I could see her mouthing what she would reply, yet not a sound came from her. Then: "It's a dream, ah shayna chulim."

With all of my passion I resisted that statement. "It's not a dream. It could happen."

"Yes, yes, but what about Jack and Lil? You didn't tell me about them."

I was prepared for the question. "They would stay in the city, work, see movies and shows. Do what they always do. You know."

"They would live in the cold apartment on Orchard Street themselves?"

"They could come to see us, like Daddy does now, a few days at a time."

"What about my business, my restaurant?"

"I told you. You would have it here instead, in the tearoom."

"You think my restaurant is where I cook and serve food? It's where I have my friends. Not only the neighbors, but the two doctors, even that stingy Yussie Feldman . . ." Her voice dropped.

"Couldn't you bear to leave them, Bubby? You were able to leave Odessa."

"I was young then, crazy in love, the two of us could eat the whole world with our hands. I've lived at 12 Orchard Street for thirty-five years, maybe more. If we moved to Connecticut, Lil and Jack would find an apartment uptown and the whole building would close down. The neighbors would find somewhere else, maybe Ludlow Street, maybe Hester, but somewhere, and with it my whole lifetime . . . Some of it was bitter, but also . . ."

I didn't cry. I waited until I could speak without disappointment. "Does that mean that we have to live on Orchard Street forever?"

"Forever? Nothing lasts forever. Not the greatest love or the worst one. Not the greatest happiness or the greatest pain. It's like water. It runs through your fingers and it's gone."

"Bubby, does this mean no?"

"Next summer, if you still love this place we'll talk again."

She caught me in her arms and rocked me. We fell asleep.

That night I realized that serving food was theater. With Lil's help, Bubby got into her corset again, and covered her bra with the blue slip from the dress she wore at Dr. Koronovsky's wedding. Over it came a white lace blouse and a long blue silk skirt, both Aunt Bertha's. The Cartier comb with its diamond rested on her braid—the one possession she hadn't hocked for our vacation. My red-and-white party dress with its billowing slip was too short but it made do.

I held Bubby's hand tightly as we walked into the dining room and her entrance created a buzz of rumors equal to the occasion.

"Have you heard, Manya Roth was an actress in the Jewish theater. Estelle told us."

"No, it's the young one, the daughter, she sang in the movies."

"Manya's husband, he died young, he was a famous writer."

"No! Was he a Bolshevik?"

"They came to America way before. From his youth he published poetry."

"So how did she come to be a chef?"

"You can't make a living from poetry."

"I thought she was an actress. She must have been. You can't take your eyes off her."

"But those grandchildren! How come they have no looks?"

"Maybe they're adopted. Maybe they're refugees from Europe, they're so skinny. That must be it. Adoption."

"You saw the little girl with her grandmother? She calls her 'Bubby.' That's no adoption."

"You heard about that girl? She never eats, she only reads."

Had my parents been listening, they would have denied nothing. They accepted whatever story was told about them, relished, embroidered, exaggerated it.

For this special dinner the med students and Maurey dressed in white shirts and black trousers. They carried out the huge challahs on broad planks, ordinarily used as table extensions. They marched around the dining area to rounds of applause. Three vast poached salmons followed, on platters surrounded by red marinated beets topped with hard-boiled egg slices.

Lil, Bubby and I had worked in the kitchen explaining how each individual plate should be presented. Years as Bubby's assistant made Lil a pro at arranging dishes. Possibly when the guests viewed the whole salmons they assumed them to be part of the New England dinner. But they couldn't ignore the beets, or the glistening sauce that I called "Holland sauce," or the pureed split peas that accompanied this first course.

The three helpers—Margie, Mrs. Gladkowski and the dark-skinned Belinda—each crossed herself as the servings went out into the dining room. Lil and Bubby prepared the first half dozen plates; after that the assistants did their best to imitate our style, with Bubby poking a finger here, adjusting the sauce there, and Lil wiping the edges of the dishes with clean white towels.

Sweat poured from Mr. Pankin's face and dampened his white shirt as he repeated over and over again, "Small portions, small portions, they're not expecting too much food." After the fish course, each entrée plate held one stuffed cabbage, two slices of brisket, a well of kasha and natural gravy, and one glorious mashed-potato pancake. Bubby, Lil and I slipped back to the dining room but not before Bubby emptied two gallons of fresh fruit compote into bowls and arranged one plateful of strudel and rugulach for each table.

I can't say with certainty that I ate anything. Mr. Pankin wanted to add his tomato slices to the fare, which Bubby vetoed. Nor did it bother her that the guests slathered the challah with butter and dipped it into the meat gravy. Many demanded seconds of the stuffed cabbage and brisket. Not a scrap of food remained in the kitchen.

To complement the dessert, Maurey and Hal brought out bottles of port wine and Maurey did the honor of the toast. "To chef Manya. No meal in France could equal this." He then played "Let Me Call You Sweetheart" on the piano.

Jack helped Bubby to her feet. She stood in her white lace blouse, her long blue silk skirt, her Cartier comb, and nodded her head from side to side. Mr. Pankin, now in a fresh shirt, declared, "To one of the best meals we've had the privilege to serve." Everyone clapped. Bubby continued to hold my hand as the guests crowded around to thank her for her cooking, for being a former actress, for having a writer for a husband, and a daughter/daughter-in-law who sang in the movies.

In the morning Estelle drove Bubby and me to the Book Barn. Because of the Labor Day weekend many people decided on the Barn as their destination, so it was impossible to browse or to have a sense of the enormity of the building with its thousands of books. A young man with long auburn hair sat on a wooden stool at the door absorbed in his own writing.

"He reminds me of my husband," Bubby said.

"Was your husband a writer?" Estelle asked.

"When he wasn't working or making love he wrote or read every minute. Those pintelach, those tiny black dots on the paper, were everything to him."

We couldn't navigate from aisle to aisle; the crowds as pushy as the Delancey Street Woolworth's on Saturday. Estelle ushered us outside.

"Did you ever save anything your husband wrote?"

Bubby's lovely black-and-white summer dress, her luminous face and white hair, were at odds with the sudden pause in conversation.

Eventually she responded, "Misha, my husband, was very sick and not having the hospital care he needed. Jack, my baby, was maybe six or seven months old. I left them together in bed and went to work. I was a baker's helper.

"In the middle of the day I ran home. We lived on the fourth floor. I thought the sun was better for him on the top floor. I ran up the steps, three at a time. The door was never locked. The whole apartment was one big room with a bed and a gas burner for cooking. Misha was on his side, his face white. I thought he slept. But the baby was covered with blood, the papers on the bed, my husband's writing, soaked in blood. He had a hemorrhage and died."

I had not heard this part about his blood-soaked papers.

"How terrible, what a horror for you."

"I couldn't save one page of his writing. I couldn't save my husband."

The sun in Connecticut was brilliant. The sky, the trees, appeared fresh as a painted landscape. The light, the softness of the late summer air, Bubby in her dressy clothes, were a universe apart from the one she had described.

A delicate moment of silence elapsed. "It must have taken a long while to forget this tragedy."

"Forget? Impossible. I try to put it in a small corner, like a box you hide with an ugly present in it. But when I'm cooking or baking, when it's summer again, and the fruit is wonderful and walking in the street is wonderful, I turn to look for him, I feel him beside me, and at night when I can't sleep . . ."

"And you didn't consider remarrying?"

"Almost once. Almost lately. It wasn't beshert. Also, I have four children. Jack and Lil, they are like a couple that's keeping company. Grown up but not. Married with children, but not. Their children are my children. I raised them since they opened their eyes."

"You've given your children everything."

Bubby shrugged. We parked at the village square. Slowly, slowly, we walked around the green, the tearoom eliciting a passing glance. My conversation with her yesterday about moving to Connecticut need not have taken place.

"I think that I held my son back," Bubby continued, following her own thoughts. "He wanted us to live together, to be together. Did you know that Lil came to me when she was sixteen? In all these years, not a bad word between us. She's baked in my heart, like my own flesh." She laughed ironically. "I don't say blood—you know why."

"How could you hold them back when you gave them so much freedom?"

"Maybe they would have done different work if they hadn't worried so much about me and my restaurant. Jack especially. He's very artistic, and shouldn't be selling women's clothes."

"Fashion is very artistic."

"Maybe he would be closer to the theater. He loves the theater. Sometimes in the winter when he has a cold or a sty on one eye, even then he doesn't stay home on his day off but runs to the theater."

To confirm this, Willy suddenly appeared, waving frantically. "Daddy is writing a play for tonight. He needs you. He wants you and

Cousin Alice to sing and me to whistle. And he's writing a song for the end of it."

Estelle's voice rose with disbelief. "In a few hours he's going to whip up an entertainment?"

"He's a brenfire." Bubby laughed with satisfaction.

It wasn't a play but a series of acts, a vaudeville that Jack prepared. He worked in the library, assigned the songs and dances. Maurey directed the rehearsal. Gabe and Ronny Glass, our other waiter, raced through the village inviting everyone to attend our show. They stopped off at Grey's Hotel, which was expecting talent from the Catskills, and posted a notice in the lobby about our early entertainment.

In his professional script Jack had written down the order of the acts:

1) Jack: Intro
2) Girls: Button Up Your Overcoat
3) Lil: Still Get a Thrill
4) Med students: Lazy, I Want to Be Lazy
5) Original song by Jack: Another Year Is Coming

"Cousin Alice and Lil are with Maurey in the dining room," Jack told me. "Do a run-through of 'Button Up Your Overcoat.' Just remember if you make a mistake, if you repeat the same line twice, keep on singing. No one will notice the difference. And forget those Eddy Cantor hand movements. This isn't a minstrel show. Hands on hips or point to the audience when you say, 'You'll get a pain and ruin your tum tum.' No matter how much people applaud, run offstage as soon as possible. Your mother is the star. We don't want people tired before she comes on. You know, like vaudeville."

For his stint as master of ceremonies, Jack selected a white-on-white shirt, open at the throat, and oxford gray pants. No tie, but hair slick as a seal.

"Good evening, ladies and gentleman, I'm Jack Roth and though I hate to begin with a complaint, I have to tell you what bothers me about Pankin's Farm." He held a cigarette between his right-hand fingers and ad-libbed the entire show, confident, urbane, relaxed as if he did this every night of the week.

He launched into the joke about getting two pieces of bread for dinner and asking for more. Reaching the punch line, where he explains that Mr. Pankin cuts an entire loaf in half to satisfy him, Jack threw away the question with expert casualness, "Pankin, tell me the truth, so why did you go back to two pieces of bread?"

The crowd in the dining room, the terraces and those listening via loud speakers on the lawn laughed and applauded. Jack went right on with the monologue. "So I say to Hal, a Harvard man, a nice college boy, 'There's a fly in my soup,' and what do you think he answers—'What were you expecting, Fred Astaire in a top hat?'"

He nodded at Maurey who improvised on the piano while Jack announced, "The Pickle Sisters." Maurey broke into "Button Up Your Overcoat." Cousin Alice didn't bother to open her mouth. She danced, she whirled, she tapped, she bounced her head back and forth without tiring. Jack had to waltz Alice off the stage. People in the audience remarked, "Are those girls cute or what? Not Shirley Temple, but adorable."

Waiting for the commotion to subside, Jack lit a cigarette, inhaled slowly and announced, "The Star of Stars, Miss Lilyan, straight from theater halls of New York."

My mother, in a smart, unadorned navy blue dress, her hair in a French knot, could have stepped into the spotlight from a cabaret. She walked to the piano, crossed her arms over her chest and through half-lidded eyes, her voice heaving with sobs, she slowly, slowly began,

"Oh I still . . . get a thrill . . . thinking of you, and I still feel your lips . . . kissing me too." Jack stood to one side against the piano. Lil gazed at the audience sitting on folding chairs that reached from the dining room to the lawn. A hush fell over the crowd. After my number, I raced to sit beside Bubby. As Lil sang I silently mouthed the words. "I still remember . . . the night . . . under the moon . . . I recall that it all . . . ended too soon."

She had been a brilliant student. "Although our love is gone . . . memories linger on . . . and I still get a thrill . . . thinking of you."

Not a man in the area failed to fall in love with Lil, desire her, want and long for that thrill. Her encore, fast and peppy, was "It Had to Be You," with the line, "For nobody else gives me a thrill / With all your faults dear, I love you still . . ." They screamed, whistled, clapped, stamped their feet.

The woman behind us exclaimed, "Didn't I tell you she was an actress?"

Her friend replied, "The whole family is on the stage. Like the George Cohans."

"That's Jewish blood for you, full of talent."

The med students came out with their pants rolled up, mops on their heads for wigs, cavorted around attempting to do the cancan, and fell to the floor singing, "Lazy, I want to be lazy."

For the finale, they stood up along with Willy and formed a semi-circle around Jack, who had written an original song that ended:

> *We're on our way, we're here to stay.*
> *We're gonna make whoop whoopee every day.*
> *Another year is coming*
> *And I don't give a darn,*
> *I'll leave the wife and children*
> *And come back to Pankin's Farm.*

Everyone joined in the singing, the guests learning the words by osmosis. They adored the line, "We're gonna make whoop whoopee every day" and shouted it out repeatedly. They clapped until their hands were raw.

Bubby and I retreated to her cottage and we talked until dawn.

We had two aching disappointments. In the middle of the night Hal and Gabe set out for med school in Boston and Maurey for New Haven, and Estelle and Philip Sullivan left without saying good-bye.

Bubby drove home with the Simons at midmorning but we stayed until Labor Day. A special train went directly to Grand Central in New York, and Mr. Pankin drove us to the station. He handed over three fresh blueberry pies securely tied in boxes, and saw us to our seats. He gave each of us a card. Jack's read, "Thanks for the unforgettable Pankin's Follies—and much more," and was signed by every one of the med students. Willy's read, "The best whistler in this or any other state." Mine said, "Complete set of Charles Dickens is yours." Lil's was from Estelle, "See you in New York."

Mr. Pankin, tears in his eyes, explained hoarsely, "Three more things." He kissed Lil on the right cheek. "From Hal." He kissed her on the left: "From Gabe." Smack on the lips. "From Maurey." He ran the length of the car and waved as the train pulled out. For separate reasons, Lil and I cried all the way to New York.

17

The Return to Orchard Street

FROM PAST EXPERIENCE I recalled but did not accept easily the need to settle back into our ordinary routine. Colchester haunted me. In the deepest sense I identified with a phrase read often in books, "She thought her heart would break."

The entire apartment had shrunk to a size smaller than our bedroom at the farm. More difficult to erase from memory was the slanted country ceiling, the large window overlooking the lawn and the barn, the leafy fruit trees that tinged the sky with green.

The Orchard Street halls had rarely seemed darker, the toilet in the hall more smelly and bleak. I missed my nightly shower, the walks with my mother, and I prayed for the sight of Estelle and the others. I opened my eyes from sleep and imagined that the two broad-shouldered women who monopolized the left side of the porch with their mahjong game were at the head of our folding bed.

The one source of comfort was the return of Clayton, who slept on the kitchen floor every night. Knowing my horror of rats, he bought rat powder and placed it on every step leading to our door. The rats ate it as if it were pistachio ice cream and the mounds of powder heaped around the garbage cans every night had been lapped up by morning with no signs of success. I hadn't caught a glimpse of a field mouse at Pankin's, but once home my rat phobia increased and I imagined that they lurked everywhere—waltzing in the skylight of the toilet, on the outside windowsill of the kitchen, grinning their evil toothy grins.

I clung to Bubby; sat in her lap; covered her face with kisses. I made desperate attempts to keep myself from crying in front of her.

As was her custom, Lil hung my dresses on nails that protruded from her bedroom door. Instead of watching them fade and grow short during the coming winter months, I wore a dress every day. Lil neither noticed nor commented on this, and possibly to hide her own sense of loss, she displayed exceptional energy.

Flat broke, we lived on Jack's last unemployment check and waited for customers who didn't materialize. For once the apartment blazed with heat and light—it was the warmest September on record. The few customers who wandered in asked for dairy dishes—blintzes, cold schav, cold borscht, priced for small change. Bubby didn't buy meat or chicken for several days and was jolted out of her confidence in the future when Weinstock, the slob agent who dumped every course onto a single plate, announced one noontime that he wanted a tuna sandwich.

"No offense, Manya," he said, wiping his face with a handkerchief that could have passed for a rag hanging from the pipes under the kitchen sink. "Excuse please, you were in Connecticut, I bought a tuna sandwich at The Grand Canal, it wasn't bad. The mayonnaise like glue, but the tuna okay, maybe salty."

"They prepared tuna sandwiches at the farm, we didn't eat them," I said loftily. "My cousin Alice, she eats anything, she ate tuna sandwiches."

"Manya," Weinstock continued, ignoring my remark. "Tuna and salmon from cans are best sellers. It's dreck, but it's *American*. Call a wholesaler, buy a few cases of tuna, salmon, Hellmann's mayonnaise. Your luck will change in this heat."

"That's it, Ma, for once Weinstock is right." Jack raised his sleek head from the racing form. "Lil should call our customers on the phone. Tell them we have a new American menu—sandwiches of every kind, cold or hot, and salads, chicken salad, green salads with tomatoes, and also . . ." My father paused, passing his long fingers over his hair. "Tell them we deliver."

"We deliver?" Bubby and I asked in unison.

"Clayton will deliver. And Maminyu, your friends at the *Forward*. Put an ad in the paper. 'Kosher American-style sandwiches. We deliver.' "

Bubby fanned her face with her apron. "Nu?" She appealed to me for help. "Vus zuched du?"

My sigh mingled with Bubby's. "Maybe Daddy is right," I said. "At the farm they served tomato sandwiches, cheese sandwiches, tuna with celery and mayonnaise, and they didn't have one left over. The Grand Canal puts a sign in the window every day about their specials. We could have our new menu printed on cheap paper. Willy and I will drop them off at all the stores."

Bubby remained silent. Jack, who had abandoned his manicurist for the entire summer, filed his nails with his personal file that he kept in his vest pocket. To prove his worth Willy tore a page from his ledger and wrote:

AMERICAN AND KOSHER SANDWICHES

SALADS   COOKIES

MANYA'S RESTAURANT. ORCHARD 4-2333.

WE DELIVER

He handed it to me and Jack.

"Very good." Jack nodded. "Only we have to print the hours, like eleven to five."

"So late? Five o'clock, who eats a sandwich?"

"It's the new America. If there's a war, God forbid, who will have time to eat four-course meals in the middle of the afternoon? Besides, this is an experiment. I think they owe me one more unemployment check. We'll invest it in food for sandwiches. It's better than betting on a horse."

The rent, the gas and electric bill had not been paid, let alone the Morris Plan, which had provided money for our vacation. Everything of value was in the hockshop. We could thank Uncle Goodman for the lavish spread Bubby had brought to Pankin's Hotel. Hours after our discussion about sandwiches, I listed my current fears in my notebook:

> Rats
> No money
> Bubby's health
> No money
> Jack and Lil not working
> Never to see Conn. again
> Missing Mother.

The last I wrote with reluctance. Lil had more or less detached herself when we came back to the city. She hadn't visited Ada. Absorbed in her own thoughts, in her private world, she behaved with no awareness of any of us.

I couldn't sleep that night, tossing in our folding bed and without realizing it, punctuating the silence with deep sighs.

"Don't worry," Bubby whispered. She indicated that she, too, was worrying when she added, "Gut vil zein unser tateh." God will be our father, said my agnostic Bubby.

No sooner did Jack prepare for work the first Saturday after Labor Day than he became a meteorologist, following the weather in the evening and morning paper with the knowledge that his livelihood depended on it. The temperature stood at ninety-six degrees the morning he set out for Division Street and Farber's.

Though he must have had a first name, no one called him anything except Farber: half the size of Jack, narrow-shouldered, with tiny hands and feet. Arms aflutter, his movements were birdlike, his head darting from side to side. Lil had once sworn she could never step foot into bed with a man whose ankles resembled pencils without erasers. Jack mocked Farber because he often bought his clothes in the boys' department.

He was tight-fisted with money, an attribute not prized by Jack, and he showed up in marked-down suits made of flimsy fabrics. Jack cried out, "Trucks turn over on the Bowery, cars crash in accidents, the Third Avenue El stops in the tracks, nothing ever happens to Farber!" Then he rushed Farber's jacket to the tailor at the end of the street to have the lapels hand stitched.

Farber's clothes mattered not a whit because his pride sprang from his wavy hair parted in the middle. His hair gave depth to his long bony face—he starved himself to save money. Yet he was incapable of operating the store without Jack. He had no eye for style, couldn't chat up women or close a sale without making an error in judgment. Two-priced selling, with the asking price printed on the tag and the final price arrived at through subtle negotiations, involved understanding women, what they wanted, how much they expected to pay, how far they could be urged to part with a few dollars. In these areas Jack was an expert. Without Jack Roth there would be no Farber's.

On this scorching day when everyone was repeating endlessly, "It's not the heat, it's the humidity," Farber peered down the street hoping to catch a glimpse of his well-dressed salesman. He hopped from one leg to another—bursting to relate something important. "Hot enough to fry an egg on the sidewalk?" he called out the moment Jack came into view.

"Hot enough to be singing, 'We're Having a Heat Wave' and mean it." Jack scowled, appraising Farber's nervous excitement, and asked, "What's up except women's hemlines?"

"What's up? A whole week you were taking care of the store while we stayed in the mountains and you didn't buy one piece of fall stock."

"What did you expect me to buy it with, Monopoly money?"

"A phone call to the mountains you couldn't make? Look at the racks, look. Shmattes from three years ago, nothing we can sell."

"Farber, even your pennies don't have faces, you squeeze them so hard, and you're telling me about new stock?"

"We need it. I want to make a good impression."

"For the yentas on a hot Saturday afternoon you want to make a good impression?" Jack drew closer and gazed down at Farber. "Never kid a kidder. What's happening, Farber?"

The little man could hardly contain himself, his arms like wind-mills, legs doing a jig. "You know Joe Brenner, he worked with Lil at Palace Fashions? His sister, aleve ah shalom, she died of you-know-what a few months ago and his brother the year before from the same. Joe was so afraid he would get you-know-what he couldn't eat or sleep, his doctor told him he needed a change, he quit his job at Palace Fashions and the whole summer he's working at Russeks on Fifth Avenue."

"What is this, you-know-what? Consumption, bleeding ulcers or the real you-know-what?"

They didn't say *cancer* out loud. Cholera was a curse, but if you pronounced the word *cancer* God might strike you with it.

"It's the real, God forbid, you-know-what."

"What's this to do with our merchandise, or whatever you're driving at?"

"We talked it over in the mountains, me and Ruthie, and we decided that what Farber needs is a partner. You know, fresh blood."

"So what are you offering this partner? Two dozen coats with lin-ings ruined from gas heaters? Green walls that haven't been painted for years, a jinxed color. The ceiling so old . . ." Jack lifted the push broom for sweeping the sidewalk and raised it on high . . . "one push with this broom the whole ceiling comes down, not to mention this fah-cockta carpet, it has so many stains the bums on Bowery wouldn't take it as a gift. To fix this place up you'd need a fortune. Maybe I'd have to bring the Persian rug from Manya's restaurant."

"Never you mind, never you mind. I hear that Joe Brenner hates Russeks. I'm meeting him this afternoon. What's to lose? He wants a partnership, he buys in for three bills."

"Three C's."

"Three big ones. Thousands."

For once Farber had the last word. Almost.

Recovering from his shock, Jack exploded. "A new Buick, top of the line, is maybe fifteen hundred dollars, you're asking three thou for your old coats and moldy walls? Surely you jest." Reaching for a fresh ciga-rette, he turned aside to steady his hand as he struck a match.

"We'll hondel a little. This is a two-price store. The partnership is also two-price."

"Joe Brenner may be worried about you-know-what but he's shrewd. He won't take your store if you gave it to him for nothing. Zero times three thousand is still zero. That's what the place is worth."

Jack spoke with bravado, with flair. Still he was shaken, his day ruined. He puffed on his cigarette and lit a fresh one. "You think we'll see a single customer on a hot day like this?"

"I have other things on my mind. You make a sale, fine. You don't, also fine. In one hour I'm taking the subway to meet Joe Brenner. And Jack, Monday you should try Seventh Avenue, pick me up some snappy garments. For this I rely on you. Why didn't you call me about buying while I was away?"

My father stared gloomily at the deserted street. "I had to take my mother to a specialist. Maybe it's nephritis. Some kind of kidney trouble."

Farber wasn't listening, busy combing his hair. Promptly at noon, he left in search of a partner. One or two women drifted into the store in the late afternoon but Jack was too preoccupied to charm them. Impatient to speak to his mother, he phoned home. "Ma, Farber is looking for a partner."

"Is that geferlach?"

"Geferlach? It's a disaster. What will he need me for if he has a partner?"

"Don't worry about catching the fish until you have the net."

"Fish, net, what are you talking about?"

"It's too soon to worry. Talk is free. Who is he trying to catch?"

"Joe Brenner. He works at Russeks now. He quit Palace Fashions. His doctor advised it."

"Then why should Brenner want to come back? His doctor told him he needs a change. He quits Russeks for Farber's? Don't be foolish."

Bubby managed to calm him momentarily, but Jack closed the store early. Despite this being their first Saturday night in the city since their vacation, my parents didn't venture out of the house. What would happen to us if Farber found, not Joe Brenner, but someone foolish enough to invest a few hard-earned dollars—and my father lost his job? Only my brother managed to sleep without waking up hourly during the night.

In the morning, as soon as Lil heard Mr. Jacob moving boxes in his store below our apartment, she stole out of bed, dressed in her sailor pants and striped top and signaled me to come with her.

We stepped over Clayton in the kitchen and he awoke immediately and ran with the broom handle to bang on the top step and scatter any animals that had lodged on the stairs during the night. My mother linked her arm in mine as she greeted Mr. Jacob.

"Can I use your phone, darling?"

I had no idea what she was up to—she didn't confide in me—but she needed my moral support.

"What, your phone upstairs is out of order?"

Lil winked and patted Mr. Jacob on the cheek.

"It's a surprise for Jack, I don't want him to know. Later, Manya is making blintzes, I'll bring you some."

Jacob was pleased. It had been a long time since we wanted his phone. He brushed up against my mother. "You're a knockout. Never looked better. What did you do, fall asleep in the sun? That tan, it's not from tar beach."

Lil could stop traffic with her golden hair, her golden skin, her trim figure. Jack may have appeared out of place as he traversed the sidewalk under the Third Avenue El in his spiffy clothes, slicked-back hair, three-pointed handkerchief perfect in his breast pocket, but Lil could pass for a society girl who had wandered downtown by mistake. Her restlessness since she had returned from Connecticut translated itself into a sexual energy that men reached for, hoping to capture. She glanced at the clock. Ten to eight. Not too early to call.

"Two minutes on the phone, Jacob dear, no more."

"Stay the whole day. Maybe you'd like to work for me, such an adorable girl, you could sell men's clothing easy."

She gave the number to the operator with great care. I waited out-side as the lookout in case Bubby came down. Then Lil emerged smiling, winked at Jacob before taking my hand and hurried across the street to The Grand Canal, acting with unusual determination.

At the entrance of the cafeteria—that great threat to our restaurant business—I hung back. After my one trip with Jack when we tried a few dishes, I had refused to walk on that side of the street. "What are we doing here?" I asked.

"I'm trying to help Bubby. Come, come, we'll be out in a few minutes."

Moe, short and hairy, who had been in class 2A with Lil, was in charge of the counter. His arms, chest and back were covered with a heavy pelt that showed through his undershirt. Maybe he had shaved before coming to work, but his face bristled with stubs of beard. His muscled arms could lift fifty-pound bags of potatoes or massive cartons of canned goods. The street urchins called him "Bluebeard" and no one messed with him. Strong, tough, fearless, a true child of the streets, he could have crossed over to Little Italy and become a big shot if he had relinquished his Jewish upbringing.

"Lil Roth!" Moe blushed, the skin under his eyes a sudden pink. "What can I do you for?" He had a quirky smile that revealed crooked overlapping teeth, some chipped or half broken. Engaged to Tzipke Goldberg for twelve years, he always replied to inquiries about why he wasn't married, "Why buy a cow when milk is so cheap?" This form of heartache was common among men in the Jewish ghetto. Moe found the idea of leaving his widowed mother intolerable and Tzipke, who kept the books for her widower father, a printer on Allen Street, suffered from the same constraints.

"Could you make me a half a tuna sandwich?" Lil asked seductively.

Moe flashed his crooked teeth.

"A half a sandwich. What's that, like a bucket of steam?"

Lil fluttered her lashes. "To tell the truth, I just want a taste. In Connecticut they made tuna sandwiches. I wanted a drop, not a whole sandwich."

Moe shouldered his way through the swinging doors to the kitchen and returned with a tray of tuna salad that he set into the counter of ice. "This hot weather is murder for salads with mayo. You don't keep it iced, you're serving poison on top of poison."

Lifting the serving spoon from the tray, Moe leaned over and placed it to Lil's lips, his cheeks and forehead tomato red.

"Feh." Lil spit the tuna into her hand. "It's pure salt."

"It's pure dreck, the worst." Moe laughed. "We buy these big cans, bits and pieces of fish, a lot of it is blood meat from the bottom of the fish that Jews are forbidden to eat. They put it in brine and we pour out the salty water, dump the tuna with a jar of Kraft's dressing. The fish is too salty, the dressing too sweet. We sell a ton of it on white bread."

"How can people eat it?"

"America goniff. Americans steal what they can. It makes them feel American. The only good thing is the celery."

"That's not what we ate in Connecticut."

"Musta been albackmore, all white tuna packed in water. Top of the line. Saperstein carries it. It's like day from night. The best."

"Thanks for the advice and the taste, Moe. You're the best, too. You think you'll come to an agreement with Tzipke?"

"When the moon comes over the mountain." He started to laugh but sighed instead.

"It's hard to leave your mother," Lil agreed. "I could never leave Manya. Never. We had some scare when we thought she might remarry. Touch wood, that's over."

We waved our good-byes. Tzipke met us on the sidewalk, yellow sheets in hand. "Here's your ad for Manya's. A hundred sheets, fifty cents."

The paper was thin and gaudy, the print smudgy. Yet the words, MANYA DELIVERS stood out boldly.

"Great. Food or cash?"

"Cash."

Years of working in dark quarters of the print shop had given Moe's betrothed a ghostly pallor and a permanent expression of despair. Whatever youthful appeal she once possessed had vanished over their conflict about marriage.

Lil put her hand on Tzipke's scrawny arm. "Listen," she said kindly, "you shouldn't wait longer. Take Moe to City Hall. A Jewish wedding comes later."

"My father says no. His mother says no."

"Two wrongs don't make a right. Get married. Even if you live in one room, you'll be together. Moe is a good boy. He loves you, you love him. Who lives where is not the question."

Tzipke began to cry. Shortly after eight on a stifling Sunday morning on Canal and Orchard streets, I lingered while Lil consoled the weeping woman. "Love will find a way," she said. And meant it.

"Don't forget the fifty cents."

"We won't."

It would have to wait. Jack's unemployment check might be in the mail—if he was entitled to one more.

When we got home, Bubby was leaning over the kitchen sink pouring warm water on Jack's hair as he washed it. "So where were you? You think it's Connecticut, you can take a walk before breakfast?"

"We sampled the tuna at The Grand Canal. Such chozerei you can't imagine. We found out that Saperstein carries the best white tuna. Moe said so. Ma, do you think he will ever marry that poor girl, Tzipke?"

Bubby couldn't answer. The phone rang. Uncle Goodman for Jack. He'd be down later for a little talk. My mother smiled triumphantly. Her early morning phone call had done the trick. She went back to bed.

Very late the night before, Jack had stumbled into the dining room, smoking furiously. Dragging a chair to the open window near our bed, he blurted to his mother, "What do you think, Ma, will I lose my job at Farber's?" He worked there for so many years that it did not occur to him to seek employment elsewhere.

Manya waited a long minute before answering. "The whole thing could be a blown-out egg. If Joe Brenner wanted Farber's business he would answer right away and Farber would tell you right away. Small men like Farber, they like to talk big. That store, it's shmutzig, it smells. Not for you, it would be closed long ago. Nothing happened. Maybe Joe Brenner even laughed in Farber's face."

Jack's cigarette lit up in the dark. "A week or two later, Brenner could change his mind," he said.

"He should leave Russeks for a whole lot of headaches on Division Street? It's a wonder the customers don't get asthma from the rotting walls. A greenhorn leaving Germany because of Hitler, he might think it's a wonderful store."

I lay quietly in the folding bed beside Bubby trying not to move, not to breathe. The air hung with their unspoken thoughts.

Abruptly, Jack announced, "You know Lil's brother, Geoff Simon? He tells me I'm a failure because I don't own my own business."

"I own my own business and we don't have two pennies to rub together. Jack darling, if you want to buy in with Farber, be his partner, think about it. You want it, you'll have it."

"And what will you use for money? Your earrings that are in hock? The back payments on the Morris Plan?"

I hoped Bubby would answer but she let the silence extend until like a rubber band it stretched and broke.

"My credit is good, but only once. You have to tell me what you want. I can ask one time, not more."

Jack lit another cigarette with his stub. "You mean Uncle Goodman?"

"He begs to help me because I brought Bertha over from Odessa when she was a child. He told you the story a hundred times. Small things I let him help me. Big, I never asked."

Jack didn't answer. Out of cigarettes, he lurched to his bedroom, hoping to put an end to the whirligig in his brain. Lil had been listening, which was why she and I rushed to Jacob's store before eight. She didn't want Bubby to ask Uncle Goodman for money for Farber's store. She asked.

I decided that with my father at work and Lil in bed I'd deliver the yellow printed sheets that announced "Manya Delivers." Clayton insisted on walking with me as soon as he bathed. He removed a pan from under the sink and reached for the old cigar box that held his personal soap, his shampoo and his hair gel. Stripped naked and shameless, he lodged his feet into the pan and poured water from the kettle over his head. He didn't like his hair to be "nappy."

His expensive hair straightener stank up the house, so to apply it, he would climb up to the fifth floor and sit on the step leading to the roof. The merchants in the neighborhood labeled him as "Manya's boy," but if some passerby caught sight of him on the roof they might call the police and report him as a prowler. On the days he applied the stinky stuff to his hair, he sat upstairs for an hour until the solution "took." What it took was clumps of hair from his scalp—the rest remained black, tightly wound springs.

Often he bathed at the kitchen sink while Bubby rattled her pans. Sometimes I peeked while he washed himself, fascinated as always by his long penis that arched from a thicket of black pubic hair. While soaping, it would stand straight out and he would gargle "Ahhhh" with a mixture of pride and joy. Bubby cautioned him from the next room, "Clayton, nisht far de kinder."

He understood Yiddish like a trouper, spoke it with ease. On this fiery day he cooled himself by pouring pans of cold water directly from the cold faucet over his torso.

Since his return from "out of town" he had taken to wearing white chef jackets. How he came by the two that he owned we didn't bother to ask—his confessions were more fantasy than reality.

This Sunday he brought forth a new one, not like the other two that he rinsed until they were spotless and then ironed. He was quite a sight on Orchard Street with his gelled hair, his sweet cologne and his white chef's jacket over black waiter's pants.

Bubby loved him fiercely, and once had a screaming fight with Markowitz from the dry-goods store across from our house because he wouldn't wait on Clayton, who loved new underwear.

Markowitz sold Bubby the shorts by the half dozen—for hard cash—no bartering for food. One Saturday when Clayton stayed out all night, he returned without his underwear. Bubby didn't mind the cost—"Ah nickel ah shtickel"—but she hated climbing up and down the stairs and crossing the street in her cooking clothes. She sent Clayton with the money and waited an hour and a half before she stormed into Markowitz's. Clayton was crouching in the corner, waiting to be waited on.

"Beautiful Manya," Markowitz announced at the sight of her. She was in no mood for false compliments. "An hour and a half my boy is here, what's wrong with you?"

"I don't wait on niggas."

"You don't wait on niggas? You're over in America a few years; the Bolsheviks should have sent you to Siberia. This boy is mine since he is seven years old, like my own child. You won't sell to him? You paskud-nock, you Cossack!" She banged the outside door in rage as she left. It broke the hinges.

Jacob tried to broker a peace between Manya and Markowitz. "Markowitz is a bulvan," Jacob declared. "What does he know? Your customers treat Clayton with respect. Even your doctors. Markowitz is a grub yung."

Sensing that public opinion was against him, Markowitz delivered a peace offering, socks for me and Willy. Bubby returned the box. Lil longed for free goodies but didn't dare cross Bubby; Markowitz kept to his own side of the street. Bubby spoke to Brody down the block, whose store was behind the pushcart that sold "Manhattan suspender-lach a quarter a pair." Brody treated Clayton royally.

Though he was determined to help me distribute leaflets, the unex-pected presence of three customers made it necessary for Clayton to stay and help Bubby. Lil had snuggled cozily in bed. Willy accompa-nied me instead.

No sooner did we hit the street than Willy burst out with his news. Having asked Clayton why he had been "out of town" a few months ago, Clayton replied, "sex raid." Dropping off the leaflets along the shops of Canal Street as we headed toward East Broadway, I asked, "Does it mean he was at a noisy party and the police came?"

For once Willy replied with condescension, "For a noisy party he would be out in a few days, a week at the most. It has something to do with sex."

"A sex party?" We regarded ourselves as both knowledgeable and unflappable when it came to sex—we heard about it everywhere, at school, at home, in the streets, at the restaurant. Can you be arrested for a sex party? we wondered. Our visualization of such events was limited to silent movies at the Loew's Canal, mostly biblical epics in which lightly clad maidens roiled on marble floors showing their thighs to insatiable men with bared teeth.

However, Willy and I were experts on the "out of town" technicalities. Some of our neighbors, a year or two older than we, didn't show up at school because they were hauled off to "out of town" juvenile facilities.

"Clayton was too embarrassed to tell us," I reasoned. We turned at Essex Street, past Seward Park High School, on our way to Delancey, throwing our leaflets into doorways. It didn't occur to us that tenement dwellers didn't know or care that Manya delivers.

At Delancey Street Willy left me and hopped, skipped and panted for home. I did one side of Clinton Street, then the other, returned to Delancey, crossed under the El, went past the Bowery into Little Italy. I was hot, exhausted and thirsty. Willy still wouldn't leave Jewish territory, but I had no fear because my father visited Rocco, his bookie, on almost a daily basis and Rocco was the law in his domain. Nothing could harm me because of Rocco.

Sure enough, as soon as his ever watchful eye caught sight of me, he gave two shrill whistles. "Hey, Jack's kid—over here."

Rocco conducted his business on the sidewalk. There may have been hours that he spent with his wife, his children, his aunts and uncles, his mistresses, but whenever I glimpsed Rocco he had his feet planted on the sidewalk outside his shoeshine stand, close to his mother's restaurant. He always wore a freshly laundered shirt and his silk jackets, made to order for him, ranged in color from steel gray to navy blue to black. You knew whether Rocco had gone to a funeral service because of his sleek black shiny outfit. Except for the mole close to his left nostril, he was handsome, with chiseled Roman features, massive hair and sensuous lips.

It was difficult to tell where Rocco began and his cronies and political friends left off. Men in hats and undershirts sat close by on folding chairs. Kibitzers and informants in garish bright yellow, green or black satin shirts hovered near, while his "runners" who took bets on horses or numbers swarmed through the streets. Sheets of the *Daily News* lay underfoot—it was the paper of choice in Little Italy—as well as butcher

paper from sandwiches, Popsicle sticks, fluted paper cups soggy from
gelato or ices, debris hurled from windows, soda and beer bottles that
rolled into the gutters. Rocco, whose connections were varied and exten-
sive, had a water truck with massive brushes come by every morning to
clean his personal street, and leave the junk on the next block. By late afternoon, though, the sidewalk was as cluttered as the day before.

Division Street lay within spitting distance of both Chinatown and
Little Italy, yet not a single merchant on the street feared robberies,
gang invasions, or random violence. By an unwritten law, the Jewish
ghetto had its own bureaucracy, its own corruption, its own petty
thieves, bookies, numbers runners, con men. They protected or abused
their own and ruled their territory like city-states, without hostilities
against the Italians or Chinese.

More than one Jewish bookie had approached Jack for his patron-
age but he resolutely refused to leave Rocco—they had attended junior
high together, in a building located on the cusp of Little Italy. The
crossover could not be severed.

"What you doing here?" Rocco asked me.

"Passing these out." I handed him a yellow sheet. He read with his
lips, moving them quietly to pronounce every word.

"What's this 'Manya Delivers'? Business lousy?"

I had had nothing to eat or drink since rising. My blouse from the
day before clung to my back, my shorts had black newsprint over
them, my sneakers were stained with grime.

"You want a lemon ice?"

I had been taught to say "No thanks" though I was dying for one.
"A glass of water would be good."

Rocco's cousins, named Salvatore and Dominic, were referred to as
Sal and Dom. Rocco put two fingers to his lips and emitted a shrill
whistle. His cousin Dom lifted his head from the ices stand. "Double
lemon ice and a big glass water," Rocco instructed.

My hands shook as I reached for the water. I drank it down without
pausing for breath. I would have gladly rubbed the lemon ice over my
face instead of licking it.

"How long you been walking?"

"An hour or two."

Rocco studied me with bemusement. "You're a gutsy kid."

I was afraid to lift my eyes to his.

"Can I tell you something?" he asked. "No offense."

"No offense." You had to hand this to Rocco—his tactfulness.

"See this street?" he asked. "Pizza parlor on every corner and one in the middle of the block." He waited for this information to sink in to indicate that he shared something earthshaking.

"You know what I say about the Jews? Brains and good food."

The yellow leaflet slipped from his fingers to the sidewalk. "In your neighborhood every street has a restaurant, a delicatessen, an ice cream parlor, a soda fountain. You get it? You got it?"

I thought hard. Tears welled in my eyes when I realized Rocco's meaning.

"No hard feelings?"

"No hard feelings."

"Hey, you want my mother should make you a meatball sandwich for the way home?"

I shook my head. Carefully. It wouldn't do for Rocco to catch me crying.

"Here's my advice," he said. "Don't say nothing to your Bubby. You gave it your best shot." He rumpled my damp sticky hair. I put out my hand stained with lemon ice to shake his. "Thank you for the ices, and what you said."

"Wait," he whistled again. "Where's Abe?"

"Around the corner," one of his flunkies said and set off at a trot. Abe Abramovitz pulled up in a brand-new black-and-white taxicab.

"Take the kid home."

"What's she doing here?"

"She'll tell you if she wants."

I started for the front seat but Abe insisted that I slide into the back. The seats were luxurious and I was afraid to stain them with my dirty hands. Abe sported a new cap decorated with black and gold braid. He had a fresh haircut, clean hands and a white shirt set off by a black leather tie.

I leaned forward. "Abe, what are you doing in Little Italy and who owns this fancy cab?"

"To make it short, I work there part-time. They own the car. I drive it."

My head whirled. Lil's early morning call, my walk with the leaflets, my conversation with Rocco and now this, Abe Abramovitz no longer in a dented filthy car but in a shiny extra large taxi.

"Abe, are you working for one of the gangs?"

"Get outta here."

"Who then?"

"They have a businessman come down to do business, I'm there to take him uptown to a hotel or La Guardia, with a new meter and a phone. You want me, you call my number. Me, little Abie who left school in 4B, a car with a phone. Real class. And here's my card. Any one of you, even Clayton, you want to drive somewhere, you call me, I'm right there."

"Is it the Cherry Street Gang? Will you be in trouble, rubbed out?"

"You seen too many movies. You think my father made me with a finger? It's strictly legit."

"Then why didn't they hire someone from their street?"

"What are you, some kind of dummy? They wanted a plain nice Jewish face, not a mug. Get it? Got it?"

Back at 12 Orchard Street, Clayton came around the corner with a bag of peaches. He handed one to Abe. "Ess a peachie," he said. "I bought these for Manya. A present. What did you do, Abe, snitch this car?"

"Here's my card. I'll drive you to Harlem anytime. I heard you were out of town. Manya, she's plenty glad you're back."

The yellow sheets already littered the streets. I dumped the rest into the garbage can. I was too tired to care. Tomorrow was the first day of school. I had my too-short skirt from last spring, and a clean unironed middy blouse. "Clayton, I need a new tie for school."

He handed me the peaches and tapped the pocket of his chef's jacket. He was the only one in the family with cash. He bought me a new middy blouse at Brody's and Orloff gave him the red silk for my tie. I didn't dare ask him for fifty cents for the worthless yellow "Manya Delivers" ads.

Not entirely worthless. The one response came from an unexpected source. The board of directors of the Educational Alliance was going to hold its semiannual meeting and they wondered whether Manya could cater and deliver lunch at twelve.

Lil, who answered the phone, said that it would be Manya's pleasure and when asked about the cost replied as Jack had instructed her, "Please let me get back to you." Jack suggested a dollar per person and Mrs. Hammond, the woman in charge of the lunch, didn't bargain. Jack wondered whether we bid too low.

On the afternoon of the luncheon, Abe drove Clayton to the Edgies on East Broadway and in one of the dingy offices Clayton placed a damask cloth on the empty table, set out a salad topped with hard-boiled egg slices and marinated beets, and unwrapped an entire steamed salmon, slices of roast chicken and Manya's famous pastries. He had brought an odd mixture of plates and silverware with him and no one complained. In fact Mrs. Hammond and the other members displayed their appreciation by tipping Clayton a whole dime. He smiled at them in his chef's coat, accepted the dime as if it were a dollar, cleared the table and didn't bother to call Abe when the luncheon was over—he carried home the carton with the soiled dishes and tablecloth.

We had a good laugh about the dime tip. Then Bubby scrounged around the top drawer of the buffet and found the pawn tickets. That's how Clayton retrieved the sewing machine, with the money from the catered lunch.

Mrs. Hammond proved to be a steady customer. Her husband had a law office on Wall Street and at least once a month Manya catered a lunch in his office. She kept the price steady at a dollar per person but requested two dollars for the waiter.

Bubby enjoyed the work. Word of her European-style catering drew a number of steady clients. With the catering money, Bubby's earrings and pearls finally were recovered from the hockshop and we paid off the Morris Plan.

Jack's foray into the business world was another matter—he turned into a nervous wreck. For one thing he wasn't certain that he wanted to become Farber's partner. He treasured his freedom, kibitzing on the sidewalk, spending an hour on the racing form, gossiping with Rocco, not to mention his Fridays with my mother uptown. The prospect of being responsible for a business—especially with a cheapskate like Farber—did not intrigue him.

Smoking one cigarette after another as he aired his grievances to Uncle Goodman, Jack finally came up with his trump card—he had enjoyed his summer off and his unemployment insurance.

"Who says you have to forget your unemployment insurance?" Goodman asked. "The partnership is in my name. You'll collect your salary like always. You'll have time off in the summer like always. Before Labor Day you'll decide if you want the partnership or not."

Jack couldn't resist the logic of the arrangement. "What's it costing you, Goodman? Tell me the truth?"

"Ah gansa gornisht. Not a penny to Farber. I'm paying for all the renovations, which is a tax deduction for me. I'm diversifying. You should think up a snappy name for the new sign. Since I'm redoing the whole building, Farber owns a fourth. You and I own three-fourths. You'll soon be a regular businessman, a big shot."

As if Jack were a reluctant music student whom Goodman dragged step by step to his lessons, Goodman had to convince Jack that he now was fulfilling his destiny. "But why now? What's the rush?" Jack demanded.

Goodman rose on his tiny feet and expanded his round chest. "Jack, you're not Manya's little boy anymore. She can't work much longer. The doctors know it and you know it. You have to take care of your mother. I'm doing this for her, for Manya. It's coming to her."

Jack swallowed hard. Slowly, he nodded. A defining moment.

18

Topsy-Turvy

THE FIRST STAGE of the renovation, namely throwing out years of junk, pained Farber. With his characteristic mania about not losing as much as a twisted nail, he scurried along the sidewalk salvaging what he could from the rubble. Jack and Goodman decided to gift him with the old limp coats and their stained linings. Farber seized upon these rags with sultanlike greed.

During the first week, the exterminators bore down with their vast tents and cylinders of gas. No one on the street had seen its likes before. John, Goodman's handyman, ripped out the ghastly smelling toilet fixtures and moldy wood boards before the store and backyard were tented and pumped full of deadly pesticide. Dressed in his black and red mackinaw and blue-striped railroad cap, John held his nose as he headed in his truck off to some remote dump to dispose of the vile garbage.

Uncle Goodman proceeded uptown to deal with lawyers and the absentee landlord's representatives, who finally agreed to pay for half the costs of a new roof. Farber maintained his post across the street the entire day, keeping an eye on the billowing tent lest some Bowery bum crawled inside for a deadly last sleep.

At 2:00 P.M. on the first Monday of the renovation, Jack, dressed in his usual natty attire, sought out his manicurist in Chinatown—a doll of a beautician with whom he flirted outrageously. The moment we dumped off our school books, Willy, Lil, Clayton and I left for Division Street carrying a pot roast sandwich on rye for Farber that must have weighed two pounds. We walked very fast, and though Lil's breath came in small gasps, it was worth it. The white tent could have been a circus for the excitement it brought us.

"Nu," said little Farber, gargling with delight. "By tomorrow morning there won't be one rat, one roach, one fly, one nothing left on the premises." He had learned the phrase "on the premises" from Jack and repeated it lavishly. Farber didn't open his sandwich until his wife, Ruthie, showed up—she had splurged on a bus ride to observe the tent.

Ruthie Farber was short, round as a matzo ball, with curly black hair parted in the middle and a childlike cherubic face. No sooner had we greeted her than Jack suggested that we snack on "chinks," in nearby Chinatown. Years later, I marveled how eagerly we consumed the slimy chicken chow mein, which consisted mostly of onions, celery and bean sprouts. But we wolfed it down with white and fried rice— Clayton ate in the restaurant kitchen—and shared fortune cookies. Lil's read, "Romance is on the way." She blushed.

The next morning, when the foreman of the exterminators put on a mask and goggles and peered inside the tent, he shook his head and told Uncle Goodman, "Sorry, there's still too many things crawling around. You need one more day." Uncle Goodman nodded his assent. Then he stopped off at our house to leave a booklet that featured bathroom equipment. "The children and Lil can't be there tomorrow when they open the tent. It's not for their eyes, and bad for their lungs. Pick out any toilet and sink from page five. I didn't buy class A of anything. The wood for the paneling, the carpet, the roofing will last a good five, ten years. The cheapest grade three is good enough, strong, clean and the few defects won't show."

I studied the white toilets and bathroom sinks and almost wept.

The least expensive appeared glorious compared to our hallway toilet with its stained water container below the ceiling, its pull chain mended with rope.

Noting my sadness, Bubby tried to make light of it. "You'll walk over to your father's store and pee on the whole world."

I didn't laugh and she didn't attempt to appease me again.

My mother had little to say about most aspects of the renovation. She had her heart set on expensive flowered carpeting for the window, together with pink spotlights, just like Palace Fashions. Uncle Goodman brought us an entire book of carpet samples and he and Jack decided on blue-gray industrial carpet for the floor. Lil selected plush red and pink cabbage roses for the strip in the window. The pattern would not have been Jack's choice, but neither did it offend him. He liked the idea of pink spotlights for the window.

Within a few weeks the store acquired a new roof, new carpeting, inexpensive paneled walls, new electrical fixtures, a new bathroom and a sign in black and gold that read Elite Fashions and in smaller print, "Where the Elite Meet."

The Thursday before we opened we hosted what Aunt Bertha called an "open house" from 5 to 7:30 P.M. Aunt Bea, Cousin Alice and Lenny, and Uncle Geoff were among the first to admire the pseudo-fancy interior. Every one of Bubby's purveyors came, as well as local merchants, my mother's brothers, Ada and her children, Jack's Chinese manicurist, his Chinese laundry man, Clayton in a rented white Palm Beach suit, and Abe Abramovitz, our cab man. Aunt Bertha stole the show in an ankle-length skirt and a tunic jacket, topped by a black picture hat with gold hat pins as large as eggs. Our doctors, Koronovsky and Wolfson, couldn't attend.

No party would be complete without Rocco, dazzling in a gray silk suit with tuxedo lapels. He had sent a basket of flowers that sat in the window under a pink spotlight. One hooded glance at me in my too-short polka-dotted party dress from Dr. Koronovsky's wedding and he whispered to one of his lieutenants. Within minutes he thrust a package into my hands and steered me to the bathroom. "Every girl needs a red velvet dress," Rocco declared.

The collar was white lace, the lines princess style with twin ribbons of white satin cascading along the front. Although the dress hung down to my ankles, Rocco was right. Every young girl needed a red velvet dress, though I felt both self-conscious and embarrassed to walk out in such finery. Bubby, seated in a baronial chair lent by Mr. L.—every merchant on the street dropped in—studied me in wonder. "Ah, Czarina," she whispered.

Farber and Ruthie stayed to clean up afterward. During the party they kept to one corner, miniature statues. Other than their wedding, it may have been the most thrilling evening of their humdrum existence.

We fell into bed the moment we reached home, and Willy and I did not attempt school the next day. No holiday in the city had been as festive as the party at Elite Fashions.

In early October, the phone rang at 7:30 A.M. and Aunt Bertha asked to speak to Lil. Saks Fifth Avenue phoned her Yonkers number; they wanted Lil to show up for orientation. Bertha explained that Lil had to spend a few hours there learning the procedures and to please call to confirm her appointment.

Both of my parents slept late and the news about Saks had them stumbling around, uncertain whether to call Saks, to ignore their request or to return to bed. Clayton made himself scarce by sloshing the steps with soapy water, sweeping the sidewalk and pouring water over the dented garbage cans.

The merchants on Canal Street envied us because of Clayton, but only Mr. Jacob obtained Clayton's services. Clayton straightened the boxes, emptied the wastebaskets, tidied the sidewalk. In addition to the petty cash, Jacob gifted Clayton with unsalable merchandise, gray with dust but appealing to Clayton's vanity: a fake leather jacket and black trousers, both cut so skimpy that the jacket wouldn't close and Clayton patiently let out the darts in the pants in order to shimmy into them.

On the day of orientation Jack walked Lil briskly to the subway; he insisted on accompanying her to the employees' entrance of Saks.

Lil found herself in a room with half a dozen women, two of whom wore cheap rayon dresses in floral prints. One of them, Fanny, over-weight, sallow and smelling slightly of underarm perspiration, sat at a desk next to Lil, a whiz at numbers and technical details.

The instructor, Mrs. Baum, who was short and short of sleep, dis-tributed printed tax sheets, sales books and bunches of sales tags held together with twine. Wiping her face with a limp handkerchief, she mumbled directions in a hoarse whisper.

Lil was the only one with no department store experience. Each of the others, including Fanny, recently from Lerner's—Lerner's!—whizzed through her sales tags and their taxes, transcribing the infor-mation to her sales book within minutes. Fanny took pity on Lil and slid over to her seat.

"See, here's a tag for $16.95. Find the number on the card, put your finger to the end of the line where it says 'Tax,' write it down, move to 'Total.' You don't add anything. Just follow the card. If the salesgirls had to add, Sophie Gimbel would be out of business."

Lil tried her best, then frustrated she let Fanny write the informa-tion in her sales book.

Mrs. Baum, still mopping her face with her handkerchief, an-nounced, "Everyone up front to practice with charge cards." The others inserted their mock Saks charge cards into their sales books with their carbon paper exactly in the right place as they slammed down the handle of the machine. Trying hard to work just as fast, Lil set her card wrong side up and on the second attempt had the name up-side down. Fortunately Mrs. Baum barely scanned the finished sheets.

Mrs. Baum continued. "Ladies, if a gentleman returns a garment that has been worn, it's the store's policy that you can't embarrass a man. Give a full refund no matter what shape the garment is in and mark the ticket MAN."

In her haste to reach the store Lil had failed to drink coffee or even a glass of water. Her head swam from hunger and thirst and the array of instructions. At Palace Fashions all she had to do was bring the pur-chased garment to the front desk and a young girl did the paperwork and the boxing.

"Twenty minutes for lunch and then we'll discuss full-length bags, short bags, boxes, gift wrap." The other women cried, "What did you bring for lunch? Cheese? Baloney?" and raced to the tiny lunchroom.

Slowly, Lil reached the elevator, pressed the down button and strode out to the street. She hurried to the subway on the verge of tears, and entered our apartment at the height of lunch hour. Clayton was packaging the takeouts, a new twist in our business, which included small cardboard boxes with the name *Manya* in script. Bubby was ladling out entrées for the seated customers.

The instant Lil came into view, Weinstock, who was gobbling every item in sight in the kitchen, asked, "Anything wrong, Lil? How come you're home so early?"

She braced her shoulders, smiled on cue and replied, "Orientation, only a few hours." She marched past the diners into her bedroom. Finishing my lunch, two bites of a lamb chop, before heading back to school, I skipped after my mother. She sat on the bed, hands to her face, weeping.

"Mother, what happened? What's wrong?"

"The worst one was me with the taxes, the totals, the charge card upside down. I couldn't bear it and I left during the lunch break."

"Why are you crying? You don't need the job there. Palace Fashions is easy for you and it's close to Daddy. Forget about Saks."

"I can't."

"Why not?"

"Because everyone in Connecticut thinks I work there and I have to."

Despite her poor showing during orientation, Lil received a call to come for the Columbus Day sale. Columbus Day unfurled not only Italian flags but banners advertising sales across the city. Schools were closed. Little Italy had a major festival with music, statues of the Virgin Mary held aloft on floats and everyone out on the streets munching on meatball sandwiches, pizza, stromboli and sticky pastries with fake whipped cream.

A few blocks away on Division Street, women with broad behinds and chunky legs or slim chippies from uptown stormed the length of the street. At Saks Fifth Avenue, a 20 percent off sale advertised in the *Times* brought out the hordes. Lil didn't have to worry about her sales book. She glowed with immediate success.

At Saks, the women selected the clothes themselves and asked for help in the form of larger or smaller sizes or different colors. A matron glanced contemptuously at Lil when she forgot herself once and uttered the phrase, "You look stunning," considered vulgar at Saks.

Quickly, Lil shifted to Jack's lines: "The color is excellent for your complexion," or, "That's elegant." Within two hours customers were asking for Miss Lilyan, and complimenting her taste and service to the floor managers. As she completed each sale, she handed her sales book, cash or charge card to the manager and sailed on to the next client. She didn't take time out for lunch, a pee, a sip of water. She danced around in her high-heeled pumps, dressed in a navy blue suit and a satiny blouse with stripes of sky blue and yellow.

Abe Abramovitz stuck his head out of the service elevator at 5:58 and called, "Miss Lilyan's cab is waiting." The other salesgirls stared and the manager, a Miss Elizabeth, holding Lil's bulging sales book in hand, nodded her approval: "Well done."

"I bet you were number one today, the most sales," Abe confided as she fell into the backseat of his glistening cab.

"What makes you think so?"

"I saw you running around like a, what you call it, a marathon runner. I heard those snooty bitches saying, 'Thank you, Miss Lilyan, thank you.' I watched from the elevator a few minutes before calling your name. You were the classiest broad on the floor."

Lil stretched out full length across the seat and kicked off her shoes. "I'm terrible with numbers. I don't know how much I took in today. If I fall asleep in your car, you'll have to carry me upstairs."

"Hey that ain't work, that's pleasure."

In fact, Abe yelled for Clayton who brought down a chair. Both men carried her up the two flights of stairs.

Bubby responded to Lil's radiant, tired face by asking, "Goot gedavened?"

"Goot gedavened."

Because Lil was too tired to undress herself, Bubby slipped off her suit, removed her silk stockings and brought her a long-sleeved nightgown, which she had warmed at the open door of the oven. Having collapsed into her bed, Lil remembered only then that she hadn't been to the toilet the day long. Bubby ran a kettle of hot water over an enamel chamber pot and, like a child, Lil crouched on the floor for a long pee. Bubby carried it out; Clayton emptied it.

Because we had so much illness we actually owned a bed tray, tucked into one of the nooks in the windowless room. Lil was finishing her soup in bed when Jack walked in. Bubby helped him off with his jacket.

"Nu?"

"We sold blue for black and black for blue. They loved the store. A million compliments. How's Lil?"

"Her heart ran fast through her nightgown. With her soup I gave her an aspirin."

"Ma, when God made you, he threw away the pattern." Jack kissed his mother on both cheeks. "Remember Maurey from Colchester? His best trick, kissing on both cheeks. Very French, sexy but not."

Lil, whom we assumed was dozing, called out, "What about Maurey?"

"Kisses on both cheeks. What a racket. No woman could take offense." Jack concentrated on his mother. His strong love for her filled the entire room. "You know what I dreamed of standing on my feet the whole day? Your breaded veal chop and mashed potatoes. One chop for two more kisses, or my marker for a hundred bucks."

"Meshugana," Bubby cried in open-hearted joy, and within minutes we could hear her pounding the milky chop.

The following morning when the phone rang, Jack jumped out of bed to answer it. He was wearing one of his sleeping sweaters that hung down to his knees.

As prearranged, Bertha relayed a number to call at Saks. In answer to the voice at the other end, Jack said, "Miss Lilyan is indisposed today. She has commitments elsewhere. Please thank Saks for thinking of her. She'll be home by 5:30."

Lil and Willy were the best sleepers in the family, though Lil could outdo anyone in shutting out the world in the lumpy cocoon of her bed. Bubby had prepared a bath for her before we galloped up the stairs from school. She smelled of soap, smiled at us cheerfully and sank back into bed with an old *Silver Screen* magazine at her side. Weinstock, who dropped in for a late-afternoon snack, ate nonstop, wiped his mouth on his chubby hand and his hand on a slightly soiled linen napkin. He addressed me.

"You know Manya, how intelligent she is? Once a year she asks me the same question and I give her the same answer. She wants to know if we can put a bathroom in the storage room. I tell her, I tell her, it's impossible. The rats would jump out of the walls but there's no space for equipment, especially on the second floor. This building is from the year of the flood. It should have been condemned years ago. I'm a friend, not just an agent, so I'm telling you to move to a new building, a place with bathrooms, steam heat, big rooms. I tell Manya the truth, she answers no, no, no. What does she love in this terrible apartment? She loves the view of Canal Street, she loves the neighbors, but mostly she loves the old shmutz and the—the degradation."

I realized Weinstock had strained to come up with the word *degradation*. He broke into a sweat after he said it.

Neither Bubby nor I had found a rebuttal to this by the time Aunt Bertha phoned with another message. Miss Sullivan at Saks wished to speak to Lil. We made the call and in her best falsetto Lil intoned, "Miss Lilyan here," snapping her fingers to signal me to write down the conversation.

"A permanent temporary position? Oh, five days a week, and no guarantee if it gets slow? I see, you want me on an 'as needed' basis."

I scribbled as fast as I could in Willy's ledger. Lil listened, then replied, "Thank you for calling. I'll let you know soon." She cried out to Bubby, "Ma, Ma, I sold more than anyone yesterday! They want me to come in five days a week. She said I was perfect for Saks. I have the job except when it's slow. Then I'm laid off."

We could hardly wait for Jack to discuss it with us. His immediate reaction was negative. "Lil, since you've been married, since you were seventeen, you've never worked five days a week. Saks means too much traveling, too much on subways, too far away from home, bad for your heart."

Then my father turned and regarded me. "Don't tell me you have no opinion," he said.

My pause was considerable. "It depends on how much Mother wants it."

Each of us stirred in our chairs around the dining room table.

"Lil, the kid is right. How badly do you want it?"

From the smallest to the largest decisions, Lil counted on Jack. It was difficult for her to answer. "Don't be afraid," he coaxed her gently. "What do you want?"

After twirling her hair, chewing her finger and crossing her legs, she stated, "I'd like two days a week at Saks. One day in the middle of the week, and then Saturday."

"Maybe they won't agree to your terms?"

"Then I'll be back on Division Street."

Everyone of us prayed that Saks would reject Lil's suggestion for two days a week. We relied on habit, repetition, sameness; we needed it. Bubby advised us repeatedly, "When a worm creeps into horse-radish, he thinks there's nothing sweeter." We wanted Lil in our horse-radish, not in a universe whose sweetness we could not taste.

But Miss Sullivan accepted Lil for Wednesday and Saturday without hesitation. Jack protested that Wednesday was their theater mati-nee day, so Miss Sullivan agreed to the odd Wednesday off. Perplexed by this new salesgirl whose taxi waited to drive her home and who needed a theater day, Miss Sullivan admitted that these oddities added to the glamour of Miss Lilyan and increased her desirability.

On Friday, they both stayed in their bedroom until they left for a movie, after which it was straight to Pandy's, a quick bite of the Friday night meal and to bed. On Sunday, Lil often didn't show up at either Palace Fashions or Elite, though on Monday, she and Jack traveled to the garment district to search for bargains for Jack's store before re-turning to the bedroom. Jack had captured Lil for himself. He didn't share her with Bubby, her children or her friends. Since she started to work at Saks, a renewed urgency existed. "Young sweethearts," Bubby called them.

In mid-September my elocution lessons began with Miss Sussman. Abe drove me there and back every other Saturday. The early sessions disappointed me. We practiced breathing, ran in circles, fell to the floor, imitated trees swaying, acquired faces and body movements to express fear or joy. We jumped from high and low places. I earned praise for pretending to be sick or injured, panicked at jumping from the stage to the floor, resisted tumbling, which everyone else in the class achieved with ease. Physical skills were my worst.

Bubby's questions about elocution lessons elicited a one-word response. "Good."

Unaccountably, I was crying. Hard. "What am I, the Little Match Girl?" I wept. "In two weeks we have to meet Estelle Solomon for lunch. What am I supposed to wear, my short dress from Dr. Koronovsky's wedding? The red velvet that's too long? Why can't you buy things that fit me? You're in the business. Don't they have samples for children?"

My father puffed on a fresh cigarette and paced the dining room. "When you're right, you're right. For ten dollars at the wholesalers, I can buy something snappy, fit for a merchant's daughter."

One minute my father had to be pleaded with, dragooned, imposed upon, to become a store owner. A breath later he doted upon his status, would have bought enough stock to fill an armory, and foisted his personal card on anyone who smiled at him. In conversation he implied that he was one of the biggest *machers* in the industry. At Cinderella Finery, a wholesale house for young girls, he ventured a step further, hinting that my ravishing mother was a buyer for Saks.

Mr. Miller, who was halfway through a stale Danish and tepid coffee when this snappy couple walked in, may have thought he had two out-of-town buyers, but he hid his disappointment when he discovered that Jack's interest centered on samples for his daughter. "You two Joosh?"

"Who in the shmatte business isn't Jewish? My wife and I are New Yorkers, born and bred."

"You do a big volume, you have branches out of town? Why fool with last year's models when we have our new line, class A stuff, high class."

"I came in for some things for my daughter. You want big orders, speak to my wife. She's with Saks Fifth."

On a rack, my father spied exactly what he wanted for me, a rose-colored two-piece suit, the skirt with kick pleats, the jacket closed with pearl buttons. A navy blue suit, virtually identical with the exception of a blue-and-white-striped knit shirt and a blue beret attached with a huge safety pin, caught his attention as well. "These two are perfect."

"But they're from last spring."

"For her elocution lessons they're what she needs."

"Perfect," repeated my mother, flashing her movie-star smile. She was bone-tired, and the lunch with Estelle at the Plaza loomed like an endurance test. She had never been to the Palm Room, didn't know what to order or how to behave, and she assured me more than once that she counted on me to prevent her from slipping up on our true address.

"Which outfit for the Palm Room at the Plaza, the rose or the navy?"

"For the Palm Room, I have a great number for you," Mr. Miller announced, "a one of a kind from France, a sample, wool and silk. The color is called 'bluebird.' If they made these in ladies' sizes I'd be a millionaire. Gloria Vanderbilt would love it." He produced a lascivious grin.

Jack leaned into the dress as if it were an art object. One piece, the top silky, long sleeved, separated by a band of blue velvet for the full skirt. Jack fondled the material, examined the hand stitching.

"I see you're a maven," Mr. Miller laughed. "Your daughter: is she a thin girl? The dress from Paris needs a thin girl."

Kibitzing, poking each other in the ribs, Jack flashed his business checkbook—Farber would scream for a week that the check wasn't written for store merchandise—and the deal was struck, seventeen dollars for two suits and a dress from Paris.

"Where did you find that incredible dress?" Estelle cried out as she embraced us at the Palm Room of the Plaza Hotel.

Lil and I were too shy to answer.

No sooner were we seated at a round table with its starched cloth and heavy silver utensils than waiters in white jackets and young busboys emerged from behind the potted palms.

Estelle smiled radiantly. "Maybe you'd like the Maine lobster? They'll provide you with a bib to keep your beautiful dress safe."

My lovely dress did not erase my ghetto background. Shellfish was forbidden to us; neither Lil nor I had ever tasted a crustacean. Jack instructed us that we couldn't go wrong with fresh fish and Lil echoed his exact sentence. Estelle suggested Dover sole, flown in from England. Lil settled our dilemma. "That sounds wonderful. We'll share one order."

Lil squeezed my hand when Estelle instructed the waiter, "One Dover sole divided in the kitchen for my friends, drawn butter on the side, please. I'll have the shrimp and avocado salad with extra dressing. Be sure the dessert cart is full. My young friend here is an expert."

My father had carefully rehearsed us on buttering a slice of bread or a roll—a small piece, not the entire slice. The rolls were cold, and I made a face at the salty butter. "Don't they serve sweet butter?" I asked.

Estelle doted on us from the beginning of the meal to the end. "I forgot I was eating with gourmets. Of course you deserve sweet butter."

Lil was grateful for the diversion about the butter. Not only did the surroundings intimidate her, but she had something on her mind that required her utmost courage. She asked softly, "How are the boys?"

Clapping her hands, Estelle announced, "Graduating from med school in June. Can you believe it? They've applied to Mass General for their residency. We're excited about that. But if one gets in and the other doesn't, it will kill Gabe and Hal. They're like twins, rarely separated. It's been such a joy for us to see them grow up without rivalry." She regarded us intently. "And what a joy for me to see you today. I couldn't sleep last night thinking of our lunch. You both look marvelous, radiant."

Radiant was the word that encouraged Lil. "How about Maurey? Does he like law school?"

"Not especially. He keeps saying he would prefer something else."

Encouraged by Jack's and her own success, Lil replied, "Would he be interested in business?" She played with her fish, forked tiny bits into her mouth, tried hard to swallow.

"You mean finance, economics? He wouldn't mind the Wharton School but Wall Street is another matter."

My mother and I tried not to stare as Estelle cut off the tail of a giant shrimp, and with quick strokes of her knife cut the body in thirds. She dipped one section into a pungent sauce and popped it into her mouth. At that moment, I longed to be able to tell Lil that someday soon I would eat seafood in restaurants, imitating Estelle's confident relaxed manner.

"Maurey needs an occupation that excites him," Estelle continued.

"He should be an actor," I said, surprised at my boldness.

"You mean in the movies, a movie star?"

"No, the theater."

"I almost forgot. You're theater people." She reached for my hands and held them. "Are you studying drama?"

"A little. My teacher isn't too good. We're having a recitation in a few weeks, mostly for new students. My lines are, 'I want to act / I want to act / I want to see the gallery packed.' Good for the Catskills."

The remark sent Estelle into peals of laughter.

Lil had excluded herself from the conversation during this exchange, but then she was able to say, "I miss everyone from Colchester every day."

"I do, too. I can't explain why it was so magical, but when I'm home, I think of something that we said or did and tears come to my eyes. It's like missing a youthful lover, a first love."

I saw Estelle's eyes mist over. I wondered if she and Lil would burst out crying. Estelle pulled herself together. From her brown luxurious purse—not like the stuff from Goodman's factory—she withdrew a packet of photographs. "I had these made for you. They're from the performance of the Pankin's Follies. We won't ever forget that evening."

I prayed that Lil's hand wouldn't shake as she reached for the photographs. We leaned our heads together to study them.

There I stood with my toothpick legs, my too-short dress, my skinny arms stretched wide. And Lil, hands crossed against her chest, showing her teeth, not smiling; and there were Hal, Gabe, Ronny, the med students with their crazy wigs and hairy legs, doing the cancan; and Jack, the impresario, his hair slick, responding to applause. Maurey gazed at someone off camera with eyes of adoration.

"Oh, I look terrible," Lil cried, though she meant the opposite.

"We adore these pictures," Estelle said. "We put them in a large frame on the piano. That's why I couldn't sleep last night, imagining this moment."

Lil sighed softly, genuinely and deeply moved. I was on the verge of tears myself. The loss of that summer lay deep within my chest. Whatever we spoke about at lunch had small meaning compared to these photographs. "I'm almost crying from happiness," Lil said, doing her best to pull herself together.

"This summer we'll be happy again, we will, we surely will," Estelle repeated.

We had difficulty saying good-bye. We stood hugging and kissing in the lobby of the Plaza, like loved ones about to depart on a long journey. We thanked Estelle for the lunch, for her friendship, for the photographs.

After one last kiss we stepped outside. Abe was waiting for us, his new cab parked in a line of black city cars and limos. We waved again to Estelle and blew kisses. The moment we sank into the backseat, Lil rifled through the photos until she found the one of Maurey staring off camera, his face transformed with admiration. No longer aware of me, Lil pressed the picture to her lips.

19

Dire Times

HAVING WORKED AT Saks on Saturday and been through an emotional afternoon at the Plaza with Estelle on Sunday, Lil expressed her fatigue on Monday by sighing and repeating, "I'd give anything for a nice hot shower." Since it was Jack's Monday off, he had an inspiration.

"Lil, let's check into the Astor Hotel, take a long soak in their big bathtubs, nuzzle a little, sleep a lot and then in the evening see a show or a movie. We'll stay overnight, have breakfast at Bickford's and come home."

"Go, go," Bubby urged. "A one-night honeymoon is perfect after working so hard."

She choked down her disappointment when Lil replied, "I'm not up to it today. It's hard for me to put one foot in front of the other. My throat hurts. Maybe I should paint it with tincture of iodine."

The cover of the iodine bottle refused to budge. Lil tapped the bottle on the sink and it cracked to pieces. Shards of glass coated with brown sludge lay underfoot. She left it for Clayton to clean and staggered into bed.

Jack's prescription for mild illness was to apply himself as often as possible to his wife's body. Bubby closed the bedroom door.

But in spite of administering what Jack called "the best medicine in the world," Lil remained unresponsive and silent. On Tuesday, still lethargic, she managed to eat and drink small portions of what Bubby hand-fed her.

On Wednesday, with some effort, she bathed and went off to Saks. Willy complained about not feeling well either and Bubby urged him to stay home. But for once Willy resisted the idea. He had a geography test and he could ace geography because of our electronic game and his large puzzle of the map of the United States.

Clayton and Bubby went off for the daily shopping and when they returned, Bubby cooked while Clayton swept the rug with kosher salt, set up two or three card tables, covered them with fresh linen and pried open the windows an inch to allow fresh air into the dining room for a few minutes.

Whenever the program changed at Loew's Canal, Clayton went to see the new movies in the late afternoon. Bubby had devised a special arrangement with the management because Negroes were not permitted. In exchange for tons of food for the ticket-taker, Clayton occupied the last seat in the back row, where the screen appeared slanted.

His kitchen chores finished, he had just started out the door for the movies when Moe from The Grand Canal shouted from the downstairs entrance that Willy had fainted on the sidewalk on Canal Street in front of the fruit pushcart. Clayton leaped down the stairs, racing with the wind. He brought Willy home in his arms shouting as he entered, "Bubby, he's a brenfire!"

Bubby found the family thermometer, as distinct from Jack's, snug in his vest pocket. She put her head to Willy's bony chest. His nonstop wheezing made her wonder how long he could keep the thermometer in his mouth. Though he coughed it up in less than a minute, it already read 103. She did her best to arrange what she called her "poker-lady face" and said "Nisht geferlach."

She fetched the ephedrine for his wheezing and found one of Dr. Koronovsky's bromides wrapped in wax paper. Willy managed to keep both down before he coughed until he vomited. Eyes closed, his wheeze sounded like a death rattle. She was about to phone Dr. Scott Wolfson, still not grasping the calamity, when she heard Lil calling to her from the living room, "Ma, I'm sick. I had to leave work. Ma, I think I'm going to faint."

Clayton carried Lil into the bed with Willy. She was almost as hot as her son. "Is it your throat?" Bubby depressed Lil's tongue with the end of a dessert spoon, and saw purple tonsils surrounded by greenish fluid. The spoon landed in the sink in an unwashed soup pot.

I slid into the apartment from school, my breath hot, my head heavy. Yellow squiggles danced in front of my eyes. Bubby said, "Clayton, let's make night."

We had acquired a sign that read Open on one side and Closed on the other. Clayton thumbtacked the Closed sign on the door, not for the customers, but to keep the neighbors at bay.

In the confusion Clayton phoned Dr. Koronovsky but forgot to leave our name or phone number. Bubby fared no better when she tried Dr. Wolfson's service. "Willy Roth is very sick. The doctor should come right now." The service assured her that Dr. Wolfson would answer his messages soon. He didn't call back.

A Dr. Solomon had taken on some of Dr. Koronovsky's practice. Bubby found his number. His wife answered in Yiddish, "Alle menschen zynin kronk."

Jack staggered in next and fell beside Lil, incapable of moving. Clayton undressed him. For the rest of the long night Bubby didn't enter the bedroom. She devoted herself to Willy, sponging him, rocking him in her arms, holding him up to the steaming tea kettle.

At five in the morning she tried Dr. Wolfson's home number. He answered on the first ring.

"Willy. Wheezing, 106. I called and called. You didn't answer."

"Oh, my God, I'll be right over. Manya, don't cry, I'm on my way."

Clayton took to the dark sidewalk with his flashlight. Dr. Wolfson must have sped through the streets because he reached us in very little time. One glance at Willy, at flushed Bubby, at me and he cried out, "Are you all sick?"

He listened to Willy's chest and phoned Dr. Koronovsky at his home. "I think Willy has aspiration pneumonia. I was out last night with Susan's family and didn't pick up my messages. Everyone is sick. The apartment is icy, beds everywhere. I don't know what to do first. I'm afraid we may lose Willy. And I can't cope."

Dr. Koronovsky spoke in a loud voice that crackled. "Stop that nonsense. Of course you can cope. You have to. I'll be right over. Do you have any emergency medication? How is Lil?"

"Lil? I haven't been in the bedroom yet."

"Take care of them in this order. Willy first, then Lil. If she has pneumonitis or strep it's dangerous for her heart. Do what you can until I get there."

"But they need blood work. They should be hospitalized. I failed them by not calling in for my messages. If we lose Willy it will be my fault."

"I don't have time for your guilt. Clayton knows how to steam up the kitchen. Let me speak to him. Clayton, how is Willy breathing?"

"Almost not."

"Please call Abe the cab driver or find another taxi. I'm taking everyone out of the apartment."

"Where to?"

"My old apartment on Grand Street. It's clean, it's warm and my sisters aren't there. Clayton, please stay healthy. And don't forget to call Abe for his taxi."

Clayton blocked the air from the front door with towels and set pots of water boiling. He carried Willy carefully into the kitchen.

"Don't worry, Dr. Scott," he said. "Dr. K., he seen this for twenty-five years or more. Whole families die. Whole buildings die. But not this one. Dr. K., he don't let it happen. The Roths, they like his family. He put his arm in the fire for them." He added respectfully, "You better see Miss Lillian."

In a daze, Dr. Scott Wolfson skirted between the beds, biting his lip. "How do you feel, Lil?" he asked. She opened her glazed eyes, closed them, did not reply. He listened to her heart before staggering into the kitchen. "I've never seen anything like this. It's a war zone."

"No, it's the Great Evacuation," Dr. Koronovsky boomed.

"How did you get here so fast?" Dr. Wolfson asked.

"Had a police escort. Called Tom O'Connor from this precinct. He arranged it for me. I'm taking Willy to Beth Israel. Dr. Rothman, Sid Rothman, will perform the trache. He's the best. Everyone else, to my Grand Street place. That includes Clayton."

No sooner did Jack understand that Willy would be hospitalized than he said, "I'm going, too." No one bothered to examine Jack. He lay next to Lil until roused by Dr. Koronovsky's instructions. Then he dressed.

By holding an unlit cigarette in front of him and keeping his eyes on its white line, Jack managed to conquer the steps without falling. Then his knees buckled and he collapsed in the outside doorway.

Bubby insisted that Willy could not leave for the hospital without her. Persuasively, Dr. Koronovsky crooned, "Manya, your temperature is high. If you step into the hospital, they'll put you in a hospital bed. You must stay with the others in my apartment. They'll need your help. Willy will have every possible care. A private nurse, whatever is necessary. You can't desert the others. They need you." Wheedling, cajoling, holding her up lest she collapse, he finally managed with the help of Clayton to drag her down the stairs and into Dr. Wolfson's car.

Dr. Scott Wolfson carried me down. Under different circumstances I would have been ecstatic. The one thing I remember was his snappish remark to Clayton, who was carrying my new suits and dress: "What are you carrying? The whole place is contaminated."

"Dr. K., he said to take these new clothes. They're not contaminated. Brand new."

The two doctors, plus Clayton and Abe, carried Lil on Willy's cot as if it were an ambulance stretcher, inching it carefully down the two flights of stairs. "We should send for an ambulance," Dr. Wolfson lamented. "All of them should drive to Doctor's Hospital, to Columbia Pres. They need first-class service."

"Except for Willy, they're headed for the Amalgamated. Scott, not everyone lives first class. We'll save them, give it our best shot."

No one bothered to lock the kitchen door. Dr. Koronovsky took off with Willy and a police escort to Beth Israel Hospital. Abe carried Lil into the elevator of Dr. Koronovsky's building and settled her into the capacious double bed in his former bedroom. Bubby and I occupied twin beds in the sisters' room. The beds felt like swansdown. If Brooklyn was the country to my mother, the doctor's apartment rated as the Waldorf.

Then a feisty young nurse showed up.

Miss Grady was very pretty, with long auburn hair and a creamy complexion. Her uniform was so starched it crackled when she walked. Somewhat upset at Clayton's familiarity and his prancing about, she asked Dr. Scott in a stage whisper, "Who is that Negro?"

"That's Manya's boy."

"Her boy?" Miss Grady gasped. "Do you mean her son?"

Bubby called out, "He came to me when he was seven, maybe nine. We never found out."

"You mean you *adopted* a Negro boy?"

"He's like my own child," said Bubby.

A blush spread over those pale young cheeks. "Well, I never!"

"He's a wonderful nurse's aide," Dr. Scott went on.

"I don't want his help, I mean I don't need his help."

Dr. Wolfson called into the kitchen where Clayton was fiddling with ice cube trays, "Clayton, I didn't bring too much money. What shall we do about that and the food?"

"Charge it to Bubby."

"Dr. K. wouldn't like that."

"Then I'll charge it to him."

"Prune Danish," Bubby reminded him. "Dr. Koronovsky loves prune Danish."

"I know where to find it. Any delicatessen? Dr. K., he's crazy about corned beef sandwiches, not too fatty."

Miss Grady asked, "Will they give you all that food without money?" Dr. Wolfson burst out, "Clayton is famous down here."

"Well, I never," she said, and to cover her confusion began to take everyone's temperature.

❖

In the late afternoon Dr. Koronovsky walked through the front door in high spirits. "Willy is fine!" he exclaimed. "He came through the surgery like a trouper, and as soon as Dr. Rothman cut into the trachea his breathing improved. Rothman said we got him to the hospital in the nick of time. He's resting comfortably, sedated, has pneumonia but he'll make it, we hope, without complications." Dr. Koronovsky sounded drunk with happiness.

The apartment blazed with lights. Dr. Wolfson stared at his older colleague. "You're dead tired, short of sleep, not eating and your adrenaline is like a hopped-up teenager. What drives you this way?"

Dr. K. zigzagged across the living room, unaware that his legs were giving out. "I've had an amazing day as a doctor. Saved Willy. That alone makes you higher than champagne. Moved the Roth family into clean, warm surroundings and no one is worse for the ride. If I can pull Lil through, keep her from real danger, it will be a triumph."

His shirt was rumpled. He needed a shave. He smelled from sweat, from hospital, from disease. Yet he was ecstatic. "Clayton," he yelled, "I'm starving."

"Corned beef on rye suit you? I cooked Bubby's chicken soup. Want soup or celery tonic to wash down the sandwich?"

"Celery tonic. Oh, God, I'm cheating on my wife. She'll kill me because I promised her, I swore, that I'd give up delicatessen. And I'm staying here tonight. My first separation from Phyllis since we were married."

Nurse Grady presented herself. "I'm leaving at four o'clock. My shift is from eight to four."

"Another nurse is on the way," Dr. Koronovsky informed her. "You have to remain and help wash the patients' hair. If you don't want to work tomorrow, you're excused. Walk out the door at four o'clock and I'll speak to your supervisor." Dr. K. caught his breath, rattled a small box with pills, extracted one and popped it into his mouth.

"I'd appreciate it if you'd make up a bed for me on the living room floor. Pillow and blanket will do."

"Wouldn't you prefer the couch?"

"I would but I won't be able to wake up if I'm too comfortable." As a peace offering, he rewarded her with a wan smile. "Clayton, where's my celery tonic, please? And take a Seconal. You've been up the whole night and the entire day."

"Where will he sleep?" Nurse Grady inquired, alarmed.

"Next to me or on the floor of Manya's room. Wherever he prefers."

Clayton placed an inch-high corned beef sandwich on a tray along with the soda.

"Open your mouth," Dr. Koronovsky commanded him and threw a sleeping pill inside it. "You've done enough work for today. Dr. Wolfson and the second-shift nurse will handle things for a few hours."

Through the encounter with the nurse and with Clayton, Dr. Wolfson had remained silent. He burst forth now.

"Why do you exert yourself with such ferocity? You don't overlook a single detail. I've been here the whole day and didn't think to have their hair washed. Of course their hair is contaminated. It's filthy with sweat. It would never cross my mind. And the expense. Who's paying for Willy's surgery, for these nurses, for the medication? You, *you*. Are these people your family, your special project, some secret obsession? I'm the one writing the paper, but I'm an observer. You're the one who rescued them. Why?"

The sleeping pill he had swallowed on an empty stomach affected Dr. Koronovsky. He laughed and laughed. He gulped his sandwich and guzzled his drink before replying.

"Manya, she's my oldest friend in a neighborhood that God may have forgotten or at least overlooked. She's my model for survival. I set myself on this course of action—doctoring for the poor—and she encouraged me. Also she kept after me to marry Phyllis. Guilt about my sisters consumed me. I was immobilized. Each and every hour I visited her, Manya repeated her refrain. 'Get married. You deserve a better life.' No one else ever told me I deserved a better life or that I had to seize it for myself. This is the least I can do for her now."

"Are you some kind of bloody socialist?"

"Is Manya? She's been giving her food away every night since I was a boy. Consider what she did for Lil, a wretched ghetto child, neglected, overworked by an uncaring mother, riddled with heart disease. The scourge of the ghetto isn't poverty, it's illness. Manya never hesitated to help Lil. She does it without effort."

"I haven't ever heard you say this much in one breath."

"I'm babbling, it's the Seconal talking. Before I pass out I'll tell you this. I'm a terrible writer. Can't cobble two sentences together. That's why I recommended you for this project and helped you with the grant. The answer is not to keep charts the way you do, but to figure out what it takes for these people to do without and cherish existence. It's touch and go, touch and go, a medical disaster in this family at every turn. From a scientific point of view Lil and Jack should never have had children. Too many genetic strikes against them. But science in one sense is bullshit. Forget their illnesses and see what they have going for them. High intelligence. Talent. An incomprehensible drive. It would help if I could pry them away from Orchard Street. I'll offer them this apartment for a year. Rent-free. I'm not sure Manya will accept."

"How could she say no to a luxury apartment rent-free?"

"Because it means giving up too much."

"You're talking in your sleep."

"Insight, Scott, is as important as diagnostics."

Dr. Koronovsky took a quick shower, wrapped himself in a hospital bathrobe, snuggled into a hospital blanket on the floor and passed out. The night nurse, Mrs. Ferguson, an older woman, proved gentler than Miss Grady. Everyone slept through the night.

In the morning Bubby left her bed.

"Where are your sisters?" she asked Koronovsky as he was setting out for the day.

"With Uncle Zelig, in Trenton, New Jersey. He's very lonely. He'd like them to live with him. The neighborhood there, it's just like here, a Jewish community." He eyed her judiciously. "Manya, try to like this place."

"It's like a fancy hotel. Only it's too finster."

"Too dark? Pull the drapes open. There's plenty of light."

"The dining room and living room have no windows. In the kitchen you see another building. Besides, what would I do with myself so far from everyone?"

"We'll talk about it later. I'll call you in a few hours about Willy."

"You shouldn't come back today. Dr. Wolfson will stay for an hour, that's enough. Go home to your wife. Make night early."

"Would it destroy you to move in here?"

"I couldn't. For a visit, you saved us. To live, no."

"Don't be hasty about saying no."

"Listen, Koronovsky, you know my brother-in-law Goodman, Bertha's husband? God alone sent such a man to us. He's begged us to come and live in Yonkers, in some nice apartment, with a little restaurant on the main street. Ich ken nisht."

He didn't argue with her. "Get some rest," he said quietly.

Against one wall in the living room stood a fake fireplace. When we pressed a button a fan went on that cast red flames against artificial logs. Bubby and I played casino on an end table between chairs angled in front of the fireplace. Dr. Scott Wolfson found us there and expressed delight that we were able to sit up for a while.

"Better, you're much better. Why do you look sad?"

"I don't have anything to read."

"There's a whole bookcase full of books, mostly medical, but some are novels. They're in the master bedroom, where your parents are sleeping."

"My father found *The Great Gatsby*. When he's finished I'll read it."

"Does he allow you to read a book like that?"

"He lets me read anything. My Uncle Geoff, he has a bookcase with a lock and key. He calls those books *erotica*. My father says it's a lot of hooey to keep books locked up."

Dr. Wolfson slapped his forehead. "This family confuses and confounds me. In other words, you drive me crazy. You should be reading children's books. You're nine going on twenty. In some ways you're older than your mother."

Dr. Scott Wolfson was my first love, the man I would marry and be with forever if I could. But I shocked him, made him uncomfortable. Even as he admired me he drew away. My whole family, perhaps with the exception of Willy, had that effect on him. I couldn't confide in him as I did with Hal Pankin. Scott Wolfson drove me to silence.

"Help me," he finally said. "I want to buy Willy a present. I still feel terrible because I didn't pick up the messages that night he got sick. What shall I buy him? A game? A puzzle? What does he love the most?"

"A radio. A small radio, the kind you don't plug in."

"A portable radio. What a great idea! As soon as I examine your parents I'm off to buy the radio."

"Is it expensive?"

He gently pounded his knuckles on top of my head. "Hey you, quit it. Be a child for five minutes and I'll buy you a doll."

When he showed up several hours later, he was exuberant. "Willy is crazy about the radio," he told us. "It's ivory color and I bought a whole box of batteries so he can play it for hours. He began to cry, he was so happy, and he misses all of you. He's still on IVs, his scar hurts and he wants Bubby. I told him tomorrow or the next day."

"Morgen. Ahf morgen," said Bubby.

"If you have no temperature we'll aim for tomorrow." He poked me with his elbow. "This is for you. It's not another log for the fire and should keep you busy for a few days."

It was *Gone With the Wind*. "Just what I wanted."

"Crazy family!" He grinned, encouraged that his two gifts enchanted us.

We stayed at Dr. Koronovsky's apartment a full week. Lil hadn't quite recovered when Uncle Goodman came to drive us back to Orchard Street. Bubby suffered terribly the last two days of our stay, restless, disoriented by the electric lights that illuminated every corner from rising to bedtime. The apartment felt like a cage to her. But an attempted early return to our own dwelling proved fruitless—Dr. Koronovsky had insisted on having the Orchard Street quarters fumigated.

"We come in and spray the floors, the walls, the furniture. It takes two days for the fumes to evaporate," the fumigator told him. "We'll open the windows on the second day. Don't rush inside before we give you the okay. The fumes can leave you sick."

On Saturday, weak in the knees though able to manage, Jack returned to his store. Uncle Goodman wanted to persuade Bubby to stay in the comfort of the Koronovsky flat. He and the doctor discussed the details by telephone.

That their cause was hopeless became evident with Bubby's first evaluation, "Dus is ein cayver."

"A grave?" Uncle Goodman could not conceal his shock at the choice of words and the emotion behind them. "Manya, people sacrifice, they scrimp and save for months and years, they deny themselves everything to buy one of these apartments. This one falls into your lap, free of charge and you call it a grave."

"If not a grave—maybe that's too strong—then a prison. I can't breathe in here. I need a place open to the world."

That ended the discussion. Nothing more could be said.

We awaited the word from the fumigator, who called to apologize for a slight mishap. The wallpaper above the telephone table had come apart at the edges. Finding swarms of roaches under the paper, he had no recourse than to tear it from the wall.

The morning we returned to Orchard Street, a light mist was falling. We sat on each other's laps in Goodman's car. Bubby applauded as we pulled up to the familiar sidewalk. We staggered up the stairs on sailor's legs. Clayton threw open the door. An arctic blast hit us with force. "Man," Clayton exclaimed, "this place is colder than a witch's you-know-what." He raced inside to light the gas stove and open the range door.

In seven days the apartment had shrunk again, or so it appeared after our recent spacious lodgings. Despite the assurances that the insecticide had disappeared from the air, the smell of poison clung to every surface. Uncle Goodman switched on the lights and plugged in the electric heater in the bedroom. He carried a new heater for the dining room in his arms. The moment the prongs of the heater hit the dining room outlet we were plunged into darkness.

"It's an overload," Clayton cried. He searched for the fuse box in the hallway and at the bottom of the stairs. Darkness. Pitch black darkness everywhere. Mrs. Ginsberg and Mrs. Feldman bolted out of their rooms screaming, "Finster, finster." Uncle Goodman remained calm and by the glow of his cigarette lighter called the electric company. We couldn't expect service for twenty-four to thirty-six hours. Two days of darkness. Two days of frigid cold, torn wallpaper, mountains of dead roaches on the floor, exterminator fumes, dripping walls.

My desperation, everyone's desperation, was as palpable as a silent collective scream. I clutched *Gone With the Wind*. Clayton wailed. Bubby cried silently.

"We'll go back to Koronovsky's. We have the keys. We'll go back," counseled Uncle Goodman, "until everything here is in order."

My father, who lived by omens and superstitions, who spit three times when he saw a nun approaching, who regarded a black thread on his clothes as a harbinger of disaster, raised his voice. "No. It's out of the question to turn back. That would bring us bad luck."

Uncle Goodman didn't argue with Jack. "Clayton," he said with authority, "take the flashlight and be careful where you step. Women first. Everyone back into my car." He drove all of us, including Clayton, straight to Yonkers.

We were held together with spit. Miraculously, Uncle Goodman brought his own electrician to Orchard Street who replaced the old fuses and installed a four-foot-high electric wall heater in the dining room. He selected the least damp wall, hammered a thick slab of wood into the perilously crumbling plaster, attached the heater to it and ran the extension cord into the kitchen. The twin coils of the heater glowed like a theatrical stage set. Uncle Goodman also treated us to a small heater for the hallway toilet. As the burly electrician packed his tools, we heard him ask Uncle Goodman, "How do people live like this?" Goodman didn't answer. The toilet heater proved a master stroke. We would have suffered from constipation for the rest of the winter without it.

Weinstock brought us a roll of wallpaper to replace what had been torn by the exterminators. "It's the latest, with sticky stuff on the back. Cut it to whatever length you want." The color and texture did not match the existing paper. No matter. Clean and fresh counted for more than decorating perfection. He also looked at the new heaters and shrugged. "Thrown-out money."

We didn't ask Weinstock to explain. On the day the fuses blew, each of us resigned ourselves to a different future. We simply plodded on because we couldn't visualize the direction it would take.

On Saturday, Dr. Wolfson drove Bubby and me to Beth Israel Hospital to pick up Willy. He wasn't coming home. Rather, we drove him to a convalescent hospital in Lakewood, New Jersey. Bubby wore her sealine fur coat and Mr. Jacob had lent me a boy's tweed jacket lined with shearling that fit over my rose-colored suit.

Pale and noticeably thinner, Willy hugged his portable radio. The warm hat with felt flaps waggled on his head like a Halloween fright wig. None of us cared. Our joy at being together erased any possible discomfort, especially since Dr. Scott was delighted with himself and the universe. He had just become engaged to Susan Laurel Newman, a chemist.

The drive seemed too short, though we stopped at a café on the way and had coffee and French crullers. If the doctor disapproved of children drinking coffee he didn't say.

The convalescent hospital resembled the posh hotels we saw along the road, with a wide veranda where recovering adults and children lounged in chairs, covered up to their chins with plaid blankets.

Heavy snow had fallen the night before and the lake, the lanes around the hospital and the boughs of the trees lay under a white blanket. Outdoors, we couldn't hear a sound. The stillness, the whiteness, the serenity were a world apart from the city.

It was painful to separate from each other. "We'll be back two weeks from today, same time, same place, same station," said Scott Wolfson, reassuring us, and handed Willy two one-dollar bills. "Treat the girls to ice cream," he said.

We didn't look back. We drove back past the snow-covered lake, the deserted skating rink, the lawns piled high with snow. None of us spoke. Perhaps Dr. Wolfson thought of his beloved. Perhaps Bubby remembered Odessa. I thought of Connecticut but didn't shed a tear.

20

Exodus

IT'S POSSIBLE THAT we would have stayed at 12 Orchard Street forever if it had not been for Mrs. Rosinski. By postponing decisions about moving, we granted Bubby the illusion that Manya's Restaurant continued to survive when for weeks on end we served as few as two customers a day. In spite of our impressive electric heater in the dining room and my grandmother's energetic return to cooking, fewer and fewer customers permitted themselves the indulgence of four-course meals at midday or ventured into our dismal hallway.

We broke even on the takeouts—beef brisket sandwiches proved our best seller. Our haphazard accounting system of placing the daily receipts under the candlestick prevented Bubby from realizing that our profits were nil. Our recent round of family illness had sent our followers not to The Grand Canal and the various delicatessens in the neighborhood, but to a brand-new restaurant, Emil's, shiny, modern, with bustling waiters, chandeliers and a sign in the window that read In and Out in 20 Minutes, or Your Money Back. Its location on Canal close to Broadway attracted a wide clientele, including women who worked in the financial district. There appeared no reason for customers to struggle up two dark flights of treacherous steps when they could frequent Emil's, which offered a large printed menu and let its customers leave with toothpicks wrapped in cellophane.

Uncle Goodman sorrowed because the site of Emil's was the one he had suggested to us well over a year ago. Even my mother's younger brothers boasted of Emil's wonders.

In truth, Bubby could not have managed a large operation, one that included several chefs, busboys, waiters and cleanup staff. She accommodated the exact amount of business that her health permitted. The early morning bustle kept her happy, and if Weinstock and her writing buddies from the *Forward* benefited from free food, it was still the cooking that shaped her days. Both Jack and Uncle Goodman indulged her and didn't press her to change, even as they acknowledged to each other that we were operating at a loss.

Bubby was following her salt-free diet as carefully as possible. She fell from grace every now and then by dashing into Saperstein's for a slice of smoked sturgeon with a dollop of caviar, but in general she obeyed doctor's orders and lost weight. Everyone except my mother recovered fully. Her convalescence was lingering, so one morning Dr. Wolfson, Lil and I descended on Dr. Bernard Frank, a cardiologist, whose sumptuous office on lower Fifth Avenue had first-rate equipment—including machines that did EKGs and took X-rays of the heart and lungs.

Dr. Wolfson had explained that the important thing about having a specialist for a doctor was his skill at accurate diagnoses. There were few medications to work with for heart problems other than digitalis and nitroglycerine tablets. Mostly doctors recommended bed rest, a healthier diet, reduced stress.

Talking a mile a minute, Dr. Frank assured my mother that he rarely had patients in his office who passed for movie stars, that he would fix her up in a jiffy, that she was too young to have anything serious.

How did I know he was lying? For one fleeting second as he wrote on Lil's chart, I saw the mask of geniality dissolve. He appeared stricken. Frank was not a two- or three-dollar doctor. He examined hearts a dozen times a day, maybe more. You sensed at once that you were in the care of an expert. "Allez oop," he then said, "now for some machinery." A nurse led my mother away for blood tests, the EKG and the X-rays.

"It's a ghetto heart," Dr. Frank said to Scott Wolfson as if he had forgotten that I was present. "Very early damage and no care. She told me she had a weak heart. Weak is not the word for it. The arrhythmia is alarming, the heart enlarged—size of a grapefruit. I'll tell you more after I read the tests." He disappeared into the X-ray room.

Within a half hour Dr. Frank led my mother back into his office. Of course he smiled, patted her back. Her purse bulged with so many free samples of medicine she couldn't even snap it shut.

"Ask for a leave of absence from Saks for a few months. The trip by subway during rush hour is too stressful and you stand in high heels eight to ten hours. Is there any chance that you could give up your career and rest?"

"Oh, I couldn't! What would I do with myself?"

"What other women do. Meet friends for lunch, shop, take your children to their after-school lessons. Fix the evening meal and wait for your husband."

"Dr. Frank!" My mother burst out laughing. "Why would I spend money for lunch when we own a restaurant? I don't prepare any meals. Manya does that. What you describe, it would last for one day, then I couldn't stand it."

"You don't know these women," Dr. Wolfson chimed in. "They are work machines. Manya stayed at Dr. K.'s apartment for one week and she described herself as a caged animal."

Dr. Frank scrutinized me carefully. "You're not as driven, are you? Are you still reading *Gone With the Wind*?"

I realized the doctors in this group shared information about us. "I finished it," I replied. "My father is reading it now."

"How does he like it?"

"He loves it. He told us he could play Rhett Butler in the movie. We couldn't stop laughing when he said it."

"Why, is he short and fat like me?"

"Oh, no, he's tall and handsome. He writes beautifully. He directed a whole vaudeville and wrote a song about Connecticut. He did it in one day."

"I hope I have the chance to know every one of you. Lil, when you're feeling better, return to your weekend job on Division Street. Less wear and tear. On days when you are wiped out and tired stay in bed. Take digitalis at least three times a week."

My mother did not return to Saks for the rest of the year. Quietly she slipped into her weekend routine at Palace Fashions. Mr. L. expressed his gratitude. The rest of us were ecstatic, especially Jack. He now regarded store ownership as his birthright. It not only provided him with additional security, but he loved the sight of his wife walking into Palace Fashions on weekends. Without fail, at the close of the day they walked home together arm in arm. Under these circumstances, the talk of moving from Orchard Street receded.

The day before Willy was to return from the convalescent hospital in Lakewood, New Jersey, Bubby was in the kitchen humming tunelessly while she cut out cookie dough with the rim of a glass. As a homecoming present, we had bought Willy a single folding bed and a new mattress. Bubby, Clayton and I couldn't wait for his reaction to the gift.

Mrs. Rosinski appeared at our door. Because of our week of recovery at Dr. Koronovsky's we hadn't encountered her for some time. Thinner and paler than ever, her transparent skin reminded me of the tiny lanterns that tourists bought for a nickel in Chinatown. The lanterns survived a few hours before their waxy paper tore and the cheap wire spines collapsed. Mrs. Rosinski's face resembled one of them, cracking under strain.

She and Bubby conversed in a combination of Polish, Russian, broken English and Yiddish—everyone on the Lower East Side interspersed Yiddish with eccentric English. Mrs. Rosinski explained that she hadn't been well—she had obviously contracted the same infection as ours—and asked whether Clayton would return her unfinished pants to Mr. Yang in Chinatown.

In her many years in our building, not once had Mrs. Rosinski failed to complete her work. She held on to our kitchen chair as she talked to us. The realization that she might not have eaten for several days came to me and Bubby simultaneously. My grandmother immediately filled a jar with vegetable soup and boiled chicken. Overcome with guilt because I hadn't distributed the mail for two weeks, I said, "I'll see if you have a letter from Poland."

Mrs. Rosinski shook her fragile head; her wispy gray hair showed patches of bare scalp. She held up three fingers. "Three weeks?" I asked. She shook her head. "You haven't had a letter for three *months*?"

Tiny tears filled the corners of her eyes as she talked. Bubby had to translate her narrative. Her two brothers and her sister had tried to leave Poland before Hitler invaded their country. She suspected that they were dead, frozen on some mountaintop.

My grandmother embraced Mrs. Rosinski, kissed her papery face, held her close. Clayton helped her up the stairs, I carried the soup. Bubby followed close behind, step by step.

Mrs. Rosinski's apartment, perfect in its tidiness, was also perfect in its cold. Frost covered the windows, lay like an invisible blanket over the sparse furniture. Once in bed Bubby fed her soup from a dented spoon. "Clayton, bring the heater from our toilet to warm this bedroom."

"There's no outlet in the apartment, only an overhead light."

"Find blankets. No. My seal coat. Like in Russia, where the blankets are fur."

"Bubby," Clayton protested, "that's your best coat. What will you wear tomorrow when you pick up Willy in Lakewood?"

"My son," Bubby answered, "will bring me a coat from his store."

We wrapped Mrs. Rosinski in Bubby's fur coat. "Like a dancing bear," said Bubby, smiling at her neighbor. "In the morning we'll see you again."

We didn't. Dr. Scott arrived early to drive us to Lakewood, Bubby ecstatic at the prospect of being reunited with her grandson. Lil spent a few hours at Palace Fashions. All together by evening, we ate dinner in the spirit of a holiday. Willy loved his new bed, the new electric wall heater, the heater in the toilet. He chattered on about the weeks of eating apple butter and white bread. We listened to the radio and the top ten songs of the week. By nine o'clock we bedded down, triumphant and exhausted by the day's activities.

On Sunday morning, however, Bubby listened for Mrs. Rosinski's light footsteps—she always walked to the Polish church on Avenue C on Sunday. Jack went off for a busy day, Lil slept until noon before setting out for Division Street. It was almost one o'clock before Clayton was instructed to knock on Mrs. Rosinski's door. "There's no answer. Maybe she's still in church."

"Maybe she didn't go to church, maybe she's too sick, maybe I should walk up. She'll answer for me."

The steps were difficult for my grandmother. Her breath came in small gasps; she leaned on Clayton. At Mrs. Rosinski's door she knocked and knocked. No response.

"Maybe she fainted."

"Maybe she's dead."

"Bite your tongue, Clayton, bite your tongue. You'll climb the fire escape from our kitchen. You'll look in the window."

Clayton managed the slippery steps of the fire escape while Bubby kept her head out of the window lest anyone on the street cry out that a Negro was scaling the building for an attempted robbery.

"The window is covered with a blanket," he called.

"Come down. We have to phone someone."

To contact my father on Sunday was like crying "Cossacks" on Saturday at shul. Out of the question. "Call Abe," Bubby instructed, "he knows what to do."

We contacted him on his car phone. "I'm phoning the police," Abe said. "Tommy O'Connor, the one who helps Dr. K. If we have to break open the door we need O'Connor."

"Maybe it's nothing, maybe it's a false alarm," Abe said when he arrived. Over his spiffy chauffeur's outfit he wore his old lumber jacket. Despite the cold, his face glistened with nervous sweat. Close to the door, he said, "I smell gas."

"Maybe she's dead," Clayton repeated. Bubby did not correct him this time. We strained to hear Officer O'Connor's footsteps.

Abe telephoned O'Connor again. "Possible suicide," he said in the manner of the movies. "The gas is leaking out. The whole building may blow up."

That did it for O'Connor. He was at our house within minutes. The three men broke down Mrs. Rosinski's door and shattered her windows. Bubby and I heard the breaking of glass, and suspected the worst.

"Sorry, Manya," Abe called down. "She turned on the gas in the kitchen."

Bubby wet her lips with slivovitz. She didn't cry but her hand shook. Officer O'Connor asked when the deceased was last seen. We told him Friday afternoon. Bubby could scarcely speak. The neighbors appeared in full force crying, "The gaz! the gaz!" Characteristically, Mrs. Feldman announced, "By you is luck. On the first floor is no gaz." Officer O'Connor, his face red with importance, asked, "Any relatives?"

"Call the priest at the Polish church on Avenue C," said Bubby. "We don't want her buried with bums. They have a Polish cemetery. The priest knows where."

"Good head on you, Manya."

She burst into tears.

And that was why and how and when we finally left Orchard Street. A suicide was the ultimate jinx, the stigma that could not be erased.

Via police car they transported Mrs. Rosinski's body to the Polish church. Money for her burial was collected nickel by nickel. Jack wouldn't allow his mother to wear her fur coat folded neatly on Mrs. Rosinski's bed. He hocked it and handed the money to his mother for Mrs. Rosinski's funeral, then tore the pawn ticket to shreds.

Bubby stuffed the bills into her apron pocket. "I called her boss, Mr. Yang, in Chinatown. She was the best worker in the factory. He's sending white flowers to the church. White flowers are for Chinese funerals."

The Polish service was held on a Wednesday. I skipped school to attend the service with my grandmother. Abe drove us to the church on Avenue C but refused to enter, superstitious about the Christ figure, afraid of bad luck.

So few people attended that Bubby propelled me to the first row.

"You don't have to cross yourself," she whispered. "The priest will understand."

The church smelled of mold, the ceiling dampened by years of neglect and covered with brown water stains. Nothing of beauty enhanced the small space. No stained-glass windows, no icons, just wooden benches and a pulpit covered with a faded red cloth. A few elderly parishioners, women with woolen scarves on their heads, sunken cheeks, mouths empty of teeth, cried quietly. Mr. Yang's white flowers beautified the altar and momentarily helped us forget the bitter cold. A broken window or an unlatched door let in the sharp wind. Bubby held my hand throughout the short service.

The priest, wrinkled, shabby, himself the victim of intense poverty, spoke in Polish and possibly for our benefit added in heavily accented English, "Our sister is in heaven with the angels."

At the end of this brief service the others rose and touched the closed coffin resting on a wooden table before they filed out.

In her new black coat with its black Persian lamb collar and cuffs and her fur-trimmed hat, courtesy of Aunt Bertha, Bubby looked like a Balkan aristocrat, a landowner who dropped into a rural village church as a courtesy. The priest came down the steps to shake her hand. He shed a few tears as she greeted him in Polish. He repeated in English that the deceased was at peace in heaven. We hastened outside.

Abe was waiting for us on the windy sidewalk, stamping his feet and blowing on his gloved fingers. The sky was low, black with impending rain. The wind cut into our necks and backs.

"Short and sweet," he said.

"Short, yes, but bitter. Not even black bread. Not a drop of wine. A mouse who crept inside that church would die of starvation. It was a shanda. I didn't think to bring food."

"Forget it. It's over and done with. Home, ladies?"

"No, let's eat. At Emil's."

"You sure?"

"Positive. Emil's. Let's see what the tsimmes is about."

Parking on upper Canal Street wasn't a problem and though I hated to admit it, Abe was right in exclaiming, "It's the cat's meow."

Lights blazed from immense chandeliers. The walls glowed with murals depicting happy peasants carrying baskets of fruit and flowers. White-jacketed waiters bustled amid the white-clothed tables. As we entered, a hostess in a short black skirt and white ruffled blouse handed us a printed menu and intoned, "Welcome to Emil's. Let me show you to your table."

The hostess was supplanted by a portly man in a blue pin-striped suit.

"Manya! Manya! Who could believe it's you?" he cried.

She stared at the fringe of black hair encircling his oval head, the front tooth trimmed with gold. "Rudnick from the shoelaces? The Odessanik with the black beard?"

"The same, the same. Now I am Emil. This is my restaurant. Come, come, the best table in the house for you. Manya, you are still a krazavitz. A beauty. And today you're dressed like a czarina. Where are you coming from?"

"You shouldn't know from it."

"From the Polachka? The worst anti-Semites."

"This person had no hate in her."

Rudnick nodded at me. "Your Bubby, she fed me for years. I was one of her schnorrers. Read the menu, read, read. No, I'll order for you."

He paused and acknowledged Abe. "I hear you have a new machine. What, you work for the mob?"

"Does Manya and her granddaughter look like the mob?"

Rudnick's eyes ricocheted around the table.

"For you, Manya, scrambled eggs with cream cheese and lox, our number-one seller. For the young lady a waffle with hot syrup and whipped butter and for Abe a steak sandwich with sautéed onions. Sounds good?"

He left us for a moment before seating himself on the fourth chair at our table. He brought a basket with assorted breads, rolls, bagels and bialys that he lathered with butter and shoveled into his mouth. "Taste, taste."

True to the sign that read In and Out in 20 Minutes, the food appeared not only quickly but on hot plates. "I learned from you, Manya. Always hot plates."

The waffle was a novel experience: crisp, sweet, the butter served in a fluted paper cup, the syrup in a miniature pitcher.

A pang of envy swept through me. I wanted us to own a restaurant with murals, with customers waiting to be seated. I wanted Bubby to be applauded for her work, rewarded for her talent. I hated Rudnick, his gold watch, gold chain and gold tooth.

"So, Rudnick. How did you come by the money for this restaurant, from shoelaces?"

"Investors. First I managed the shoelace factory, a dump on Houston Street. I heard someone else was after this property. A Goldstein, Goldberg, a Goodman, something like that. I grabbed it right away. Six of us put in a little cash, but enough to open. The name, my idea. Something classy, like French. We have a gold mine here." He paused. "You still in business, Manya?" As if he didn't know.

"Mostly catering," I answered boldly. "We have several Wall Street accounts."

His eyes flashed up to his flashy chandeliers. "How did you get the accounts?"

"My mother works at Saks Fifth Avenue," I answered defiantly. "She meets a lot of professionals."

I hated myself for playing my parents' game, but I wasn't bad at it.

Rudnick winked at Bubby. "You want to come work for me? Who can cook like you? Who? Nobody."

"Thanks," she smiled. "The business I have right now, it's perfect for me. Not too much, not too little."

"You're still cooking four-course meals?"

"Out of style," she admitted, "but we do takeouts. Clayton delivers."

"He is still with you? I'll send him lunch." Rudnick ran off again. Abe wolfed down his steak sandwich, in a hurry for us to leave. We ate very fast, lower-class Jewish style, utensil to mouth, no pauses until done.

"Rudnick, the check please."

"For you, Manya, never. It is my pleasure, my pleasure." He held out two boxes. "One is filled with desserts. The apple strudel we sell twenty-five pieces a day, maybe more. Tell Jack and Lil they should come for dinner. That's what they call the evening meal, dinner. I want they should have a beautiful evening."

Abe hurried us out and we sped home. "What do you think?" Bubby asked him.

"You know yourself. It's a mishmash. Jewish, American, Italian steak sandwiches, but that momser has it right. It's a gold mine."

The moment Clayton heard us on the stairway he called out with relief. "Where have you been, you're so late!" Like my father, Clayton suffered acute anxiety when Bubby left the apartment. She handed over the boxes. Lil, just awakened, strolled in. "What's in the boxes?"

"You remember Rudnick from shoelaces? He's Emil's."

Without washing her hands or brushing her teeth, my mother bit into an apple slice covered with a thick crust and white icing. She quickly spit it out. "It's canned, not fresh apples. It tastes like Mrs. Wagner's nickel pies."

"Clayton," Bubby asked, "any orders?"

"The lawyers called. Lunch for Friday. What did they have at Mrs. Rosinski's service?"

"Nothing. Not a drop. I can't bear to talk about it."

It started to rain, heavily, the sky murky as dusk. We listened to the rain beat against the windows. The day was over for us.

"When Willy finishes school, we'll make night early."

The storm would keep any potential customer away from our door, let alone the news of a suicide in our building. My mother crept back into bed. Every electric heater was blazing, but none of us felt warm.

Without discussing it, my parents began their search for a different apartment. On their day off they walked to Battery Park to the complex where Mathias, the hat man, had moved. "Not for us," Jack announced.

Their fall-back position was Dr. Koronovsky's apartment at the Amalgamated. He consistently repeated his generous offer of free rent for a year.

New buildings with fancy facades began to change the landscape of the Jewish quarter. Like a hero out of a Horatio Alger novel, my mother was consumed with ambitions. "Do you realize that we never had a sofa, an armchair, a living room set?" she exclaimed. "Only beds and dining room chairs. Is that how stock should hang?" The last was a quotation from Mr. L., who inspected his clothing every morning and if one of his garments was askew, roared, "Is that how stock should hang?"

A tacit understanding existed between my parents and my grandmother: no discussions about apartments until they found a suitable one.

One Friday my parents returned from their search and broke their silence. "There's a new building on Grand Street, not far from here, beautiful, with an elevator. We thought we saw Orloff, the silk man, out in front. What would he be doing there?"

"You went inside the building?"

"No," Lil answered. "It will be finished in a week or two. They tore down an old grocery store and built this tall skinny building."

"Not skinny," my father corrected, "narrow, with high windows. The architect was standing on the sidewalk, supervising everything. Imagine, an architect on Grand Street."

Bubby went right on rolling dough for taglach. We couldn't tell if she accepted this information seriously.

A week later however, Orloff himself telephoned. "Manya!" he shouted. He regarded speaking into the phone from a distance of three blocks as a transatlantic call.

"Manya," he repeated, "I have a surprise for you. On Friday I am coming with my machine to drive you to Grand Street. The whole family should be there at 3:30. New York time, not Jewish time. Tell Jack to call me."

"Who was that?" Jack asked, looking up from the racing form. He and Lil had walked their feet off searching for apartments with no results.

Jack returned Orloff's call immediately. He said, "Jack Roth here" and then three "yeses" in a row. My grandmother dropped chunks of dough in boiling honey. "I'm dying for those taglach," Jack said. "Hot out of the pot is the best."

My father invariably ate food out of sequence, so it was not unusual for him to start with honey-coated pastries that he retrieved with the slotted spoon. He winked at Lil lasciviously before he walked her to Pandy's for her weekly shampoo and set.

The following Friday Jack took it upon himself to keep us together. "Ma, change your dress. Nothing fancy, just not your cooking outfit."

It wasn't like Bubby to acquiesce without asking questions, but her son exuded such enthusiasm that she washed her face, recombed her hair and slipped on a wool dress without protest. The entire family stood in a row like schoolchildren, waiting for Orloff. His face was shining with pride when he drove up.

We crowded into his car and drove the half dozen blocks to 444 Grand Street. There, a tall slim man with unruly auburn hair was waiting for us on the sidewalk. He had an uptown accent, wore a tweedy coat and no hat. He extended his hand to Jack. "I'm Peter Peterson, the architect."

My father held to several provincial attitudes. One of them was that men who didn't wear hats were Communists or at the least Socialists. He eyed the architect warily because his hair tumbled over his eyes and his striped wool scarf circled his neck like a barrier against a sore throat.

"It's a secure building," Peterson explained without preliminaries. "You buzz and if no one answers, you stay out." Orloff grinned widely, opened the door with a key and we trooped inside.

The building was indeed narrow. But its elevator held four of us, so Bubby, Jack, Peterson and I went up first and got off at the fourth floor. Willy, Lil and Orloff followed.

"Only one apartment on each floor," Peterson explained. "The walls are noiseproof and insulated. This apartment is the best one. Mr. Orloff had your needs in mind when I designed it. He insisted on space for folding tables."

We entered into a long hallway, which Peterson referred to as a "foy-ay." Self-conscious, we hesitated before walking on the polished wood floors with their intricately patterned inlays. To the right at the end of the foy-ay was a large kitchen with blond wood cabinets, a double sink, a contemporary refrigerator and a restaurant stove complete with a griddle and two ovens. Across the length of one wall there was a highly polished counter, installed in place of a table, where Bubby could chop, slice, beat and mix food. Its surface was impervious to heat, so she would be able to remove roasts directly from the oven to the counter.

"A half-bathroom." Peterson opened the door of a white-tiled room with a white commode and a small white sink. We understood the meaning of *white* for the first time; it was as dazzling as a jewel.

The prize of the apartment, however, filled us with awe. This was an immense room, divided by what Peterson referred to as "Dutch doors," a few feet in height but high enough to separate the dining area from the living room. In the living room, the floor-to-ceiling windows gave onto a view that encompassed not only Grand Street, but because this was the top floor, glimpses of the spires of the financial district.

The sun broke through the winter sky and flooded the apartment with a golden aura. My father heralded this as a lucky omen. On either side of the central space were bedrooms, each larger than our entire Orchard Street flat. Only in the movies had we observed anything like the master bathroom, with a massive tub and a separate enclosed shower. "Nothing on West End Avenue or Riverside Drive equals this bathroom," Peterson announced.

My mother, who had not once in her life gone to an art museum, an opera house or any cultural center, was overcome by the beauty of her surroundings. This vision of how life could be lived, not in some distant reaches but close to recognizable streets and people she knew, moved her to tears.

With lips trembling and eyes brimming she implored Bubby, "Ma, please don't say no to this."

The rest of us grew as hushed as in the moment before Kol Nidre on Yom Kippur eve.

"How could I say no to what would make you so happy? It's Gan Edan. Orchard Street was my home. This is yours, for all of us."

My mother fell on Bubby's neck. Orloff clapped his hands and cried, "Mazeltov, mazeltov!" at our change of fortune.

Perhaps made uncomfortable by our intensity, Peterson managed to grin. My father bit his lip. Not one of us asked about the cost of the rent.

Orloff, who planned to occupy the apartment below us, seized the opportunity to kiss Bubby full on the lips. Bubby announced, "If you live long enough, you live to see everything."

Flushed with success, Lil decided to bring nothing from our old apartment to Grand Street except our best clothes. The recently acquired kitchen table and Willy's new folding bed were given to Clayton, as gifts. For perhaps half an hour we considered taking the dining room table, the scene of hundreds of meals and years of festivities. But moving it to the center of the room, we discovered that it was worm-ridden and its legs uneven. Pulling strudel dough over its surface for so long had left lumps of pastry embedded in the crevices and along the back. It was a pitiful mess.

Clayton had been off watching movies at Loew's Canal when we inspected the Grand Street premises, but the moment Jack suggested him as the superintendent of the new building Orloff jumped at the idea, pending the architect's approval. Clayton's interview was scheduled for the next day.

Bubby beamed at him when he appeared with his hair pomaded, dressed in one of Jack's slightly worn but serviceable white-on-white shirts, his black leather jacket and black trousers. Bubby assured him that Pete Peterson would be impressed. He was.

After the interview and a discussion about the furnace and garbage disposal Clayton came back to Orchard Street elated, twenty feet off the ground, bubbling, laughing, tap-dancing in the kitchen, spilling over with ideas.

"I'm buying a doorman's jacket, and I'll stand outside with my whistle and call for cabs, open and close the doors for the tenants, the only doorman in the neighborhood."

Clayton, like the rest of us, had been weaned on movies. He conceived of his new role with Hollywood grandeur.

My father signed the lease with a flourish. The rent was forty-five dollars a month; he told everyone he paid sixty. Aunt Bertha in her mink jacket and dashing mink beret steered my mother away from middle-class decorating mistakes. No flowered drapes trimmed with red velvet, no maroon carpets with flowered patterns. No shag rugs—too difficult to clean. The rooms lent themselves to neutral colors; pale lined drapes that hung from ceiling to floor. A contemporary apartment required contemporary decor.

The fact that we didn't have two dimes to rub together did not enter this theoretical equation. Scott Wolfson, who wandered in, recognized our state of poverty when Jack suggested a new loan from the Morris Plan and the rest of us with one voice shouted, "No!"

Nevertheless, Uncle Goodman sent us three twin box springs and mattresses to use until my parents could afford a bedroom set of their own. I snuggled in one twin with Bubby, my parents in their luxurious bedroom in another, and Willy in a real bed for himself at last—his first since the cradle. Doctors Koronovsky, Wolfson and Frank contributed a gift certificate for a dining room set at Jones Furniture and Jack opted for an oval-shaped table in teak, with six matching chairs padded with a nubby fabric in the lightest shade of tan.

My mother, who had spent years raising and lowering hem lines, adjusting collars and saving out-of-fashion clothing toward the day when the style would be revived, tossed the rejects from her closet to Clayton. Some he slept in, others he sashayed in, the rest he sold to a secondhand store. Uncle Goodman insisted that Clayton keep the electric heaters. He stored them in his one-room studio in our new building.

I had little to pack, although I could not leave behind Mrs. Rosinski's gift to me: her sewing threads, needles and hoops of various sizes. Clayton had found the box beside her door with the words *Jung Gul* pasted on her one significant possession. We hid it in a hatbox, together with the three dresses she had embroidered for me. Jack didn't discover them, so he couldn't decry this legacy as a jinx. Rough cord tied together the notebooks with my stories and the books bought for me in Connecticut.

Abe made two trips to the new apartment—one with fewer than a dozen boxes and then with our family. Not one of us turned to look back. We feared that Bubby would cry but she didn't. We never stepped inside 12 Orchard Street again.

21

Up from Orchard Street

BY THE TIME the intercom bell announced the entire Simon family on
Saturday morning at nine o'clock, Manya and Clayton had been roasting meat and fowl since daybreak. They were preparing for our new
catering business for merchants as far away as Second Avenue.

Jack could not conceal his pride when he conducted the Simons on the
grand tour. Even Uncle Geoff, usually reluctant with his compliments,
openly admitted, "West End Avenue has nothing to compare to this."

Jack boasted, "Architect's name is Pete Peterson and this is his
maiden voyage into the slums. He says an architectural magazine is going to photograph the building and especially our apartment."

Uncle Geoff nodded impatiently. Obviously he had a secret to share
with my father, and obviously he couldn't wait to be alone with him.
Also obviously, my father understood "offen glance."

"Come on," Jack said, "I have to open the store but I'll treat to coffee and Danish at Emil's."

Geoff mounted his usual high horse. "It's not Em-il's, it's French.
Aye-meel, as in Aye-meel Zola."

"I stand corrected." My father winked at me.

I was too miserable to respond. As always, Cousin Alice's presence cast a cloud over the private jokes between my father and me.

"See you in an hour," Geoff told Aunt Bea. "Then we'll drop in on my mother." Over his shoulder he asked me, "Want to come with us to visit Grandma Rae?"

"I have a run-through of our play today; the performance is next week."

This polite answer to my uncle testified to my performing skills. My avoidance of Grandma Rae, Lil's mother, was no secret.

The mystery of the Simons' visit burst upon us when Aunt Bea, unable to restrain herself longer, announced in megaphone tones, "We're not going to Connecticut this year. It's Florida, Miami Beach, to the Roney Plaza."

"To *Florida*? A million miles from here and sitting up all night in the train. What for?" Lil exclaimed.

"Summer rates," Aunt Bea replied smugly. "You know Geoffy. He finds out about these things. The Roney Plaza, it's for millionaires. Swimming pool, tennis courts, dancing every evening to live bands."

Then she said, "This is for Manya. For your new home." She handed Bubby a large carton.

Clayton cut open the tape and removed wads of tissue paper. Inside a small box lay measuring spoons: tablespoon, teaspoon, half and quarter sizes. Staring in disbelief at the four spoons on their tin ring, Bubby silently blessed Clayton for exclaiming, "Just what we need for our snazzy kitchen."

"There's something else." Aunt Bea smiled modestly.

Clayton withdrew a translucent salad bowl in a nonbreakable material, not glass, but not cheap plastic, complete with serving spoon and fork.

With relief, Bubby seized upon the bowl, perfect for raising yeast dough.

"You heard about Lil?" Bubby said, laughing. "Everything from Orchard Street we left behind. Jack, he went to a special wholesale store to buy me new pots and pans. The old ones I was used to, the burned bottoms and no covers, didn't bother me. With these new ones, my hands have to learn again." The recitation brought her to the inevitable graciousness. "A nice bowl like this I really needed."

"Don't throw out the box," Lil instructed and Bubby and I read her mind—she intended to return the presents. In a moment, though, her plan was dashed. The box read "Abraham and Straus," located somewhere in Brooklyn. It could have been Timbuktu.

"What's in the garment bag?" Quick recovery was one of Lil's virtues and she had seen it when the Simons walked in.

Bea had brought her summer wardrobe to show off and spilled out shiny blue shorts and a short-sleeved blouse in a matching fabric, pajama pants edged in white, midriff halters, short jackets in rainbow hues to cover her bathing suits, all made of garish satin.

"Gorgeous. Out of this world," cried Clayton.

"I never saw the likes," admitted Aunt Bea.

As she folded and repacked her outfits, Bubby added under her breath, "Perfect for a nafka."

As usual, Bubby wasn't far from wrong.

I went off to my spring show rehearsal, a hodgepodge of scenes from *Peter Pan* and individual recitations. I was responsible for a sonnet from Shakespeare. In the grand finale for the entire company each student recited assigned quotations that ranged from Shakespeare to Maxwell Anderson. Miss Sussman's notion of dramatic delivery, not based on Stanislavsky, emphasized breakneck speed, the better to conceal the deficiencies of her less talented actors.

Sensing my impatience to get home afterward—I didn't want to miss any information about the Simons' trip to Florida—Abe ran a few red lights, and a few blocks from Grand Street we spied Jack and Lil, walking home arm in arm from their respective stores.

"I decided to let Farber close up," Jack explained as he climbed into Abe's taxi. "Only mad dogs shop late on Saturday night." He withdrew a single from his pants pocket. "Believe me, getting into this cab saved us after standing all day."

No sooner did we cross the threshold of our apartment than Lil burst out, "Ma, can you believe it? Jack swears it's true. Geoffy has a girlfriend, a manicurist, her summer job is in Miami Beach, that's why they're going there. He's crazy for her brand, she gives him French. He's so worn out from sex he can hardly stand. Ma," Lil continued, perplexed, "what's French?"

"Me you're asking? If Jack knows, let him tell."

"Jack says it's a man's favorite."

"So if it's Geoff's favorite, Bea can do it, too."

My father changed into his at-home clothes, the shirt he had worn to work and the bottoms of his pajamas.

"What's with you two?" he demanded. "Listen, you wear the same pair of shoes day after day, you don't give the shoes a thought. You buy a new pair you walk on air, feel like a million bucks. It's the same with a woman. If she's new, it makes your heart beat faster. Maybe it's the excitement, maybe the danger. For the first minutes a man goes crazy. How long does it take, five minutes, ten? But it's fresh. Even if it's worse, it's better. That manicurist must have some technique."

"Technique. What's from technique?" cried Lil.

"Ma, are we eating or not?" Jack announced. "This discussion is over."

"I'm not going to Florida, Roney Plaza or not," Lil said defiantly.

"Lil, do what you want. Maybe you should stay home and spend the money on a bedroom set. My back is killing me on that single bed. Or we could buy a couple of soft fancy chairs!"

"The children and I are spending two weeks in Connecticut," said Lil, and dug into her roast chicken basted with Bubby's own apricot jam.

Pandy came to the house to help me with my costume and makeup on the night of Miss Sussman's dramatic presentation. We were touched that she had closed up shop at four thirty to prepare me for the stage. To disguise the dark circles that ringed my eyes, she applied green and yellow powder base.

My eyebrows, a wilderness of unplucked hairs, grew manageable when she spit into a box of mascara and applied the softened soot to my brows. With a black pencil, she outlined the eyes, and pasted fake lashes to my own. From the edges of my eyes into my forehead she drew a wheel of black lines.

"The lines look goofy up close," Pandy laughed, "but on stage you'll be Cleopatra."

"How do you know so much about stage makeup?"

"You think I was always on Clinton Street? Before I fell for Jimmy Paglia, before we run away to Trenton to get married, I was studying stage makeup at a studio on Thirty-ninth and Seventh Avenue. Number-one student. Only my parents, they sat shiva for me. I married an uncircumcised goy. I'll give Jimmy this, he was, pardon me, you're so refined, a screwing machine, could go on day and night, alls he needed was a little water to drink. I was passing out from happiness, so when he told me, when he said, 'Forget Broadway, come back downtown, then we can do it standing up in the broom closet while the women's hair dries.' The idea of him and me in the broom closet during work hit the right spot. That's how I landed on Clinton Street and stayed there."

I donned a costume from Miss Sussman's dilapidated wardrobe. Some of the young girls wore Elizabethan-style empire dresses stuffed with tissue paper for breasts. Others twirled velvet capes trimmed with fake fur and wool silk berets with plumes of feathers.

For the occasion Miss Sussman had put on a black evening gown with a bolero jacket and adorned herself with chunky costume jewelry.

A few of the younger performers threw up, wet their pants, could not move a leg forward from fear, but I didn't miss a cue. I delivered my speeches with authority, and captured the audience packed with relatives and friends who cheered every young actor who appeared on the stage. Even Shirley Feld, who stuttered through "Sweet are the uses of adversity," basked in her share of applause. Then Miss Sussman joined our ranks and, as instructed, we applauded the audience.

She was glowing like a klieg light as she urged the audience, "Please do stay for refreshments." An urn of coffee, cookies with sprinkles and small squares of yellow cheese pierced with toothpicks did not stimulate the appetite. Yussie Feld had contributed a basket of fruit, but it remained pristine under its yellow cellophane wrapping. I heard a few ask, "Is there any wine, any soda?"

Our family was the first to leave. "Congratulations," Jack called out to Miss Sussman and blew her a kiss.

On the ride home Abe informed us, "I heard that two agents, two scouts were there. They thought Clayton was one of them."

"What a bunch of klutzes," Jack remarked. "Not for my own daughter the critics would leave in a hurry." Bubby showered me with kisses.

But the next morning the phone rang as my father ran for the door. Having overslept, his mood was less than sanguine.

"Speaking," he said curtly. "Today is very inconvenient. It's our busiest day on Division Street. Tomorrow is my day off." He listened impatiently.

"If it's just a half hour I'll do my best. Between five thirty and six. You have my address? We'll buzz you in."

Bubby wiped her hands on a towel. "Abe was right? About the critics?"

"They'll be here tonight. About a drama scholarship. You know, free lessons. Don't mention it to Lil. It may be a whole nothing." He wanted no further distractions.

My grandmother and I had no knowledge of scholarships—the idea was foreign. Bubby suggested that Lil remain in bed for the day, but she laughed at the suggestion; a few hours at Palace Fashions wouldn't kill her. Later I wondered whether the events of the evening were due to her lack of rest.

Work that day yielded small rewards for both my parents—scores of women but few buyers. They were home by the time the downstairs buzzer sounded at five thirty, before they could change their clothes. Lil kicked off her high heels and took a chair at the table. She showed so little interest in the arrival of the two dark-suited men whom Bubby greeted at the door that she didn't even bother to apply fresh lipstick or comb her hair. Still, her natural beauty shone through, and the taller of the men, who introduced himself as Bill Schneider, seated himself opposite her. He reminded me of my father—slick, fast thinking, fast talking.

The shorter one with massive wavy hair let out a cry of recognition. "Manya, I'm Saul Green. I ate in your restaurant years ago. The best chef downtown. Are you still cooking?"

"Sit, sit. I prepared our Sunday special."

Bubby hastened to serve them cheese blintzes sizzling from the frying pan onto heated plates.

Bill Schneider wasted no time in coming to the point: competent, no-nonsense, straightforward. "Saul and I represent a union that sets aside money that we distribute for worthy causes. Some of it is for poverty-stricken families, some for illness and of course money for the arts. We don't accept applications but when we saw your daughter last night we agreed she could be a candidate for our drama program. Lessons would be paid for by us, for classes or individual instruction at least twice a week. Depending on her skills, she could start auditioning within a year. In other words we will prepare her for a professional career if she wants it." He did not tear his eyes away from my mother. "Any questions?"

"Who pays for the carfare?"

"If something is bothering you, and I think it is, please share it with us."

After a moment of hesitation Lil blurted out, "She doesn't have the looks of Elizabeth Taylor, she can't sing like Deanna Durbin. She's plain, skinny. What I mean is, maybe she's not—" Flustered, she broke off.

Bill Schneider smiled broadly, said nothing. The silence stretched around the table, taut, oppressive. Finally: "You're talking movie stars," he said. "We're discussing theater. The ability to project, to reach out to an audience, means more than conventional prettiness."

Jack, restless in his chair, took over. "The question is not about carfare or beauty. We're a theater family. Our daughter has been to Yiddish and American productions for years. She has talent, brains and she's a fast learner. You were right to choose her.

"But we don't have a stage mother or father to take her to lessons, to auditions, to rehearsals. That's the story. Manya runs her catering business. My wife and I have our jobs, and our daughter is too young for late nights on the subway on her own. Maybe in a year or two . . ."

There was an edge of weariness in my father's voice. He leaned across the table and placed my hands in his. "What do you say, darling? We haven't even asked you."

Darling. "I agree with you, maybe next year would be better." I stood up and shook Bill's hand first, then Saul's. "Thank you for coming." In spite of myself, my voice broke. "It was deeply appreciated."

Bill Schneider produced his card. "If you find someone to accompany your daughter, or change your mind, call me."

The instant they left, I raced into the darkened bedroom. Bubby stretched out beside me and stroked my hair.

"You were wonderful the way you spoke. Just like you were on the stage. Do you want acting or maybe for you writing is better?"

My mother showed her head at the door. "Maybe I didn't say the right things," she remarked.

We lay quietly without answering. The strain seeped away, like drops of water off a rainy roof. At the moment of blessed sleep, Bubby whispered, "To love with an open heart you have to let the pain in."

I hid Bill Schneider's card in my drawer. We didn't speak of it again.

At least once a week Lil treated herself to a day of bed rest, dozing on and off, daydreaming. On this particular Monday she had slept without interruption until the phone rang and I answered.

"I bet on two long shots, won the daily double for two hundred and fifty dollars." Jack's shouting could reach from Rocco's to Grand Street without the intercession of the telephone. "Two hundred and fifty big ones. Call Lil."

She heard.

"Is it really true? You won a fortune?"

"Get dressed. I'm sending a taxi for you. Meet you at Jones Furniture. We're buying a bedroom set. Is fifteen minutes enough for you?"

"Do I have to take a shower? I could walk to Delancey Street in no time."

Since we moved to Grand Street my father's two favorite maxims were "Never leave the house without a shower" and, when particularly delighted, raising his tea glass in a toast, "Up from Orchard Street."

"A five-minute shower, yes. A walk in high heels, no. Look snappy. One of your best suits. You can't expect good help in a store if you don't look a million bucks. Let's make it twenty minutes, outside of Jones."

"Twenty minutes is perfect."

They bought a mahogany set, real mahogany, not imitation, on sale, reduced because some of the brass fittings on the chest were screwed upside down and a scar ran the length of the left sideboard of the bed.

"With a long bedspread no one will notice that little scratch," the salesman reported.

Had he been able, Jack would have rented a truck on the spot and brought home the entire bedroom suite. Jones provided free delivery, forcing Jack to wait.

He did his best to control his impatience, while Farber handed some profit money to Uncle Goodman who turned it over to Aunt Bertha who called her drapery man who came to measure our extra tall windows that required two pull cords and two sets of fabric: a filmy one to cut the glare of the sun, the other, a nubby beige-yellow to provide complete privacy at night.

What with the custom-made drapes and the search for the oversize bedspread in a diamond pattern of beige and café au lait—the saleswoman's phrase—almost a month passed before we could study the completed bedroom, all of us standing in a row as Jack exclaimed hoarsely, "Up from Orchard Street."

In keeping with Bubby's notion that our parents were still honeymooners, she willingly accepted Uncle Goodman's plan for a Saturday morning trip to Yonkers.

"No cooking, no patshkying in the kitchen," he said. "Lunch at our house, then a movie. A relaxed easy day."

I brimmed with excitement. Willy dug in his heels and refused to leave.

Equal to his love of whistling was his recent enchantment with Elite Fashions. Business was slow, so store owners and sales help tended to stand on the sidewalk and reminisce about the old days, gossip about new fashions. During those moments they referred to themselves as "sidewalk salesmen" and Jack joined them. He'd say to Willy, "Half an hour with the sidewalk salesmen." At Elite Fashions, on a street full of laughter to compensate for the lack of sales, Willy discovered ease.

On this special early summer Saturday, Bubby, Goodman and I laughed all the way to Yonkers. A tray covered with tiny crustless sandwiches waited for us in the garden. They were large enough for no more than two bites, they were filled with chicken salad, turkey, cucumbers and especially for Bubby, egg salad sprinkled with caviar. A tomato carved into a rosette sat in the center of the platter.

Aunt Bertha emerged from the back door of the kitchen carrying a crystal pitcher jiggling with ice cubes and sugared tea.

"The secret to good iced tea is hot tea poured over ice. No tea bags, real tea. Manya taught me that."

She smiled at her white-haired sister, old enough to be her mother. "Sorry about the commercial mayonnaise. Not like yours, homemade, but we asked for as little mayo as possible."

As Bertha poured the tea, I whispered to Bubby, "What is this called? What kind of food is it?"

"Tea sandwiches. Bertha loves them."

I gobbled a half dozen, washed down with two glasses of icy tea. The garden, eating outdoors in the sunshine, the Goodmans' generosity, their desire to surprise and delight us—all tripped my heart into cartwheels, made me giddy with laughter.

Then Aunt Bertha called out, "Shopping in my closet" and Goodman added, "That's my favorite," as he cleared away the remains of lunch.

Uncle Goodman had converted the sewing room at the rear of the house into a walk-in closet suitable for his wife's elaborate wardrobe. In addition to floor-to-ceiling shelves for her hatboxes and shoes, her coats hung from a rack and three wide compartments marked the seasons for her dresses. The space was mildly cooled, protecting her furs.

Bertha threw open the doors of her summer closet and reached for a dress with its price tag affixed to its sleeve.

"I bought this for you, Manya. The style and color will suit you. Goodman loves it, too."

"A pink dress? What will I do with a pink dress?"

"It's not pink. It's called 'summer rose.' "

"Pink, summer rose, it's the same thing. Where will I wear it, in the house for looking out the window?"

"To the doctor or if you drop in on your clients, to introduce yourself as their chef. Isn't Dr. Wolfson giving an engagement party? You'll wear it there, or this one, or this."

Two or three more dresses flew in Bubby's direction—one-piece, two-piece pastels, dark colors, a short coat for cool evenings, long skirts, silken blouses.

"Bertha, what are you doing? Five years it would take to wear them all. Or maybe you think I should open a dress shop with so many beautiful things."

Uncle Goodman laughed and laughed. "It's for your new life. Those cooking clothes, the cardigans for shopping, forget them. One thing I'll say for Lil, always with a pretty dress, high heels, ready to step out like a swell. You, too, even for a walk, a drive, people should say, 'It's Manya, the society lady.' "

At that moment the phone rang. Insistently.

Insistently is subjective, it comes from within. The phone always rings in the same tone. Still, later when I related the story about Clayton, I repeated "The phone rang insistently" because his voice chilled and frightened me so.

"Where's Bubby? I'm beat up, cut. Blood, lots of blood. Swole all over."

"Where are you? Where are you?"

"Jail, Harlem Jail."

I shrieked at the last two words. Uncle Goodman grabbed the phone from my trembling hand.

"Don't worry," he shouted. "Harlem jail? We'll come right over. Bubby, too? Of course Bubby is coming. I have plenty for bail money, plenty for graft. You have no clothes? I'll bring, I'll bring. Wait, Bubby is right here."

Clayton had already hung up.

We didn't dillydally. Aunt Bertha shoved the box with Bubby's clothes through the open front window of the car. "Be careful in Harlem," she cautioned.

No one spoke after that. Goodman concentrated on driving as fast as he could without attracting the attention of the police. He had enough to deal with worrying about Clayton's release. At the Harlem turnoff, he slowed down and at Lenox Avenue, densely populated on a Saturday, he called out, "Where's the jail?" A young man in a short-sleeved sport shirt and too-long shorts pointed his finger straight ahead.

We inched our way to the stoplight. The street was crowded with small cars with large dents, small trucks with large dogs chained inside the open cabs, men and children riding inexpensive bicycles long past their prime, and our black Lincoln created a stir.

Still, none of this was that different from any street on the Lower East Side: children on fire escapes, men squatting on stoops, babies in carriages watched by two or three older siblings, girls drawing squares in soft chalk for potsie, girls jumping rope singly or for double Dutch. Nothing except the presence of a squat, rust-colored structure, its doors and windows dark and unwashed, and a half-eroded carving on the front: Harlem Jail.

Keeping his hands in his lap, Uncle Goodman counted out several five-dollar bills, wadded them into his left fist and stepped outside. "Lock the doors and stay inside the car," he told us, then ran across the street and disappeared inside the decayed building.

No sooner had he vanished from sight than Bubby and I stepped outside, leaning against the Lincoln, our feet in the gutter. Children played on the sidewalks. A dark-skinned girl about my age asked, "Wanna jump? A my name is Anna and my husband's name is Al, we come from America and we sell apples."

I shook my head.

"Someone in trouble?"

I nodded.

"Riot last night."

"About what?"

"Cops. Just for fun."

Because of her early years in Odessa, dodging Cossacks, dodging police, Bubby was fearless anywhere in New York. Now she ignored rumors about Harlem, though her white hair and pale skin contrasted sharply with the people around her. The two of us moved toward the middle of the street and stood waiting.

Clouds closed like heavy curtains over the sun. We kept peering into the dismal entryway for the slightest flutter, passed an agonizing hour, and decided to go inside. There we halted and Bubby let out a cry of despair.

Lurching toward us was short Goodman holding up tall Clayton. A raincoat thrust over Clayton's shoulders did not conceal the blood-soaked rag of an undershirt. Most horrifying of all was his face, especially the swollen left temple, oozing blood from a gash as large as my hand. He stank of piss and vomit and shit.

We folded him into the front seat of the car.

"He needs a hospital, but I don't know where," said Goodman.

"We'll take him home. We'll call Koronovsky," Bubby announced.

Clayton sat in a daze, a black stone figure covered in blood. It must have required every ounce of his strength to call us in Yonkers.

Goodman didn't waste a minute, this time driving with reckless speed from Harlem to Grand Street. I opened the front door of the building with a key and we dragged Clayton into his studio apartment down the hall.

My little Bubby had the strength of a she-lion, a she-wolf, an inflamed tiger. She would have lifted the entire building to save Clayton.

His apartment was neat and orderly, furnished with Willy's folding bed, a small table and one chair. Our old blankets, thin but clean, were folded on top of the bed.

Gently Bubby tore away the stained rags of his clothes and dumped them into a paper bag, biting her lip at the purple welts covering his body.

Dr. Koronovsky answered on the first ring.

"I'll be right over," his voice boomed. "How bad is the cut?"

"Bad. Very bad."

"Listen, Goodman, I'll be there in twenty minutes. I sewed up dozens of juvenile delinquents downtown. I'll bring everything. Who's with him now?"

"Me, Manya, the girl."

"Good, good. I'll sew him up. You and Manya will assist."

"We have to wash him." Manya could barely speak. "Goodman, help me put him under the shower."

Next to the sink, there were two walls of tin enclosing a shower head mounted high above a drain on the floor, and a shower curtain. An up-ended cardboard box held squares of old towels that served as washcloths. Though our family was wedded to Rokeach non-animal-fat soap for our dishes, Clayton, who adored new products, had a bottle of liquid detergent on his sink. Cupping her hand over his face wound, Bubby sprinkled the liquid over his hair, shoulders and feet. The bloody suds ran like melted tar down the drain.

At the sound of Koronovsky on the outside bell, Bubby shut off the water and wrapped Clayton in a clean blanket. He fell on the bed like a mummy, his eyes closed.

Unusually cheerful, Dr. Koronovsky rose above our fears. "You reached me at the perfect moment. My in-laws are in our little garden with Phyllis. We're leaving for Martha's Vineyard in the morning. I have to be back by Thursday night. I'm on call all next weekend." He leaned over Clayton, appraising the gaping flesh. "Nasty. Really nasty. You two scrub your hands and slip on these medical gloves."

He lifted Clayton onto the kitchen table. Limp and motionless, Clayton had fainted.

Nevertheless, the doctor spoke to him soothingly.

"I'm putting you to sleep with this shot. Also an antibiotic. Bubby is here and so am I. You'll be fine. Have a good sleep."

Uncle Goodman kept his hand steady, holding up a roadside flashlight from his car that had a wide range and an intense yellow light.

"Manya," Koronovsky instructed her, "when the disinfectant is on his face, wipe it off with the sterilized gauze, then discard it immediately."

She didn't flinch, standing on her feet, assisting as if she performed this task a dozen times a day.

"My God!" the doctor cried as he worked on the wound, "it's full of shit! I can't believe it!"

Carefully, he applied disinfectant, and with Q-tips and sterilized tweezers he removed dirt and particles from the open flesh. His intensity was fierce. "That's about as clean as it will get. I'm using sulfanilimide powder as an extra precaution. Okay, Manya, relax. Sit down and rest. I'll suture this now."

Bubby's shoulders slumped. Her arms were trembling from the exertion.

"How many stitches?" asked Goodman.

"Thirty, forty."

"Forty!"

"One of these years we'll use clamps instead. Less chance of infection."

"Clamps? But you're such a good sewer. You could be a tailor."

He finished stitching and gently wrapped miles of white bandage around Clayton's head.

"Manya, do you want a nurse for the night?"

She roused herself—her first smile since Clayton phoned us. "You remember that beautiful nurse when we were sick in your apartment? Scott Wolfson told her Clayton was my boy and she said, 'You adopted a Negro as your child?' This I don't need."

"Clayton should have someone looking in on him every few hours."

"We'll take him upstairs. On the kitchen floor."

"Like old times on Orchard Street."

"Pain, heartache, they don't change. They're the same everywhere."

Dr. Koronovsky didn't argue with her. "He's a dead weight, but we'll sit him in the elevator. After that Goodman and I will carry him into the kitchen."

The appearance of my parents and Willy, tired from their day on Division Street, created a fresh commotion.

"He could have been killed!" cried Jack.

"He could have died!" cried my mother.

"He could have died in jail and no one would know!" cried Willy.

"I thought when he was on the kitchen table that maybe we would lose him," Bubby admitted.

"You should see Manya helping," said Uncle Goodman. "A regular Florence Nightingbird. Manya, dear, you remember which pills are for what?"

"White for pain, yellow for no infection."

I hadn't eaten since those tea sandwiches hours ago, but when Bubby said, "Let's make night" we scurried to our rooms. All except Bubby, who sat in the kitchen, leaning forward every hour to listen to Clayton breathing.

The next morning Dr. Scott Wolfson bounded into our apartment, a medical textbook in his hand.

"Manya, Dr. K. said you were a super nurse."

"Ah glick is mir getrofen."

"What does that mean? You found luck? I love Yiddish. I studied French from the age of ten. I hadn't even heard of the existence of Yiddish until I came to your house. Now I have a whole vocabulary. Goniff, meshugana, tsures, gevald. I want to be able to speak whole sentences, whole paragraphs." He opened his textbook. "How's the patient? What was the last time you medicated him?"

"Four in the morning."

Scott paused as he scanned the textbook. "Any excess bleeding?"

"That's how you'll take care of him? From a book?"

"I never worked head injuries, but I can deliver a baby and I know dozens of children's diseases. Manya, if you have a baby, I'll deliver it free."

"When you see me pregnant, you'll see the Meshiach walking in the sky!" She stood up and hugged Scott. "I'm glad you're happy. I'm glad love is giving you so much happiness."

"If I lost Susan, I don't think I could love again."

"I thought after Misha, there's no love. But each love is different, like each meal is different, like each play is different. How many times have I seen *The Old King*? Different actors make it different. It's not the same twice."

Unaccountably, she burst into tears, her chest heaving.

"Manya, Manya," Scott consoled her. "You won't lose Clayton. Remember how he cared for all of you when you were sick? Now you'll care for him and he'll be handy-dandy. Why are you upset when the worst is over?"

When Dr. Koronovsky returned from his long weekend, he suggested no work for Clayton and bed rest. If he couldn't sleep or had night terrors, Bubby was to give him a magic pill—the doctor set aside a half dozen Seconals—and she squirreled them away in the cinnamon jar. And Orloff took mop and broom in hand to clean the lobby.

On the night of Scott Wolfson's engagement party, Clayton wept copiously as we set out—Bubby in her new summer rose dress, I in my Parisian blue outfit and Willy in navy blue slacks, a long-sleeved white shirt and a V-necked sweater vest that matched his slacks. I was happy that the years of indifference to our attire were over.

Nor was Bubby upset that for once we were not hauling cartons, bags, boxes and cauldrons of food. Dr. Koronovsky had informed us firmly but kindly that the Wolfson and Newman families were providing food and drink.

The Koronovskys lived on the upper floor of a brownstone that faced lower Fifth Avenue. We could hear voices and laughter as we stepped into a setting of very high ceilings, bookcases lining the entrance hall, prints in gilt frames, end tables piled high with art books. A chess set with jade pieces caught the pale light.

Phyllis wore a long, Mandarin-style satin hostess gown the color of the chess set. She extended her arms to us, smelling of a subtle perfume, her narrow intelligent face radiant. "We're thrilled that you're here." She kissed Lil and Jack, whom she had not met before, on both cheeks, shook Willy's hand and said, "Will, I'm glad we finally met," and kissed Bubby and me.

Kisses and conversation filled the evening.

We spent no time worrying about our part in the conversation. Bernie Frank embraced us in his usual tipsy kissing mood, followed by

Dr. Charles Newman, Bubby's kidney specialist, who proved to be Susan's uncle. Was that how Scott met Susan, by bringing Bubby to this famous urologist?

We couldn't bother to speculate because Scott and Susan dominated the room. Straight-backed, long-legged, clearly the product of excellent health, vigorous sports and the confidence of privilege, Susan displayed her love for Scott as her birthright.

At last I gave myself permission to stop loving him. Liking him forever, yes, purging him from my fantasies, also yes. I remembered the first night Bubby and I talked about him in bed on Orchard Street, when she explained to me about mismatched worlds.

A gentle tap on the shoulder turned me around to see the benign face of Dr. Koronovsky. "I want to show you something," he said, and led me into the entryway. He nodded toward a small painting in a simple modern frame.

"This was my wedding present to Phyllis, a real Edward Hopper."

I gazed at the picture of three rust-colored buildings, identical in size and shape, with a pale slash of light at first dawn illuminating the lower half of the houses. "It's our tenement," I exclaimed, "our building on Orchard Street!"

"Or any decaying building in the city, standing in dead silence. Urban sculptures," said Dr. Koronovsky. "Come into our bathroom. I'll show you our Roualt. Bubby says it's King Lear, the one she calls the Alta Koenig."

"You have art in your bathroom?"

"Of course, that's where you need it most. The human body is far from perfect and seeing yourself undressed may cloud the day. When you step out of the bathtub and your eyes meet a masterpiece, you greet the new day courageously. Aren't those paintings lovely?"

It was an inspiring evening, and it wound down with the rustle of people leaving, more kisses, more congratulations to the golden couple. Near the door, I saw a table I hadn't noticed before covered with beautifully wrapped gifts.

"We didn't bring anything," I protested as we sank into Abe's cab.

"They have everything," Lil chimed in. "What could we get them, a coat at wholesale?"

"We brought ourselves," said Bubby. "That was the gift."

One Saturday evening a month later my parents came home to Grand Street by cab as daylight waned. Lil had worked at Saks, Jack at Elite Fashions. They ate schav and strawberries with sour cream—nothing more.

Then the phone rang. Pete Peterson, usually soft-spoken, spoke loud enough for all of us to hear. "Jack, good news at last! The architectural magazine is short of one article. It's going to be 'Grand Street Renaissance.' The shoot is early Monday morning. Are you game?"

"We'd love it. We'd be honored."

"We have to start while it's dark so the outside can be lit better. We'll have a crew of lighting men and we'll bring the furniture from Boucheron et Fils. Also two security guards, armed, in the truck and on the street. We're photographing the living room, the bathroom, the kitchen. We'll bring flowers, plants, an entire case of prime fruit. Please, let me speak to Manya, to Bubby."

Bubby's hand was shaking as she grasped the receiver.

"Hello dear, I don't want you to fuss. No baking, please. Three colorful dishes. Can you whip up a pâté? Do you have a mold?"

"Yes, yes, the mold is from a wedding I catered."

"Great. Perfect. Russians do beets. What do you suggest?"

"Beet borscht?"

"We'll bring the tureen."

"A whole salmon, no skin, black caviar."

"That's it! Molded pâté. Beet borscht with sour cream. Whole salmon, caviar topping."

"Where can I buy a fresh salmon on a Sunday?"

"The camera doesn't know fresh from day-old or hot from cold. The camera understands color. Is this too rushed for you?"

"No. It's maybe two, three hours' work."

"Good. Perfect. You'll be compensated for your time and the food. Thank you. Thank you so very much. Any questions?"

"What about the art?" I whispered.

"Who's that buzzing in the background? Put her on."

"What about the art?" I asked again.

"Sorry, I failed to mention it. A ravishing piece, wrapped in tarp, heavily insured. It will cover one entire wall opposite the windows, and has to be returned to the Cassette Gallery before 9:00 A.M. Monday."

"I meant for the bathroom."

"Thank you for reminding me. Where did you see art in the bathroom?"

"At Dr. Koronovsky's apartment. One artist was French and the other Italian. And he had an original Edward Hopper."

None of us had heard Pete Peterson laugh before. "I can't promise you an original Hopper but I'll do the best I can. And also, Orloff is a wreck. Try to calm him down. I've alerted the police. They know we're coming."

Jack phoned the Goodmans and on Sunday they brought down an electric coffeemaker that could brew twenty-four cups.

The rest did not run like clockwork. It was more like a disjointed dream, repetitive, bustling, anxiety-producing, heart-racing. Trucks drew up at 4:00 A.M. Monday. One lighting crew scurried onto the roof; another set up equipment on the high top of the truck.

Every room of our apartment was suddenly illuminated with glaring track lighting. Peterson hadn't decided whether to suggest darkness or early morning, so he photographed in two time periods, one with night and one with a day atmosphere.

Once inside the apartment, Blake, the dark-haired assistant who wore cotton footlets on his shoes and weighed about a hundred pounds, directed all the movements. He glided rather than walked, jumped on and off the furniture like a mountain goat, and gave instructions in what seemed like sign language, pointing, waving his arms, nodding his head for yes or no.

He selected the master bathroom first, hanging two framed prints of women in elaborate and futuristic gowns, both backgrounds red, the gowns lilac and yellow. He told me the artist's name was Erté.

He unfurled an off-white Swedish area rug, its edges tinged in lemon and milky cocoa brown. By the time the blue-black sky was showing a distant layer of gray, a couch had been moved in sideways through the door, cream-colored, the throw pillows with strips of satin that matched the edges of the rug. Lil gasped at its beauty.

The family, which included the Goodmans who had slept at our house that night, two or three in each bed, stood bunched in the doorway of the bedroom, watching.

In came two armchairs, one in front of each window, facing the sofa.

Worldly Aunt Bertha asked, "How much does a chair like that cost?"

As Blake hopped from one chair to another, he replied, "Five hundred dollars each. A thousand a pair."

Two chairs cost as much as a small car!

Flowers and exotic plants blossomed on a small table between the chairs and in unexpected spots—on the floor, in odd corners. Blake produced a bolt of ivory cloth, mounted a ladder, draped it across the top of one window and let the rest fall naturally to the floor.

Then they unwrapped the painting, a Miró with abstract baubles in a massive black frame.

"Careful with the frame. It costs three hundred dollars," Peterson warned. It was the first time he had spoken.

None of our minds could accommodate these numbers: five hundred, a thousand for chairs, three hundred for a frame. Peterson called on Clayton for help.

As Peterson had promised, the miraculous painting covered almost the entire wall. Two men photographed everything, crouched on the floor, on the chairs, on the arm of the couch, perched on the first rung of the ladder, on the last: ten, twenty, thirty views of the windows and the painting, the quietly elegant furniture . . .

"Where's the coffee table?" Lil asked.

"No coffee table. Never a coffee table. It's clutter. It serves no purpose, especially for knees and feet." Peterson's tone was not harsh, just authoritative.

He directed the kitchen shoot. Clayton stood at the window, in profile. Bubby, in her summer rose dress, leaned against the long counter. Peterson appraised the two of them. "Bubby needs rouge, needs brow darkener, her hair slightly mussed. I want her and Clayton out of focus, maybe double takes. The food is straight on, crisp and clear."

I thought Bubby looked gorgeous—her theatrical makeup and her natural gray hair, the smile in her eyes rather than on her lips.

"That's it. Don't look at the camera but think of . . ."

"Lil and Jack dancing," suggested Bubby.

"Perfect. Great. Done. We're done. Everything to come down in reverse. Outside lighting last."

Peterson kissed Bubby on both cheeks, shook hands with Clayton, Jack, Goodman, pecked Lil and Aunt Bertha on both cheeks. He applauded the crew. We applauded the crew.

They worked fast and skillfully, especially Blake, whom everyone called the A.D., assistant director. They retrieved the Italian ceramic dishes but left us the food and the flowers. In less than an hour, the art and furniture were gone and the trucks, the security guards and the police cars left.

Orloff hadn't slept the entire night, and he staggered in, rumpled, sweaty, and unsteady on his feet. "Manya, slivovitz." He knocked back the fiery liquid in one gulp.

For breakfast we drank Cafe Royale, the heavy cream high in the glasses, and ate French pastries.

"If you could keep one thing and one thing only, what would it be?" Jack asked.

"The white couch," said Lil.

"The thousand-dollar chairs," said Bertha.

"The big painting," Willy and I said in unison.

We waited for Bubby, who placed small value on material things.

"Maybe that Italian soup bowl with the handles. Not for using, just to look at."

Jack raised his glass. "Up from Orchard Street."

We noticed that he made no requests. Either he wanted it all or none of it.

22

Return to Connecticut

THE CHECK FROM the magazine brought us some relief. The rent was paid and at Bubby's suggestion, my father bought Willy an inexpensive record player for his records. And on a slow Monday, we set out for Jacob's store on Canal Street to buy a new outfit for Clayton—his fake leather jacket, his black skinny pants and his shiny shirt had been destroyed in the Harlem riot.

"For you, something special," Jacob exclaimed, "very uptown stuff. College kids and the young men with new jobs, they love them. I have exactly one suit left and for you, Manya—I can't tell you how much I miss you upstairs—for you a super bargain: a seersucker suit."

He slipped the pale blue single-breasted jacket on Clayton. Bubby applauded. "Perfect! He must have it."

My father had taught his mother long ago that clothes had little to do with protection from the elements. They were magic, to fulfill fantasies. Did Clayton require a seersucker suit to haul out the garbage cans, mop the steps, sweep the sidewalk? Yet in the most profound sense, this suit belonged to him. His image depended on it.

"Bubby," he pleaded, "I love it, but can you afford it?"

"If I asked what I could afford, I would be living on the Bowery." She retrieved the money from a *knippl* in her stockings. She still had voluptuous thighs and when she untied the knot Jacob sighed from suppressed arousal. Tears ran down Clayton's cheeks at the prospect of his new finery.

"Vayn nisht," she told him. "It's coming to you."

Clayton understood—he spoke Yiddish as well as I did—but he still didn't think he was entitled to such largesse.

Having completed the successful purchase, we rounded the corner to 12 Orchard Street. "Want to see the old neighbors?"

The sidewalk was unswept, the hallway dark—no one had bothered to change the lightbulb. "I'll help you up the stairs," Clayton offered, but Bubby couldn't step forward, immobilized either by memories or by dread. We hastened away from the building.

Before we reached Grand Street, Orloff spied us from his upstairs remnant shop, where a large sign declared, Going Out of Business.

"Manya, Manya!" He clattered down the battered steps. "What are you doing on Orchard Street?"

"Shopping for Clayton, a few things after his accident. I see you're having a sale."

"It's no sale. I'm selling the whole facockta business. Peterson and me, we bought another building on Grand Street, down from the Amalgamated. Peterson named the new building The Garden Terrace. Very fancy. Every apartment has a view of the East River and a terrace. In front is a fountain. Should I save an apartment for you?"

"Orloff, what are you doing? Buying up all New York?"

"Three houses on Grand Street because Peterson, he likes the idea of the Grand Street Renaissance. Then uptown. Already for the building you're living in, we could sell for a big profit. But not yet. I just spoke to Peterson, he tells me the photographs of your apartment, they're gorgeous." His billiard-ball head shone in the sun.

"I have to learn these new words," he said, laughing, "Renaissance, photo shoots, architecture. I know from fire sales, from burned dreck. Now it's Orloff, Real Estate." He paused and searched my grandmother's face. "You miss Orchard Street? Everyone came to your door."

"Like love, like children growing up, you close your eyes for one minute, nothing is the same. It was time, more than time, to leave."

"You can't leave this minute. My new tenant, he has girls' clothes, you will cholish when you see them. Five minutes. Hand to God."

With Orloff pleading and protesting, we walked down to the basement, a windowless space with a single lightbulb hanging from the ceiling. A young bearded Hassid, his skin pale as alabaster, with an enormous black hat on his head, reigned in the midst of chaos. Clotheslines extended from wall to wall, the garments attached with clothespins.

As was the custom, you never tried anything on over your head, you held it up to your chin. Orloff appraised me and pulled down lollipop-colored blouses, shorts, two or three dresses. "Take, take. I hear you are going back to Connecticut. For Connecticut you need these things."

"Orloff," Bubby protested, "for two weeks in the country it's too much. I don't know if I brought enough money, discount or not."

In this miserable space where we had difficulty breathing, Orloff stopped in his tracks. "Manya, you're a good giver, but a bad taker," he said firmly. "I'm giving your granddaughter a present. Manya, I've loved you many years. You thought it was a joke. Maybe you thought I was a joke. Don't shame me talking about money."

"Thank you," Bubby and I said simultaneously.

We held my outfits in our hands—the makeshift store had neither bags nor paper—and we trooped upstairs in silence. Bubby didn't protest when we reached the street and Orloff's lips grazed her cheek. The outing had exhausted her. We hailed a cab for the few short blocks up Grand Street.

Lil had been shopping. When she heard the taxi door slam, she greeted us in the lobby wearing a white two-piece sunsuit. "Ma, how do you like this? Isn't it stunning?"

"Twenty years old you look, not a day older."

"Would you believe the halter has a built-in bra, a halter with an uplift? You know what that proves? You can't believe anything you see in the movies."

Finally, finally, we left for Colchester, Connecticut. Abe's taxi glided to a stop in front of our house at 5:30 in the morning. Since the meter wasn't running Willy sat in the jump seat beside Abe while Lil and I stretched out in the back.

Driving with Uncle Geoff the year before, tension and fear had overwhelmed us. Each mile became an endurance contest. With Abe, the reverse was true. He told jokes and recited off-color limericks. The one that sent him into peals of laughter concluded with the line, "He put it in double / without any trouble / and instead of coming / he went," then excused himself if he offended Lil. He read the Burma Shave ads along the road with gusto. We laughed or yelled, "I have one! I have one!" meaning a joke or a funny story. Once we grew alarmed when he swerved off the highway. "Why are you stopping?"

"We're halfway there," he answered with pride. "I'm treating to cherry Cokes."

We didn't enter the truck stop—Abe took his duties seriously and didn't want the family in contact with tough men and their sour-smelling armpits. Willy slurped down his Coke in a few gulps and smacked his lips.

"It's the caffeine," Abe explained grandly. "One cherry Coke has more caffeine than two cups of coffee. On the road, a couple cherry Cokes, you stay awake and don't fall asleep at the wheel."

He jingled change from his pants pocket and headed for the public phone booth. We thought he had been checking in with Rocco, but he smiled. "I called the farm, said we'd be there in two hours, tops. I called Jack and told him the same."

"That was very nice of you."

"Hey, you folks from Westchester County expect service."

I wondered: where had he heard last year's lie, that heavy burden, about our living in Yonkers? Happily, this season we could declare that we moved downtown to relieve my father of the long commute to his business.

But despite this freedom, the closer we drew to Colchester, the more silent we became. Not out of shyness or fear, but because this place was our enchanted hideaway and we had endowed it with storybook quality.

Abruptly, the village green rose before us. We clapped and cried, "We're here, we're here!"

A creature of habit, I wanted every detail to remain the same as the year before. But a few yards out of the village we saw change.

"The road is paved. It'll be paved straight to the farm," I protested.

"I'm glad. I hated the stones in my sandals when we walked," Lil replied.

"That's what I liked. Roads with ruts. That's what made it the country."

"You and the country! Brooklyn is the country with sidewalks."

"Don't drive too fast. I want to see everything. Look, Gladkowski's farm is gone—the trees, the rocks, the fence for the cows. No more cows."

"I say it's an improvement. Not a farm, but a real hotel," Lil observed.

I hate it, I thought, but restrained myself.

We edged to the entrance of the hotel and halted. Estelle was leaning against the railing of the porch, peering down the road. "They're here!" she shouted. Her red-orange hair matched her orange shirt. She wore white shorts held up by white suspenders.

"How you children have grown! You're both ten feet tall." Estelle couldn't say more. Lil had fallen into her arms. They held each other.

Emerging from the shadows of the tiny lobby, I saw him, in his shorts with multiple pockets, his chest bare and brown, his long wavy hair bleached by the sun as if the skies had poured peroxide on it. He walked toward us in slow motion, taking small measured steps in his sandaled feet, half wild, infinitely beautiful.

Men are referred to as handsome but Maurey was beautiful. He dominated the canvas and crushed the frame around it. Squinting his eyes against the brilliant light, he delivered a heart-stopping, hypnotic message to Lil as she stood entwined in Estelle's embrace.

Standing on the lowest step of Pankin's Farm at the noon hour as Maurey approached, I resigned myself to one unwavering fact: my mother was in danger, our family was held together with spit. In one second she could leap into Maurey's arms. I was afraid.

The sudden appearance of Hal and Gabe bearing a straight-backed chair decorated with wildflowers broke the spell. Gabe looked taller and thinner to me, rusty-haired and befreckled; Hal sober and sad-eyed. Neither had had his hair cut since graduating from med school. They hoisted Lil into the chair, and cried, "Hold on tight!" and carried her up the long flight of stairs to our old room. Lil whooped, "Don't drop me, don't drop me!" until she was out of breath and the young men announced, "We did it! Top of Mount Everest. You're the tops."

To my joy, the smell and furnishings of our old room had not changed. But when I ran to the window, instead of the barn I saw three new cottages with wide terraces, their ledges filled with window boxes full of blazing flowers.

"It's beautiful, but where's the barn?" I leaned so far out the window that Hal drew me back. Then he led me to the end of the hall and up a half flight of stairs to the attic room.

"This is yours. We fixed it so you can read and write in privacy. How do you like the window seat? We killed ourselves to finish it on time."

In the room there was a single cot, a small table piled with yellow legal pads, an entire box of number-two lead pencils, a pencil sharpener and a lamp. A hand-lettered sign on the door read, Quiet, Genius at Work.

"I could stay here forever!" I cried. I meant it. The young men who bestowed this enormous gift on me laughed and clapped their hands. I dug my nails into my palms to stop my tears.

After a snack, they persuaded Abe to nap in Aunt Bea's old room before returning to the city. Then, one by one, the young men drifted downstairs, but not before Gabe checked Lil's pulse. "I'm the resident cardiologist this year. Hal is changing his specialty." He smiled at Lil. "You're doing just fine."

"Mother, I'm so very happy to be here," I told her.

"Me, too." Her face was soft, loving, luminous. She cradled in her bed with closed eyes. I went upstairs to my attic room where I slept.

❦

Compared to our shower on Grand Street with its mauve tiles and magnetic shower head that poured hot water like sizzling champagne, this country contraption was a sorry affair; the old-fashioned hexagonal floor tiles smelled of disinfectant and the water spurted in a mere trickle. But showers didn't matter. Tiles didn't matter. Wrapped in the thin towel, I didn't glance at myself in the mirror. Tall now but still shapeless, with no indentation to mark my waist, I still had a straight up-and-down body, skin and bones. I said a silent thank-you to Mr. Orloff for providing my white shorts and navy blue knit shirt.

Willy rolled off his bed and held his head under the faucet of the sink, shaking his face back and forth like a baby seal, drops of water dribbling down his shirt. That was his way of indicating his happiness at being in Connecticut.

Once outside we oohed and aahed at the new cottages, but mostly at the site of the uprooted garden patch, now covered with fresh grass. Glass tables with colorful umbrellas provided shade. The wicker chairs had been replaced by lightweight aluminum frames webbed with yellow and green.

The two mahjong ladies greeted us effusively. "We thought you'd never get here," they told us.

"We couldn't stay away. We wouldn't dream of it."

The plumper of the two, in her usual sack dress, asked, "How do you like the improvements? They'll be calling it 'Pankin's Country Club' next."

My mother stretched out on an aluminum chaise. "Our room is the same."

Not surprisingly, the evening meal was disastrous: meatloaf thickened with oatmeal, succotash on the side. We settled for their famous tomatoes topped with sour cream. But Estelle saved the evening by telling us about her recent trip to California with her husband and Gabe—a present for Gabe's graduation from medical school.

"Two weeks of sheer heaven." She blushed at the memory as though regaling us with details about a new lover. "We flew to San Francisco, rented a car and did the city as they call it, then drove to Los Angeles. Now that's something. Palm trees tall as mountains, hills the color of clay in the daytime, blue at night. And the houses. The mansions in Beverly Hills and Hancock Park. The movie theaters are like palaces. Everything is oversized, gaudy. You know the line in *The Great Gatsby* about Daisy? Her voice had the sound of money? Los Angeles thunders with the sound of money."

Lil admired Estelle's ability to speak vividly and well. Though Jack tutored her without cease, this was beyond her.

"Did you see any movie stars?"

"Not in Los Angeles. But we drove to the Del Mar racetrack and at a table at the Turf Club, right beside us was Walter Pidgeon. Talk about handsome and a deep voice! I said, 'It's a pleasure to sit near you,' and he answered, 'Well, thank you.' I didn't want to embarrass my husband or son but my knees were weak."

We loved that anecdote. We wanted Estelle to repeat it again and again.

"The Pacific Ocean is everywhere, and the surroundings take your breath away. I was in tears when we left. I could imagine myself becoming a painter or a writer, maybe a poet, if I lived there."

Not knowing how to respond to this declaration, Lil presented her own recent worldly experience. "We had a photo shoot at our apartment. It's coming out in an architectural magazine."

"No!"

"Our architect lent us the chairs and the art, and an armed guard brought the furniture into the building. The armchairs were from Boo-cher-on ay Fees. One thousand dollars for two chairs fit for movie stars."

After dinner, on the strength of the lively conversation and the inedible food, we walked toward what was formerly the dilapidated house with its many unkempt children. The tumbledown shack was gone; in its place stood a charming Cape Cod cottage.

Willy ran ahead. "Where is it? What happened to it?" he cried.

"Destroyed," said Estelle. "Hank, Mr. Pankin, bought the land from here to the fork in the road. He built this new house for the Gladkowskis in exchange for their land. They're now in the produce business together and sell vegetables for miles around. An entire staff cultivates the produce. Hank is very restless. These projects keep him busy. The Pankins are a restless breed."

"Hal isn't," I said.

"True. But Maurey expects each day to be an adventure."

As if to prove it, we heard the steady honking of a truck horn.

Maurey yelled into the wind, "Ladies, ladies, it's Monday, movie night. I've come to fetch you."

"What's playing?"

"Boys Town."

"We saw it a hundred years ago."

"Then see it a hundred and one. Or not." Maurey let the motor idle. "Hey, you missed Jack's phone call. He called on the dot of six and you were out walking. He said to tell you he bought a coat with a swing back. What's a swing back? How would you like to swing into the truck and accept my treat for ice cream? The dinner was pretty awful . . ."

"You can say that again."

"The dinner was pretty awful." Maurey whirled my mother around before seating her, breathless, in the front seat. Estelle was hoisted up next and Willy and I sat on the women's laps.

Exuberant, restless, irrepressible, Maurey nibbled on my mother's ear without shame. "I'm hungry for ice cream but I'd like to dive into the new pool we're going to build. I wish it would appear by morning. Did you know that I'm going to be the swimming instructor when the pool is finished? You'll be my first pupil. I'll cure you of your water phobia." He tapped my bony knee.

"I don't have a water phobia."

"Of course you do. You don't wet your toes, let alone splash in the lake."

"It's not because I'm afraid. I can't stand the noise. The children scream and the mothers scream. It gives me a stomachache."

"What do you suggest for that beautiful space that used to be the old Gladkowski farm? A reading room? A library?"

"A library with an aquarium would be restful. Not a big aquarium like Battery Park, but small with little fish."

"Your daughter is a number-one eccentric," he told my mother. He didn't slap her thigh, only pretended to play the piano on the thin fabric of her slacks. "I have a great new song for you. First lesson, tomorrow morning at nine."

After the ice cream in the village, I retired to bed. The day had overwhelmed me; too much talk, too many people, too much to figure out and understand. I must have dozed off when a slight noise awakened me—the sound of our bedroom door closing.

"Mother!" I called. "Mother!"

She could have left for the bathroom, returning in a minute. The clock read 11:10. I concentrated on the slightest noise. Not a murmur. Five minutes went by. Ten. Half an hour, each minute increasing my anxiety, my dread. I considered searching for her, but where? In my private attic, the dining area, outdoors? The prospect of finding her was possibly worse than waiting. I breathed with difficulty.

At last, a movement no louder than a summer's breeze.

"Mother?"

"Are you up? I couldn't sleep either. I stared out the window at the end of the hall."

Her voice was calm and steady. She slid beneath the sheets. As an insomniac of long standing I could sense a person who lay awake, eyes gazing at the ceiling. I turned in the direction of the yellow cottage lights. Miraculously, they helped quiet my savage heart.

We drank our breakfast coffee with Estelle, who then excused herself. Every day, including Sunday, she wrote to her husband. "It's the same as keeping a diary," she explained, "and Philip enjoys my letters. He can hardly wait to read them." She liked to take a quick walk to the post office in the village to mail them, after which she spent her leisure hours reading or talking with the guests.

For her first day in the sun, Lil had selected her white sunsuit with the built-in bra. Since she had slept fitfully during the night, she dozed in the aluminum chaise after breakfast until she felt a gentle tap on the shoulder.

"Ready for our singing lesson?" Maurey squatted beside her. "That's a fantastic outfit you're wearing."

"It was hard to find."

"And well worth the effort. Now let's start on our new song."

He gathered her to her feet, held her hand in a steady grip and trotted toward the main house. "My heart, my heart," she gasped.

"I'm sorry. I truly am. I forgot about your heart." As if no other soul inhabited the hotel, he lifted her in his arms and carried her up the porch steps. Then he settled her on the piano bench in the dining room, and with his hair flying and his eyes alight with mischief, he placed his ear to her heart and listened to its rhythm, not stirring his head from her chest.

At midmorning, guests were walking to and fro, the porch was filled with card and game players, the dining area was set up for lunch and children amused themselves by jumping from the railing of the porch to the grass below. But Maurey was oblivious to the other guests, acting in the belief that he and my mother occupied a magically invisible private realm.

"The song is 'Take Me in Your Arms Before You Take Your Love Away.' " His singing was flat and toneless but his piano playing was like liquid cascading over smooth rocks.

"Take me in your arms before you take your love away / take me in your arms before we part. Lil, we need lots of vibrato in the middle section, the lowest tones possible, and try to cry a little. Female European singers sob on cue. Americans don't because jazz has taught them to belt it out. Try very husky. When you sing *fast* and *past* it's the British *a*. Not too exaggerated or it's phony, but not New Yorkese either. Pahst. Fahst." He held her with his daring blue eyes.

"I don't know if I can do it."

"Of course you can. You have enormous vocal range. It's just that you haven't been trained to take advantage of it." His long suntanned fingers rested at the base of her throat. "Begin: 'One hour of sadness that we knew in the pahst . . .' "

Lil hadn't sung much during the year—too busy, too sick, too involved with moving, too emotional about our store and her work. But she desperately wanted to please Maurey. "One hour of sadness . . ." Off-key. Awful.

Maurey could not be faulted for lack of patience. Not a negative word escaped his lips. "A bit rusty. That's to be expected." He faced her without playing. "From the top, without music."

"Take me in your arms before you take your love away."

"That's it. Much better. Once more."

"It's a sad song."

"You were made for sad songs. They were written for you. You've been spoiled by too much 'I'll be down to get you in a taxi, honey.' You're good at fast tempo and you've been doing it for a long while. Try to think of what you're singing. You want to tear the listener's heart out. 'Take me in your arms,' pause, 'before you take your love away . . .' It's a true experience. A terrible farewell. You're not seeing this man again. Ever."

My father could have sung this duet with Lil, led her in dramatic presentation.

"Close your eyes. Sob a little. Not over the top, only steady, from the bottom of your toes. Let's hear it slowly, slowly, one word after another."

"Take me in your arms before you take your love away."

Her effort touched him. Without self-consciousness his arms embraced her. She leaned into him with no resistance.

Instinctively I fled, down the steps, past the patio and into the cornfield. Not on the path along the side of the corn but into the corn itself, scrambling over irregular patches, zigzagging, heading for the fruit orchard. Glad to be alone, my heart pounding from the exertion, I recognized a familiar call: "Hey, you funny duck, wait up!" I didn't stop, but Hal's legs were longer than mine. He caught up with me.

"Are you practicing for a cross-country marathon?"

The pear tree under which I read *Jane Eyre* last year welcomed both of us. I sank back against the gnarled tree trunk, breathless. My spindly legs were covered with bits of greenery, corn silk, damp earth.

"What's the rush?"

"Just felt like it."

He tossed a manila envelope into my lap whose return address read *Architecture*. It was addressed "Roth Family" and marked "Do not bend."

"The photo shoot! The pictures of our apartment."

"It came in the early mail. I thought you'd like to see them first."

The photographers had performed miracles. There was our narrow building in an urban setting—not downtown, just anywhere sophisticated in New York. The spotlighting had re-created the architect's vision; the morning sky resembled dusk, the sun setting rather than rising.

"That's Bubby in her summer dress at her kitchen work table and Clayton, her assistant, behind her," I explained to Hal. Bubby with her white hair and Clayton in his white jacket were out of focus as planned, the food in the forefront clear and sharp.

The living room was spellbinding, the elegance of the furniture immediately apparent. The killer photo was the half-draped window and the wall dominated by the Miró painting.

"What a snazzy apartment. Incredible."

"The architect borrowed everything. We cried when they carried out the painting. The living room is still not furnished."

Hal regarded me for a long moment.

"How did you become so honest?"

It was impossible to return his scrutiny. I loved Hal dearly. Not kisses and hugs, but with reverence, admiration. I basked in his understanding, his depth; I could tell him anything without fear. If I were double my age I would throw myself at him and beg him never to leave me.

Then he handed me a stapled green paper bag stamped "Harvard University Book Store." My fingers twitched as I tried to loosen the staples.

"For heaven's sake, tear open the bag!"

"No, I want to save it. It's important to me."

"All right. But hurry it up. I want you to see what's inside. It's a boxed edition. Last year I gave you two secondhand books. This year you deserve better."

In a heavy gray box separated by a partition lay Tolstoy's *War and Peace* and *Anna Karenina,* leatherbound, the titles embossed in gold.

"Only you could buy me such a beautiful present."

"The moment I saw this in the bookstore, you flashed into my mind. Gabe and I went to the Sullivans' for Thanksgiving and showing Estelle and Philip these books made the evening."

He took both my hands in his. "You have to promise me one thing. Don't save these books as sacred objects, the way you said your Uncle Geoff keeps his books under lock and key. Take them everywhere. Let cookie crumbs fall between the pages. Let these books save your life. That's what they're for."

His hair flopped over his eyes. He was not tall and slender or appealing to both men and women, the way Maurey was. Not a movie star. Just a loving, lovely man. I was too overwhelmed to speak. He enjoyed my wonder.

"I told you, didn't I, that when my mother died the three of us were half crazed? Maurey, my mother's darling love, stopped speaking. He'd say a few words and start howling."

"Did it bother you, that he was your mother's favorite?"

"Does it bother Willy that you are your grandmother's favorite?"

"Why don't you ask about my mother's favorite?"

Hal nudged me with his elbow. "Hey, this discussion means no holds barred. Lil's favorite is Jack. You and Willy accept it. I accepted Maurey's position with my mother and every stranger he met because my father adored me."

I smoothed out the Harvard bookstore bag, folded it carefully in quarters and placed it inside the back cover of *War and Peace.*

"I have something else to tell you. I went into therapy this year. Like Willy."

"What for? You're perfect. Scott Wolfson takes Willy for long drives, buys him ice cream, talks about this and that. Is that what your doctor does?"

"No ice cream, but lots of talk. That's why it's called the talking cure. Sybil wounded me deeply when she accused me of not being able to free myself of old habits. More important was the issue of my medical specialty. I found out I didn't have to study cancer in order to save my mother."

"Your mother is dead. How can you save her?"

He grazed his knuckles on my head. "It's all in the mind, dear, all in the mind."

Hal taught me the power of silences. I sat quietly, not sure of the meaning of this conversation, but realizing its importance.

"By the way," he asked, "how was Willy's year? He seems less anxious, freer."

"He had emergency surgery, a tracheotomy, but he liked the radio Dr. Wolfson bought him."

"How did he adjust to the move from Yonkers?"

Again a black cloud suddenly appeared in an otherwise faultless sky. Hal had complimented my honesty. Would I ever be able to tell him the truth about Orchard Street?

"Willy loves the movies downtown and my father's store. He's terrified of Little Italy, Chinatown, the crowds in the streets and the subways."

"Any bad traumas, things that frightened him, sent him into a panic?"

"Clayton was almost killed in Harlem. It was scary for all of us, and Willy couldn't stop crying. He cried and cried."

"Willy is lucky that you're his older sister."

This mistake would last a lifetime; I lost interest in correcting people.

"Would you still like to live here?"

"I asked my grandmother last year; maybe she could open a restaurant in the village. But they're New York City people. My mother calls Brooklyn 'a day in the country.' They couldn't live without Manhattan."

"And you?"

"I'm leaving New York as soon as I can. The sky is always dark there. I'm afraid it will fall on my head and crush me."

"You are a funny duck. I missed you all year."

"You mean my family?"

"No, you."

We walked side by side toward the main house. "I've decided on pediatrics," Hal confided. "I think I'll enjoy taking care of children."

"That will be better for you, less depressing."

He bumped into me deliberately, throwing me off my stride. "Last year you told me you couldn't be a doctor, it was too depressing. Now you assure me pediatrics is less depressing than cancer studies. What's with you and depression?"

"I wish I could be like my mother. A musical comedy makes her happy. Singing makes her happy. Also a sunsuit with an uplift bra."

"Lots of things make you happy. They're different than your mother's. The books I gave you . . ."

"They made me very happy."

"Remember what I told you. Read them again and again. They'll save your life." He ran off, darting toward an errand he didn't share with me.

I wandered into the hotel's kitchen because it reminded me of Orchard Street. I missed our old kitchen there, it's intimacy, the heady smell of cooking food, the presence of my grandmother's friends. I missed our open door, the merchants, the gossip that flowed in several languages.

No, I didn't miss the rats and roaches, the windows thick with frost, the cold. But I longed to see my grandmother pouring hot water over my father's hair before he left for work. I longed to peek at Clayton as he washed himself in the kitchen, and how his chocolate lollipop stuck out from beneath his fuzzy bush as he oohed and aahed. I missed everything about that kitchen, even the charred, dented pots and pans that new ones could never replace.

The farm kitchen delighted me because of its chaos—not to mention the baskets of newly harvested tomatoes, string beans and baby cucumbers.

"My grandmother would love those baby cukes!" I confided to Belinda.

"You help with the cooking?"

"No, never."

In a gesture reminiscent of Bubby, Belinda fanned her face with her apron. "Your grandmother spile you?"

"She spoils everyone. My mother is a great helper with pastries but she doesn't cook either."

"You find the food here funky?"

"Very. We lose weight in Connecticut." I studied the crusted gas burners, the oven doors with a summer's worth of spilled gravy on them, the sticky floors. "Don't you have anyone help you clean this place?"

"What for? Either next week or next year, they tear the whole kitchen out. Throw it all on the junk heap. Like we should throw out these chickens. Kosher chicken, she's dry as an old lady's satchel."

We laughed and laughed. This year when the phone rang I no longer had to stand on a stool to reach it.

"Pankin's Farm," I said.

"I'd like to speak to Lil Roth, Mrs. Roth."

"Daddy! Is it really you?"

"Where's Lil? I have news that will knock her out of her socks. Aunt Bea and her children are here on Grand Street with us. She walked into her room at the Roney Plaza and found Geoffy with the manicurist. Dead to rights. In the act and in the flesh. Bea started screaming. Geoffy told her he would never give up Sharon, that she could take it or leave it. So Bea left it and came to us."

"Why didn't she go to her house in Brooklyn?"

"She wants to give Geoff a hard time. Says it's the principle of the thing. She hasn't been sleeping or eating, just crying. Her children hate it here. I'm sending her to Connecticut. Abe is finding her a driver. She'll be there tomorrow afternoon."

"Daddy, I want to speak to Bubby." I poked my head through the kitchen door. Gabe stood in the lobby. "Gabe, please, would you find my mother? It's important." Then I shouted, "Bubby, what do you think?"

"He was a fool to tell her he wouldn't give up the manicurist," Bubby replied. "She was a fool to say she was leaving on principle."

"They were just being honest."

"Honest? Honest gives heartburn, heartache, hartz-klopinish. The worst pain comes from honest. They both should say less. Where can Bea go and what can she do with two children? And that other woman, the manicurist, in a few months it's over. You can't eat kugel every meal."

"Bubby, is this a don't-tell?"

"One look at Bea's face, the whole world will guess."

Gabe yelled, "Your mother is waiting in the library. She's on the phone now." I hung up the receiver in the kitchen and zoomed into the library, where I stowed the envelope of photos and my new books on a low shelf for the moment. I saw Lil cover her heart with her hand as she listened to Jack.

"Dead to rights? In the act and in the flesh?" she repeated. "What does Manya say? Forgive and forget? How can she make believe it didn't happen? How could Geoff be so foolish to do it in his own room? What do you mean, maybe he wanted to be caught? How could he want such a thing? Jack, you're too deep for me. Yes, Bea should have come to Connecticut in the first place and my brother kept his pants closed in the second." She hesitated and added, "Jack, when we're here and you're in New York, no flirting."

From where I stood, I could hear his answer: "Flirting? You think I'm a no-goodnik like your brother?" It may not have been the truth, but the words calmed her.

Gabe came up to Lil with an aspirin in hand as she hung up. "Take this and walk over to my mother, Estelle. You two may have a lot to talk about." I gathered up my possessions, told Lil about the architecture magazine, and crossed the lawn with her.

You could see evidence of Estelle's calm self-assurance in her cottage. Along the window seats were pots of fresh wildflowers, and every surface—the chest of drawers, nightstand, small table—was covered with new books, paperbacks, magazines.

Throwing herself at the foot of the bed with its white coverlet, my mother recounted what she regarded as the messy story of her brother's misbehavior, and her fear that it might lead to divorce, or to "terrible public opinion."

"Public opinion is not at issue," Estelle told her. "Only what happens to Bea and the children."

My mother began to cry. Too many Hollywood movies and tabloid articles had convinced her of the horrors of divorce.

"These infidelities happen." Estelle spoke carefully, smoothing her hair away from her face. "It even happened to me. I was unfaithful to my first husband, to Joe, on the very day he died."

My mother sat up, eyes brimming with astonishment. I was stunned. Estelle recounted her story without asking me to leave the room or resorting to language that masked the truth.

"Joe was at home with a nurse around the clock and enough equipment to put most hospitals to shame. The doctor told me it was a matter of hours, not days, and he suggested that I speak to our son, to Gabe. I expected Gabe from school at any minute—but when the door opened it was Philip, Joe's partner and best friend.

"I couldn't stop crying. Phil tried to comfort me. One minute I sobbed into his neck because Joe was dying, the next Phil was kissing me, saying how much he loved me, that he hadn't married because of me. Suddenly we were making love standing up, with Joe in an oxygen tent and the nurse in the next room. It was the most amazing sex I ever had—I thought the top of my head would come off.

"Then the front door slammed and somehow we straightened up. Phil said to Gabe, 'I'm sorry, son, your dad is in a bad way and your mother is taking it hard.' Phil, the trial lawyer, gave an Academy Award performance.

"I staggered into my own bedroom and called Hank's wife, Paula Pankin. Paula was like Manya, very open-minded and wise. She said, 'Don't feel guilty. Death and sex go together, one takes away the pain of the other.' Then she advised me, 'Out of respect for Joe you should follow the Jewish law. Wait one year and one day before you marry Phil.'

"But he hasn't asked me," I said.

"Of course he did. The minute he opened his pants."

"And did you wait a year and a day?" asked Lil.

"To the minute. Gabe was thirteen and our best man. A Reform rabbi officiated. Hank and Paula and their two boys were the only others at the ceremony."

My mother sighed. "I love happy endings." She debated her question. "No offense for asking, does Philip ever have a nosh?"

"A nosh? You mean a sweet?"

"I mean . . ." My mother stumbled and forged ahead. "Does he have a quickie, like with a client, a secretary?"

Estelle could not suppress her laughter. "We were unfaithful to Joe that one night. Enough for a lifetime."

Lil had the good sense to change the subject by taking out the architecture magazine with the photographs of our home. I scampered out, my head a jumble of all the sexual stories I had heard over the years. Despite the open talk in our house, I never really absorbed them. Pandy, the hairdresser, and her grief over her unfaithful husband, my father's criticism of Ada Levine, even his confession to my Bubby about his noshes—all sailed in and out of my head. Clayton's saga about three in a bed, Hal's puppetlike lovemaking with Sybil last year, Dr. Wolfson's hugging and kissing at his engagement party—the images came to me from a distant shore, through mist and fog, and vanished as quickly as they appeared.

As I headed for my room, I wondered why my idea of an intimate evening consisted of talking to Hal Pankin about books. No question about "all the good things" was left unanswered at my house, and now I watched my mother lost in a dream state with Maurey, but it never occurred to me to seek these emotions for myself.

Of the many incidents of lovemaking that I heard, I realized that the one that moved me the most was the story of Estelle and Philip as her husband lay dying in the next room and what Paula Pankin said: "Death and sex go together. One takes away the pain of the other." As quickly as I was able, I climbed to my quiet attic hideaway. Carefully I opened *Anna Karenina*. My eyes glazed over and I fell into a deep sleep on the cot.

The following day Aunt Bea, Cousin Alice and Lenny spilled out of a hired car. Aunt Bea looked dreadful, puffy-eyed, wan, her hair disheveled. The moment she greeted Lil they went up to our room to talk undisturbed, two childhood friends with no friction between them. Their dinner was sent up on a tray. Neither touched the food.

In contrast, there was Cousin Alice, impervious to her mother's despair, who emptied out what she had stuffed into one of Lil's old purses. "Look at what Bubby Manya bought me." Onto the porch floor fell a half-dozen lipsticks in colors ranging from near white to deep purple, a clutch of nail polish bottles in varied hues, polish remover, a box of mascara, another of rouge, a wand of eyelash enhancer, barrettes, colored bobby pins, an eye pencil.

"They're all for me," Alice cried. "Bubby Manya said I didn't have to share. We went to Woolworth's and I picked out whatever I wanted."

In my many years with Alice she had never talked as much as she did while we sat on the floor of the porch. Since we had last met, she had grown taller and thinner, and two points blossomed from her blouse. She cupped her hand over my ear and whispered, "I have cucumber hair. I'll show you later." Then she rouged her cheeks and her knees. "Flapper dapper," she sang out and turned a somersault. Alice may have had no interest in reading books, but she certainly seemed to have acquired or inherited her father's appetites.

Pankin's Follies was performed on Saturday night. It wasn't the same without my father, but he was stuck in New York this year, preparing for the fall season. Hal acted as master of ceremonies, and while the program was ragged and often chaotic, its success could not be denied.

Reluctant as I was to recite the Shakespearean sonnet that I had memorized for Miss Sussman—it didn't seem appropriate for the evening—Hal persuaded me that it would set the tone for the other performers. My red velvet dress, the gift from Rocco, no longer grazed my ankles but it was much too hot. Still, it did have a Shakespearean air, and when I concluded with, "For thy sweet love remembered such wealth brings / that then I scorn to change my state with kings," the applause gratified me.

Willy whistled "I Can Dream, Can't I" with absolute pitch and tempo. The med students, led by Hal, roared, screamed and sang off-key, "I can't give you anything but love, baby" until they grew hoarse. Alice pirouetted alongside them.

The star of the show, "straight from the heart of New York," appeared in a long black dress, her hair parted in the middle and fashioned severely in the Spanish manner with a giant red silk flower tucked over her right ear. Estelle had created the costume and hairstyling.

Maurey's generous instruction enabled Lil to sob on cue, "Take me in your arms before you take your love away." She and the audience were captivated by the lament and she sang it twice to satisfy her admirers. Miraculously she remembered every word, every nuance, and the throb of her voice depicted her heartache. Calls of "Bravo!" resounded until Hal announced "Our theme song, written by the one and only, the talented Jack Roth." The entire ensemble broke into, "And another year is coming and we don't give a darn / we'll leave the wife and children and come back to Pankin's Farm."

The house shook from the hours of dancing and the piano-playing of Maurey and Hal, who alternated at the keyboard. The mood was carnival-like.

Everyone, male or female, insisted on one dance with Lil, who floated across the dining room floor without holding her heart, without fear, without caution. She accepted each person's kisses as if they were her birthright. Most especially from Maurey, who again drew an invisible curtain around the two of them, and murmured, nibbled, licked, touched, whirled, dipped, kissed short, kissed long until, out of her head with emotion, it was a marvel that Lil did not faint.

When the dancing finally ceased, Gabe and Hal carried her up the stairs. Estelle removed her dress and Lil passed out amid her finery, smelling of the Chanel No. 5 on the scarlet silk flower pressed against her cheek.

Willy and I dropped our clothes to the floor. Drunk with the desire for sleep, I forced myself awake from hour to hour to certify that my mother was in her bed, that she hadn't crept out the door like a sleepwalker. Once, to anchor her, I even reached out for her leg. She didn't stir. Remarkably her breathing was serene, as if in a hypnotic trance. At last I allowed myself to sleep undisturbed.

The sun loomed high in the sky when I awoke to a shrill piercing whistle, a New York whistle, the whistle petty thugs used to mean, "Cheez it, the cops."

Why was a whistle like this invading our country privacy? It sounded again and yet again. I heard the scuffling of feet, the slam of a car door, the whoosh of tires on the gravel.

Lil and Willy slept on. I leaned on my elbow and surveyed the mess on the floor, towels, clothes, shoes, no space to walk. It seemed an enormous effort to leave my bed. Then I heard slow, labored footsteps, a tentative knock on the door.

"It's me, Hank Pankin, Hank."

I debated sending him away, reporting that my family was still sleeping. Except that the owner of our beloved farm had never before come to our room.

"Just a minute."

I gathered up the stuff on the floor and threw it into the closet, while rousing Lil. "Mother, Mother, it's Mr. Pankin." I shook her awake. "He's waiting outside. Maybe Daddy is on the telephone." Quickly I brushed my teeth and splashed water on my face.

"Just a minute," Lil repeated.

No time to remove last night's stage makeup. She rinsed out her mouth. Her hair a bird's nest, strands stuck together with pomade from the Spanish hairdo.

"Open the window, open the window."

"You mean the door?"

"No, the window. It must smell awful here."

Chastely she drew the sheets to cover her bosom and told me, "Smooth the covers, then let him in."

"Sorry if I disturbed you." Hank lumbered over to the one vacant chair in the room.

"I came to tell you. I thought you'd better know that your brother was here. Mr. Simon. He drove a new black Cadillac, very big, top of the line. He whistled. His wife and children heard the whistle, they jumped right into the new car. No hello, no good-bye, they drove away."

"Did they pack, take anything with them?"

"Nothing. He whistled, they went with him."

Hoarse from last night's exertions, Lil's voice had a falsetto edge. "That's how Geoff made up with her: he bought a new car. You must have heard . . ."

Willy yawned. Mr. Pankin did not acknowledge any talk but his own.

"One more thing. Maurey, Hal, Gabe and Estelle, they left right after they put you to bed. They didn't want any fuss, any good-byes. I'm telling this to you because you're family, so you know how I felt when I waved good-bye. Hal doesn't want any changes in the farm, neither does Estelle. I don't know what I want, what I'm doing or why.

"Listen, standing there when it was nearly light, waving, smiling, a piece of my heart tore out of my body, it was such a wrench, such a pain to watch them go. I didn't know how to comfort myself. I didn't. I couldn't."

I couldn't do anything either, just try to create a safe place for myself by rocking gently in the bed with the pictures from the photo shoot and my Tolstoy books locked to my chest.

23

The Circle

AGAINST HER CARDIOLOGIST'S advice, Lil returned to work at Saks, Saturdays only. Her one concession was to eliminate the subway ride in favor of taking Abe's taxi to and from her job. Always punctual, she walked into the department store refreshed and with a private thrill of condescension because she hadn't struggled on the subway or the bus like the other salespeople. This aura of superiority impressed the store's managers, and in early November she was transferred to evening wear, a mark of status.

Lil's happiness at selling evening gowns served to compensate for her minuscule salary—taxis and the need for handsome clothes ate into the stash of money that she was saving for living room furniture. Her conversation now centered on satin gowns, or taffeta or georgette, off-the-shoulder or jacketed, low-backed, decorated with seed pearls, bugle beads or discreet sequins.

Customers had to make an appointment to view the latest gowns. Since my mother had a mannequin's figure, at work she wore a long silver lamé dress with a black velvet bib, along with flat-heeled silver

sandals. She decided to buy the dress, which she paid for on an install-
ment plan. Her hair, parted in the center, was enhanced by an added
braid of real hair placed at the nape of her neck. Every Friday night
Pandy washed and adjusted this elaborate hairstyle, appropriate for the
opera or charity galas, and wrapped it in a heavy net to keep it in place
while Lil slept. When she stepped into Abe's cab in the morning, my
mother came as close to representing a movie star as she ever would.

Upon her return early each Saturday evening, Bubby helped her remove her elegant dress, no matter that its wear and tear came out of her
salary. She would sink into bed immediately and amuse herself while still
awake by adding the sum of her day's wages to her account book.

There was a hectic period before New Year's Eve, followed by the
postholiday clearance sales. Then she took the following weekend off
and accepted the invitation from the architect of our building, Pete
Peterson, to attend a wholesale furniture sale on Saturday morning.
She decided that I should go with her to bolster her morale.

Peterson selected an ivory-colored couch with a skirt that fell over the
legs. It was covered in a linenlike fabric treated to withstand dirt, and its
deep cushions were edged in bands of satin. We had not encountered a
sofa of such subtle beauty before and the possibility that she might own it
brought my mother to tears. She barely managed to nod her head when
Pete asked whether she liked it. He put a sold tag on it immediately.

As we searched for two armchairs to be placed in front of the windows, Peterson spied a low, long teak table, the exact length of the
couch. "We'll take this, too," he said.

"I thought you hated coffee tables," I said.

"It's not a coffee table. It goes behind the sofa for the display of a
few choice art objects."

"*Behind* it?" Lil repeated.

"Yes. It's both a room divider and a display table, for art books, a
few whatnots and of course a vase with fresh flowers. Fresh flowers are
a must in a civilized home. A few daisies will do the trick."

Finally catching her breath, Lil said, "Jack should have come
with us."

"He'll love this sofa and table," Peterson assured her. "Jack is a man of innate taste. I sometimes think taste is an inherited characteristic. Don't you?"

My mother grew dizzy from having to assimilate this lesson in esthetics.

In a dark corner labeled "Twice Removed" Lil spied a square deep chair with an ottoman. Peterson winced at its faded purple color and brocaded fabric.

"Macy's basement," he declared.

"It's for Manya. For her bedroom. She can look out the window and rest her feet."

"There's one almost like it in dark blue velvet."

"It's more expensive and I've run out of money." Unexpectedly, my mother began to cry. Out of frustration. Out of embarrassment. Out of longing.

"There, there," Peterson said gently. "I'll put it on my account. You'll pay me back when you have it."

When these words were spoken by Goodman, they signaled a gift, phrased to save my family the humiliation of seeming like shnorrers, people who exploited Goodman's generosity. But Pete Peterson, the uptown architect, wasn't from Lil's world. Adrift, but not wanting to disgrace herself, she desired his good opinion of her.

For once, honesty came to her rescue.

"It's taken me months of waiting on women and zipping up evening gowns on Saturday and then selling coats and suits on Sunday, and saving every penny, every cent. My cardiologist would be upset if he found out I worked Saturday and Sunday, but we need the couch and of course the stunning table. I don't have a penny more, or know when I can pay you back."

"It's not a Russian bond," he laughed. "The Bolsheviks won't come after you. Besides, you're right. Manya needs this chair. We mustn't let numbers stand in our way." He paused. "The Roth family helped smash my stereotypes about downtown inhabitants."

She didn't understand his vocabulary but his tone and his courtesy soothed her. "Thank you," she replied.

The day the furniture was delivered Willy and I stayed home from school and Jack from Elite Fashions. The sofa emphasized how far we had traveled from Orchard Street, but it was the table behind it that caused an uproar.

"What a knockout, what style, what class!" Jack announced.

The ring of the outside bell heralded two gifts from Pete Peterson. Inside a box stamped "Breakable: Handle with Care" was a hand-blown vase with a tiny sticker that read "Made in Denmark." Pale blue swirls thin as fine ribbons encircled the delicate glass. The second box had a florist's label and within were two exotic flowers as long as swan's necks: deep orange surrounded by equally deep green fronds. Pete's enclosed card read, "May these birds of paradise symbolize your new surroundings." When the vase and the flowers were placed on the table behind the couch, we looked at them enthralled, possessions we hadn't conceived of in our dreams.

And yet! Ah, but for that yet!

Lying in her bed with its splendid headboard, an unopened *Silver Screen* magazine at her elbow, Lil was resting on her side, her legs drawn up and her green eyes small pools of sadness. I wondered if her thoughts were with Maurey. It wasn't their age difference that stood between them, but their backgrounds. It was one thing to steal a walk, a quick embrace, a kiss—my conscience did not allow me to envision more—but suppose they had an entire day together, a weekend, a week?

In October, we received a picture postcard of the Harvard Quad. It was addressed to The Roths, 444 Grand Street, Apt. 4, and it said, "Miss you, love you, wish you were here. Dead tired from work." Signed "Hal, Gabe, Maurey."

The card revived Lil. Her lethargy eased. She started to sing again, her step quickened and she reported to Dr. Frank that she was less tired than she had been. He urged her not to give up her medication or her rest periods. She replied, "I may be taking a short trip to Boston soon."

That shook me: didn't she realize that Maurey studied at Yale, was in New Haven? That the card had been written by Hal? She showed it to everyone she met and when the edges began to fray she placed it in her underwear drawer. Before she left the house she would kiss it as if it were a mezuzah on the door.

I also worried about Bubby, who was doing her best to accept her new role as caterer. It kept her busy, but so much of what she loved in her old life had been lost. Her business came from more distant merchants, so we rarely encountered customers, and our open door that had once welcomed Yiddish poets and journalists, local merchants and new arrivals from Europe, Negroes and Caucasians seeking a free meal—all these had vanished. Either they didn't make the effort to find us—Mr. Jacob would have provided our address in an instant—or the world now revolved on a different axis in which Manya no longer starred.

It had been Uncle Goodman's idea that we lease a food vendor's truck and park it at the Garden Terrace. The truck was manned by Clayton and two of his local associates. At midmorning Clayton's helpers used the truck to make deliveries of prepared lunches to distant merchants. They returned in time to restock the truck and sell Manya's food to the people who gathered in front of the building at noon.

We bought the ingredients for the lunches that she provided from wholesalers. Clayton laid out four kinds of bread on the long kitchen counter, slapped tuna salad, kosher bologna, egg or chicken salad on the bread, doused the second slice with a mixture of mayo and mustard, added lettuce and tomato and slipped the results onto squares of waxed paper. We sold out each weekday.

Bubby cooked two days ahead for Friday, when the menu consisted of brisket of beef, roast chicken and Russian-style hamburgers. The *Forward* did a feature story on the best Friday lunch in town, but the diners went to our truck at the Garden Terrace, where Bubby did not appear.

The article in the paper inspired Lil and me to walk over to the paper. Ostensibly, we wanted to thank Shimon Gross for writing the review, but our real intention was to seek out the old buddies who had frequented our Orchard Street kitchen.

In the pressroom I recognized one former acquaintance and asked him for Avrum Liebowitz, who answered letters to the editor and wrote feature stories. "Don't you read the *Daily News*?" came the reply. "He's now A. S. Lang and he covers obituaries for them. He sits the whole day in the basement called The Morgue and you can reach him there. He'd rather be in the basement of an American paper than stuck here."

The poet Zalman Glick, who thought years ago that Manya had literary connections, sat at a corner desk. He was sweaty and distracted, and we could see he was annoyed by our appearance. So after circling the pressroom and noting all the writers pretending not to recognize us, we abandoned our scheme. Manya and Aunt Bertha did call on our Wall Street clients, whose polite handshakes and compliments lasted five minutes.

One Sunday, James Feld, together with his wife, daughter and Mrs. Feldman, appeared at our apartment and were disappointed to find that Manya no longer cooked on that day except for the family. From the moment we left Orchard Street, Yussie had approached several matchmakers for his mother. One candidate caused him to boast to us that he had bagged an American widower, and he spent almost an hour describing their soon-to-be wedding and their apartment in a newer project on East Ninth Street. But these plans collapsed when the daughters of the seventy-year-old groom-to-be revealed that their father had recently undergone surgery for prostate cancer. The one quality Mrs. Feldman could not abide was impotence, and then there was the prospect of taking care of a sick man. The marriage plans evaporated.

Riddled with envy at our apparent prosperity, Yussie Feld moved his mother into a studio apartment in one of the more modest buildings on East Broadway. She visited Bubby twice a week, placed a sugar cube between her teeth as she sipped tea and chattered like a schoolgirl about possible marriages her son hoped to arrange for her. Bubby tolerated these monologues with a straight face.

One by one the other tenants from 12 Orchard Street also came by, marveled, stuttered and spat softly to ward off the evil eye. They gossiped in the kitchen in hushed tones, slightly in awe of their surroundings, eager to rush back to their familiar squalor. More than once I found Bubby in our bedroom, sitting in her velvet chair and staring out the window, enveloped in unspoken loss.

Ironically, when the time came for me to enter junior high school the person who spoke up with the greatest intensity about my future was my mother. Jack and Bubby took it for granted that I would select an academic program that led to college entrance. Lil, on the other hand, envisioned me as a secretary—the very word brought a blush to my cheeks—and she spoke up vociferously for courses in bookkeeping, typing, and shorthand.

"Just think," she announced seductively, "you can buy all the clothes you want, have lots of spending money. You might marry a businessman, a man in business who will take good care of you."

The fact that she had met the Pankin brothers and Gabe Solomon, two brand-new doctors and a would-be lawyer, did not alter her thoughts about my prospects. What did shorthand and bookkeeping have to do with me?

"Just try it," she cajoled. "In six months, if you don't like it, you can switch over. I'll write you a note and you can change."

My homeroom teacher in junior high was white-haired Mrs. Wilson, whose glasses dangled from a chain around her neck. She had a vacant sweet smile derived from years of not listening to the hysterical babble of her multilingual charges. On one side of the blackboard she wrote Algebra, History, English, French, and on the other Basic English, Accounting, Typing, Civics. I refused to look at the latter side.

Then, a magical event occurred. Mrs. Wilson clapped her hands for silence and read out loud from a typed sheet of paper. "The following students are in rapid advancement classes. They will complete three years of work in two." My name was called. Academic classes qualified students for the advanced program. Saved! Saved by the system.

My favorite class that day was French. With adrenaline urging me on, I ran the full length of Grand Street to share my high spirits with Bubby. By the time I threw myself into her lap in the blue velvet chair, I had erased the memory of my mother's preference for me. A repetition of the scene with the men who offered me a drama scholarship was unthinkable; beyond endurance.

Lil, who had forsaken Ada as no longer "in her element," was now spending hours with Jack at Elite Fashions. After nervously rehearsing what I would say about my school program, I picked up the phone, praying that my father would answer. I drew back when I heard Lil's voice, and told her quickly, "Mother, I'm in the rapid advancement program, all academic subjects."

"If you want to break your head with that stuff, that's your business," she answered and never mentioned my classes again.

After our second summer in Connecticut, I had written careful letters to Hal, Gabe and Estelle and a postcard depicting a rosy red apple, the Big Apple, to Maurey. No replies.

In late March the weather turned springlike: warm, sensuous days, unaccustomed sunlight. One Friday, the phone rang in late afternoon and Lil answered. She reached for a chair, sat down hard and put her hand over her heart. The veins in her neck pulsated; her voice quivered.

"Yes, it is short notice. Yes, I usually work on Saturday. Yes, I'll take the day off. Lunch is fine. Yes, I'll bring my daughter. Twelve thirty would be perfect. Across the street from Saks on Fifth Avenue." Pause. "Maurey, I can't believe it's you. You sound like you're in this room. You have a surprise for me? Can you give me a hint?" Pause. "All right I'll wait until tomorrow. We'll see you then. Without fail." Pause. "Me, too."

Lil drew my hand and held it to her heart. It thumped savagely. "Mother, do you need your digitalis?"

She attempted to raise herself from her chair without success. "Don't be silly, no pills. Just water." I ran to the kitchen. "Don't bother with the water. Dial Saks. No, I'll do it myself. What's Mrs. Dixon's extension? I have it. It's here in the phone book."

"Mother, take some deep breaths, let the air out slowly. Count from one to ten. You have to calm down." I brought her an aspirin and water.

"Mrs. Dixon? Lilyan Roth here. I'm terribly sorry. We have a family emergency. It's my mother-in-law. I won't be in tomorrow. I'll work Friday and Saturday next week. Thank you for being so understanding."

Bubby wiped the flour from sugar cookies from her hands and came into the dining room. "Who called you?"

"Someone from Connecticut."

"Estelle?"

"One of the Pankin boys."

"The doctor?"

"I'll call Pandy and find out when she can take me. What should I wear for lunch uptown?"

"One of your designer suits," I suggested.

"I'm tired of my suits. A dress would be better. More feminine."

No one could deal with Lil when she became agitated, lost focus, changed her mind from minute to minute.

Unfortunately she rejected every outfit my father selected from her closet. One was too severe, the other too matronly, still others too long, too short, too wrong. Jack declined further involvement. She picked a red dress with a gold thread, a deep V neckline, a peplum front and back.

"Mother, that's a cocktail dress. It's not a dress for lunch."

"I'll tone it down with my hat and purse."

The hat consisted of a brown beanie placed on top of the head like a yarmulke, from which hung a veil decorated with brown felt circles that cast an unbecoming shadow on her skin. The envelope purse had a gold chain, making it a casual accessory that clashed with a cocktail dress.

Neither my grandmother nor I had the courage to disparage her outfit. We shared one thought; one of her magnificent coats—she owned a closetful—would obscure the pieces of her costume that didn't go together. We hadn't counted on Lil's stubbornness—she refused to wear a coat.

"It's summer weather. Who needs a heavy coat? It's not the season." Translation: she wanted to show off her eye-catching figure. She radiated confidence; she believed her outfit was ravishing.

Promptly at 11:30, Abe picked us up in his taxi. As a result we were a half hour early. Because of the unseasonable weather, Fifth Avenue bustled with shoulder-to-shoulder strollers, New Yorkers basking in the fame of their most renowned thoroughfare.

I held my mother's free hand as she craned her neck, searching in the direction of uptown for Maurey.

"What do you think the surprise is?"

"Maybe a comb that he bought in Paris."

"Maybe it's Chanel."

"Maybe it's something we never imagined."

I thought the wind was lifting me on high. Two strong arms whirled me around. It was Maurey, hair trimmed though curling at the neck, a flash of a navy blazer, a red and blue rep tie, light gray trousers. His face was still suntanned, the lips full, receptive, the eyes piercing. He turned heads as he set me down, lifted my mother and spun her to the sky. She could have been a thistle in his hands, light, airy, ready to be blown away in the unseasonable breeze. "And this," he announced, "is Linda."

We saw flaxen hair, a mile of white teeth, a pale pink sweater highlighted by a thin rope of seed pearls. A red and pink plaid skirt fell almost to her ankles; her feet were shod in flat-heeled ballet-style shoes. She wore a maroon blazer that echoed Maurey's. She smiled and said nothing. I didn't dare contemplate what she thought of my mother's attire, though it's unlikely she gave it more than a glance. Her eyes were fixed on Maurey. Both of them gave off ferocious heat.

"Isn't she wonderful? What do you think of her hair?"

"Corn silk," I replied, as I recalled the sunlit afternoon during the summer when we stood in the cornfield and devoured fresh young corn plucked from their delicate green husks.

"Exactly." He buried his face in Linda's hair.

"Linda and I study together," he said. "Can you picture me studying hour after hour? With Linda there, it's relativity. An hour passes like a minute." He leaned over and sucked her eager mouth into his.

The wind sharpened. My mother's hat with its absurd veil seemed on the verge of flying off. She had the sense to remove it and jam it into her purse. I threaded my arm through hers.

"Hey, where's your coat?" Maurey asked.

Lil nodded in the direction of Saks across the street.

"What a couple she and her husband are," he said to Linda. "Talent, talent galore."

I could feel the quiver in my mother's arm. Whatever fantasies she had indulged in about this afternoon lay underfoot like dust.

Maurey emitted his charming laugh. "Which brings me to a slight change of plans. Would you two lovely ladies forgive us if we didn't join you for lunch?" He dangled house keys that he extracted from his blazer pocket.

"We discovered Chip Richmond isn't coming in this weekend so he's lending us his parents' apartment on Park."

We weren't sure whether he meant Park Avenue or Central Park.

"We thought we'd catch up on some sleep, then have a snack before we take the train back to New Haven."

Both Linda and Lil remained voiceless. Linda continued to smile. Lil's mouth was frozen, clenched.

To break the silence Maurey asked, "Where were you planning to eat lunch, the Carnegie Delicatessen?"

"That's for tourists," I said.

"Where then, Longchamps?"

"No, the new French Pavilion in Rockefeller Plaza. We read a review and thought you would like it because of Paris. Our treat."

"Wait until I tell this to Hal! He sends his love." Even as he spoke, Maurey had stepped off the sidewalk and raised his arm for a taxi. The moment it drew up, he helped us inside, pressing his cheek against my mother's and kissing the air. "It was truly wonderful to see you. Until this coming summer in Connecticut."

My mother pulled herself together and with as much jauntiness as she could muster replied, "See you in Connecticut."

Her words hung midair. We beheld Linda and Maurey hasten into the next cab and watched as it drove away.

"Where are we going?" Lil asked me.

"Home. Let's take this taxi home."

"No," she replied firmly, "get out! Driver, we've changed our minds."

Luckily, the Forty-second Street subway station wasn't crowded. Luckily, the car we selected had dozens of empty seats. I put my arm around my mother's waist. She dropped her head on my shoulder.

In retrospect, it would be simple to admit that during the ride from Forty-second Street to Canal Street I became the mother of my mother, that my protectiveness, my empathy, my sorrow for her sorrow reversed our roles. The unadorned truth, hardly a surprise, was that she had rarely mothered me—she had left that to Bubby. People liked Lil immediately. They admired her, enjoyed her presence, yearned to soak up her vivacity. Say her name out loud, "Lil Roth," and the response was almost always: "Isn't she terrific, wonderful, enchanting."

These remarks always reached my head, not my heart, though had I been asked, I would have said I loved my mother. But that day, on the rackety train ride that hurtled us home, suddenly and unaccountably, I fell in love with my mother, and all the bad and silly stuff tucked itself away in some remote corner of my heart.

Approaching Canal Street, my mother instinctively sat up, found her compact, freshened her lips, combed her hair and asked, "How do I look?"

"Beautiful."

We climbed the steps slowly. A sharp wind came off the East River, whipping the silk dress around her shapely legs. I moved in the direction of our apartment, shivering from the cold.

"It's early," my mother said. "I'll walk over to Daddy's store. Maybe I'll make a sale."

"Mother, it's freezing. Come home. You'll catch a cold."

"Not yet."

The wind blew abandoned newspapers into the air and motes of dust into our eyes.

"What shall I tell Bubby?"

"You'll think of something."

"I'll tell her they had theater tickets and didn't have time for lunch."

"Good. That's very good."

"Mother, you need a coat."

"Jacob will lend me a jacket until I get to our store."

I clung to her for a second without crying. She ran a finger over my cheek and walked on, resolute. At the first corner garbage can, I saw her remove the hat from her purse and drop it into the can. Then she walked on, a scarlet dot against a black landscape.

❦

The next day it rained but we could not prevail upon Lil to stay away from Palace Fashions. Bubby appeared to have swallowed the excuse about Maurey's theater tickets, but as she prepared soup for my parents' return from work she asked, "Nu, vuz hut zach pasert?"

I didn't lie to Bubby. There was no need.

"He brought along his girlfriend from law school, some tall shiksa, and he dumped us. He wanted frya libbe with his girl and after he put us in a taxi, they went off. From start to finish the visit was over in ten minutes, on the sidewalk across from Saks."

"She needed a coat." Pouring barley and dried mushrooms into the soup pot, Bubby added, "It happens. It happened to me. You were there. You saw."

"Do you think of him?"

"No. That person doesn't live for me anymore."

Whether that applied to Lil and Maurey we never knew.

It rained for the rest of the week. Lil's scratchy throat escalated into a wheezing cough and in one middle of the night we awakened to the sound of a brief, hoarse conversation, followed by a phone call. Bubby and I, whose sleep vanished faster than wet snow on a sidewalk, arose as one and dashed to my parents' bedroom.

"She can't breathe. She can't catch her breath."

"Steam?" Bubby asked.

"I turned on the hot water in the bathroom full blast but I can't carry her. She's like a dead weight. Dr. Koronovsky and Dr. Frank are on their way."

"It's four in the morning."

My father pulled on his trousers and shirt. Lil lay inert, gasping, leaden.

During emergencies my grandmother glided about like a ballerina. In a few minutes, hair combed and face washed, she was prepared to greet the doctors. Her hands trembled. The sound of the downstairs bell brought her to the door. To our surprise the man to step out of the elevator was Scott Wolfson.

"I came first to do whatever is necessary." He had never forgiven himself for his unavailability when Willy needed his tracheotomy. The other two doctors soon followed. It required no more than a few minutes for

Dr. Frank to announce, "She needs oxygen, blood tests, whatever modern medicine can provide. I think Doctor's Hospital because it's where I work." He picked up the phone and instructed firmly, "This is Dr. Bernard Frank. Emergency ambulance service? 444 Grand Street, downtown. Immediately. That's fine. Straight to Doctor's Hospital."

"She has a broken heart," I said. Fortunately, no one heard me.

Clayton brought us the coffee in Bubby's tea glasses with their filigreed bottoms. Lil had gifted him with a mountain of old dresses, possibly to sell in secondhand shops, and he chose to sleep in some of them; in his haste to bring the doctors up to our apartment quickly, he forgot to remove Mother's old polka-dot summer dress, a perfect nightshirt.

Tears were running down Clayton's cheeks when the ambulance appeared. Since I invariably accompanied my mother to her doctor's appointments, I had dressed quickly and I started out with my father as the hefty ambulance assistants carried my mother in the gurney. Dr. Koronovsky understood and whispered softly, "Not this time, darling. You have to comfort Bubby and Willy. Lil is going to the ICU—the intensive care unit. No children allowed there."

"I'll phone as soon as I can," Jack told us. "Wait for my call. When I hear anything I'll let you know." He held an unlit cigarette in his hand to guide him down the elevator and into the ambulance. Dr. Koronovsky added, "Manya, she'll have the best care, the very best."

Bubby and I didn't meet each other's eyes. Willy, who hadn't left his bed, was sobbing loudly. Scott went in to comfort him.

The worst of it was that we had nothing to do, nothing to occupy the leaden waiting. There was no food to prepare, nothing bearable on the radio to divert us. For a while we sat quietly, immobile. We didn't use the bathroom, or attempt to eat or drink.

At last Scott Wolfson came out of Willy's room. "I have to drive home and sleep for a few hours," he said, and like magic, we roused ourselves. Clayton, now aware that he was wearing my mother's polka-dotted dress, said, "I'll change my clothes." Bubby commented, "Food in hospitals, you can't eat it. Maybe I should cook something."

Scott replied, "I'd like some more coffee with lots of cream and sugar. I need the energy." He kissed Bubby good-bye and carried the coffee with him. I followed him into the elevator. He sipped his coffee in silence as we went down.

To my surprise I asked Scott, "What's wrong with Willy?"

"Angst," he answered. "You remember the day you were chased by those boys? That's how Willy feels every minute of every day. Terrified, haunted, in flight from what he fears most."

"What is he afraid of?"

"He listens to news of the war on his radio. But it's more than that. He's afraid of everything, everyone."

"Not of Bubby."

"No, not of Bubby."

"Not of me."

"Yes, of you."

"Of *me*? How can that be? I take care of Willy. I always have."

"He envies your boldness."

"What does that mean?"

"All the things you've done—that you do. Who you are. You walk in Little Italy and Chinatown by yourself. You take a shortcut home under the Third Avenue El. You're not afraid of Harlem. Bubby told me that you stood in the street and didn't show the slightest fear."

"But I cried when the gang chased us. I fell down. My new muff fell in the slush. I pulled Willy all the way."

"You pulled Willy. Think about that. I try my best for him. He's my first psychiatric patient. But the damage, there's layer upon layer of it."

"Like Bubby's strudel?"

"If only it were a strudel," he said, and he handed me the glass. The front door closed behind him. Both of us avoided mentioning Lil.

Jack could not stop praising the wonders of Doctor's Hospital. Lil was suffering from double pneumonia—both lungs were filled with fluid. He was permitted at her bedside in the ICU for half an hour and then told to stay away for three hours. During these periods various doctors came to examine her, specialists in pulmonary diseases. They didn't speak to Jack. Dr. Frank and Dr. Koronovsky consulted with them about her vital signs, her blood tests, her temperature. Jack relinquished one of his visits to Uncle Goodman, who had come down from Yonkers, and he refrained from smoking on the pulmonary floor. Uncle Goodman kept repeating, "Jack, with everything you need luck. You found gold with these doctors. A movie star couldn't have better. A queen. Ahf allah Yiddishe kinder such care."

On Friday evening, Jack staggered home, watered himself in his beloved shower stall until his skin wrinkled, then dropped off to sleep in Bubby's bed in the room she and I shared. He couldn't bear to sleep in his own bed without his wife.

Two weeks later Uncle Goodman brought her home. The house was filled with baskets of fruit, boxes of candy, fresh flowers, plants. The get well cards couldn't fit into our mailbox and Clayton waited for the mailman to slip the cards inside a fancy box that had come with a bed jacket "From the girls at Saks."

"She looks sixteen," Bubby repeated endlessly and indeed Lil did. Slim to begin with and having lost weight, her legs were as thin as a teenager's, her hair hung straight to her shoulders, and like leaves in the fall it had turned reddish-brown. Pandy would have been pleased to color it but the doctors forbade it. "No dye, no makeup, no artificial products on her skin until she's stronger." This news created a stir, as if it were a medical instruction of the highest order.

"You heard about Lil Roth? Not a drop of lipstick on her lips. To bathe her, soap without perfume. No Chanel. Everything pure. She lost twenty, thirty pounds. A regular stick. Every day Clayton walks her up and down the foyer three times. That's her exercise. It's the latest. Did you ever? And the newspaper! Only the back where there's entertainment and ads. Nothing from the front with bad news about war or love nests. From those she doesn't need."

Another ten days passed before Clayton led Lil into the street in a short stylish summer housecoat. He chose his black pants and white chef jacket for the occasion and he flashed a watch with a silver stretch band given to him by Lil's doctors: Wolfson, Koronovsky, Frank. The inscription read "For service beyond the call of duty." Holding Lil under the arm, he walked her exactly five minutes before he reversed and brought her inside. The onlookers applauded. The neighbors and passersby who had heard about her illness called out, "Keep up the good work." I stayed across the street, nervous about her every movement, until she and Clayton returned inside. I praised every baby step of her progress. But my concern and anxiety for her rarely lifted. I had become as obsessed as Jack in devoting myself to her every movement.

Clayton, Bubby and I catered to her every whim. It gave me the greatest satisfaction to read to her from *The Great Gatsby*. Several times she dozed off while I read and I watched her sleep as if she were my child. Nights I'd strain to hear her, calling softly, "Mother, Mother." I didn't allow myself to fall into a deep sleep, yet I lacked the courage to confide my pain to Dr. Wolfson.

She cried at the ending of *Gatsby*. "Does such a love really exist?" she asked.

"Daddy loves you that much," I replied.

A flash of guilt streaked across her eyes.

I rarely left her side. Bubby said, "When is a poor man happy? When he loses something and finds it again." A found mother! Imagine that!

We agreed that she would be able to manage *Gone With the Wind* on her own, but we still discussed it chapter by chapter. It no longer bothered me that she was a slow reader. It increased our intimacy.

Beaming at her progress in walking, Jack reported a surprise for her. Pandy came to the house and applied a nonperoxide rinse to Lil's hair before setting it, and brought over a hand-held dryer to prevent her from sitting around with damp hair. And a few hours later the true surprise burst through the door. Estelle Solomon.

Of course they both cried; of course they both laughed; they started sentences and broke off without finishing. To hide my own emotions I took the advice I gave Lil: deep breaths, letting them out slowly. I longed to kiss both of them at once. Estelle related most of the news while Lil and I listened raptly.

The Pankin boys, Gabe, and Estelle and her husband, Phil, were taking a trip together to California. Would Lil and her children like to come, too—first week of June, on the Twentieth Century Limited? Three days in Los Angeles. Three in San Francisco. For Maurey, it was a business trip. He was planning to leave Yale and enter UCLA Law School. He had decided to become a lawyer for movie stars—contracts, divorce, any problems with the law. He would be bigger than Greg Hauser. Smarter. Make more money.

"What about Linda?" I asked.

"Didn't you read about it in the *Times*? She's marrying a wealthy financial adviser. Did you think her family would seriously consider a Jewish boy whose father is a dirt farmer?"

Lil and I exchanged a swift, meaningful glance. For Linda, Maurey had been an afternoon quickie, to be discarded like a corn husk.

"And Sybil? Whatever happened to Sybil?"

"She's with a Frenchman. They're in the Resistance. No one knows where." Estelle in her spring frock and straw hat encircled with multi-colored silk flowers reached over to hug me. "Hal and Gabe are waiting for you to grow up. Didn't you know that?" Lil smiled benignly, not really aware of the implications, but enthralled by our easy chatter.

Clayton brought the tea tray to the table—silver on loan from the Goodmans.

When Jack told Bubby and me that Estelle was coming to visit Lil, there had been some behind-the-scenes to-and-fro about what to serve her. Aunt Bertha had pressed hard for an English high tea with cucumber sandwiches, potted meat with crust served in clay tureens, petit fours. In the end Bubby decided on three styles of blintzes: cheese, fresh sautéed apples, and her own strawberry jam laced with lightly sweetened sour cream. Clayton's table setting brought praise and so did his centerpiece of daisies. Estelle could not stop tsk-tsking about the tall windows, the floor-to-ceiling draperies, the eye-catching sofa. "No wonder you moved here from Yonkers! It's an enchanting setting, so modern, so contemporary."

She produced her present, a large square, heavily wrapped in brown paper. Clayton cut the intricately knotted cord.

"What is it? What is it?" Lil exclaimed.

"It's a miniature Miró—the one lent to you by the art gallery when your apartment was photographed for the architectural magazine. Pete Peterson found it for me and had it framed."

If the ride home in the subway after Maurey left us for his tryst with Linda altered my love for my mother in ways that defied mere logic, that gift of the Miró, *L'Arc de Terre,* with its abstract free forms in brilliant colors to signify the universe, sped my mother across a new threshold. I held back my tears as I watched her study the reproduction.

She held it out at arm's length. She pressed it to her lips, to her chest. Once she had referred to the Koronovskys' Fifth Avenue apartment as a library and barely noted his small but exquisite art collection. Now Estelle's gift moved her as no other present.

"I love art," she exclaimed. "I love it. I do."

The throb in her voice was genuine; tears filled her lustrous green eyes.

"As soon as you're completely well, we'll try the Museum of Modern Art," said Estelle. "Not as many steps as the Met and we'll have lunch in the roof garden."

Lil's response was ardent. "I'd love that."

Estelle burrowed into her spring straw purse. "And another thing." She held up a newspaper clipping. "It's from the business news. Didn't you once work at Palace Fashions? The owner's daughter, Rosalind, is opening a high-fashion boutique on Madison Avenue. Before the war she scooped up dozens of Parisian dresses and coats, handmade designer items, very chic, very expensive. The store is called Panache and it's opening on Madison Avenue in September."

"Rosalind is opening a high-fashion shop during the *war*?"

Clapping her hands with excitement, Estelle ventured the thought that Lil did not have the courage to express. "I'll bet she'll ask you to work for her because of your experience at Sak's."

"We grew up together. My daughter wore her daughter's outgrown clothes. Why would she consider me?"

"Because you're perfect for the job."

"Yes, you are," I echoed. "They would be lucky to have you."

Gathering her things, which included a package of blintzes expertly wrapped by Clayton, Estelle kissed Lil. Bubby and I added our hugs to the departure.

"I'm sorry you're not coming with us to California. Let's make a date for Labor Day weekend in Connecticut. The boys were promised those three days."

It was a perfect visit: the conversation, the food, the gift. It catapulted my mother from a long sorrowful sleep into a world filled with potential wonder. The promise of the museum visit and the opening of Panache by Mister L.'s daughter sped her recovery. "If only I could stand on my feet, if only I could walk!" Her laments made me realize how much I feared her return to work and how much she needed it.

"You will, you will," Dr. Frank assured her. "But you must be patient. Relax. Allow your body to heal."

"This whole long summer, what will I do with myself? What will the children do?"

For a week the entire family stayed in Yonkers. Like Bubby, Lil had never been as enamored of the old house as I was. She slept on the sun porch, took walks and grew lively only when the Goodmans went house-hunting. Now that their children were away at college, they longed for more modern quarters. We scoured the new houses in Westchester County; we drove to West End Avenue where Pete Peterson and Uncle Goodman were searching for buildings in foreclosure that they could renovate. I despaired at the prospect of losing the old Yonkers house.

"You don't like progress," Aunt Bertha told me.

"I don't care for change."

"Do you miss Orchard Street?"

"No, not that. Too much cold. Too much illness. But other things—the restaurant, the house full of people . . ." I broke off, fearful of hurting Bubby.

"You'll love our new home. You'll learn to love it."

"The way Bubby loves Grand Street."

Aunt Bertha pretended not to hear.

The days of summer stretched on, golden-hued but lifeless as a desert. Bubby, Lil and I walked to Orloff's Garden Terrace building daily, marveled at its terraces, its vistas from the upper stories, and its kitchens with double ovens. We did not consider an apartment there.

One day Abe drove Bubby and me to Battery Park while Lil was taking her afternoon nap. I longed for the smell and sight of green grass, which the river did not satisfy. I spent long afternoons trying to amuse Lil and fill her vacant hours. I wept easily and every night I told Bubby that when I grew up I would leave New York forever.

"It was the same in Russia," she admitted. "Some artists needed big cities, others hated it. Look at Levin in *War and Peace*. He would rather work with the peasants than live in Moscow." Among her many endearing qualities was my grandmother's ability to perceive characters from fiction with the familiarity she felt for people she knew.

I made my third visit to Connecticut by myself. Lil was too frail to travel and Willy didn't want to go. He had agreed to visit the Simons, who planned to stay home in Brooklyn that year because Uncle Geoff was preoccupied with the start of a new business. I pestered my parents until they agreed to let me visit Pankin's Farm alone. Scott Wolfson drove me to Grand Central Station, where a clerk from Phil Sullivan's office met me and accompanied me to Colchester on the Labor Day Special. The only ones at the hotel were Gabe, the Pankin brothers, Estelle and Hank. All the guests had left the day before to make way for the carpenters hired to renovate the buildings.

Sun filtered through the leaves and an immense stillness enveloped my every hour. In the distance the fruit trees with their winter pears seemed to descend directly from the blue sky. The patio furniture had been put away so I lay in the hammock in the shade, half dozing, my thoughts drifting among the new paradoxes in my life. Once all contradictions focused upon Orchard Street: its physical harshness, the lack of money, the illnesses that continually attacked us—yet, there we thrived on rich and varied cultural experiences. And above all, we were always together.

Now I was in Connecticut, alone, proud of my independence in one sense, but plagued by a dull aching fright. What was to happen to this farm I loved, which would soon be torn apart and changed beyond recognition? The adult friends I held so dear—would they be scattered on both coasts and seldom come together again? My own family was a long way from Orchard Street now, but my terror of losing them one by one never left my consciousness. I sought refuge in dreams.

From early morning to summer twilight it felt as if the golden light shed its radiance especially for us. The universe became a painter's vision of warmth and comfort and stillness, a suspension of time and place that I would recollect forever.

We didn't speak much except at dinner. In the kitchen with its hotel-sized stove, Gabe prepared coq au vin and blanquette de veau. We drank white wine, mine mixed with water, and all of us got drunk, slipped off our chairs and slipped into bed. Above the remodeled lobby, the upstairs rooms where we slept before remained intact. My bed was still beneath the window from which I could view what had once been the barn flooded with yellow light.

In the fall, as Estelle predicted, my mother went to work for Panache on Madison Avenue, Saturdays only. I accompanied her to her first day's work, kissed her as she entered the store and recited "Knock 'em dead." With my nose pressed against the glass, I studied the mannequins in the window, painted gold and dressed in filmy gowns that took my breath away. Lil floated through the boutique and out of view. I could no longer see her, but I remained there, filled with pride and with sadness, searching for the sight of my mother, waving my fingers discreetly, like a toddler who has recently been taught to wave bye-bye. It took me awhile to make myself leave.

Not too many weeks later, while in Panache, happy and as full-throated as a lark, Lil pivoted on her high heels, reached toward the plush floral carpet and died.

As Jewish custom dictated, she was buried within twenty-four hours. The funeral service was held in the funeral parlor on Canal Street. Every store on Division Street closed for the day in her honor.

Passing the open casket everyone remarked on her youthful beauty. Willy kept repeating, "It should have been me. It should have been me."

Clayton wept uncontrollably, crying out, "Miss Lillian, don't leave us," causing everyone to sob.

Jack removed the handkerchief from his breast pocket and wiped the lipstick from Lil's cold lips.

At the grave site it started to rain. I caught a fleeting glimpse of Estelle and heard her say, "Look at the way his daughter holds the umbrella over Jack's head."

My father never remarried.

AFTERWORD

———◦《◦》◦———

Up from Orchard Street is part memoir, part social history and part fiction. Nevertheless, every word is true.

The Jewish ghetto on the Lower East Side in the 1930s, with its culture, traditions and restraints, no longer exists. As with many diasporas, when the inhabitants of this enclosed, tightly knit universe scattered, they rejected its old customs and possibly attempted to wipe their struggles from memory.

Not I.

Though by now I have lived in Southern California for several decades more than I lived in New York, the sights, smells and physical images that haunt me are of Orchard Street and the overcrowded thoroughfares that surrounded it. In dreams, I am in the tiny freezing apartment, or I walk the streets in the dark, heart pounding, in search of the old tenement that I cannot find.

Today, Orchard Street and its environs are enjoying an esthetic and financial renaissance, and the scenes of my childhood are now filled with trendy clubs, fashionable restaurants and expensive condos. My Bubby was right: "If you live long enough, you live to see everything."

In 1976, the year of America's bicentennial and the tall ships, I flew to New York to rediscover 12 Orchard Street. My eyes lit on the water tower that came into my childhood view every morning when I peered out of the window from our folding bed. I began to cry behind my California sunglasses.

The men's store on Canal Street that I called Jacob's in these pages was still there, still situated on the ground floor of the derelict tenement. I walked into the store and said in Yiddish, "Excuse me, is there any way I can get inside the building?"

The owner, an aged man, short and grizzled, was arranging boxes of socks on a shelf. He answered, "One time I went with the fire inspectors. I stood on the ladder and we looked inside. Rats and bats, they ate everything. Nothing but shmutz, a few pieces from bedsprings. I wouldn't look inside again for no amount of money."

I turned down Canal Street to the funeral parlor from which my grandmother and mother had been buried. Across the street, on the site of Loew's Canal, with its red-carpeted lobby and gilt-framed movie posters, there was now a shop that sold inexpensive cameras.

I reversed my course. The Third Avenue El was gone, the Bowery remained the same. A street sign indicated that I stood on Division Street, but I saw little that was recognizable. There was a public school on the right side of the street.

I whirled around as a man's voice asked, "You looking for someone?"

"A store," I answered. "My dad's store. Elite Fashions."

"You're in the wrong place. I been on this block thirty, forty years, never heard of that store."

"My mother worked where the school is. My father started his business close to where you're sitting."

The man shook his head. "Nah, nah, it happens all the time, mistakes in location."

I grew exasperated. "Listen, our name was Rackow. My grandmother had a private restaurant, Manya's. Everyone knew her."

In an instant he shed fifty pounds, rose from his chair and spread his arms. "Oh, my God, it's Jack the horse player's daughter! I didn't make a nickel on a nag after your father moved away."

It would be inappropriate not to report on some of the people who appear in these pages.

My extraordinary Bubby, whose influence on my life never faltered, died of a kidney ailment that today is curable. At her funeral, Clayton wept piteously, "Bubby, don't leave me." He ran out after the services and did not accompany us to the burial site. In the confusion of getting in and out of cars, we didn't realize he had gone—forever. Our search and inquiries led nowhere. For years I kept insisting he had traveled to California and in my mind he remained as he had appeared in his youth. I bless him still.

During my adolescence I spent many an afternoon with Lil in the offices of eminent cardiologists. Often I would be asked, "Why isn't your father here?" and I would answer truthfully, "He's too anxious. He can't bear to hear bad news." If I heard the sirens of an ambulance I automatically started running, assuming my mother was on the way to a hospital. The lines from Webster's *Duchess of Malfi* echo still: "Cover her face. Mine eyes dazzle. She died young."

As for my brother, Willy shuttled between various psychiatric hospitals and Jack's house, where he occupied a small bedroom whenever he was deemed well enough. The last time I saw him he was living in a nursing home in West Sayville, Long Island. I took him to an elegant restaurant for lunch; he ordered lobster and cheesecake for dessert. We sat outdoors; dappled sunlight came through the branches of tall stately trees. We held hands as we talked about his favorite philosopher, Bertrand Russell. Suddenly he said, "If anything happens to me, promise that you won't mourn because my personal torment will be over." That winter he suffered a stroke, and a few days later died of aspiration pneumonia.

Jack passed into legend. After smoking three packs of cigarettes a day for all those years, he gave his last breath to emphysema. My sons,

Matthew and Jonah, and I still speak of him as if he were alive, especially during the Belmont Triple Crown race, a track he frequented for years. Once I had dinner with one of the leading horse trainers in the United States, and my regret was that I couldn't tell Jack about it.

I extend my gratitude to my cadre of California doctors for their devotion to me: Dr. George Dennish, who enjoyed it most when I brought a few pages of my novel and read them out loud to him; Dr. John Hassler, whose optimism never faltered; and Dr. Herman Serota, who provided me with an excellent mantra: "When you're tired, hungry, lonely, sleepless—write." And Dr. Donley McReynolds, who joked, "I'll pay you to sit in my waiting room and just tell stories to my patients."

I extend my deep thanks to my companions Carmen Palacios and Samuel Calvarios; my cousin Professor Edward Turk; my dear friends Julia Sundt, Kira Kaufman, Jan Percival, Vita Sorrentino and Ilan Shrirer; and my editor, Mariam Kirby. But most of all, I appreciate the unfailing love of my daughter-in-law, Colleen, and my two sons.

—Eleanor Rackow Widmer
La Jolla, California
October 2004

ABOUT THE AUTHOR

ELEANOR WIDMER, who grew up on New York's Lower East Side, had a varied career as a scholar, a critic, a teacher, a passionate defender of freedom of expression, and for twenty-six years, a noted food and restaurant critic in the San Diego region, where she made her home.

She earned her master's degree at Columbia University and a doctorate in English literature at the University of Washington in 1956, writing her thesis on women novelists of the nineteenth century. (It was when she was studying for her Ph.D. that she won a cooking contest in Seattle for her apple pan dowdy recipe.) She was an expert witness in an obscenity trial involving banning the sale of Henry Miller's novel *Tropic of Cancer* in San Diego, a case that culminated in 1964, when the Supreme Court ruled that the book was not obscene.

Eleanor Widmer died in La Jolla, California, on November 8, 2004, at the age of eighty, not long after she had completed revisions on *Up from Orchard Street*. Two sons and two grandchildren survive her.